MW01257867

This book is a work of fiction. References to real people, events, establishments, organizations, or locales are intended only to provide a sense of authenticity, and are used fictitiously.

Cover Design and assistance:
Isaac Peterson of Emerald Design Company
isaac@emerald-design.com

Copyediting
Tammy Conley
tconley12210@gmail.com

A Midwife's Song
Oh Freedom
A Hope River Novel

by

Patricia Harman

Other books by Patricia Harman

The Runaway Midwife

The Midwife of Hope River

The Reluctant Midwife

Once a Midwife

Arms Wide Open: A Midwife's Journey

The Blue Cotton Gown: A Midwife's Memoir

Lost on Hope Island:

The Amazing Tale of the Little Goat Midwives

Readers Reviews

A Midwife's Song: Oh Freedom

"Racism, unconditional love, the unbreakable bond of mother and child...**A Midwife's Song** is a beautifully written account of two time periods in Appalachia that will have you asking for more. Patricia Harman is a brave and masterful storyteller in this continuation of the Hope River Midwife series." Lisa McCombs

*"Thanks to Patricia Harman for giving a voice to my people in her new book, **A Midwife's Song.** The author's writing reflected several of my thoughts, and it's taken me a while to process that the she wrote this, not me." Venay Uecke, Certified Nurse-Midwife, Midwives of Color*

A Midwife's Song: Oh Freedom is an amazing narrative. I absolutely loved it for all the honesty, history, humor, and surprises it offered. The story was real, entertaining and thought provoking. It helped me have a glance of two eras in time for people of color. There are so many quotes that resonated with me...like this one... *"Looking up, my mouth falls open. The sky is a parachute of silk, lined with silver clouds. When the moon peeks through, I raise my arms in a prayer; only two words, Help Us, but I feel the moon answer. "Here is the truth," the smiling orb says. "Children grow in their own mysterious ways. And just because they seem broken, doesn't mean they won't heal."* Karen Bryant, Educator

"**A Midwife's Song** was intriguing. I read it in about 10 hours. Exciting and very knowledgeable on the history of my state of WV. So good!" Bonnie Starcher

A Midwife's Song is really a first of its kind. From the beautifully drawn characters of Mrs. Grace Potts, Patience, and Bitsy to the historic timelines of pre-civil war and the civil rights movement, I feel so honored to have shared so much of these courageous women's lives in another wonderful novel by Patricia Harman.
Kim Vanderwert

Having read the other books in the Midwife of Hope River series I could not wait to find out what adventures Patience Hester would embark on in **A Midwife's Song**. I was not disappointed. Patricia Harman has a gift of storytelling and as a reader I was transported once again to Patience's doorstep and into her life. Historical fiction is one of my greatest loves and I was transported twice in one book! What a treat....I would recommend this book to anyone who's interested in learning about West Virginia in the 1950's, traversing the Underground Railroad in the late 1800's as a runaway slave, or just a historical fiction lover in general. I pray the series continues.
Tara Bodine

I have read all of the Hope River novels over a span of years. I think they just keep getting better. Within the first chapter, the characters come back to me, just by the way they're depicted. Even if A Midwife's Song was the only book a person read, the characters would jump off the page. When I read Patricia Harman's books, I feel like they are my neighbors or friends. Having grown up in a small rural town in Ohio, I can relate. Mary Jane Rings

Literary Acclaim for

A Midwife's Song: Oh Freedom

A Midwife's Song: Oh Freedom!
The latest novel by Patricia Harman, *A Midwife's Song: Oh Freedom!* weaves together TWO fast-moving historical midwife tales, one set in the 1850s, with the heroine escaping slavery via the Underground Railroad, the other set in the 1950s, with the heroine joining the early Civil Rights Movement. Patricia presents astonishingly accurate historical details, none of which bog down the assault of adrenaline running under the story. The author proves again that people dedicated to selfless service make far more compelling action heroes than spies and hired guns. *Alicia Bay Laurel,* New York Times bestselling author of Living on the Earth.

"Patricia Harman has a wonderful way of weaving modern and past history within **A Midwife's Song: Oh Freedom**, a captivating story that is rich with intimate details about people's lives and the land. I enjoyed every part of the novel and learned things about both the Civil Rights Movement and slavery that further opened my eyes and heart. I will recommend this book to young women as well as adults who love historical fiction and a great story."
Suzanne Arms, author of Immaculate Deception II: Myth, Magic and Birth and other books, photojournalist and activist. Founder of the nonprofit, Birthing The Future.

Acknowledgements

I would like to thank the many friends who have supported my writing over the years and the many readers who reach out to thank me.
Life is not easy; I've said this before, but every day I get a note from someone telling me how much they like my books and this keeps me going.
I write books for people like you.

A Few Words from the Author

When I began the first Midwife of Hope River book, set in the 1930s, I fell in love with the characters and didn't want to leave them, so I wrote another book about the Hope River and then another. There was one character from the first book that I couldn't forget, Mrs. Grace Potts, the elderly black midwife who befriended the younger midwives, Patience and Bitsy. At 85, she passed away and it wasn't until I was imaging her funeral that I realized by her age that she was quite likely born a slave. For ten years, I've thought about Mrs. Potts and asked myself, how did she get to Liberty, West Virginia? Where did she come from? Did she escape her master or was she emancipated after the Civil War? In 2017, I began to imagine her story, did extensive research on the pre-civil war period and started to write *The Midwife's Song*.

As a midwife I have known and loved strong women of all races, women who are intelligent, courageous and kind. I want my books to be inclusive, to show people of all skin tones and cultures struggling for dignity, for freedom, for love, for inner peace. This book was written in their honor and to celebrate the contributions of the slaves who built the United States. It is also to honor Mrs. Grace Potts, a fictional woman, who lives only in my mind and soon in yours.

"If there is a book you want to read,

but it hasn't been written yet,

then you must write it."

Toni Morrison

A Midwife's Song

Oh Freedom!

*"If you ever feel alone," the old woman said,
"Remember, a great river of Hope connects us."*

From the journal of Patience Hester,

Midwife,

1956

And the diary of Grace Potts,

Slave girl

1859

Winter

1

Authorized Only

A woman's scream. *"No! No! I can't. I won't!"*

"Lordy!" Bitsy says as we push through the glass doors of the newly built hospital in Liberty, West Virginia and are greeted by One Arm Wetsell, a ruddy-faced carpenter, with short thinning gray hair. His name is actually *Holly Wetsell*, but twenty years ago he lost his lower arm under the roller of a sawmill and it had to be amputated.

"Upstairs!" he says pointing. Then he follows with, "The elevator isn't working yet."

The cries of protest continue. "No! No!"

"What have we gotten ourselves into?" I mutter. Only thirty minutes ago, I'd received a call from the desperate nurse. "Are you a midwife? Can you help us? The hospital's not open yet and we don't have a doctor."

Bitsy, my partner, takes the steps two at a time, but I limp along. I don't need a cane anymore, but still when going up steps, I have to stifle a moan. On the second level, boxes of supplies and hospital beds without mattresses are everywhere.

Delivery Room: Authorized Personnel Only!
says the sign on the green tiled wall. For a moment
we hesitate. We aren't used to hospitals, but the
door is ajar and another scream follows, so we push
on through.

What we see is something out of horror movie.
An almost naked young woman with long red hair
hanging over her face is kneeling on all fours.
When the next pain hits, she leans back and howls
like a trapped wolf. Two nurses dressed in white
with white cloth caps and white surgical masks over
their lower faces are pulling on the patient, trying to
get her up on a narrow steel table.

There are gleaming metal stirrups attached to the
table and a searchlight overhead. A tray of
instruments has been knocked over and a bottle of
strong smelling antiseptic is pooled on the floor.

"Are you the midwives?" one of the nurses
shouts over the wail of the labor patient. "Thank
God, you're here. She's been out of control since
her family dropped her off. As you can see, we
aren't set up for deliveries, yet. I'm Head Nurse
Frost by the way, and like I said on the phone, I've
never delivered a baby. We're trying to get her in a
hospital gown and up on the table, but she's
behaving like an animal. Gretchen already has
scratches on her arm."

"Get your gol darn hands off me!" Quick as a
wink, Bitsy kneels on the floor in the middle of the
mess and whispers something in the girl's ear. If
the patient even notices Bitsy's brown color, it
doesn't seem to bother her and she stops screaming.
Then the nurses begin to pull on her again. "Stop,"

I order, holding up my hand. "Can someone clean up this mess? Do you have a broom and a mop?"

"I hardly think that's a priority," says Nurse Frost. "The baby's about to come out."

"If that's true, we'll need some clean linens, but I insist that you not pull on her any longer. She's scared and doesn't know what's happening." I glance around the room, looking for something soft to place on the floor, but all I see are gleaming metal instruments, knives and scissors of all kinds and a pair of long forceps that I recognize from the OB text my husband, Dan, got me for Christmas. Also on the table are two huge stainless steel bowls full of cotton. *Now why would anyone need that many cotton balls?* the thought comes to me.

While Bitsy is soothing the patient, I pull on one of the pairs of sterile gloves laying on the steel table and begin (just in case Miss Frost is correct) to get ready. The younger of the two nurses, a small woman with a very pink face and wide blue eyes, who must be Gretchen, is frozen against the green tile wall. The head nurse hovers over me, waiting to see what I'll do next.

Frost is a tall woman, mid-thirties, I'd guess, with dark brown curls shooting out of her cap and she gasps when I dump the cotton balls in the trash and begin to put what we'll need in the larger of the bowls; a pair of scissors, two hemostats, the red suction bulb, a stack of gauze and a piece of sterile cloth tape for tying the cord. That's pretty much it, except for some oil from my birth satchel in case it looks like the patient might tear.

I kneel down with Bitsy and introduce myself.

"Hi, I'm Patience, the other midwife. You're doing fine. We are here to take care of you. You don't need to be scared anymore." Up close I can see that she's younger than I thought, fifteen or sixteen, and I wonder where her husband or family is. Strange to just leave her here. "Did you get any history?" I whisper to Bitsy.

"It's Kitty's first baby," Bitsy summarizes. "Her pregnancy's been uncomplicated. She's from Elkins, West Virginia. When her parent found out she was pregnant, she was sent here to live with her uncle on Snake Run. The uncle took her to a clinic in Torrington just once, where a doctor said she was due mid-January."

"Water bag broken?"

"I don't think so, but she feels a lot of pressure."

"Oh, no! It's coming. It's coming! Something's coming and it burns so bad!" Kitty cries. She tries to get up, but falls back on her knees, clutching her vagina as if to hold something in.

"Nurse Frost. Please. I don't think she'll move, but if you'll get me a clean sheet, she can give birth right here. I need your help."

"Aghhhhhhh!" Kitty bellows low in her throat, beginning her birth song.

"Slow it down, honey," Bitsy instructs. "Slow it down. Blow the pain away."

Miss Frost, realizing there's no way this is going to be a routine delivery, whips into action and spreads some sterile white drapes on the floor. In that moment I realize I don't even know if this baby's alive. "Did you listen to the infant's heart tones?" I ask the nurse.

"We didn't have time; she's been thrashing around ever since she got here."

Bitsy assists the girl to roll over and it's then that I get a good look at her face. She has very green eyes, freckles across the nose and a bruise on her cheek.

"You're doing great, Kitty. Your baby's right here," I say, tucking a strand of her long red hair behind her ear. "Do you have a warm blanket, Miss. Frost?" The nurse is attempting to put a white surgical cap on my head, but I shake her away.

Finally, she gives up and gets three infant blankets out of the closet. "As I said, we aren't set up for deliveries yet. Gretchen and I were working in here, trying to get things ready, when Sheriff Bishop showed up with his siren blaring. The girl's his niece. He just left. Said he had police business to attend to."

"Can you open our birth bag and find me a bottle of oil, pour a few teaspoons in the steel cup on the table and bring it over?" The nurse's assistant moves quickly, does what I say and I wipe a little oil around Kitty's vagina.

"Push a little…" I say.

"Blow a little," Bitsy urges. "Then push a little more."

Swish! The water bag breaks! The infant is coming now. There's a trickle of blood that I wipe away with gauze and then put my hands around the head like a crown.

"Don't you do an episiotomy?" Nurse Frost asks holding out a pair of sterile scissors in her gloved hand. I shake my head no as a little blue-gray head pops out of the young mother's vagina. There's a cord around the neck, but it's loose and I loop it over easily and wait for the baby to turn in the pelvis. Then down for the top shoulder, up for the bottom and the baby slides out.

Bitsy reaches over and takes the slippery infant, cord still attached, and lays her on a rectangle of sheet that she's prepared and I notice how we work so gracefully together, her brown hands and my freckled white hands moving like dancers in a dance we've done together so often we don't need to think about it.

"Here you go. Your new baby!" Bitsy says, wrapping a blanket around the female infant and stimulating her gently until she cries. "Go ahead, take her."

Kitty seems shy, but she reaches out anyway. "Is she ok?" she says quietly. "Is she really ok?"

An hour later, after cleaning up and giving Kitty postpartum instructions, we head out of the almost completed three story brick building and I make note of the black and yellow civil defense symbol on the glass door. There must be a bomb shelter somewhere below.

"How'd it go?" One Arm Wetsell asks when he sees us. "We heard a lot of screaming and then a baby's cry."

"Everything went fine," I say laughing. "By the time we got the placenta delivered and the baby on the breast, Nurse Frost had the medical instruments picked up and the floor mopped. In truth, it was one of the wildest births that I've been to and there have been many, but in the end all was well. It was a girl."

"It wasn't just wild," Bitsy mutters as she helps me into the sidecar of her new Harley motorcycle. "I still feel shaky inside, like I've been in a train wreck. If all births were like that, I wouldn't be a midwife."

"But they aren't. That was an exception. The poor patient was scared to death. I don't think she had a clue what was happening. And did you hear what Nurse Frost said? She's been staying at the Bishops' on Snake Run."

Bitsy adjusts the throttle and kicks the motorcycle to life. "And?"

"Well Aran Bishop is Sheriff now, but he and his brothers have been trouble in Union County for forever. They're the men who beat Dan up and blamed him for the death of their horse, Devil."

"Yeah, I remember," admits Bitsy. "Aran Bishop was also the leader of the mob that dressed up as the KKK and terrorized us twenty-five years ago." She pulls away from the curb and cruises down Main where we wave at Mr. Bittman, hauling boxes into his grocery store and Ida May, closing her hair salon.

At the stone bridge we stop to stare over the rail at the Hope River, running clear and wild below. On the other side, bare maples shiver and ice forms at the edges.

January 18, 1956,

Called to the unfinished Liberty Memorial Hospital by the head nurse for a precipitous delivery. The young woman, Kitty Bishop, age 15 or thereabout, was in quite a state and the nurse knew little about calming her. Baby Girl, 7 pounds, born without difficulty at 3:00 pm. Blood loss minimal. No tears. The mother named her Mary. Present were Bitsy Cross, Nurse Abigail Frost, her assistant Gretchen and myself. Kitty wouldn't get onto the delivery table, so Bitsy and I sat on the floor to help her give birth. We were not paid, but I didn't expect to be.

2

A Million Tears.

I close my leather bound journal and lock it with the tiny key before I turn out the light. Five minutes later, I switch the light on again and unlock the book.

I've kept a diary for over two decades. I don't write every day, just when I feel like it and there were some times in my life when I wrote rarely. This was back when the kids were little and I was doing four or five births a month. It's 11:30 pm and my husband, Daniel Hester, isn't home from his rounds. Strange. He usually calls when he's late.

Dan, a country veterinarian, and I have been married for 26 years and I am a fortunate woman. I live in a sturdy stone farmhouse with a man who loves me and have four grown children, all healthy and strong. On the bedside table is a framed family photo taken last year and I sit up in bed to inspect it.

There's Dan and I with our arms around each other, a middle aged couple, smiling into each other's eyes. He's a tall man, handsome and rugged. I'm smaller, wear glasses and my auburn hair is tied back with a ribbon. The photo is black and white, but it was Easter and I have a yellow dress on with a daffodil behind my ear. I remember because Bitsy, who took the picture with her Kodak, told Mira to put it there.

Mira is our youngest. She's employed at Woolworths in Delmont, ten miles away, and shares an apartment with her girl friend from high school. She was a firecracker when she was little, but has settled down now and is dating a boy who sells cars at his father's Ford dealership.

Danny, the jokester, our only son, stands behind her, making a face. He's employed, part-time, by his father, as a vet-assistant and has been a great help. He took a break from Torrington State six months ago, but we know he'll go back. He's a smart boy and will someday run his dad's vet practice.

Our two other girls, twins, Sunny and Sue, adopted after their parents perished in the forest fire of '35, are now in Martinsburg, West Virginia, studying nursing and even though they didn't come from my womb, they're my daughters all the same. I touch each child's face in the picture frame and I know why my having such a beautiful family is so important to me…

My life wasn't always so tranquil.

I was born Elizabeth Snyder, in Deerfield, a small town North of Chicago. My mother was a teacher, my father a first mate on a freighter hauling iron ore across the Great Lakes. As a little girl, I was a treasured only child, but then everything changed.

When I was thirteen, my father's ship, *The Appomattox*, on its last run of the season across Lake Michigan, floundered in a November fog. The freighter, the longest wooden ship on the Great

Lakes, carrying a load of iron ore, was grounded on a sand bar in the dark mist. Papa was the only crewmember who died, swept overboard by a wave.

In our first months of grief, things went from bad to worse. Mama was shocked to learn that we were destitute. Our savings were gone, gambled away by my father in high stakes card games out on his freighter. Because of his debts, the bank foreclosed on our home and we moved to a rooming house in Deerfield. Those were hard times.

Only two years later, Mama developed a cough and came down with consumption. She was spitting up blood when she died. Because I had no family left, I was shipped to Chicago to stay with the sister of our solicitor and eventually sent to the St. Mary's House of Mercy, an orphan's asylum.

Now here I am, two or three lives later…having once been a nanny, a suffragette, a chorus girl, a thief, a union radical, and now a midwife. There's one other thing and I try not to think about it…

I look again at the Big Ben alarm clock on the dresser, wondering again where Dan could be. It's now after twelve. Why doesn't he call?

We didn't always have such luxuries as the telephone. When I first came to the Hope River Valley on the run with Mrs. Kelly, my midwife teacher and patron, we lived without a phone *and* electricity. This was back in the twenties, just before the Great Depression, when thirty percent of rural Americans lived the same way.

It's funny how, in just a few minutes, you can

review your life, the highs and the lows of it; births, deaths, celebrations and funerals, but embroidered through those times are a million smiles, a million tears, a million deep breaths and sighs.

I gaze around the bedroom one more time, taking in the framed photographs of my husband's horses, the white curtains I made ten years ago, the homemade rocker Dan built me when I got pregnant with Danny. Then I switch off the light. Where could he be? Why didn't he call?

Without Warning

At 2:40, I wake again, listening. Was that a door closing?

"Dan?" I call. "Daniel?" No answer. I must have dreamed it.

What could have happened? This isn't the first time he's disappeared. He took off for two days back in the forties. No explanation. No warning. He just drove to Philadelphia to get advice from some Quakers about his pacifist beliefs. This was right after Pearl Harbor, a difficult time for us.

With Germany and Japan hell bent on world domination, I felt we had to oppose them, but Dan, who'd served in World War I, had long ago promised his Maker he'd never kill again. In the end, he went to prison for resisting the draft.

Finally, I get out of bed, pull on my old pink bathrobe and pad down the stairs. It's a cold night and I throw another log in the fire. Dodger, our old hound who sleeps in a box behind the wood stove, lifts his head and gives me a wag. At the kitchen door, I peer through the window. Though the roads are clear, something must have happened. Dan could've been run down by a coal truck or swerved into a ditch to miss hitting a deer.

A few minutes later, I step out on the porch to get strength from the stars. It's a cold night; frost on the ground; quiet as an abandoned coalmine; no night birds singing, no call of an owl. I search for the Big Dipper ...wondering what the North Star will tell me and then I hear from far, faraway the low purr of a motor.

"Where the hell have you been?" I greet my husband as he opens the door of his old Ford pickup. His face is strained as he struggles to get out of the driver's seat.

"I'll tell you about it when I get inside... I may need some help bandaging my back. I think it's bleeding."

My flare of anger is immediately extinguished. As a mother and wife, I'm given to bouts of anxiety and anger, but in a crisis, especially as a midwife, I pull it together. "What is it, Dan?" I say hurrying across the frozen grass in my bare feet.

"Just get me inside and I'll explain." He leans on me with his arm over my shoulder as we shuffle back into house. The three steps up the porch are the hardest and Dan makes a grunt with each one.

In the kitchen he supports himself on the back of a chair while I take off his coat, which is ripped into shreds. "My God!" I say when I remove his

shirt. His back is bleeding and torn in two places.
"Do I need to take you to the new hospital?"

"They aren't open until next week."

"Boone Memorial in Torrington then?"

"Hell no. I can't stand another two-hour drive.
Just get my vet kit out of the truck, clean the wound
and suture it if it's bad. You can manage, can't
you?"

"I guess….Yes. Do you have an anesthetic?"

"Lidocaine…in my bag. Also, morphine; draw
some up in a syringe."

An hour later, the two long lacerations are
cleansed and stitched. I've given Dan an injection
of Morphine; 10 milligrams, the amount he said
he'd use after surgery on a good size sheep. When
the pain shot kicks in, I'm at last able to get him
upstairs to bed.

Dan lays on his stomach, eyes half closed. "Can
you tell me what happened now?"

"It was after dark when I finished the de-
worming on the Spragg's farm, but before I left
there, Mrs. Pettigrew called. Somehow she'd seen
me pass earlier in the day and knew where I was.
Her old man is in the VA hospital for a flare up of
his emphysema and she had a bull that wasn't
eating. Since she suspected colic, I went over to
their place on my way home.

"I was out in the barn observing the animal
when she came over from the house and said a
nurse had called and her husband was poorly, so she
had to leave.

"I could have come back the next day with

Danny, but it seemed silly, so I slipped into his stall. As I was listening to his bowel-sounds, Midnight decided he didn't like it and tried to swipe me with his horns. I jumped for the rail, but the rail splintered. That's when I fell right in front of him and he gored me twice.

"I'll tell you, Patience, I thought I was a goner. For what seemed like hours, I lay as still as stone while the massive black beast stood over me. He'd sniff me and snort, sniff me and snort. Finally, when he turned around to munch some hay, I managed to run out and collapsed in the barnyard."

"Did Mrs. Pettigrew come back and find you?"

"No, she never did. I fainted and hours later, when I came to, I crawled to my truck, pulled myself in and drove home. I guess you should phone her in the morning and explain what happened. Tell her Midnight is fine. If he could eat hay over my almost dead body, he doesn't have colic."

I sat in the rocking chair as Dan fell asleep. I'd done my best with the stitching but my experience is limited. If everything healed ok, he'd have two impressive scars, ten inches long. Finally, I crawled into bed beside him.

"I'm glad you're home," I whispered, as the gray light of dawn seeped into the room.

Back of the Bus

"Have you been following the Bus Boycott in Montgomery, Alabama?" Bitsy asks sipping a cup of peppermint tea. It's been almost a week since we've seen each other and I've been a little down.

The truth is, I get that way after Christmas every year. The twins, Sunny and Sue, were home from their nursing program at the hospital in Martinsburg and Mira got two days off her job at Woolworths. Danny hung around with Daniel and I, playing board games and singing carols around the piano. It was a house full of laughter and song, now it's empty again.

"Boycott? Is it some kind of strike?" I ask. As a former union member and radical, such things interest me.

"No, nothing like that. I'm surprised you didn't hear. It's been going on for over a month and it's all over TV."

"We don't have TV, remember." I smile. "And Dan hasn't been to town since his accident with the bull. What's it all about?"

"You know how in the Deep South, there are laws if you're Negro, you ride at the back of the bus. Well this woman, Rosa Parks, a seamstress for a department store, was on her way home, sitting in the colored section like she was supposed to. A white man got on and since the seats for whites were full, the driver told Rosa to stand up and give him hers. I figured she'd just had it with white people, so she refused. There was a big ruckus, and she got arrested and thrown in jail.

"Now most of the Negroes in Montgomery are boycotting the buses. On the news they showed them walking to work, or biking or sharing cars; it's going to hurt the city's budget big time. J. Edgar Hoover, the FBI director, claims it's part of a

Communist plot, but he sees Commies everywhere.

"There's a new organization called the National Association for the Advancement of Colored People supporting the boycott and it has a chapter in Torrington," Bitsy goes on. "I'm going to go to a meeting. You want to go with me?"

"Do they allow whites?" I ask. "I wouldn't want to intrude."

"Sure they do, the NAACP has had white progressives since it was founded."

"I guess I could. It seems like we should be supportive. What's the old saying? 'If you won't work for justice, don't complain about not having it.'"

"Is that an old saying?" Bitsy asks.

"It is now." And I can't help but smile.

3

February 1956

Throw Away Boy

I stand in the kitchen looking down at a recent copy of *Look Magazine* that my husband had left on the table when he went to work. There's a photo on the cover of a smiling boy sporting a straw hat at a rakish angle. His shining eyes look back at me out of his handsome brown face and I immediately recall the details of his murder last summer.

The story was in the papers for weeks and the facts of the case were simple enough. In August, fourteen-year-old Emmett Till was sent from Chicago to visit his mother's family in rural Mississippi for a few weeks vacation. From all accounts he was a brash young lad, full of himself and funny, unused to the strict racial mores of the Deep South.

On a dare, at a rundown country store, he flirted with the storeowner's pretty white wife, Mrs. Bryant. Some say he touched her hand, some say he gave her a wolf-whistle. When her husband got home, she told him what had happened and in a rage, he and his brother, kidnapped young Emmett and proceeded for hours to drive around in a pickup, terrorizing the boy and pistol-whipping him in the face whenever they felt like it. Eventually, they killed him. Fourteen years old and they killed him for touching a woman's hand.

The lynching of Negros, in both the North and the South, is common enough; it was the trial and the age of the boy that outraged me. Despite clear evidence that the two brothers had committed the murder, an all-white male jury, in only one hour, declared them "Not Guilty".

The sound of a familiar vehicle crossing the wooden bridge over the creek and into our farmyard interrupts my dark thoughts. It's Bitsy on her red Harley motorcycle.

"Knock. Knock," she slams through the back door, almost breathless. "Did you see the new *Look* about Emmet Till's lynching?" she asks.

"I was just looking at the pictures. Did you read it? Any new angles?"

"I'd say! The killers *confess* to the murder right in the article! Milam Bryant says he never hurt a Negro in his life, that he actually likes them, *in their place*...but listen to this..." She picks up the magazine, opens the article and reads a few lines.

"Me and my folks fought for this country, and we got some rights. I stood there in that shed and listened to that burrhead throw poison at me, and I just made up my mind. 'Chicago boy,' I said, 'I'm tired of them sending your kind down here to stir up trouble. Goddam it! I'm going to make an example of you -- just so everybody can know how me and my folks stand.'"

"Then he describes how they beat Emmett with a pistol, stripped him, shot him in the head and threw him in the river for the catfish to eat." She throws the magazine back down on the table.

"So will there be a new trial?"

"No, there won't be! That's the most disgusting part. According to the story, there's a legal principle called *double jeopardy*. It means you can't be tried twice for the same crime! There's talk of arresting the men for kidnapping, but the Mississippi state prosecutors aren't enthusiastic about it. Either they're on Bryant's side, or they figure the two killers will be found not guilty again, so what's the point."

I can see Bitsy is really upset and I understand. Racial incidents aren't much of an issue in northern West Virginia. She and I are midwife partners of different colors and best friends. We socialize with neighbors of different skin tones. To see the racist killer's confession in print and know that there is no justice for Emmett is a slap in the face.

I study my friend as I get two cups out of the cupboard; light brown skin, almond eyes with long lashes, short curly hair, a beautiful woman in her mid-forties. It's the worry lines across her forehead and around her mouth I hadn't noticed before.

It's been a hard few years for Lou and Bitsy Cross since their adopted son Willie was sent to Korea. Despite being of white heritage, he told the draft board he was one-eighth Negro so he could join the all-black 24th Calvary with two of his colored friends from Fredrick Douglas High School in Delmont.

While most of the regiments at the end of the conflict were coming home, his unit was sent to the 38th parallel and he was shot in the leg when North

Koreans tried to cross the Demilitarized Zone.

Since then, Willie has been recovering from a wound infection at Walter Reed Hospital in Washington. Lou, Bitsy's husband, a veteran of the Spanish Civil War, says it was out and out racism that the colored troops were sent to the most dangerous area and he's probably right.

"Danny didn't come home last night," I tell my friend as I pour our coffee.

Bitsy flashes me a look. "What's going on?"

"I don't know. It's the second time it's happened. Dan says he's a grown man; he doesn't have to report to us. *It's not our business*, but he could at least call."

Bitsy blows on her tea. "Speaking of calling, I was thinking about the girl, Kitty. We should probably make a home visit."

"I've thought about that, but she wasn't really our patient and I'd rather have a tooth pulled than go out to the Bishops."

"That's what I meant. We could *call.*"

"Would you do it? I don't want to."

"Ok," says Bitsy. "You get her on the line." I look in the phone book and dial the number.

"Hello," comes a low woman's voice.

"Hello," Bitsy says. "This is the nurse from Liberty Memorial Hospital. Is Kitty available?" She sounds so much like Mrs. Frost I'm choking with laughter.

"Kitty's resting," the woman says. "I'm her aunt. That's about all she does anymore. Sleep. She won't even come to the table and she's getting right skinny too."

"Rest is important after a delivery. I hate to bother you, but would you mind asking her to come to the phone? I need to ask her some questions."

"Ok, hold on," the aunt mumbles, dropping the receiver.

"This may be some kind of a crime," I whisper, giggling. "Impersonating a nurse."

"Hello?" comes a feeble voice.

"Hi, Kitty. It's Bitsy. Patience and I were just wondering about you. I told your aunt I was the hospital nurse because I wasn't sure she'd let me talk to you. Don't let on, ok?"

"All right..."

"She says you aren't eating."

"I'm not hungry."

"Is the baby nursing?"

"Yes, all the time."

"You have to eat, Kitty. If you don't eat you won't be strong enough to take care of her and you'll also lose your milk."

"Ok. I'll try."

I listen while Bitsy asks more questions. "How's the bleeding? Any cramps? Are your bowels moving normally? Any fever or pain?"

I can't hear the answers, but Bitsy seems satisfied and then she asks a question I hadn't thought of. "Have you had any sad or gloomy thoughts?" Holding the receiver up, she beckons me over to hear Kitty's answer.

"Oh, I'm sad all the time. I don't think I'm a good mom. I feel like giving up, but if I do, what will happen to Mary?"

A door slams and a man's voice fills the room. "Who the hell are you talking to, girl?

"The nurse from the hospital," Kitty squeaks. "She called to ask me some questions."

"Well she can mind her own damn business!" he shouts and the line goes dead.

"Yikes. That was really so rude!" Bitsy comments, placing the receiver back on the base. "Physically, I think she's doing all right. Bleeding just a little. Breastfeeding well. Maybe we should call again in a few days. Maybe do it when we think the Sheriff's in town."

I let out my air. "Yeah, probably. I just wish it wasn't the Bishops. If it was anyone else, I'd go over there, but those people scare me."

Wanderer

"By the way, Danny won't be home again tonight." Dan says as he comes in the back door. He flashes me a look out of gray eyes, yellow around the middle, then he plops down in one of the kitchen chairs and runs his hands through his hair.

"What's going on?"

"Well, he slept in the truck on the way out to the Dresher's to dehorn a bull, but once we got there he pulled himself together and was a lot of help."

"Does he tell you where's he staying when he doesn't come home?"

"He says he's with friends in Delmont, but he's a grown man now, Patience. He doesn't have to tell us his plans. At his age, I was a soldier in World War One."

"He should have stayed at Torrington State. He could have graduated by now and be on to vet school. Maybe when Willie comes home he'll straighten up. Willie used to be a good influence on him. Not everyone who wanders stays lost."

Early in the morning, Bitsy and I went into Liberty to buy red, white and blue banners for Willie's homecoming party. In front of what used to be Stenger's Pharmacy, a couple of workers were putting up a new sign, **Dixon's Drugs and Soda Fountain**, with a big red Coca Cola symbol in the middle.

A stocky man in his forties with a large mole over his right eye stood on the sidewalk. "Greetings, ma'am!" he said to me in a pronounced southern accent. Under his white lab coat, he was dressed in gray pants with bright blue suspenders and a wide red bow tie. "I'm the new proprietor and pharmacist of Dixon's Drugs and Soda Fountain. Name's Dixon. Robert Dixon. Just moved here from Tennessee…How can I help you?"

"I'm Patience Hester and this my friend Mrs. Cross…" Bitsy sticks out her hand, but Dixon doesn't take it. "We're having a homecoming party today for her son, a vet who's just back from Korea and we want to buy some decorations."

"Just some inexpensive crepe paper, in red, white, and blue," Bitsy explains as she wanders up and down an aisle with Mr. Dixon following her as if he suspects she's going to pocket something.

Finally the man says, still looking at me, "I

think I know just the thing."

"We'll need twenty yards of each," my friend responds. "Quite a lot. Do you have that much?"

The pharmacist leads us to the back of the store, but again when he speaks it's directly to me. "What do you think of this, Mrs. Hester? Three red, white, and blue banners already made up."

I can't tell what's going on. Is the man intentionally treating Bitsy like she's invisible because she's black? If he is, he's getting on my nerves. "Mr. Dixon, is there a problem? Mrs. Cross is the customer today. If you don't want to serve us, we can take our business to Delmont."

Except for the thump of a radiator, the shop is dead quiet. Finally, he speaks. "No problem," he says and he rings up the sale, but when Bitsy pays he doesn't reach for the money, just indicates with his hand that she should drop it on the rubber pad on the counter.

"That was weird," I comment as we hurry down the sidewalk to the church. "The guy acted like you were gonna pinch something."

"That's what it's like when I go to some place where people don't know I'm the wife of a white man and owner of the Hope River Woolen Mill." Bitsy raise her eyebrows and pokes me in the ribs with her elbow, laughing. "It's the race thing. You've just never experienced it. Come on. We're running late."

When I look back over my shoulder, the pharmacist is still standing at the glass door, his jaw clinched, eyes narrowed.

Walking Wounded

The basement of the AME Baptist Church is one of the largest public spaces in Liberty and it's frequently rented for celebrations, meetings and private parties. A big yellow civil defense sign on the door, like the one at the hospital, says Fallout Shelter. Since the Communists now have the atomic bomb, everyone's sure they will come for us. They are already testing it and we are testing ours too, ready to send missiles across the world if needed.

In only a few hours Bitsy and I lay out the refreshments, decorate the church basement with our red, white and blue banners and set up the tables. Then, when we hear the train whistle in the distance, we head over to the railroad station across the street where Lou and Dan and a few of our friends are waiting.

Liberty is a small settlement that looks a lot like a model village that comes with a toy train set. There's a bank on one corner, assorted small stores, a diner, a pharmacy and a courthouse. There's the red wooden train station and a coal train waiting. Even with the one stoplight they put up last year, it takes only five minutes to traverse the whole town.

The incoming B & O locomotive slows and there's a blast of steam as the boxcars crash into each other. A Negro porter, dressed in a sharp gray uniform with silver buttons, steps out of a passenger car and assists a young man down the steps. It's

Willie in a dress uniform, pale and unsteady, a ghost of himself.

At the party, it's like the guest of honor isn't even present. Willie stands for a while at the bottom of the basement stairs, leaning on his crutches, greeting the guests with a hand that trembles, but eventually he lowers himself to a chair.

B.J. Bittman, the owner of the town grocery store, strolls over to me with a cup of coffee. "Think we'll get snow this week?" he asks to make conversation.

"Snow?" I respond.

B.J. chuckles. "That's what the weather report *says*, but they're only right about half the time." We stand watching the group of young people, both black and white, in the corner by the phonograph.

Lilly Bittman, the grocer's wife, is cutting a cake. "How does she do that?" I ask B.K. "She's been totally blind since she was three years old."

"Darned if I know," he responds. "She cuts cake better than I do even with two good eyes."

Shake, Rattle and Roll

Our son Danny puts a platter on the church phonograph. It's *Maybellene* by Chuck Berry, a new rock and roll song that I actually know because they play all the time on the radio. I watch him with affection. He's a good looking young man, funny and smart. Three girls surround him, looking up with big eyes and flirting as he asks them all to dance. Funny he isn't dating. Dan says he's just picky.

"Maybellene, why can't you be true? - Oh Maybellene, why can't you be true? –

All the young people, except Willie, are congregated around the record player.

Willie still sits alone. He's a handsome youth too, as tall as Dan, but thinner with high cheekbones and curly dark hair that was blond when he was young. My husband saunters over to him and holds out a china plate with a piece of red-velvet cake. "So how you doing?" he asks. Willie takes the plate with hands that shake so bad I think he might drop it and Daniel sits down next to him.

"I'm good," Will answers, staring at a yellow and black civil defense sign on the wall across the room.

"How's the leg?"

"It's just my ankle. They had me on IV penicillin for a while. Wanted me to stay a couple more weeks at Walter Reed, but I couldn't stand it, so they put me on pills and let me come home."

When the first record ends, our daughter Mira picks up another. *"Shake, Rattle and Roll!* It's Bill Haley and the Comets"* she yells and begins to waggle her behind.

"I said shake, rattle and roll," Danny sings. *"Shake, rattle and roll!"* With his sandy hair slicked back like Elvis, he could be a performer and I begin to wonder if one of the boys at this party has brought in some booze. *Surely this kind of music and dancing isn't really appropriate in a church basement!*

I look around for Bitsy. Maybe she has the authority to put a stop to this… but she's already doing the jitterbug with her husband Lou, a man with the smooth good looks and charm of another Fred Astaire.

Years ago, I worried about Bitsy and Lou because they were an interracial couple. Though they were in love, with the miscegenation laws in West Virginia, I couldn't see how they could marry. This was back in the forties. Then Lou solved the problem by announcing he was one-eighth colored on his dead father's side. Who could prove he was wrong? In the eyes of the law, one drop of colored blood and you're a Negro, so *then* they could marry. They had a big celebration and everything.

Now Lou, once the manager of the woolen mill, actually owns it. He was always a hard worker and when old man Vipperman, the previous owner, died from lung cancer five years ago, he willed his company to Lou; quite a windfall. Turns out Mr. Vipperman, a widower, had only one child, a son killed in the Great War and no other heirs.

"Shake, Rattle and Roll!" Mira comes jiving across the room making eyes at the guest of honor.

"Want to dance?" she asks sweetly. He shakes his head and points to his foot, which is still in a cast. "Oh, come on! You can do it. Just lean on your crutch and swing to the music!" She reaches over and takes his arm to help him up.

"I said NO," he rages over the music. Danny lifts the needle off the record and the basement goes quiet.

"Ma!" Willie barks. "I want to go now!" And the wounded veteran limps home.

Vanished

"Oh, no!!" I say to my husband as we sit in front of the fire reading the newspaper. "Did you see the front page? Mother and Infant Disappear, Foul Play Suspected"

"What's it about?" Dan asks sipping his coffee. He's reading the letters to the editor section.

"It's Kitty, the girl Bitsy and I helped give birth at the new hospital. Remember I told you we called the Bishop place a few weeks ago to check on her and she seemed so sad and withdrawn. I was worried about her, but didn't want to go visit because her uncle, Sheriff Bishop, is so hateful?

"Listen, to this. It says in the paper that Kitty Bishop of Snake Run and her infant girl have been missing for three days. According to the Sheriff, she went for a walk with her baby snuggly wrapped against the breeze and never came back. It's possible she planned to hitch a ride to Liberty and catch the Greyhound, but foul play is suspected because she didn't take any of her belongings. The Sheriff is offering a reward for any information leading to her return or any clues that can help solve a possible kidnapping or murder.'

"Then there's her description. '15 year old white female with long red hair and freckles, wearing a blue coat and carrying a baby in a white blanket with a pink knitted cap.'"

"How many days has she been gone?" Dan asks.

"Almost a week."

"I bet she'll turn up. Kids run away all the time."

4

Pandora's Box

"My mother was a white woman and I believed, until I was twelve, that I was white too".

Bitsy looks up from the old journal. "That's quite a beginning!" she says. "When we met the old midwife, Grace Potts, during the '30s, everyone knew she was colored. I always thought she kind of favored me because of that."

"She did favor you! Remember your first delivery? She set that up. You were only nineteen and we were called to assist that teenager who wouldn't stop screaming, what was her name, you know the one, the maid's daughter at the Judge's home." We both smile, remembering.

"So where did you get this?" She runs her fingers over the worn paper notebook.

"It was on my front porch this morning in this carved wooden chest. Look..."

My friend takes a sip of coffee, adds more thick cream from our cow, and lifts the lid. When she sees the contents, her mouth falls open. Inside are *twelve* notebooks with Grace's name on the front, written in old-fashioned cursive. "A Pandora's Box," Bitsy laughs. "Perfect for winter." Then carefully she opens the first book again. The pages are dusty and smell faintly of mold.

Hintonville, Virginia

June of 1857

My mother was a white woman and I believed, until I was twelve, that I was white too. Pray, let me explain!

Dr. Richard Coffman, his wife Miriam, and I lived comfortably in a large brick house just outside of Hintonville, a small town in Virginia, and I was so doted on as a girl I didn't know I was chattel.

Then one morning, in early summer, passing the doctor's desk, my eye fell on an open ledger and I was shocked to see my name listed, along with the livestock and the three household slaves, under "property".

Thelma, cook (Chestnut colored, age about 40)
Belle, housemaid (Mulatto, age about 26)
Jammy, stable hand and healer (Dark black, age about 42)
Grace, girl (Quadroon, fair-skinned, age 12)

Further down the list were the field slaves, all twenty-two, ages 5 through 54. Up until then, I'd believed the story they told me, that a white patient of my father had died in childbirth. Mrs. Coffman had raised me as her daughter, taught me to read, to do sums, to sew, to embroider, even to ride a horse like a lady, but the moment I read my name in the slave ledger, the gold and pale blue papered walls of my parents' library collapsed on me.

That very afternoon, as soon as we were alone in the sewing room, I posed my question. "Mother," I said. "Am I a slave like Jammy, Thelma and Belle? Are we all slaves?"

"Why ever would you ask such a thing? Haven't Doctor Coffman and I offered you every advantage?"

"Passing through the library this morning, I noticed his ledger open on his desk. I didn't mean to pry, but I saw my name. I was listed along with the horses and cows."

Mother Coffman swallowed hard and then the words flew out of her mouth like bats from the barn, fast and hard, as if that was the only way she could say them. "It is true. You were born a slave because your real mother was a slave, not a planter's wife as we implied. I didn't tell you the truth because...because I don't believe in slavery. I didn't want you to think like a slave. You're my daughter as much as if I gave birth to you.

"As you have long known, my people are from the state of Pennsylvania and were Quakers. The Quaker Society of Friends believes that no man has the right to own another man. All men are children of God. Doctor Coffman became a Quaker too before we married, but he is a lapsed Quaker now and we don't agree on what in the South is called our "peculiar institution".

"But if you're a child of God, why can't you speak your own mind?" I challenged, though I knew it was impudent. "And don't worry about me thinking like a slave. I will not be a slave much longer!"

"You are only twelve, Grace. Let's not talk of it again," Mother Coffman said very softly. "When

you're eighteen, Father will set you free. Come here." She reached out her arms and pulled me into her lap, me a big girl with my legs dangling down over her full long skirt. Then she rocked me while I sobbed...."Amazing grace – How sweet the sound - That saved a wretch like me," she sang. "I once was lost, but now I'm found – Was blind, but now I see."

"Shall we go on?" I ask, pushing my wire rim glasses up to look at my gold pocket watch.

"What time is it?" Bitsy wonders.

"Two o'clock."

"Oh, no! I've got to get home to check on Willie. Let's start up again next week."

This evening for dinner I have leftover potato soup and a glass of cold milk from our cow. Dan is staying the night with a client, so after I clean up my dishes I go upstairs and open my journal. It's a comforting feeling putting my thoughts down, as if I'm writing a letter to some sensible woman who lives far away. I wonder if that's how Grace Potts felt when she wrote.

"Patience!" the little carved box calls, in a seductive voice, from down in the living room. *"Patience! Don't you want to read more? Bitsy won't care. Come on! You know you're fascinated. Someone left these diaries for you. Come on. Take a peek. Just read a few more pages."*

Finally, I give in. The voice is right. Bitsy won't care. I'll just start reading where we left off.

Hintonville, Virginia,
July 1857

Up until the summer of 1857, when I discovered I was, by law, a slave, I lived the innocent life of a planter's child. Each morning, after an ample breakfast, school began in the library under the tutelage of Mother Coffman who had once been a teacher.

It was illegal to teach a slave to read, but since the Coffmans were raising me as their daughter, no one made comment. If the weather was sunny and pleasant, after eating a mid-day meal with the doctor, we would go out for a horseback or carriage ride.

Riding a horse as a young girl or even a grown woman was somewhat unusual in those times and I'm sure Dr. Coffman must have taken some ribbing when his wife and young daughter were seen trotting along the back roads on side saddles wearing broad brim bonnets.

I had no friends, because mother didn't socialize with the other planter's wives. Sometimes, as we traveled around the countryside, I would see white boys and girls in their shady yards, batting shuttlecocks, rolling hoops down the drive or playing marbles on the porch.

Even brown children had someone to play with. Small clusters of young Negro girls, usually under six, watched as we passed, standing together at the edge of the road with cornhusk dolls. Troops of boys dressed in rags chased after the carriage on their homemade hobbyhorses.

I asked my mother if those children were slaves

and she said, "Yes, but when they're young they usually only carry water, run errands, or help in the kitchen, so they have time to play. When they're older they will work in the fields."

"How much older?" I asked.

"Oh, ten or twelve," she answered staring straight ahead.

My age, I thought. That's my age.

A few weeks after the revelation of my true place in the world, I found Old Jammy in the barn. Jammy was a stable hand, a blacksmith and a general house servant with shoulders as wide as an axe handle. He slept in a cozy stall he'd fixed up with a bed, a table and a fireplace. Sometimes I visited him in the late afternoons when it was raining and I couldn't ride.

"Jammy?" I began quietly. "Did you know I was a slave?"

The man studied the bridle he was oiling. "What do you mean, Miss Gracie?"

"I saw my name listed in Doctor Coffman's ledger under "property." When finally I confronted Mother, she admitted I'm actually father's bondswoman. Have you known all this time?"

Finally, the man looked up and his brown eyes met mine. "All the house slaves know. That would be me, Thelma the cook, Belle the housekeeper, and Mister Blunt, the overseer, of course."

"Where is my real mother?"

Jammy looked toward the open barn door as the rain poured down in gray sheets, "Dr. Coffman's brother, Andrew, sold her South two weeks after she gave birth to you. She wasn't even through her lying-in period. He sold her to a trader on his way to the Carolinas. Sold her as a proven breeder. Then they brought you here to your Ma because your Aunt Glenna couldn't stand the sight of you..."

"Why did she hate me?"

Jammy hesitated..."Because you were evidence of interbreeding..."

"But my true mother, what was her name? Did she love me?"

The old man ran his hands over his head and let out a long sigh. "I never knew her name, because your uncle's family lives in Richmond, but I'm sure she loved you. They say she cried for two days when they took you to the big house and gave you to a wet nurse. Later, they told her you died"

Just then a rider galloped through the yard and pulled up near the hitching post in front of the house. He hurried up the porch and called for the doctor. "Looks like trouble," Jammy muttered.

"Who is it?" I asked.

"Mister Ashby of Edgehill. Someone must be mighty sick or dying. The Ashbys never call the Doc unless the grim reaper's at the door. They're a tight bunch and don't want to pay for a physician. Also, look at the horse. See the lather on his legs. Your father will soon be leaving."

"You mean our Master?"

Jammy gave me a sharp look. "I said, your Father! You best mind yourself, Missy."

5

Arrested

"Did you hear the news on the radio this afternoon?" Dan asks as he puts his sock feet up on the ottoman. He's exhausted from traveling all over the county doing tuberculin examinations on cow's udders.

"What?"

"The Reverend Martin Luther King and eighty-nine people were arrested recently in Montgomery, Alabama."

"Who's Martin Luther King?"

"He's a young Baptist minister who's become the leader of the Bus Boycott. He agrees with Gandhi that social change, even revolution, can be achieved without violence."

"Why'd they get thrown in jail?" I continue my mending.

"It said on the morning news that King and the Montgomery Improvement Association were holding a protest and the law just scooped them all up. I didn't realize the Reverend King's house was bombed a few weeks ago. He has little kids and a wife…Things are really heating up."

"Seems like every other week, something happens down South. I feel like a storm is coming. It's peaceful here."

"West Virginia isn't the same as the Deep South, Patience. Because of coalmining, blacks and whites have worked together for sixty or seventy years. Come over here." He pats the sofa cushion beside him and when I sit, he puts his arm around me. "What have you been doing for the last few days?"

"I've been waiting for you to ask me. Look at this." I rise and bring him the hand-carved chest.

"It looks old. Where did it come from?"

"I don't know. I found it on the front porch the day you left. It's a box of Grace Potts' journals. Remember her, the old colored midwife that lived on Horse Shoe Run. Since we almost always use the back door, the chest could have been sitting there for a week."

I hand him the first little book. "I figure someone found the box and thought, because I'm a midwife, I should have it. Want me to read a little?" Dan gives me a nod and lies down with his head in my lap.

I quickly summarize how Grace Potts had been told she was the adopted white daughter of a plantation owner, but learned when she was twelve that she was actually a slave; then I begin...

Hintonville, Virginia, at the base of the mountains in the Great Shenandoah Valley, is a pleasant village surrounded by rich farmland. The doctor owned a modest plantation that he'd inherited from his father. It was only a small spread, named Oak Hill, but it gave him a comfortable income. His brother, Andrew, lived near Richmond where he'd taken over the family tobacco business.

A white overseer, Mr. Blunt, who occasionally came to the house on business, managed the slaves and the farm. He was a thick man with one cloudy eye that seemed to follow me and I usually went upstairs to sew when I saw him.

On his 500 fertile acres, four miles north of town, father's slaves grew corn, wheat, oats and cattle, but no cotton or tobacco. The foothills of the Alleghenies were too cold for those crops and they also required too many field hands.

I once heard the doctor tell a friend his philosophy of controlling slaves. "There are three steps in molding the character of a valuable bondsman; strict discipline, instilling a sense in the darkie of his own inferiority and, finally, inculcating in the man a deep sense of helplessness." He and the fellow planter were sitting in rockers smoking cigars and I was standing there serving lemonade, a ghost listening in.

"I do not whip them, you understand," the doctor went on, barking a laugh, "I leave that to the overseer, and I don't believe in branding, that's dangerous and inhumane."

The fact is I had never seen a slave brutalized until I was eight. Then one spring, when our family made a trip to Charlottesville, I saw a black man being whipped in front of the courthouse and felt sick.

The muscular slave with a brand burned on his cheek, was stripped to his waist and chained to a post on the town square. Blood dripped down his scarred back while a man in a bowler hat wielded the strap. All around him, white men smoked and conversed with jocularity as if they were at a summer picnic. There were even some darkies watching.

Mother grabbed me, pressing my face into her long skirt and headed the other way down the cobblestone street. "You didn't see that!" she said.

"But I did!"

"You did not," she remonstrated.

That was the last time I was taken to the city. My world narrowed to Hintonville and the curtain dropped around the rest of the South.

"Wow," Dan says. "That's incredible. I mean you know it's true, but when you hear someone who was actually there write about seeing a slave being whipped…"

"You want me to go on?"

"Sure. It's not exactly a bedtime story, but it's interesting. This was written a hundred years ago, right?"

It must have been near the end of that summer when I cornered Jammy, the stable man, again, and begged him for more information about my real parents.

"Do you not see it?" he asked as he saddled my horse. "Your resemblance to your cousin Blanche, your uncle Andrew's daughter?" I shook my head, unsure what he meant.

"Look at her the next time she comes to visit."

Jammy's answer left me bewildered, but when

Uncle Andrew's family stopped with us for a few days in August, on the way back from their holidays in the mountains, I stared at her with new eyes. Blanche was just two years my senior and in days gone by, when she came from Richmond we would play dolls.

I could see the resemblance now. We were both slight with narrow shoulders and bony fingers. We both had wide smiles and the same wide eyes with long lashes. But Blanche had blue eyes, pale skin with freckles and golden hair that she parted in the middle and let hang in sausage curls around her face. My skin was olive; my hair dark and curly, so unruly it would often spring out of my braids, and my eyes were light brown.

Sitting around the table in the wood paneled dining room, my attention was diverted by my father's coarse oath.

"Well I'll be damned. Pardon my language ladies." he shook the newspaper and read to us from the front page. "Richmond planters report that the number of escaped slaves has doubled in the last two years."

"If Buchanan wins the presidency, he'll crack down on the abolitionists." Uncle Andrew responded. "They're the ones who are encouraging this. It's their hypocrisy that bothers me. They know damn well the wealth of this country, North and South, depends on slavery. Cotton and tobacco are the main national exports and they can't be grown without massive free labor. I read in Harper's Magazine, last week, that slaves in this country are worth more than all of the rest of America's wealth,

railroads, workshops, and factories combined." He stopped and drew a deep breath. "Do you know who the slave patrollers are in your area?"

"Okey Layton and his clan," Father responded. "A bunch of poor whites and they couldn't find a needle in a haystack if they tried. Any darkie with half a brain could outsmart them. Lucky most of my slaves are like children, completely dependent, witless, really."

I was so incensed I almost threw my crystal goblet at him. Witless! He was talking about Jammy! He was talking about me! As if a person's skin tone affected their brain!

"Do you want to bring in the peach pie, Thelma?" Mother called to our cook, trying to change the subject.

"Just last week on a Saturday night, two of Malcolm Moore's best bondsmen stole away," Father went on, not responding to Mother's signal. "They've never been found."

"Well, I'll tell you this," Uncle Andrew stood up and paced the dining room. "If any of my slaves escape, the first thing I'll do is hire a tracker. A good field hand is worth $1000, but the price of a slave catcher with slave dogs is only $150 a head. Trouble is, the slave catcher has to be able to pull his dogs off the man before they tear him to pieces."

Thelma cut the pie and served us, but after imagining myself as a runaway slave being torn to bits by savage hounds, I had no appetite.

The day after Uncle Andrew and his family left, I located Jammy in the barn again. "Is it true, that Miss Blanche and I have the same father?"

The stable man scratched his head and looked toward the big house. "It wouldn't be the first time a master forced himself on a comely slave girl in an empty shed."

The air went out of me.

"So Blanche is my half-sister? Uncle Andrew forced my mother? Forced her?" Jammy was silent as he continued to curry the tail of one of Dr. Coffman's beautiful Morgans.

"It's not uncommon, Grace. Look at the skin colors of the slaves. Notice the different shades of brown. There's white blood in most of us. The embarrassment of your birth nearly killed your Aunt Glenna. That's why she hated you and they sold your real mother down the river. They were going to sell you too, until Mrs. Coffman asked if she could keep you."

"I hate Uncle Andrew! I hate Blanche! I hate the whole family! And I understand now why Aunt Glenna looks at me as if I were an abomination." Tears ran down my cheeks. Then the dinner bell rang and Jammy pulled out his red kerchief and wiped my face.

"I know. I know. Don't think of it no more," he whispered. "We must live for today. That's all we have...the gift of this day and a few moments of joy."

"What joy is there?" I asked obstinately. "When we're captives owned like beasts of the field."

"You think animals don't feel joy? Look out across the meadow. See those colts leaping in the air. See the barn cats curled up the sun. Hear the birds sing."

He was right.   A robin sat on a fence post chirping its heart out for no reason at all.

"It's taken me years to come to this," the blacksmith went on, "But I'll save you some time. Here's what I've determined. I am a slave. I can never be rich or famous, but I can be kind. I can do my duty to God and my Master. I can comfort. I can heal and I can care for the animals in my charge.   That is my reward until my Maker calls me."

I looked at my old friend, his simple broadcloth pants and shirt, his strong dark hands, his graying hair and I was struck by how eloquently he spoke. Still I wasn't satisfied and knew I couldn't be... until I was free.

"We should quit for tonight." I said when I noticed Dan's eyes drooping.

"Yeah, thanks. I think I must have dozed off for a moment, but it's interesting. I read Frederick Douglas's autobiography years ago. It hurts to hear firsthand about slavery, but it's part of the nation's history. Slaves built so much of our country, not to mention the wealth of so many southern families and northerners too. Are you going to read all of the diaries?"

I stand up to bank the fire for the night. "Of course, even if they're painful, I want to read them. I want to understand."

6

Compulsion

I'm at it again. I can't help myself. As soon as I finish the morning chores, feed the chickens, water the stock and milk the cows, I return to Grace Potts' writing...

Hintonville, Virginia
November 1857

I turned thirteen in November of 1857 and began to intentionally listen to conversations between the house servants to glean what I could about their lives as slaves. One thing in particular I wanted to know... how a slave might get free.

There was an old black couple that Mother Coffman knew and liked, Agnes Washington, the laundress and her husband, Jim, the barber, in the nearby town of Staunton, who owned his own shop. They appeared to be free and independent. Every few months, Mother Coffman took her quilts and blankets to Agnes because they were so heavy and hard for Belle to wash.

How much she paid for the service I don't know, but she was always so happy when she came back with the coverlets all wrapped in brown paper that I guess it was worth it. Usually the trip took all day and she sat around with Agnes and talked while

Agnes and her helper did the laundry.

One evening, as she was telling Belle that she planned to take the bedding to town in the morning, I inquired if I could go with her. She seemed taken aback, because I'd been so sullen since I'd learned of my slave origin, but she agreed with pleasure.

It was a beautiful day, the maples already turning red, wild asters and golden rod waving along the ditches and fencerows. With the rhythm of the swaying carriage, I was almost asleep when a commotion up ahead awakened me. Two white men with pistols in holsters were blocking the road and Jammy was forced to halt our conveyance.

"Where you headed, boy?" the shorter of the two yelled to him. Mrs. Coffman and I were sheltered in the closed carriage and could not be seen.

"Slave catchers!" the gentle woman whispered.

"To Hintonville to take quilts to the laundress, Massa." Jammy answered.

"Let's see your pass, darkie!" the second man demanded.

"I got no pass, Massa. My mistress rides with me." I hated to hear him talk like that, like some ignorant old man.

The patroller approached and peered in the windows.

"Ma'am..." said the larger of the two, tipping his hat, a rough fellow dressed in black and covered with road dust. "We're seeking two runaway slaves, a well-built black man of about six feet, age 26, named Ben and his mulatto companion, Pious, a

female around 18 with light gray eyes. They escaped the Auburn plantation last night and are believed to be traveling along this pike."

"Captain Boggs commanded us to guard this bridge and search everyone who passed," his partner declared without a hint of regret. "You will need to step out." I sucked in my breath. Nothing like this had ever happened before.

Mrs. Coffman was offended. "You know who I am don't you?" She didn't wait for an answer. "Dr. Richard Coffman's wife. Dr. Coffman of Oak Hill in Hintonville." The two slave catchers looked at each other and almost laughed, apparently not impressed.

"All the same, Ma'am. We have a job to do. Mr. Auburn's lost six slaves this year and we have to put a stop to it before all the Africans in the country think they can runaway. I'm sure you understand..." He nodded at Jammy, implying that the Coffmans owned slaves like all the other well-to-do whites in the area, then he boldly opened the carriage door and held out his dirty hand to assist us down.

I could tell Mrs. Coffman didn't want to touch him, but there was nothing else we could do. We had to get out and with our long skirts and petticoats we needed the help. Then we stood in the rutted road while the men stuck their heads in the coach and our driver stared at the ground unable to do anything to protect us.

The patrollers ripped through all the quilts and bedding and pulled up the gray velvet seat to look underneath, but of course there was no large black *man and his woman hiding there. Then without a word of thanks or apology, they let us go. Mother Coffman held her head high through the whole thing, and I do commend her.*

For a while, after we got back on the road, we were silent. "I don't know what Dr. Coffman will say…" Mother started out. She never called him by his first name in public, always, Dr. Coffman or The Doctor. "Treating us that way…the patrollers aren't usually on the roads in the day time. Someone must be paying them extra."

"Maybe the Auburns," I offered. "If that many slaves got away from Father, he'd be mad too. Where do they go anyway?"

"North to Pennsylvania or Ohio or New York, but more and more they're running all the way to Canada since Congress passed the Runaway Slave Act. Now, even if a slave can make it to Ohio, a slave owner or his representative can cross the state line, track down the fugitive and bring him back in chains. Not only that, even a person who doesn't believe in slavery can be forced to help capture the fugitive. It's a federal crime if they don't, punishable by a prison sentence or a $1000 fine."

I swallowed hard imagining myself sprinting through the dark woods, hounds baying after me. It seemed impossible, but I vowed that one day I'd try.

7

Rage and Sorrow

How's Willie settling in?" I ask Bitsy when she comes over to read again. Outside it's snowing, big white flakes, whirling like feathers through the cold air. She twists her mouth as if biting an unripe persimmon.

"Not so great. It just makes me so sad, Patience. He was such a good kid. Now he's a shadow of himself. He just picks at his meals. If I push him to eat or talk, he gets angry and shuts me out. He just lies around, complaining that his foot hurts and referring to himself as a cripple. He won't even read or watch the TV. Lou says, give him time... He's still in a lot of pain."

"You told me his leg isn't healing."

"It's his foot and ankle now. He's at the VA every week and they're giving him penicillin shots again. His old cast comes off in another ten days or so."

"Are you happy with his care? Do they treat you any differently because of your color?"

"It's hard to say. We always have to wait for hours. The VA isn't a great model of efficiency and everyone else seems to wait too. The doctors don't tell us much, either. If Nurse Becky and Dr. Blum were still around, I could ask them some questions."

"I got a Christmas card from them postmarked in North Carolina, but I think they've moved again and I lost the envelope. It's funny how people drift out of your life. You left me once and I'll admit, I'm afraid you'll leave again someday." Bitsy reaches over and lays her warm brown hand over my cool white one.

"Don't be silly, girl. Come on, let's read about Grace."

"Wait, I want to ask you something... Did your Mom, Big Mary, ever talk to you about the slave days? Some of your relations might have been slaves."

"I know my Great-grandmother was. She was a fancy lady from New Orleans and was freed during the Civil War. I've seen photos of her all dressed up in a high-necked black dress, her hair braided and wrapped around her head. I actually look a little like her."

"My great-grandparents were from New Orleans too. Go figure! Maybe we're related. Maybe our family trees touch."

Bitsy rolls her eyes. "It's possible. What do you know about them?"

"Not much. They died in some epidemic, yellow fever, maybe. What else did Big Mary tell you?"

Nothing really except she eventually ended up in North Carolina and married my Great-grandfather, a free black man. I didn't really ask anything more."

"You weren't curious?"

"Not really. It made my mother sad to talk about it. She wanted to think about the future and the good days to come. Did *you* want to know about your family's troubles when you were young?" Bitsy returned my question.

"I guess not. I was only thirteen when both my parents died so there was no one to ask."

"Well, see what I mean? I'd heard about the slave ships and Harriet Tubman and cotton plantations and all that... but nothing personal. The real history of slavery is hidden even from the ancestors of slaves."

I bring out another journal.

"You've skipped ahead haven't you?" Bitsy gives me a knowing look.

"Yeah, I couldn't help myself."

"It's ok." She stares out the kitchen window. "With all my worries about Willie, I don't have much time."

Hintonville, Virginia,
February 1858

After the new year, during the gray days of the winter, in the year of '58, I acquainted myself with every book on the institution of slavery in the Coffman's library, including George Fitzhugh's Sociology for the South, a dreadful book that rationalized why whites must be the caretakers of the black man.

The Negro, Fitzhugh wrote, is a grown child who needs the economic and social protections of a master. Without it, he would be a beast. Slavery ensures that blacks will be economically secure and morally civilized. I thought of Jammy and gritted my teeth. The Negroes weren't beasts, the slave owners were!

Because I was sure the doctor would object, I tried to conceal my research. Sometimes when I read, I'd hide in an alcove under the stairs. Sometimes I'd put a book about slavery inside one of the schoolbooks Mrs. Coffman gave me to study. I also began to inform myself first hand of the South's "peculiar institution", by talking to the house servants whenever my parents weren't around.

One day, I took Jammy aside in the barn. "Mr. Jammy. I want to apologize if I have ever treated you with disrespect. I know it's no excuse, but I thought of myself as the master's daughter and believed it was my right to order you about, but now that I know I am a slave too, I greatly regret my manners. Please forgive me."

The groom paused in his work and looked me over and then he laughed. "Oh, Miss Gracie, you've never been a tyrant. You're the nicest little white girl I know."

"Really?" I said. "I've been worried about it night and day. Can I ask you a question? Do you want to be free?"

"Hush, Miss Grace." He looked around and motioned me into one of the empty stalls. "You could get a slave in serious trouble talking like that. Men, and women too, have been whipped for just talking about freedom. Some have even been sent South in a chain gang."

"You mean to the Carolinas?" I asked. "Where my mother went."

"No, further south... Louisiana, Alabama, Mississippi, Georgia, where they work black men

like dogs in the cotton fields and you can never come back."

The conversation ended when Mr. Blunt the overseer came across the yard and headed straight for the barn. "You there! Stable hand," he shouted. "Ready my horse. I have to get back to the plantation. Make sure the bridle isn't tight or I'll have your hide."

"Yes, Sir. Yes, Sir. Right away, Sir!" Jammy bowed and scraped. "You go on now, Missy," he whispered to me. "Go and play. This old fellow has work to do."

I slipped by Mr. Blunt, who smelled like garlic and tobacco, and ran toward the house, then stopped and hid behind a big oak in order to study my enemy. Blunt was dressed all in black with a wide brimmed black hat and his face looked brittle with hate.

It was strange. I'd never had an enemy before. Mother Coffman taught me, from the earliest age, to love my neighbor as it says in the Bible. Now, with squinted eye, I glared at the overseer and felt a dark fury, ready to defend what I thought of as my people.

I was fooling myself, of course. I was no Harriet Tubman. The overseer mounted his horse and with out so much as a thank you to Jammy, rode away, leather whip in his hand.

Hintonville, Virginia
April 1858

Early in the spring of '58, we had an exciting event in the stables. Jammy had pointed out weeks before that one of the doctor's favorite horses, Fancy, a rare chestnut Morgan with a golden tail, was in foal. He'd even let me lay my hand on her side to feel the unborn baby horse move and my eyes grew big as hen's eggs.

It was on a cold afternoon, windy and gray, when the commotion began. Doctor Coffman, returning from his medical rounds, went straight to the stable and few minutes later stormed into the house.

"It's happening!" he shouted to no one in particular. "Fancy is bagging up and milk is beading at the end of her teats. It won't be long now." He paced the front hall. "I just hope she's ok. Maybe I should sleep out in the stable tonight."

Mother floated down the front stairway in a long sleeved brown day dress with a lace collar. "Now Richard," she said. "Jammy is perfectly capable of handling it. He's been a midwife to horses as long as we've owned him. Remember, you paid twice what any other slave was worth when you purchased him years ago. You just sleep inside and stay warm."

"I suppose you're right. I'll tell Jammy to call me if there's a problem. He can take the cold better than me. He's used to it."

That night I heard doors opening and closing and several low voices calling. I was certain the conversation was about Fancy and I suspected that things were not going well. I cracked the window, but could hear nothing. I needed to know what was happening, so I dressed quickly, wrapped a cloak around me and tiptoed down the back stairs. At the bottom, I slipped on my shoes and crept out the door.

It was a dark moonless night, with a wind that whipped the trees and I moved through the shadows to the side of the barn. Through a small window, I could see the horse. The first thing I noticed was that Fancy's beautiful golden tail was bound and knotted like a thick rope and her back legs were trussed. The poor thing lay on her side panting and groaning softly. Old Jammy was on his knees near her backside, pulling on something.

"Good girl! Good girl!" I could hear him murmur over and over. Dr. Coffman paced back and forth.

"Dammit, Jammy! Let me in there! Don't just pull; rotate the legs a little. Use a corkscrew maneuver. Do you even know what that means? The lower shoulder must be stuck. I don't want to lose this foal or the mare either."

"Now don't you worry, yourself, Master. Old Jammy knows what to do…"

When Father moved a little to the side, I could see better. Two small legs were coming out of the mare and part of the head. Every time Fancy strained, Jammy pulled the legs with all his might, then in between he rocked the legs back and forth as if working the foal into a better position. "It's ok, girl. It's ok. Good Mama. You can do it," he crooned.

Once, Fancy struggled to get to her feet. "Hold her down. Hold her down!" Dr. Coffman yelled, but Jammy remained calm and kept patting the horse's rump until she settled. "It's ok, girl. It's ok," he continued his song.

With the next push whatever had been improperly positioned, came unstuck and the whole mass of wet animal swooshed out in Jammy's lap. I had seen kittens born, but nothing this big. The foal, covered in membrane just lay there and I held my breath.

"Is it alive?" Dr. Coffman asked bending down. "Yes! Look! It's trying to cough. It's a filly!"

"Here, Master. Let me put her up near her Mama." Jammy took charge. "She can lick the membrane off. It's good for them both." He grabbed the new baby by its back legs and pulled it up to Fancy's face, and then Fancy went to work on it. Lick. Lick. Lick. The little horse nickered and sneezed.

I wanted more than anything to go inside the barn and touch the baby horse, but I knew I'd be in serious trouble, so I silently retraced my steps and crawled into bed.

In the morning, Dr. Coffman could not say enough about Jammy's skill as a horse midwife. "I got one fine animal man when I bought that African!" he bragged. "He's gentle and smart. I think I could hire him out as a horse doctor and animal healer and make some silver."

"But would it be worth it, worrying about him

out on the roads with the patrollers prowling about?" Mother wondered out loud.

"Most owners of slaves with special skills rent them out," Father argued. "The bondsman brings you his pay on Sunday and you give him back a few coins he can keep. Jammy wouldn't run. He knows he has it too good."

"I didn't mean that," Mother said, patting her lips with her napkin. "It's the patrollers. They have license to whip or to beat any suspicious slave they find on the road. Some just pummel a black man for the fun of it."

Dr. Coffman raised his eyebrows, conceding Mother's point and I was glad that the talk about renting-out Jammy stopped right there. The old man was my friend and I depended on his counsel.

A few days after the birth of the foal, I went to the library and looked at Dr. Coffman's books. There was a row of The Farmer's Almanacs, along with a leather bound volume of The Gentleman Farmer, but I couldn't find anything about the husbandry of horses.

I turned next to his medical books and pulled down Churchill's Midwifery, a worn text published in Dublin and the woodcut illustrations showed human babies lying in the womb in all kinds of positions.

Though the author reassured that nine out of ten infants came out head first with little fuss, there was so much variation in those that weren't headfirst! Some foals presented by the legs like the one I saw; some by the arm or the forehead or face.

There were also several copies of the Southern Medical and Surgical Journal. In one, I found a detailed description of how to do a delivery through a woman's belly. Astonishing! The mother-to-be was cut open, the baby lifted out and then she was sewn up again. Dr. Francois Prevost had finally perfected his procedure by experimenting on thirty slaves. It didn't say how many bondswomen had died before he succeeded... or how many babies.

In another article, I found an item by a Dr. Charles White declaring that blacks bore surgical operations without ether.

"I have even amputated the legs off Negroes where they held their limbs up for me," he wrote.

A dark cloud of fury passed over me again. Not only were Africans enslaved, branded, worked to death, whipped and separated from their families, but they were cut open and experimented on as if they felt no pain.

"Let's stop," says Bitsy. "I'm so angry, I'm ready to spit." I put the second journal back in the chest.

"I'm sorry Bitsy," I say looking into her brown eyes wet with tears, not falling yet. "I'm sorry for every cruel and stupid thing the whites did to the Negros, every vicious, stupid thing."

"It's not anything to do with you, Patience. All that nonsense about the African being unable to feel pain, too primitive to learn was just justification for one group of people using another group of people as *farm machines*. Racism is a product of American greed. The nation got rich on the scarred backs of

Negroes."

My friend lets out a big breath, overwhelmed by her speech. "The saddest part is that a hundred years later, the lies they told each other about the Africans still affect some white people's view. You aren't part of the problem, Patience. You're part the solution."

Bitsy stands up and shrugs on her orange and brown plaid jacket. "I guess you can read the journals on your own for awhile. I need a break." Then she's gone, roaring away on her red Harley motorcycle.

Spring

8

March 1956

Fracture

Tonight Dan and I went over to watch television with Lou and Bitsy at their house on the hill at the end of Wild Rose Road. We've thought of buying a TV of our own, but it just seems so extravagant. Then again, way down in the hollow we probably couldn't get reception.

About once a month we accept their invitation to watch *The Ed Sullivan Show* on Sunday night. It's as fun as going to the movies. Bitsy makes popcorn and I bring cold apple cider. Lou even gets out a few bottles of beer.

Before the show, Bitsy asked me to come upstairs to look at Willie's foot and it was worse than I ever imagined. There were two gaping wounds on his ankle as if the bone infection was worming its way to the surface and the profuse pus smelled horrible. No wonder the poor kid wouldn't come down and join us. He knows he stinks.

"That's where he stays most of the time," Bitsy whispered after we'd gone back downstairs. "I'm supposed to check his circulation every day. I try not to worry, or at least not show it, but I do."

Before our program started, there was a special

called *The South Rises Again.* Apparently the southern states are once more challenging the 1954 Supreme Court decision requiring schools to integrate.

Virginia, Mississippi, Georgia and Alabama are invoking state's rights and claiming, "The Court drove a knife through the very heart of the Constitution."

"Damn racists," Lou choked out. "Looks like the bigots will go down fighting tooth and nail."

The T.V. special continued with a clip of white men marching in Georgia with confederate flags and signs that said Save Our Children from the Black Plague.

"I need another beer," groaned Dan. "The whole South's going nuts."

After the special segment and a commercial for Old Gold Cigarettes, Ed Sullivan strolled on the stage to a roar of fans. Then with a wave of one hand, he introduced the featured guest singer, Harry Belafonte, performing a new hit, *The Banana Boat Song.*

"Work all night on a drink of rum - Daylight come and me wan' go home"

During the next commercial, Bitsy and I went to the kitchen to make more popcorn. "Belafonte is great, isn't he? I've never heard him sing before," I commented.

"He grew up in Jamaica, but he's a civil rights activist behind the scenes in the U.S. now, supporting the bus boycott and Reverend King."

"Now I like him even more!"

"Hey, want to stay and watch Hitchcock when

Ed Sullivan's over?" Lou asked. "It's another great show."

"Who's Hitchcock? It's not more news, is it?" I asked. "The news makes me so depressed."

"You mean the stuff about the boycott and the racist protestors?" asked Bitsy as she fooled with the dials on the back of the TV to get a better picture. "People need to see it."

"I'm all for the boycott and people standing up for themselves. It's the backlash that's getting to me. I didn't know how deep prejudice was in America."

"You're naïve, Patience. If we want to change things, it's going to get ugly. For too long Negroes have taken the back seats. We've eaten crumbs while white men sat at the banquet table. It's time to stop with the 'Yes Sir and Yes Ma'am. We're going to have to shove our head in the lion's mouth!"

Lou puts his hand on his wife's knee. "Come on, honey. You're under a lot of stress. Don't get upset."

"But did you see those white faces on the screen?" I said. "They're beasts full of hate. The lion is about to bite down…hard!"

"Well, that's a risk we'll have to take," Bitsy flashes back. "Negroes have fought for this country and died for this country and the whites aren't going to oppress us much longer!"

Dan pulls himself up and fakes a yawn, indicating he's ready to go home before we get in a real fight. "Well, thanks for the evening folks. It's late and I have a long day tomorrow. Have to be up at five."

As we stand at the door, I want to get one more word in. I want my friend to understand how it makes me feel watching those racists, full of ignorance and self-righteousness, but my husband helps me into my coat. "It's late," he says again, gently pulling my arm.

"Here let me get the porch light," Lou says, stepping in front of Bitsy to separate us. "Watch your step now, folks. Drive safe."

Hintonville, Virginia
August 1858

It was in later that summer when I saw my first human birth. It was an accident to be sure and I had no knowledge of obstetrics other than the pictures in the medical book.

Dr. Coffman was called to a home a few hours away, where a long time patient was ill with dropsy. I knew the doctor would be gone most of the night because he planned a long session of bloodletting. Mrs. Coffman, Thelma, and Jammy had gone to Hintonville in the carriage to pick up supplies, and I was allowed to stay home with Belle. This was a treat, because it meant I was free to explore the library and read anything I wanted.

As soon as everyone was gone, I went to Mrs. Coffman's selection of abolitionist books and pulled a worn copy of Uncle Tom's Cabin from behind a stack of Godey's Lady's Books. Then I curled up to read the wildly popular novel written by a Connecticut woman who Dr. Coffman disparaged as knowing nothing of the South. In a fit of rage, he'd once thrown the book in the trash, but Mother had recovered it.

It was almost dark and I was deep into the novel when I heard a horse coming fast then pounding on the door. "Dr. Coffman! Come at once. There's trouble in the slave quarters!" It was Mr. Blunt.

There was nothing else for it. Belle was in the washhouse out behind the kitchen, so I stuffed the book behind the Godey's magazines and went to the door. "I'm sorry, sir," I answered, trying not to look at his one cloudy eye. "Dr. Coffman and Mrs. Coffman are gone. There's no one here, but me and our servant woman." I had never spoken to Mr. Blunt directly before.

"Then you'll have to do. Get your cloak, Miss."

"I don't understand. What's the trouble?"

"A slave woman's having a baby; she's screaming something fierce and the other darkies can't do a thing with her. If I lose her, the master will blame me. She'll listen to you if you command her to lie still because you're a white woman." He took off his wide brimmed black hat and put it over his heart, beseeching me. "Come, now. There's no time to lose!"

I didn't know what to do. The overseer revolted me, and I'd have to ride behind him on his horse and hold on to him. I knew very little about childbirth and doubted the screaming mother would obey me.

On the other hand, I'd wanted to visit the slave quarters since I'd learned I was a slave. This might be my chance, so I wrote a hasty note for Mother, ran back to the library, grabbed Dr. Coffman's book on midwifery and tied on my cloak.

The journey to the farm, five miles away, was accomplished swiftly as I clung to the back of the overseer's coat. Soon we turned into a tree lined lane that ended before a pleasant white farmhouse that I took to be Mr. Blunt's lodging.

The overseer didn't stop at the house, but continued to urge his horse across the farmyard past two large barns, a stable and a granary. We eventually halted in front of a row of 10 low wooden shacks, each with a stone chimney and one window. These were the slave quarters and from the one on the end came a scream that would curdle milk.

Mr. Blunt helped me down and led the way toward the woman in travail. As we rushed by the slave cabins, the residents, wearing only the crudest of garments, silently bowed and took off their hats as if I was someone important.

Many of the cabins didn't have doors and as we passed I tried to peek in. Most had sparse furniture and only loose pallets of straw on the floor. A few had stools made of logs and some had crude tables. In the middle of the complex, there was an outhouse and a well with a rope and a bucket for dipping.

Finally we stopped in front of the cabin from whence came the screams. A rough plank door stood slightly ajar. "Hannah!" Mr. Blunt yelled in a rough way.

A stooped woman wearing a white apron over a worn gray dress stepped outside. She looked at me with suspicion, but curtsied, then turned when the mother inside began to scream again.

"This is Doctor Coffman's assistant," Blunt lied. "The doctor is attending a sick bed and Miss Coffman is here to see if she can help Lottie." It sickened me to see him act like he cared when I knew it was only the dollar value of the slave woman and his reputation that mattered to him.

I peered in the door of the dim shack and saw there was only one candle. "We'll need better light," I said to the overseer. "Have the men bring two kerosene lamps, a cake of soap and another bucket of hot water from the house. We'll also need clean linens, sheets and towels."

These were things I'd heard Dr. Coffman discuss with Mother. He complained that many of the pregnant slave women he attended had no supplies for their deliveries and he blamed their masters. The poor white women, he said, had even less. It wasn't that Father truly cared about the Africans either, but he knew the women would sell for $1000 and he didn't want the plantation owners to lose confidence in him if one of them expired.

Mr. Blunt looked surprised when I made my requests, but he followed my orders and headed for the farmhouse calling two boys to come with him.

A few minutes later, I was alone with the two slave women, but I reminded myself that I was one of them and there was work to be done. Every few moments, Lottie screamed and screamed.

Finally I spoke. "Miss Hannah, how long has the new mother been in travail?"

"Since last night," the old lady informed me. "She commenced bleeding at dawn. Some terror is holding the baby in and though she strains and strains she can't overcome it. I'm afraid if she doesn't give birth soon, she'll tear herself apart."

I took off my cloak and sat down on a tree stump that served as a chair. "Lottie," I said softly as if talking to a wild animal. "If you can stop yelling for a few minutes I want to ask you some questions." The girl, who wasn't much older than I was, opened her eyes. When she observed I was white and probably from the master's family, she tried to hold her cries in.

"Can you tell me where it hurts? In your stomach or lower down?"

"Aaeeeee!" she started to scream, but cut the wail off by biting her hand.

I kneeled next to her and patted her back. "It's ok. It's ok. Don't push. Don't strain." I tried to talk like Jammy when the mare was foaling. "That's a good girl. There you go now. The pain will soon be over. Just rest." If I had been worried about what to do next, those worries were gone. I was here for Lottie. That was all. I was here for the mother.

"It's so bad, Miss. Something way down below burns like fire," she answered me.

"Is there no midwife here?" I asked the old lady.

"No. And Lottie's suffering has driven away her familiars. I'm the only one that could stand it. Is Dr. Coffman coming?"

"He's away on a case and Mr. Blunt said I

should come."

I wished I could tell Hannah that I'd never seen a human baby born before, only one foal and two kittens, but I didn't want the young woman to hear.

"Has Lottie had anything to eat or drink today?"

"No. She refused all my urgings."

"I'll have Mr. Blunt bring some broth from his personal kitchen immediately. How about a sip of tea? Mother says peppermint is soothing for the stomach."

"I'll make her some straight away," the old lady promised. "But I don't think she'll drink it."

When I stepped to the door, Lottie began to cry again, so I made my errand quick. A small boy in a short shift made of gray linsey-woolsey was standing in the yard out in front.

"You there, child. What's your name?"

"Samuel, Miss," he said with a lisp.

"Do you know Mr. Blunt?" The boy nodded but didn't say a word or make any eye contact.

"Well run quick and tell him Miss Coffman needs warm chicken broth from his house and she needs it right now. Tell him Lottie is poorly. Can you do that?" He nodded again and ran like lightning down the row of shanties.

When I got back inside, Hannah had a chipped porcelain cup held up to the patient's mouth, but Lottie pulled her head away. "See, she won't take it!" the old woman complained. I took the cup and sat down next to the girl.

"Here, Lottie. Take a sip. It's good for the baby. The baby needs some strength." She took a

sip and then a few more. "If I help you, can you walk around the cabin?"

Lottie shook her head no, but when I gently pulled on her arm, she stood and we paced the room together. Soon, a mulatto house slave, wearing a clean blue dress with a white collar, came from the overseer's house with a cast iron pot in one hand and a carpetbag that contained linens in the other. She looked around at the miserable conditions of the shed, set the broth on the table, nodded to me, then left in a hurry as if coming into the dreadful slave cabin offended her. No one had returned with a lamp and hot water, but we were doing ok without them.

The minute I lifted the lid off the pot, the rich smell of the chicken soup filled the room. "How long do you think Lottie's been in labor? You said her pains started last night. At sundown or near dawn?"

"Sometime in the middle, I would say. Generally, us slaves collapse around nine. Mr. Blunt insists on it and walks through the quarters to make sure all the lights are out. Says we can't work if we burn the candles at both ends. He don't really care how tired we are; it's all about the work in the fields.

"Sometimes my bones ache so bad, I can't sleep." She bit her lip when she realized who she was talking to. "Sorry, Miss. You're just so comfortable like, I forgot my place."

Just then, Lottie leaned over as if she was going to drop to the floor, but I caught her in my arms. She let out a moan and bent over the simple wooden table. *"Something's coming!"* *she howled and squatted down with her hand between her legs.*

I helped Lottie to lie down on her side, as Jammy had positioned Father's horse, Fancy.

"Soap and water!" I requested, looking around the room for Hannah. "I need soap and water. Don't push, Lottie. Please, don't push!" But the girl couldn't help it. Lying on her side, she grabbed her upper knee and pushed so hard veins bulged in her neck. That's when I saw it, a small hairy head.

"Ow! Ow!" she wailed again as if she had been branded with a hot iron. A few faces peeked in the door, their eyes wide with concern and I swallowed hard.

"Here, let me hold you," I said, dipping a cloth in the warm soapy water and placing it over the top of the baby's head with my hand. The head pushed out a little more and when I took the cloth off for a peek, the mother's skin was blanched as white as Hannah's porcelain cup. Not knowing what else to do, I just kept on using my soothing voice. "It's ok. It's ok. The baby's coming. Be easy now."

Lottie huffed and she puffed and little by little as I watched, the head slid out and the little face wrinkled up as if wondering what had happened.

"Oh Lordy!" the old lady exclaimed. "It's alive!"

The baby's head was just sitting there, one life coming out of another and its eyes were wide open. Was it stuck? I wondered. "Push again, please," I asked politely as I placed a hand on either side of the head and tried a gentle rocking maneuver as Jammy did with the foal.

Side to side... and up and down... and that's when the whole infant slid out on the pallet, first the shoulders, then whoosh, the whole body, trailing its cord.

Lottie looked down when the infant let out its first cry. "A baby," she said. "It's a baby."

"Of course, child. What did you think was going to come out, a new lamb?" Hannah joked. "Here let me chop the cord." She brought a sharp kitchen knife, dipped it in the soapy water and sliced the curly blue rope of blood vessels with one whack.

Now blood began to spurt all over the place, but quick as a wink the old mammy ripped off a piece of clean towel and tied the cord on baby's end and I let the other end drip into a bowl.

"Can I hold him?" That was Lottie. "It's a boy, isn't it? I dreamed it was a boy."

"Yes. He's a man-child and a feisty one too. See him throw his little arms wide?" Hannah chuckled. "He's ready to take on the world."

"There's still one more thing to do, Lottie," I interrupted. "The afterbirth must come and then you're done."

(This is something I'd learned from Churchill's Midwifery. The organ called the placenta was supposed to deliver in a few minutes. If it didn't, I wasn't sure what we'd do, since I didn't read the whole chapter.)

While we waited I inspected the birth canal to see how badly Lottie ripped and was surprised that, at least on the outside, her opening looked fine. Then another trickle of blood came out.

Lottie looked down, then turned toward me.

"Am I ok?"

"Yes. This is normal," I answered, though in truth, I had no idea, until a wrinkled shiny ball of flesh slid out on the pallet.

"Oh!" Lottie said. *"That's feels a sight better."* She rubbed her stomach and laughed, a nice sound after all the wailing. *"Look!"* she said, smiling. *"My belly has gone from the size of a watermelon to the size of a sugar beet."*

"Here's your babe," Hannah announced, bringing over the infant swaddled in an old white towel. *"I'm sorry we don't have any clothes for him."* Outside, I heard singing.

"Swing low, sweet chariot comin' for to carry me home - Swing low, sweet chariot..." It began, with one man's deep voice and soon other's, until the whole night rang with music. They were singing to the baby.

"Shall I tell them to hush?" Hannah asked.

"No, I like it. I've never heard that song before."

The sound of horses at a gallop broke the peace and soon I heard Father call. *"Where is she?"*

"In here!" Mr. Blunt pushed open the door, followed by Dr. Coffman. They didn't even knock, but then I guess they didn't need to. These people were slaves, mere possessions.

Hannah jumped up and bowed, but Lottie didn't move and neither did I.

"Are you ok?" Dr. Coffman said to me, before he even asked about Lottie and the baby.

"Of course."

He reached out his hand to help me up, apparently distressed to see his adopted daughter *sitting on the dirt floor in a slave cabin. Then his eyes turned to Lottie.*

"A male?" he asked. "It looks healthy. Let me examine it...I think I'll call him William," Father thought out loud. "We don't own a William do we, Blunt? Who's the father?"

Lottie looked away. Hannah sucked in her lips.

"Master Coffman asked you a question, girl," Blunt yelled with more force than needed. "Who's the father?" When she didn't answer, he drew back his arm as if to slap her, but Dr. Coffman stopped him.

"That's not necessary, Blunt. Lottie's a good girl. She'll tell Hannah later. Any trouble with the birth, dear?" He asked this as if I delivered babies all the time.

"No," I answered politely. "Things seemed to go well. The baby cried right away and Lottie didn't tear. I don't think she did anyway."

"Good. I'm sorry you had to be here, but I couldn't come until Mr. Wilson expired. I knew the bloodletting was futile. The dropsy had already encompassed his heart." He described these things as if I was another physician, then he scrubbed both his hands and reached for the baby. But Lottie didn't let go. Finally, he pulled the infant off her breast and I heard a little pop.

I could see it hurt her nipple, but she didn't complain. When you live a life of misery, I imagined, a little tug at the breast isn't worth fussing about, especially with Mr. Blunt and his big fist hanging over you.

The baby began to holler. "Where's my milk?"

he cried. "Where's my Mama?"

The doctor laid him on the cold hard table, without even a towel between him and the wood. He stretched out the baby's legs, all the while explaining what he was doing. "His limbs look fine. No deformity. If a slave is born deformed, they're of no use to us. Sometimes I have to drown them. It's a kindness to the mother, really."

He put his finger in the infant's hand and checked his grip. "He's strong and has good reflexes." He checked the baby's mouth with one finger. "Palate intact." (I didn't know what a palate was, but I planned look it up later.)

Finally, he clapped his hands and the infant startled and cried. "Good," he said. "He can hear....Now let me examine the mother.... You say you checked for vaginal tears?" he asked as he washed his hands again.

Hannah helped Lottie roll on her back and open her legs, but Mr. Blunt didn't avert his eyes or turn away, as a respectful man would. This is not how the doctor would treat any white woman. The girl stared at the ceiling. When he was done, he washed his hands one more time and then said, "Let's go home. Your mother will be worried."

I didn't want to go home, but of course I had to. "Goodbye, Lottie," I said to the new mother. "Thank you Hannah. Goodbye, William." I bent down to touch the baby's beautiful soft brown face and he grabbed my finger.

9

Day of Prayer

Yesterday, Dan and I went to the Hazel Patch Chapel where there was a big surprise. A new young preacher, Reverend Jerome, was introduced and he gave us a sermon, which was more about freedom and justice than humility and forgiveness.

Jerome Jackson, tall, thin, and handsome with a little mustache like Martin Luther King, was taking over the church from the Baptist circuit preachers that have served since Reverend Miller passed away in '54.

As I looked around the congregation at the brown and white faces, I noted it had grown from about thirty people when we used to come with the kids every Sunday, to fifty or sixty today. Hazel Patch is an isolated village where mostly blacks live. Back in the twenties, a group of them migrated up from the southern part of the state to work the Baylor Mine then stayed on after the cave-in and now make a living as subsistence farmers.

I sat there in the pew, barely listening to the pastor's prayers and thought about Bitsy. She and Lou were sitting up front and she waved as we came in, so I guess our spat is forgotten and she's not mad.

"Help us to walk together, pray together, sing together, and live together as one family," the pastor winds his long prayer down. "Until the day we come home to be with you in your kingdom. In the name of the Father, the Son and the Holy Ghost..."

"Amen," we all say as I mentally join the rest of the parishioners, but it's not time to leave yet.
Reverend Jerome steps in front of the pulpit and begins to talk informally about his life and beliefs. "I grew up in the mountains of Tennessee, a place called Leadville, a one horse town if there ever was one!" he laughs and we all chuckle with him.

"Racism was the status quo in Tennessee back in the thirties and it's still the status quo in too many places. As a child, I felt the longing to be respected as much as anyone, but my father warned me to keep my eyes on the ground, to manage the white man by pretending to be docile. We made that choice to survive, but those days are now over, folks."

"Amen!" a few dozen of the women in the congregation shout.

"It's time to *make* some noise! To *make* some trouble, but we'll do it *non-violently* and we will win because God gives us courage and God wants all people to be free."

"Oh Freedom!" a woman up front begins to sing. (It's Bitsy!) *"Oh Freedom..."* we all join in, jumping to our feet. *"Oh Freedom over me!"*

Sweet Chariot

Daniel has gone to bed early, tired from mending fences on the farm all day, but I stay up reading the

headlines in the local paper, *The Liberty Times*.
Tunisia Gains Independence.
Union Workers End 156 Day Strike.
Russia Performs Nuclear Test.

All over the world, people are demanding their rights and at the same time, the snakes are coming out of the walls. There's danger in walking the protest line, but there's even more danger in walking away. Silence in the face of injustice makes us complicit. My mind is on fire, but not just my mind, my heart.

It's a warm evening, and when I go to the door to let the dog out the spring air rushes in. There's the smell of growing things and wet dirt and the peep of the little spring frogs along the creek. Above, the nearly full moon has a small golden halo as it sails between big white islands of clouds. "Hello, Moon!" I raise my hands in salute.

After Dodger comes back, I return to the living room to turn out the lights and notice the old wooden chest on the table. Once again, I can't help myself. I sit down on the sofa and open Mrs. Potts' journal. Are they just a distraction? I wonder… or are they a message from the past trying to tell me something?

"That was brave of you, Grace," Father said after the birth in the slave camp. I was riding behind him on his horse, exhausted, and I leaned into his back to keep from falling. "To attend a delivery in the slave quarters when you had seen nothing of birth but two kittens born in the loft of the barn. That was brave."

"The overseer didn't leave me any room to refuse. He described the situation as quite grave and said because I'm the Master's daughter, I might command some respect and get Lottie under control. All the slaves thought she was going to die and I think Mr. Blunt did as well."

"Regardless, you did a good job. There's no midwife in the county now. Judge Morgan sold Comfort, to a slave trader heading south. She was a big help to me and I asked if I could buy her, but he declined to sell her to me, just to punish her."

"For what?" I asked boldly, unsure if he'd answer.

"She refused to be bred with a man from another farm, a stout fellow, ten years her junior."

"You mean the Judge breeds people like horses?"

"All the plantation owners do, Grace. You're almost a woman; you should know that, just like I'll breed the girl Lottie, again, in a year or so. Owners or overseers just pick two strong slaves and tell them they're married, but you have to do it before the slaves get a will of their own. Trouble with Comfort Morgan was, she had too much self-respect. That's not good in a slave. You want them to be docile, like a family dog. You want them to try to please you."

At this point, I was sorry I even asked the question, so I changed the subject. *"The singing tonight was beautiful. Did you hear it? I've heard the cook singing in the kitchen, but never heard a group of slaves singing in chorus."*

"Slaves sing all the time. A happy slave is a

singing slave. They sing at worship services. They sing at their frolics. They sing when they work. Mr. Blunt insists upon singing in the fields. Slaves even sing when they march toward Georgia in the chain gangs."

I was quiet after that and soon the lights of home came into view, slanting golden out the windows on the wide lawn.

Mother was sitting up in the parlor and she clucked like a hen when we came in. "Oh, my Lord, Gracie! What were you thinking, going into the slave quarters like that? I'm furious at Belle for allowing it."

"She didn't know, Mother. She was in the laundry shed. Mr. Blunt was quite insistent that I come right away and I left a note. Anyway, I've always wanted to see the slave quarters."

"Well, now you've been there and you don't need to go again," she responded taking my cloak and giving me a hug. "I just can't believe my thirteen-year-old daughter was subjected to such a thing."

Father defended me. "She did right, Mother. A breeder woman is a valuable commodity. If the slave had died in childbirth, we would have lost one thousand dollars and to get a live infant out of her was a blessing. That's another five hundred if he survives."

He turned then to me. "Half of all slave infants don't make it to one year old, Grace. It's usually an infection of some sort, but perhaps they can't be blamed. Dr. Sam Cartwright proved in his recent journal article that the small skull of the African compresses the brain. Their mental defects make it impossible for them to survive or raise children properly without the guidance of the white man."

Mother was still on her high horse. "That's ridiculous! They did fine in Africa before they were shipped across the Atlantic against their will. And more slave babies might make it if Mr. Blunt fed the women and children better. How can the mothers give birth to healthy infants if they don't get meat and milk? And how can babies grow strong enough to survive on nothing but gruel?"

Dr. Coffman lit a cigar. He was irritated, and he knew she hated the smell. Myself, I just wanted to go to sleep, but Mother ordered Belle to help me wash up. Finally I fell onto my feathered bed, exhausted. Belle pulled the quilt over me, but before she left she stood in the doorway holding a candle. "Did the mother live?" she asked.

"Yes, she and the baby are fine. Beautiful, both of them."

When she smiled, I could see her white teeth in the dark. "You did good, Missy," she said.

10

April 1956

Secret

Something happened on Easter Sunday that upset me. Mira took me aside asked if we could talk.

"Sure, but what's going on?" I asked, sitting down on the sofa.

"What do you know about feminine hygiene?" she asked.

This took me aback, but I kept my face calm; it's a habit midwives have, to always appear unsurprised, even when we're secretly shocked

"I know about *marital hygiene*," I answered, implying that only married people had sex.

"Do you know about douching for birth control and where I could get a douche bag?" my daughter asks.

"Oh, Mira! Is this something you want? Your boyfriend isn't pressuring you is he?"

"No Mom! It's just..." She shook her auburn curls in frustration and I saw tears in very blue her eyes.

"Well, are you engaged? You should at least be engaged."

"Come on, Mom. You know you don't have to

be engaged to have intercourse."

Her boldness shocked me, but I addressed her with respect. "Certainly you're right, but no method of birth control is perfect. Until they invent a pill or a shot to prevent pregnancy, the diaphragm is the next best option."

"Mom! I know all this, but there's no way I am going to go to a doctor and ask for a prescription for a diaphragm! They probably wouldn't give me one anyway, unless I lied and said I was married. What I need to know is where to get a douche bag, you know, like if the rubber comes off or breaks."

I take a big breath. "Lordy, let me think. Don't they have them at Woolworths where you work?"

"Yes, but I can't buy one there, in front of all the other sales girls. The boss, Mr. Holland, might find out."

"Maybe you could get one at People's Drugs in Torrington."

"That's a good idea. I'll get Ron to drive me, but this is strictly between you and me, ok? *You can't tell anyone. Please!"*

"Not even your Dad?"

She rolls her eyes. "Especially not Dad."

As she leaves, I recognize my hypocrisy. I was pregnant at 15. Most people don't know this, only Bitsy and Dan. I've never told the kids. This was back after I escaped the House of Mercy Orphanage and got a job as a chorus girl in Chicago.

The father's name was Lawrence and we were in love. He was an art student and a scene designer at the theater, but he died in a train accident on his way to tell his parents we wanted to marry. I lost our baby a few days later. It was the grief, I'm sure of it.

The placenta came loose from the womb and I was rushed to the Chicago Lying-in Dispensary pouring blood, but it was too late for the baby. When you think of it, it's amazing I even survived.

Still, I never in the world thought Mira would have extramarital sex, other girls, maybe, but not Mira.

Sighting

"Did you see in the paper that someone spotted Kitty Bishop in Delmont?" Bitsy asks.

"Really?"

"Yeah, and the reward has gone up to $300. That's a lot of money."

We're sitting on the porch of the house with the blue door on Wild Rose Road, the one I lived in when I first fled with Mrs. Kelly from Pittsburgh in the twenties. It's funny how I felt about these mountains then, as if I'd been banished to the wilderness of Siberia.

On the run, after the United Mine Workers march on Blair Mountain and the war with the mine owners and their Pinkerton goons, we were hiding from the Feds. Nora, Mrs. Kelly's lover, had already left her, running away to San Francisco with her new girlfriend, an author of steamy romance novels.

Those first few years were rough, but gradually people learned we were midwives and folded us into the community. Now the Hope River Valley is my home and I wouldn't want to live anywhere else. Across the field, yellow mustard blooms in the very green grass and two robins court on the lawn.

"Three hundred dollars! Did you hear me?" Bitsy whistles to get my attention.

I bring myself back from memory lane. "Do they *know* it was Kitty?"

"The witness just described a girl with long red hair getting on a Grey Hound Bus with a baby. Sheriff Bishop was quoted as saying they continue to search."

"I guess I've been putting her out of my mind," I admit. "I've been so busy getting ready to plant the garden I haven't even looked at the paper. You going to plant anything?"

"With taking Willie back and forth to the VA Hospital, I haven't thought much about gardening or about Kitty either."

I gaze at my friend. It's been weeks since I've seen Willie. My world has narrowed to my own family problems; Mira and her secret; Danny's withdrawal. All over the U.S., all over the world... people are suffering with difficulties much more serious than mine.

"What's the story? Are the doctors making any progress?" "What exactly do they say?"

"The diagnosis is osteomyelitis, an infection. Apparently it's spreading up the leg again. I'm beginning to think it's hopeless. Willie is too."

"Is there anywhere else he could go? Any orthopedists in Torrington?"

"The nearest other specialists would be Pittsburgh, but the VA is already consulting with them. They've even sent copies of his x-rays by courier to the radiologist at West Penn."

"I guess it's down to prayer then," I offer.

"People are already praying for him at the Hazel Patch Chapel and the AME Church in town."

"Does Willie know?"

"I told him a few weeks ago that Reverend Jerome mentions him at every Sunday service."

"What did Willie say?"

"He said they could just keep their GD prayers to themselves and then he stomped away in a huff." She rolled her eyes. "Did you know it's possible to *stomp* away on crutches?"

Bitsy gets up to pour another cup of coffee. "I've been thinking of going back to work at the mill."

"Why? Lou must make good money as the owner and men need those jobs to feed their families."

"Lou wants me to stop hovering over Willie; give him some space to cope on his own. He also says he could use help in the office. It would be a sit down job a few days a week, dealing with employees' arguments, hiring new workers and keeping people out of Lou's hair so he could take care of manufacturing."

I make a non-committal noise in my throat, sort of a grunt. "If it will make you happy…"

"I liked working back in the forties, liked having the responsibility. We even thought of getting a small place in town. We'd come home on the weekends. It would be better for Willie in town too. He's so isolated from people his age; never goes anywhere, just lies around and snaps at me."

Now alarm bells are ringing. For years, Bitsy has lived on Wild Rose Road, just over Hope Mountain. She's the sister I never had. She's family. I've spent my whole life looking for family.

11

The snow came deep and heavy the fall of '58, the year I turned fourteen. Father stayed in the parlor smoking one cigar after another, a decanter of golden spirits at his side. Mother sat on the other side of the fireplace, watching him out of the corner of her eye. Being a Quaker, she couldn't abide the alcohol and tobacco, but she was too stubborn to leave the warm room. Meals were now silent with only the scrape of the silverware on the fine china plates.

One afternoon in late-November there was a commotion outside and we all went to the window. Jammy was talking to another darkie out the yard and a few minutes later, they came to the door.

"Master!" I heard the stable man say. "They need you for a birthing on the other side of Hintonville."

Father came back to the parlor and stood in the archway. "How would you like to see how white ladies have their babies, Grace?" he asked me. "Jammy's hitching up the sleigh."

Mother threw down her knitting. "Really, Dr. Coffman!" she choked out. "Have you no shame? What kind of an education are you giving Grace?"

I was so tired of being cooped up inside for a

week, that a sleigh ride sounded wonderful. "I'll be fine, Mother. I'm sure this delivery won't be like the other one. Maybe I'll be a nurse someday. I may learn something useful."

Soon we were on our way. "The Parkers are new to this area," Father explained. "They purchased The Hermitage when the owner, a recent widow, sold out to pay off her debts; Mr. Parker got all the plantation slaves for a song.

"The wife is young and this is her first baby," he continued as the bells on the sleigh rang merrily. Then he took a little silver flask out of his pocket and tipped it back. "Want some?" he asked

I shook my head no.

"Oh, come," he teased. "It will keep you warm."

"No, thank you," I said once again formally. "Mother doesn't approve." He slipped his arm around my shoulders and held the flask to my lips and forced me to drink. There was no getting around it.

"Echhhh!" I sputtered. "It burns."

"That's why the Injuns call it firewater," he chuckled.

"Echhhhh!" I said again. "Why do you men drink it?"

"Not just men. Ladies will have a cordial now and then and the female slaves drink whiskey at Christmas when they have their winter frolics. Your mother is just a teetotaler."

"Because she's a Quaker? You were a Quaker too."

He took another drink from his flask and laughed again. "That was a long time ago. I'm a fallen Quaker now."

In time we arrived at a large white stone home with four columns in front.

"Thank God you're here, Coffman," a young bearded man shouted when the door flew open and yellow light spilled like lemonade out on the snow. "I hope I didn't call you too soon."

"Better to be too early than too late," Father joked and shook Mr. Parker's hand as a Negro groom took our horse and sleigh. A house slave took my cloak and muff and offered me a chair so I could undo the dozen tiny buttons on my boots and step into slippers.

"This is my daughter Grace. I'm teaching her to be a nurse and I thought she'd offer some consolation to your wife. Let us warm ourselves by the fire and then we'll go see the mother-to-be."

The owner of the plantation led us into a spacious parlor where he offered Father a hot drink. "Can the young lady join us in a rum cordial?" he asked.

"It will warm us both," Father said nodding yes and I dared not contradict. Mr. Parker rang a little bell and an another slave woman, dressed all in white with beautiful black braids wound around her head, came in with three cut glass goblets on a silver tray. Each goblet contained amber liquid and had a slice of lemon in it. She offered me one and I took it, but only held the drink in my hand.

The men waited politely for me to take a sip, so finally I pretended. To divert their attention from the drink in my hand, I inquired after Mrs. Parker. "How is your wife doing, sir?"

"She was still sleeping a few hours ago," he informed us.

"Could Hoppy take me up to her?" I asked. "Maybe it would help to have some company. My Mother says a hand to hold is fine medicine."

"Excellent idea, daughter," Dr. Coffman agreed. "Here, I'll finish your cordial."

Hoppy led me up a long curved stairway. "You the midwife, Miss?" she asked. "You look awful young."

"I'm in training," I hedged.

"It will do Miss Emma good to have another white lady with her. Since she has no mother nor sisters around, it's a lonely time for her."

"Dr. Coffman said there was a very experienced midwife in Augusta County until a few months ago, Comfort Morgan, but she got sent South."

"Bad business," mumbled the cook. "Terrible bad business. Last time anyone saw her she was chained to a line, on her way to Mississippi." She shook her head and tapped on the first door we came to. "Miss Emma, honey? It's the little nurse to see you." Pleased to be introduced so importantly, I smiled and waited for a response, but only a groan came from inside.

The groan came again. "Ma'am? Mrs. Parker? It's Grace Coffman, the nurse. I'm coming in." Boldly, I stepped across the threshold and what I saw shocked me more than my first glimpse of poor Lottie curled up on the straw in the slave quarters.

Emma Parker was standing in the middle of a four poster bed in a long white embroidered night

105

dress, hanging onto the cross pole and the white lace trimmed canopy was torn to shreds. She was biting the cloth with her teeth, as a bondsman might bite a stick while being branded. She thrashed her head back and forth, ripping the cloth, her eyes shut tight.

Hoppy, looked at me with wide eyes. "Oh Lordy!" she whispered. "Should I get Dr. Coffman?"

"No. Wait. Let me try to calm her first." After Lottie's delivery in the slave camp, I felt a slight confidence. If nothing else, I could give comfort and inspire courage.

"Emma Parker," I said, trying to sound sure of myself. "Emma, it's Nurse Coffman. When this pain is over, I want you to open your eyes and look at me." She thrashed for another thirty seconds, tossing her long brown curls back and forth then dropped to the bed in a heap of sorrow, her eyes still shut.

"Hoppy, bring us a little of that warm rum with lemon. Don't let the men come up yet. I know Mrs. Parker wouldn't want to be seen like this."

"Yes, Miss."

I sat on the edge of the bed and touched the patient on the shoulder. "You can open your eyes a little now, Emma, and while you have a break, can you tell me what hurts?"

"It's my back," she whispered, her eyes still closed tight. "It feels like a knife is stabbing me and then when my belly gets hard the knife goes deeper and twists. Oh, I know I'm making a mess of this!"

"I see that there's blood on the bed and on your gown. This is called bloody show and it's normal, but I wonder if when Hoppy comes back you would let us clean you up and change the sheets so the doctor can examine you." I reached for her hand. "Emma, please look at me. I'm here to help."

Finally, the young woman opened her eyes, a startling pale blue, and pulled her hair out of her flushed face. "Oh, you look so young! I pictured someone like my governess back in Delaware. Please forgive me. It's ungracious not to greet you like a lady, but this is so hard. I had no idea!...Oh, no! Here it comes again." She pulled up on the bedpost once more, grabbing the lace canopy in her teeth.

Without even thinking I kicked off my short healed slippers, jumped up beside her and began to rub her back. "It's ok. It's ok. The baby will come and you will be happy. Quiet now. Let the baby come." From the sound of me, you'd think I'd seen scores of births, when in fact there have only been four, one human, two kittens and a horse.

At the end of the contraction, Emma flopped on the bed again, curling on her side, so I could continue kneading her back. My hands seemed to give her some peace. With the next pain she moaned, but the moan was more musical, more like a song. Finally, Hoppy returned with a silver tray and two cups of warm liquid.

"Did the doctor inquire how Mrs. Parker is?" I whispered as she put the tray down.

She raised her eyebrows. "The Master and Dr. Coffman didn't notice me pass."

"Why so?"

"The gentlemen are fast asleep by the fire. I believe they've had one too many."

I pressed my hand to my forehead as if to hold my brain in. Father was inebriated and I was tending a woman in labor, but this time it wasn't a slave girl; it was a rich planter's wife.

An hour later, things got more intense. "How long will this go on?" the lady asked me as I braided her hair. "I don't think I can do it much longer...Oh, no. Here's another one! Where is the good doctor? Can't he help me? Can't he give me some laudanum or spirits of ether? Oh! Oh! Oh!" she cried.

This time, instead of standing on the bed and pulling on the bedpost, she planted her feet on the floor and leaned over the feather mattress, a better position, at least for me, and I went to work on her back again.

"Let's get through this one and we'll call him, Emma. Just breathe and sway. I'll rub your back."

(Hoppy had already told me she wasn't going to wake a sleeping white man. That left it for me and I was a little scared myself. I've seen the doctor growl at Mother when he was drinking and it was not a pleasant sight.)

Emma's wail turned into a growl. Her face turned red, she shut her eyes and she gave a long grunt. When the pain was over her eyes opened wide. "Miss Grace. Oh, help me! Something's coming."

I had no doubt what was coming. Dr. Churchill

described it perfectly in his book on midwifery. The involuntary pushing stage had arrived.

"It's ok, Emma," I announced, as if I knew what I was talking about. "This is all very normal. The baby is moving down the birth canal. If you feel like pushing you may, but only if it feels better. If it hurts more, stop."

I could wait no longer and I hurried downstairs where I found both men snoring softly. "Dr. Coffman." I shook his shoulder. "Father! Please wake up. We need you in the bedroom. The baby's coming."

"Good. Good," Dr. Coffman murmured, but he was still not quite awake. When I got him upstairs, he rolled up his sleeves, washed his hands and moved next to the bed.

"You were absolutely correct, Grace. It is time," Father exclaimed, after a quick examination. And with six more long pushes, the baby emerged, wet and gray, but eyes wide open. The doctor grabbed his tiny ankles and swung him up like a slaughtered chicken. Whack! He gave the infant a smack on his butt and he let out a howl. "It's a boy, Father announced.

"What did you do that for?" I whispered.

"What?'

"Hang the baby upside down and spank him."

"You want to drain the infant and you spank him to get him to cry. Never delay the spank. It doesn't hurt a baby. Like the darkies, infants have little sense of pain."

I watched closely as the doctor expertly tied the

cord in two places and cut in between. "Later I'll trim it and apply alcohol to prevent infection. In fact, I will let you do it."

"Can I hold him?" Emma wanted to know, pulling herself up on her elbows.

"Here's your little sugar-man," Hoppy gushed, holding the infant out to the mother. He was swaddled in a white flannel blanket with white lace trim.

"Oh, my baby!"

Just then the husband appeared, rumpled and groggy, but able to walk. "Oh, sweet darling. You did it. Marvelous! And with so little fuss!"

Hoppy and I looked at each other. So little fuss? The new father had missed all the sweat and the tears, but he'd also missed the joy of hearing his son's first cry.

As we left the Parker's house, Father put his arm around me and helped me into the sleigh. "You did a fine job Grace and I enjoyed having someone accompany me. Maybe we'll be a team. Mother won't approve of course, but she's not in charge. Would you like to learn more about obstetrics?" He gave me another affectionate squeeze then took the reins with two hands as we went down the lane.

"I've been looking at the pictures in your text, Churchill's Midwifery."

"Good! To be honest you are ahead of many so-called physicians. Did you know that half the men who call themselves doctors never even went to college? Some can't even read. Any questions you have, don't hesitate to ask me."

In the moonlight I could see his teeth when he smiled, as white as the snow that lay all around. Father was not an old man. Forty-two, mother said. She was only thirty-eight, but her hair was already graying.

When we got back to the house, Jammy, wiping sleep out of his eyes, ran from the stable and took the horses and sleigh. The sky was pink at the edges and dawn was soon coming. On the porch, father held out his arms. "A new day," he said.

12

Klu Klux Klan

It's a clear spring morning and the air smells of honeysuckle. Up on the mountain, redbud trees bloom and at the edge of the woods there are white clouds of dogwood. I'm just putting on my old garden shoes, when I hear the first geese flying over Hope Mountain, the rising sun, turning them gold. Honk. Honk. Honk. Their cries are a harbinger of spring and this migration is holy to me. Twice a year we see the long Vs, spring and fall. "Hello geese!" I call, raising my arms.

A few minutes later the phone rings. It's Bitsy. "Did you see the geese?"

"Yes, I was just outside watching as they flew over. What are you doing at home? I thought you were starting work at the woolen mill."

"Lou said I should stay here another week."

"You ok?" I ask. "Is Willie ok?"

"No... not really. His foot still isn't healing. He's depressed. He's losing weight and looks like something the cat drug in. Lou took him into town today, just to get him out of the house. I think we really have to move into Liberty, Patience. I don't know if we should rent or buy..."

I bite my lower lip, while Bitsy goes on about the benefits of various neighborhoods and if her skin color will be a problem. It sounds like the move is really going to happen and I'm hurt, but I don't want to show it. She has to make decisions that are best for her family. She's my friend, not my lover or wife.

Later, trying to shake the blues, while I iron Dan's shirts, I turn on the radio. *"Shake Rattle and Roll! Shake Rattle and Roll!"* sings Chuck Berry and I wiggle my butt like I'm Bitsy doing the boogie-woogie.

When the news comes on, the announcer tells us that the NAACP is now illegal in every state in the Deep South. He also reports that West Virginia Congressman Robert Byrd just gave a speech to a state Rotary Club conference, encouraging every white man to be prepared for rioting Negroes.

"As a former recruiter of the KKK," the politician said to the community leaders, "the Klan is needed today as never before and I'm eager to see it reinstituted in every state in the nation."

Great! I think. Just what we need; the Klu Klux Klan in every state in America, including West Virginia.

When I finally get back outside, a Blue Jay on the fence post, thirty feet away, looks over and I notice he has a little white patch on one wing, a defect in his beautiful blue feathers.

"Hello," I greet him. "I'm Patience Hester."

"Jay!" "Jay" "Jay" he answers, cocking his head, so I give him a name.

"Morning, Howard. Fine day, don't you think?"

"Jay!" he squeaks, fixing me with his beady black eye, then he flaps away.

Hintonville, Virginia
March 1859

Over the winter of '59, weather permitting, I attended four more deliveries, several sick calls, and a bloodletting. By spring I was traveling from town to town, plantation to plantation with my father, something unheard of for a young girl like me.

Johnnie Layton, a ten-year-old boy with an inflamed foot, had languished for days before the family called Dr. Coffman. When we arrived the patient lay in a dark bedroom, delirious, his foot as red as the sunset over Spruce Mountain. The young fellow fought the doctor when he tried to take his pulse and cried in pain when the doctor examined his toes.

"Can you arrange my instruments on a tray?" he asked me, indicating with a nod an ivory box he'd laid on a table. There was a silver lancet in the case, a steel blood bowl and a set of three clear glass suction cups attached to a small brass pump.

Since leeches are expensive and hard to get, father had told me, he used the cupping method for bloodletting, which took longer, but was, in his opinion, just as effective. My job, after he made the three deep cuts and attached the glass cups to the boy's back, was to keep the little hand pump going. Within a few hours we removed almost a liter of the bad blood that was making him sick.

Johnny cried and gripped my hand when the

doctor first wounded him, but later he fell into a faint. "I need to talk with the family," Father advised me. "You just keep pumping."

When he got back we sat together at the bedside while the shadows crept across the wooden bedroom floor. As we watched, the lad got weaker and then turned white and passed on. I had never seen anyone die before, and it had a profound affect on me. I wasn't sad, though the family cried and carried on. I was happy. Johnnie was free of his feverish, painful body.

On the way home, Dr. Coffman told me if he'd amputated the foot the young man would have lived, but Mr. Layton, the boy's pa, wouldn't let him.

Soldier's Home

For the last few days, because of the planting season, I've had no time to read the journals. They were becoming too upsetting anyway. Then yesterday, Bitsy asked me to go with her to Willie's doctor appointment at the Veteran's Clinic.

I had never actually been to the Veteran's Administration before and was surprised at the size of the place. The complex of brick buildings included the hospital, doctor's offices and the Old Soldier's Home. Before we could get to the clinic we had to walk through the manicured grounds past dozens of men, who despite the chill day, sat in wheel chairs playing cards or smoking, wearing pajamas and robes and taking the sun. Most appeared over sixty, but a dozen or so were young fellows Willie's age, many with missing limbs.

One old guy, with hands so scarred by burns that they looked like knots of wood, was actually wearing a World War One uniform. Another man had bandages all over his face, but the worst was a young black soldier with only one arm and no legs. His body, tied in a wheel chair, was wrapped in a gray wool blanket and I thought about what Bitsy had said that night. "Negroes have fought for this country and died for this country, and the whites aren't going to oppress us much longer!"

Willie stopped in front of him and gave him a smart salute. The soldier saluted back and I almost cried.

"Do you want to sit down while Bitsy and I register you?" I asked Will, when we got to the clinic, but he was too proud.

"No," he snapped hopping on his crutches to the back of the line. "The people at the desk already know me." For over an hour we waited and I was beginning to think they'd forgotten us when finally someone shouted Willie's name.

"Can we go in with you?" Bitsy asked. "You know your Father and I are very concerned."

"No. I'll be fine. They just want to examine me and do another x-ray. You can come when I get my medicine. It's another long hike to the pharmacy."

Sequestra

While we wait, I try to amuse myself with an out of date copy of *The Post*. "Look here," I whisper. "Did you know they're working on a vaccine for polio?"

"How can they? I'd be afraid it would *give* me polio. That would be terrible," she whispers back, looking up from her old issue of *True Crime*.

"The article says the polio vaccine can be inactivated, but it still protects you. In a couple of years kids will get the shot for free at health clinics."

"Mrs. Cross?" an RN wearing fancy gold cat-eye glasses with little rhinestones in the corners, calls across the crowded waiting room and my friend jumps up. "The doctor would like you to come back to his office."

I start to go with her, but the nurse bars my way. "Just family," she orders.

"I *am* family. Willie's aunt," I tell a white lie. She looks me over; apparently suspicious I might be planning to steal all their cold bedpans, but finally relents and leads the way down the hall.

At the end, she opens a door and escorts us into an exam room and office where the physician is slouched behind his desk and Willie sits on a bench with his foot elevated while a medic changes his bandage. The doctor rises when we enter and I'm surprised he isn't dressed in a uniform, but wears a white coat, over a white dress shirt with a brown tie and slacks.

"I'm Dr. Spiggle, Board Certified Orthopedist," the man announces, indicating with his hand where we should sit.

"I'm Mrs. Cross, Willie's mother. This is Mrs. Hester, his aunt."

The doctor, a small man with receding dark hair and a long forehead, nods and addresses us both. "Do you know anything about osteomyelitis?" he asks, opening a chart on his desk.

Bitsy speaks first. "A little... It's a bone infection, isn't it? That's what I wanted to talk to you about. Will gets better for a while and then his ankle gets red and festers again. You can see it's bad now."

Willie stares out the window, his face as gray as the walls of the room. When I glance over, I see that Bitsy is right. The red open area now extends from the ankle to below the knee.

"Osteomyelitis is a bone infection," the doctor intones. "The x-ray we did today confirms that the tibia and fibula have become necrotic as a result of diminished blood supply and now sequestra are forming..."

"Can you interpret that?" I break-in; irritated by his uppity tone.

"The tibia and fibula are the shin bones that connect the ankle and the knee. Lab tests show that there is pus in the bone marrow. Do you know what marrow is?" We nod. "The type of bacteria is called staph. The infection is decreasing the blood supply and the bone is dying around it. Willie has what's called *chronic* osteomyelitis, which means it comes and goes."

"I thought penicillin, the new wonder drug, could kill anything," Bitsy interrupts. Willie's eyes are hard and distant. He seems to have checked out, as if this medical discussion doesn't concern him.

"Well, in the 1940s penicillin *seemed* to kill everything, but already we're seeing some strains of bacteria that are resistant, thus the extensive sequestration." He turns up his hands, implying the situation is very difficult and possibly hopeless.

"What's this sequestration, you speak of?" Bitsy grills him, a mother fighting for a son who appears uninterested in fighting for himself.

Spiggle sighs, taps his pen on his desk, tilts his head back and looks down his long nose at us. "Sequestration means that pieces of dead bone have become separated from the healthy bone and are causing more necrosis."

"So what is your recommendation?" I ask, as if I'm a medical person.

"Well, we need to do another exploratory surgery to debride the dead bone, clean it out, and then we'll try more antibiotics."

Willie takes a deep breath, kicks the stool aside with his good leg and growls. "I'm sick of this!"

"Willie!" Bitsy scolds, but the young man picks up his crutches and hobbles out of the room.

"Don't worry doctor, we'll do whatever has to be done." I stand up too. "Could you write a few words down for me: osteomyelitis… debride… necrotic… penicillin resistant… staph… and sequestration. My husband is a doctor of veterinary medicine and a surgeon and will know what they mean." I say it like that, instead of *my husband is a country vet,* because "doctor and surgeon" sounds more like something Dr. Spiggle would respect.

"When do you want to do the exploratory surgery?" Bitsy asks.

"My next opening is one month," the doctor says, consulting a clipboard. "Not a day longer."

13

Obsession

My fascination with Mrs. Potts' journals goes on. Dan has no idea how often I read them, nor does Bitsy, and I wonder if I'm using them as a diversion from my own troubles. Each week we see less and less of Danny. He's stopped working for Dan. Who is he living with? What is he doing for money?

Except for a few minor worries about one of our twins, Susie, when she used to wet herself at school and the conflicts Dan and I had over his pacifist beliefs during World War Two, our family and home has been a safe and tranquil harbor. Now I feel like part of my heart is being slowly ripped off. I let out my air in a long sigh and unplug my iron. I can leave Dan's shirts for tomorrow. Grace Potts is waiting for me.

Hintonville, Virginia
July 1859
As we traveled the countryside in the buggy that summer, Father often sang. "Oh, the sun shines bright on my old Kentucky home - 'Tis summer and

the people are gay." It was one of his favorite Stephen Foster songs and he had a strong voice. Often I joined him.

Father was different when he was out seeing patients. Sometimes, he hugged me and told me how pretty I was. Once as we traveled through Staunton, he stopped at the dry goods store and bought me a new bonnet. It was much too fine for a fourteen-year-old girl, cream in color with lace and flowers around my face and a long fancy pink ribbon.

I asked him to buy one for Mother too, but he said the bonnet was a reward for my services as his nurse and that Mother hadn't done anything.

"I'll tell you, Grace," he confided. "It's got me down. All she does is sit in her sewing room and work on her needlepoint. She doesn't even make clothes for the bondsmen like other planter's wives; just buys the broadcloth and thread in town and gives it to Blunt to hand out to the slaves so they can make their own shifts and trousers."

It was true what he said about Mother. She no longer went with Father on carriage rides and she looked at him with slanted green eyes. I asked her what was wrong, if she disapproved of my learning a useful skill and she tightened her mouth.

"It's Dr. Coffman's decision," she snapped. "I'm only his wife of twenty years, his ornament and not much of that. You're now the apple of his eye." I didn't know what to say, so I just sat there, but she went on... "It breaks my heart, Grace. Your father and I were once so much in love. He's stopped going to church. He drinks and he gambles.

He sends you out to the slave quarters on errands. You see things no fourteen-year-old should see. I can hardly stand to look at him.

"And you might as well know this right now, Grace. A female in Southern society has no power but her looks and her feminine ways. It's not like in the Quaker's Society of Friends, where women are considered equals. Here in the South, if a female isn't ruled by her father, she's ruled by her husband or grown son." Then she started to cry. I had never seen Mother cry before.

Hintonville, Virginia
August 1859

One day in late August, when I was in the barn watching Jammy, I got up my courage and asked him something I'd long been thinking about.

"Jammy, can I ask you something?" The man didn't answer, just continued to sweep out a stall. "Can you read?"

"Why do you ask such a thing? You know it's against the law for a slave to read."

"But you seem to know so much. Does Father realize?"

Finally, he answered. "He knows I read a little. Your mother knows I read a lot. She taught me and still gives me books and old newspapers. She could be fined one hundred dollars and imprisoned for it and I could get 39 lashes."

"I can't comprehend it. Mother's not usually so rebellious."

"It didn't start out that way. This was a long time ago, when she first came to Virginia from

Pennsylvania. Your mother often read the Bible to Belle, Thelma and I in the evenings when Dr. Coffman was gone. She was young then and lonely.

"At the time," Jammy went on. "I knew nothing of books or the printed word or what they could do for me. In my ignorance of the law, I asked her to teach me and with her being almost as uninformed as I was, she agreed.

When your father found out, he was furious and informed her that it was both illegal and dangerous. 'Give a slave an inch and he'll take a mile,' he said. 'Teach him to read and he's forever ruined. Give him knowledge and he'll want freedom.'

"So that was the end of the lessons. The rest I've taught myself. A bondsman caught reading is a grave danger to us all, so I must beg you never to say anything or demonstrate that I am any more than an ignorant old man."

"How old are you Jammy?" I asked shyly.

"I don't know, because slaves don't own family Bibles to record births and deaths, but I think I am around forty."

"That's about Father's age," I said. "And do you think a slave has rights, Jammy? Is a slave a person? Have you read about the Dred Scott Case? Father and Mr. Parker were discussing it."

"Lordy, Miss Grace, you ask so many questions...In the Dred Scott Case the highest court in the land ruled that slaves have no rights as citizens in the United States and can never be citizens, even if we are freed. We're non-persons.

"Worse yet, slaves can be brought into every state now, even the free states like Ohio,

Pennsylvania and Delaware and still be held in bondage. Now, even if a slave can escape, there's nowhere he can be truly free in the whole United States, not even further north, in Massachusetts, New York, or Vermont. Nowhere."

"But Mother had me memorize the United States Declaration of Independence. I remember the first line. 'We hold these truths to be self-evident, that all men are created equal, that they are endowed by their Creator with certain unalienable rights.'"

"Oh, Miss Gracie!" Jammy sighs. "Seems like those men in white wigs didn't mean black folk."

"Why do people think it's ok to own another person, Jammy? I don't understand."

"Some say God intended it to be that way, made black men to be slaves and white men to be masters."

"How could anyone know what God intended?" I argued. "And anyway, not all black men and women are slaves. Look at Agnes Washington, the laundress in Staunton and her husband. They're free and independent, own their own house and barbershop. Are they going against God's will?"

"You ask too many questions, Miss Gracie. All I know is that every time Master Coffman gives me a silver coin for doing a healing in the slave quarters, I'm putting it into my hiding place so that some day I can buy my freedom. I don't know if that will happen, but I'm trying."

"Could I buy my freedom?"

Jammy laughed so hard I thought he would choke. "Oh, Missy!" he said. "You are so innocent."

Winds of Change

Today, Bitsy had time to come over and read. It was such a special occasion I made gingersnaps and we sat outside on the porch with ice tea. All around us birds sang, the apple trees were clouds of white and Howard watched us from high perch in a Willow.

"See that Blue Jay?" I asked pointing upward. "The one with the white patch on his wing. That's my friend. I even know what he's thinking."

"Like what, for example?"

"Well, he wants to know who you are." I grin. "This is Bitsy." I address the bird loudly. "She lives on the other side of Hope Mountain in a little house with a blue door." The bird cocks his head as if nodding. "See! He recognizes you now!"

"Jay!" The bird says as he flies off to the West.

"Bye, Howard! Come again."

"You are losing your marbles, Patience!" Bitsy laughs.

"I miss you, Bitsy…" I feel my face flush. "I miss talking to you every day, and joking, and working together."

Bitsy lets out a long sigh, but doesn't say anything at first. Finally, she speaks.

"I know you're worried about us moving into town, Patience, but we're still friends; it's just that things change."

"It makes me sad, is all, but I understand. You're right. Nothing stays the same…You have your own problems. I have mine. I'll cope."

Bitsy looks at me sideways, then takes another long breath and begins to read softly.

Hintonville, Virginia
September 1859

Can you give me a hand, honey?" Father asked me one early autumn evening when he'd had too much to drink. "I'm going to need a little help getting up the stairs."

Since I'd been accompanying him on his rounds, we'd become closer, but he didn't usually call me Honey. While I stood next to him so he could put his arm around me, I smelled the strong spirits, but that was nothing new. What alarmed me happened a few minutes later. We were half way up the stairs when his hand slipped down to my breast and he squeezed it. I paused, shocked, but I couldn't get away without dropping him, so we struggled upward.

At the door to his bedroom he invited me in. "Come on, Sugar. I want to show you the new medical book I got this week. It has the best original anatomy illustrations I've ever seen!"

"I'll look at it tomorrow," I demurred. "I'm tired and cold and just want to go to bed."

"I could warm you up." He laughed low in his throat and pulled me toward him.

My own father! I laughed too, but scurried away. Once in my room I remembered there was no lock on the door and I hauled a heavy chair in front of it. The chair wouldn't keep Father out, but it would slow him down and the noise if it moved would wake me. Mother's bedroom was at the far end of the hall and the women servants slept in the kitchen, so I felt very alone.

For a long time, I lay staring up at the ceiling, quilt tucked tight up to my chin. It's the drink, I decided, trying to excuse my father. He didn't know what he was saying. Then I remembered his hand on my breast.

As the month went on I tried never to be alone with Father. I was a young woman now; old enough to be a breeder and my body was changing. I had earlier started using rosewater for a skin tonic and beet juice on my cheeks, but I decided maybe I was giving my father the wrong impression and I stopped at once. The truth is, I felt a great shame.

If I hadn't so enjoyed getting out of the house and learning about medicine and childbirth, I'd have begged off or made excuses, but instead I went back to my little girl look and played cat and mouse with the doctor.

"Oh shit!" I said. "This is getting sick. Can you imagine?"

"Actually, I can easily imagine it," Bitsy said, "You remember old Mr. Warren at the barbershop in Liberty? This was back when I was eighteen, before I came to live with you. Wall Street had just crashed. The mines were all closing. All the people that had servants were letting them go...and then by luck, I got part-time work, helping Mrs. Warren with cleaning and laundry."

"Yeah, they left West Virginia during the Great

Depression."

"I'd only been there one week when Mr. Warren started the same kind of funny business as Dr. Coffman, grabbing my breast and pressing himself against me. It was disgusting and I spent every moment in that house trying avoiding him. Filthy old goat! Finally, I quit and went back to my mother at the Macintoshes, but I could only stay one week and I had nowhere to go until she talked you into taking me."

"I had no idea what was going on. I'm so glad Big Mary convinced me. I can still remember what she said. 'I've studied it out. Bitsy could learn to help you with the women in labor and on the farm. She'd work for room and board. No salary. My daughter is thrifty and smart. She'd be company for you out there in the sticks. You'd like her.' She also added that you'd finished four years of high school, knew how to sew and could fish and hunt deer. How could I refuse?"

"If I hadn't been able to get out of there, it's hard to imagine what would have happened to me. "

14

May 1956

An Education

The next day I was surprised when Bitsy came over again. "Willie was so depressed I had to get out of the house. Let's read some more out on the porch."

"Wait, what do you mean, depressed? Like *how depressed*?"

"It's the pain. He's either so knocked out from the drugs that he's drooling or he hurts so much he can't even watch T.V. I just needed to get away"

"I'm glad you could come. Look," I observed, "Howard, the Blue Jay, has a girlfriend. They're building a nest in the old lilac bush." We watched as the two bright blue birds went back and forth from the barnyard to the top of the twenty-foot shrub carrying mouthfuls of rootlets and fresh twigs, dried grass and long pine needles. Sometimes they carried so much they dropped it and had to go back for more. It was only because of the quarter sized white patch on Howard's wing that I could tell them apart.

"I didn't know that the male Blue Jay would be so involved in nesting," Bitsy said. "I thought that was a female thing, like pregnant women go through *nesting* a few weeks before term."

"Dan told me Blue Jays mate for life and that the fathers care equally for the young."

"I wonder how long it takes them…to make a nest, I mean."

"I guess we'll see!" Then I opened the diary and began to read.

Hintonville, Virginia,
September 1859

It was later in September of '59 that I assisted Father with another bloodletting. This time it was for a ten-year-old child who cried through the whole thing. After we left and were in the carriage, I told him I didn't want to see anymore of such things. I knew it made him angry because he pulled out his silver flask and threw back a drink.

"Now that you've become a useful nurse, you're abandoning me, you ungrateful bitch!" he yelled and I think he would have hit me if I'd been sitting closer.

The rest of the way home we didn't speak. For days we didn't speak.

Looking back, I'm convinced that part of Dr. Coffman's downfall was not just his love of hard spirits. The whole South felt threatened. In Congress, the abolitionists and pro-slavery proponents had actual fistfights.

About that time, Abraham Lincoln gave his famous "A House Divided Against Its Self" speech. There was even talk of cessation.

Still there was no excuse for what he did next.

Walk, Run, Dance

As I planted the beans, carefully dropping them into the furrow at every three inches, I couldn't stop thinking about Willie. After his recent exploratory surgery, Dr. Spiggle told the family the fragments of bone still aren't knitting.

In Grace Potts' journal, she wrote of a young man who needed his foot amputated, but his father forbid it. That boy died of infection, but is Willie's situation that dire? When I told Dan the latest, he was concerned.

"What would you do if a horse had chronic osteomyelitis and its leg wouldn't heal?" I asked him. "Do horses ever get it?"

"Yes, occasionally."

"And what would the treatment be if the infection was resistant to antibiotics?"

"You don't want to know."

"Yes, I do."

"I'd have to put him down."

"But Willie's a person! You can't put him down."

"Then the leg will have to go."

"Oh Dan!"

Later, I went into town to see the house Lou and Bitsy are thinking of buying. It's on Third Street, only a few blocks from Main, one of those Sears mail-order houses that was sent in pieces on the train and put together by a group of neighbors and friends back in the thirties, a cute little three-bedroom, with one bed and bath on the main floor that doesn't require stairs.

"How's Willie doing?" I asked as we walked into the kitchen. It already had everything a family needed; fridge, stove, sink. The cupboards looked a little old fashioned, but they could be painted and the previous owner had even left a nice Formica table.

Bitsy turned on the water and waited while the rust cleared. "His leg is worse if anything. He knows we're moving because of his health and he's fuming. Says he feels babied and he's sick of it. Says he wants to be treated like a man."

Not knowing what to say, I peeked in the pantry then wandered out on the front porch. The locust trees in the yard were in full bloom and a white shower of petals blew across the big yard. "So what does Dr. Spiggle think, now? Does he have a new plan?"

Bitsy stared out across the grassy front yard. "One more course of antibiotics and if no improvement, they'll have to amputate." This was the news I was dreading…and I felt my heart drop to my feet.

I remember Willie as a boy, running through the fields, playing army. I see him sprinting around the bases at the town baseball field. I see him rescuing Mira when she fell in the Hope River. I see him walking through the snowstorm with his arm around his mom after they had a motorcycle accident. I watch as he proudly boards the train for his army training at Fort Lee. In every picture he has two legs.

After we walked through the house, we sat on the front porch swing and Bitsy talked about how nice it would be to live in town, but it hurt me to hear it. Finally, I got out my pocket book. Inside was one of Mrs. Potts' journals. "I brought a surprise. Want to read?"

Slave Quarters, Oak Hill Plantation
September 1859

It was a warm autumn day in '59 that Father decided the field slaves should be inspected for lice and he wanted me to go with him, saying he needed a woman present when he examined the females.

I was going to refuse, but when I saw the look on his face, I realized it would be too dangerous. He grabbed my wrist and pulled me out to his horse. Jammy had taken Mother to Hintonville and Thelma and Belle were nowhere around, not that they could have helped me. A slave doesn't disobey her master without significant punishment.

Father rode his mare hard, whipping her with the reins, while I bounced along behind him. When we got to the slave quarters he ordered all the bondsmen to come in from the fields. Blunt seemed annoyed, but he didn't argue. His job was to enforce his employer's commands.

When the slaves were assembled, Dr. Coffman ordered them to separate by gender and then to strip. I was shocked and stared at the ground as the people began to disrobe, laying their worn gray garments in a pile at their feet.

"It's come to my attention that there is an outbreak of lice in the camp." Father shouted so that all could hear.

"Lice will lead to disease. Today we will inspect you and tell you how to get rid of them. After this, we will inspect frequently and anyone who still has lice on his body or in his hair will

receive ten lashes."

Blunt didn't say anything. How could he? I imagined that this new policy must have caught him off guard. Though he may have enjoyed whipping a lazy or impudent slave on occasion, I doubted he wanted to do it for an offence as small as having lice.

I looked up for a minute and noted that there were roughly the same number of women and men in the group, along with 6 youngsters and Lottie's baby in old Hannah's arms.

It turned out I was not there just as a female chaperone. Father wanted me actively involved. He started with Lottie, the girl that he bought for a breeder. She had gained weight since the delivery and had got back her beauty.

"Here's what you do," he took me by the arm and pulled me toward her. "First look at the back and check the crack in their buttocks. To get the best view, you will need to sit down....Can you get us some chairs, Blunt?

"Then have the slave turn and you examine their pubis. Afterwards, you will take this comb and rake through their hair. If you find any lice, have the slave stand over there and Blunt will treat her with kerosene.

"Now pick one of the women and I'll watch." When I sat down on the crude wooden bench that Blunt had provided, my father put his claws on my shoulders and I felt he was punishing me, either for rejecting his advances or possibly for refusing to go with him on his medical rounds.

I went through the process, trying to convince

myself it was medically necessary "Stand please." I motioned to one of the women I didn't know. "What is your name, Miss?"

"Clara, ma'am." Her eyes were averted.

"Turn please, Clara....Bend please" I opened her butt cheeks.

"Turn again please," I looked under her arms and combed through the hair around her woman parts, then "Bow please." I looked through the hair on her head, which I had to unbraid.

"Thank you, Clara." I said at the end. "You may remain over there."

"Well, done," Father pronounced. "But you can drop the please and thank you. Also you're going to have to speed up, since you have to unbraid the women's hair."

"They can unbraid each other's hair," Blunt growled his opinion.

Then Father sat down beside me and called an elderly man. The naked old gentleman held his hands in front of his private parts and kept his head low. Father was efficient and rough and finished the exam in only a few minutes.

I called on old Hannah next because she had the least hair. She was standing with the little girls and they came with her while Lottie took the baby, so after I finished examining her I thanked her profusely and did the children. They weren't embarrassed because in the warm weather they often ran naked.

Even though Dr. Coffman had instructed me to stop saying please and thank you, I continued. It was a small rebellion, but to outright defy him in front of the slaves would be too risky. I had no idea what he'd do. Slap me perhaps or make me stand naked with the other slaves. I saw now that there were no limits to his malice.

"Come forward, please," I said to the next bondswoman. "What is your name, Miss?" "Turn, Please." "Pardon my fingers." "Turn, again." "Bow, please." I examined slave after slave, noting the thinness of the bodies and the whip scars on their backs. One woman had a lump in her breast. Another had pick marks on her arm. There were boils and scabs, signs of dropsy and open sores. They were not a healthy lot, yet every day they worked twelve hours in the hot fields.

Half way through the lice inspection, Father stopped what he was doing and called my attention to a man's flaccid organ. I knew such things now, things no girl of fourteen would know unless she read anatomy books from her father's medical library.

"Look at this, Grace. It's a French Pox, a sign of syphilis. Don't touch one if you see it, but show me. It's very contagious and slaves, because of their sexual proclivities, are rife with it.

"I'll need to get this man some mercury ointment, Blunt," he said to the overseer. "And be sure he doesn't lay with any of our slaves. Mercury isn't a cure, but it will slow the disease." He was playing the professor now to impress me.

"Ultimately, syphilis is fatal, Grace. It destroys the brain and results in flesh rot and paralysis. Many white gentlemen get it too, from lying with

their loose slaves. Then they give it to their wives when they have marital relations." I looked once at the sore on the drooping organ then averted my eyes, but in my future exams I did what he said and began to watch carefully for such lesions in females. I definitely did not want to touch a French pox by accident and die of syphilis.

A few minutes later, Father broke out in a jolly laugh. "Observe this, Grace," he ordered. I glanced over and saw a young man, about my age, standing before Father, trying to hide his erect male organ. I knew about these things, because I'd seen Father's stallion mounting the mares.

"Here feel it. It's as big as a toddlers arm."

I glanced up at the young man's face and for a brief second our eyes met. "I'd rather not. Mother wouldn't approve."

"To hell with your Mother. Touch it. I want you to touch it!"

"I'd rather not," I repeated.

"I'm your father and I said for you to touch it." He grabbed my wrist, pulled my hand toward the boy's male part and folded my fingers around it. Hot tears of anger sprang from my eyes. I wanted to scream. I wanted to run, but Father had hold of me.

That's when it happened. He wasn't my parent anymore and he would never be again. I was only his slave. I tightened my mouth and made the tears stop. Finally, he let go of my hand. Even though I was of African descent, my fingers looked so white against the boy's brown skin.

"I have an idea, Blunt. Let's show Grace how

darkies mate." Now, even Blunt looked uneasy.

"Get that comely girl, the breeder." He pointed to Lottie.

Oh, no, I thought. He can't have Lottie! Father threw my cloak on the ground, the beautiful blue silk one he'd brought me from Charlottesville and Lottie started to run.

"Get her Blunt!" The overseer caught the naked girl as she tried to jump the spilt rail fence and pulled her back to the yard. "Lie down!" he ordered, pointing to my blue cloak and threatening her with his whip. Then he grabbed the young man. "Ok, Leonard, mount the wench. Show the Master what that black cock can do."

Lottie lay on her stomach, her face turned toward me, our eyes locked. "I'm sorry," I whispered. "I'm so sorry."

Leonard positioned himself on top of the girl and inserted his still erect organ. He just shut his eyes and lay there, trying to support himself on his elbows to take his weight off her. Lottie didn't try to get away again.

"Now watch this, Grace. It will be an education for you, so when you marry, you won't be as reluctant as your mother is." He stood behind me, placing his hands on my shoulders, holding me there and I felt his own bulge against my upper back.

"Let's see some action, boy!" Blunt yelled, holding a whip over the couple.

Leonard began to pump and it went on a long time. Some of the slaves were mumbling prayers.

Some stared at the ground. Some looked at the sky.

"Pump harder," yelled Blunt. "Give it to her, boy! I don't want to take the strap to you."

Leonard pumped and pumped. Finally his whole body went rigid and he let out a roar. Lottie just lay there sobbing.

Meanwhile, Dr. Coffman, no longer "Father," was rubbing against me and when it was over, the back of my gown was sticky and wet...

Ok, that's it," says Bitsy slamming the journal closed. "This isn't good for me. I have to take a break again. You take the journal home and read it if you want to."

"It's not like I actually *want to*. It's more of a compulsion."

Bitsy shakes her head as if tossing off a bad dream. "Don't make yourself sad, Patience. It's not right. We need to focus on finding hope and happiness when we can." She points to the flowering trees and the daffodils along the walk, but I think she's trying to convince herself, not me and she goes on…"Remember, Grace Potts survived all this cruelty. We became her friend when she was a proud black midwife, a leader of her community. Life is too beautiful to spend our days being angry and sad."

May 12, 1956

Mother's Day

A box has arrived through the mail and I sit on the back porch unpacking it. In small envelopes with colorful pictures on them are all kinds of seeds. My own dried seeds, saved from last year, corn, beans, pumpkins and squash, are still in their jars.

A warm wind comes up bringing the scent of the apple blossoms and something else; the good smell of dirt. Though I've had gardens for decades, I still wonder at the miracle of placing seeds in the ground and watching them grow. The seed opens and sprouts; it makes leaves that reach for the light. It is the light that sustains us.

Yesterday was Mother's Day and Susie and Sally came home for a visit. Both girls looked so grown up, but in different ways and I'm proud of them. They're identical twins, but Sally wears her long blond hair up on her head in what she calls a French twist and Susie has a short Doris Day cut.

Nursing school is going well and they gossiped about their favorite doctors, nurses and friends, all people I don't know, in a world I've never entered. Sally will start her OB rotation next month. Susie will be doing pediatrics. I asked if they were dating anyone and they both just giggled. Mira was home too. We didn't hear from Danny.

Years past, I could almost count on a patient

143

going into labor on Mother's Day, but it's not like that now. So many women want to give birth in the hospital with all the latest equipment and medicines. Too bad actual childbirth is still so old fashioned! If couples could buy a baby at Woolworths, they probably would. For a minute I imagine it; rows of babies in colorful cardboard boxes; white babies, brown babies, some with curly hair, some bald; some crying, some smiling in their sleep.

"Oh, how precious, honey!" a woman says to her husband. "Isn't she cute? Let's take that one."

"Does she come with instructions?" the man wants to know. "Kind of pricey."

Middle Passage

While I sit on the porch, I recall the conversation I had with Bitsy the day we decided to stop reading the journals. "Just think about it," she said. "The captive slaves had to be incredibly strong just to survive the Middle Passage."

"I don't know what that is... *the middle passage*," I said, feeling ignorant.

"It means the trip from Africa to the New World. The voyage usually took a few months. Under the deck of the slave ship, men and women in wooden bunks were stacked four or five tiers high, with their legs chained to a post and also to each other. There was no way to walk around, no way to stand up, no way to go to the bathroom." Bitsy had tears in her eyes.

"What did they do?"

"When they peed, the urine would just drip down on the people below. If they got seasick and threw-up, their vomit would seep through too. Sometimes disease spread and a captive might end up chained to a dead man."

I wanted Bitsy to stop and I held up my hand, but she went on. "There were sometimes as many as 700 slaves on a ship, stacked like firewood. By the time they got to the Americas, especially if bad weather extended the trip, a third of them were dead and they were just dumped in the ocean. Can you imagine?

"Captured, taken away from your family, branded with a hot iron like a horse. The Africans had no idea where they were going. Some committed suicide by jumping over the side when they were allowed up on the deck for fresh air. Others, who never got the chance to go on deck committed suicide by not eating." Bitsy was no longer crying, but I was. *How could anyone think this was right? How could anyone?*

Stayed on Freedom

"There's an NAACP meeting in Torrington tonight, do you want to go with me?" Bitsy asked on the phone this morning. "Lou says I need to do something besides fuss about Willie." This strikes me as strange, I know she's very worried, but in the past Bitsy has always been so upbeat and sure of herself and strong.

People *think* I'm strong too, but that's just

because I'm a midwife, defender of mothers and babies, calm in emergencies and ready to fight against injustice. It's only lately that I've felt weak and I think I know why. My family is unraveling. The twins are grown up and living two hundred miles away. Danny never comes home. Mira only visits on holidays or when she needs something.

As an orphan I had no family, now I'm orphaned again. The circle of love I'd created to protect my heart now has gaps so wide a bear could run through.

"So I think we should go, don't you?" Bitsy continues her sales pitch about the NAACP.

"Are you sure I'd be welcome?"

"Don't you know the history of the NAACP?"

"Remind me." (The truth is…I have no clue.)

"It was started in 1909 by the Negro writer and civil rights activist, W.E.B. Dubois, two white suffragettes and a white lawyer from Boston. Injustice to black Americans is everyone's problem, Patience, not just the Negro's. It's important for both races to be involved."

"Ok," I finally agree. "I just hope it's not awkward."

By the time Bitsy arrived on her red Harley, Dan still wasn't home from work, so I scrawled him a note. It was a beautiful afternoon, with towering white clouds scattered across the sky like mounds of whipped cream. We followed the wooded ridge on the paved county road past waterfalls that cascaded down sandstone cliffs and around coal trucks, five of them. I was surprised there weren't more.

Sitting in the sidecar, I could lean back and stare up at the light streaming down through the leaves. My only complaint was the occasional bug that spattered my face.

Equality and Justice

When we got to Torrington, it took us awhile to find a restaurant that served both black and white diners, but we finally heard about the Riverside Café, the only integrated restaurant in Torrington. After cokes and burgers, we headed over to the campus to locate the meeting on the second floor of the Journalism School. Another yellow and black Civil Defense sign on the door pointed toward the basement.

Taking seats near the aisle in the back of the room, I was able to observe the crowd. They were mostly brown skinned gentlemen, with short cropped hair, dressed in suits and ties, who seemed to all know each other, plus a few colored mothers with toddlers in their laps.

As Bitsy predicted, I was not the only white person present. Sitting up front was a bald headed priest with a very pink scalp, next to an olive skinned fellow in a corduroy jacket who might be a professor. In back were a handful of white co-eds dressed in purple T-shirts that said Lutheran Student Association.

A young man walked up to the podium and cleared his throat. "Greetings everyone, I'm Wally Richards and I want to welcome you to our third NAACP meeting in Torrington. Reverend Wilson will open with a prayer."

An old black man with bushy white hair and a white mustache walked with a cane to the platform and we all bowed our heads. "Father, we thank you for giving us this chance to meet together, to bring equality and justice to those who've been oppressed...."

When he was finished, Wally Richards took the podium again. "This is our best turnout yet," he announced with a grin. "It's nice to see so many new faces and I hope you'll come forward and sign our mailing list before you leave." He was a tall fellow over six feet with a deep musical voice that carried to the back.

For the rest of the meeting we broke into four groups to brainstorm about actions we could take to further civil rights and integration in West Virginia as well as in the South. The younger people were all for hiring a bus and taking a bunch of students down to Alabama to help with voter registration. Those over forty were more concerned about working for integration on the local level.

In the end we decided to do both and started a collection to charter a bus. The co-eds felt they could find a few dozen students, black and white, who would go down south for a month in July to help colored people register to vote. By the fall, they'd be back and ready to do whatever we needed to help the mandatory integration of the public schools go smoothly. Bitsy's group was more radical. They planned to picket all the racist businesses in Torrington.

At the end of the meeting, the group broke out in song. *"Well, I woke up this morning with my mind stayed on freedom - I woke up this morning with my mind stayed on freedom!"* Everyone knew the words except me.

15

Blue-green Eggs

Today when my Blue Jay friends, Howard and Lulu, were out foraging for acorns and insects, I pushed the porch bench next to the rail and climbed up while holding onto the post. Lying in the lilac bush, in the perfect grassy nest, were four beautiful pale blue-green eggs!

Within minutes the parents were back and I was in for a scolding. "Keep your shirt on," I told Howard as he raised his pointed crest and screamed at me.

"Jay! Jay!"

"I was just checking. No harm done." Then I carefully climbed down.

Dan wouldn't approve of my antics. Ever since my accident, I have to be careful. It's amazing how sharp a cow's hooves are and how one kick to the leg can age a woman. When Dan was in prison I once crawled up on the house roof to repair a loose shingle. Now I tremble if I'm three feet off the ground.

After lunch, I searched for our bird book and finally found it on top shelf of the pantry. The guide said that Blue Jay eggs take 18-21 days to hatch. Since I don't know for sure when the female laid them, I just marked the eighteenth day on the calendar.

My research was interrupted by the sound of a

motor coming down Salt Lick and when I stepped out, I saw an unfamiliar green Ford.

The Baby Cabin

The car stops near the house and a dark man in his forties gets out. In the back sit two girls, one just a kid and the other about Mira's age; up front there's a woman with curly black hair.

"Hello. Can I help you?" The vehicle's license plate, says Ohio. *They must be lost.*

"Are you the midwife?"

"I am. Can I help you," I ask again.

"I surely hope so. We just moved into a little cottage down the road from Hazel Patch. Reverend Jerome sent us. My older daughter might be in labor, but we can't tell."

"Did you take her to the doctor in Liberty? The hospital is open now."

"I did, but they don't provide care for coloreds."

"That can't be right. I heard they were going to have a Negro ward in the basement."

"We just left there. The nurse said they do have a colored ward, but not for maternity, so we would have to go to Boone Memorial in Torrington."

"That's ridiculous! What's your daughter's name?"

"Rose… but there's something else." Inside the auto, the older of the two girls, a moon faced young woman, stares back at me. "Well, our daughter is poorly today, worse than she has been."

"You better bring her in. I have a little bungalow behind the house called The Baby Cabin,

151

but it hasn't been used for a while. Let me run ahead and turn on the lights and make sure it's tidy. My name is Patience, by the way. Patience Hester."

"Fred Lincoln and my wife, Lacy Lincoln, and Rose and Daisy," he makes the introductions.

Quick as I can, considering my bum knee, I hurry across the yard to the kitchen, get a clean bucket of warm water from the sink and trot around back to the cabin. Luckily, it's in pretty good shape. The bed's made neatly with a blue and white quilt. The cradle is layered with white flannel and my birth items are all neatly stored.

Daniel and our friend, Dr. Blum, built the little building for me when we adopted the twins and our family went from two children to four. At the time, Bitsy was in Paris and I was running all over Union County delivering babies, but with the little lying-in-home right in my own back yard, I could attend more women without exhausting myself.

The one room cabin is made of poplar logs planed smooth to show the golden wood. The shelves and floor are of pine. Everything looks as ship-shape as a little boat, ready to go to sea.
Only one thing is out of place, three empty beer bottles on the rolling maple birth table that Dr. Blum made and I quickly put them in a bottom cupboard. *Danny!* I think. *Over Christmas, he must have been drinking out here.*

Minutes later, there's a tap on the door and Mr. Lincoln assists the pregnant girl in.

"Hi, Rose. I'm Patience," I introduce myself. "Nice to meet you." I make the right sounds, but what I'm thinking is, this girl is sick!

Land of Prayer

"Sorry if we interrupted your day," Rose says politely as the whole family troops into the Baby Cabin. Her face is as round as a pumpkin and her feet are so swollen I think they might burst. "I just don't feel good; I have a headache and I'm sick to my stomach. I might be in labor, but I don't know what labor feels like."

"Well, let's get you settled and then I'll examine you. Have you had any doctor visits this pregnancy?" The father and the younger sister stand back by the door and I notice the little girl leans on a crutch.

The mother takes the rocking chair and begins to tell me how Rose's husband is in the army and how Mr. Lincoln lost his job as a maintenance man at Republican Steele in Pittsburgh when they hired a white man to replace him, but her husband cuts her short.

"Honey, the midwife doesn't want to hear all that…The bottom line is, we were short on cash and no doctor would take us without paying first. We've been short on funds since little Daisy got polio in '52. The good news is the March of Dimes paid for her brace and Morgan Mining just hired me as a coal truck driver, so whatever your fee is, we're good for it, as soon as I get my first pay check."

I lay out a clean nightgown, silently reviewing

the symptoms of toxemia, a disease of pregnancy. (*Headache, swelling, visual changes, nausea,*) but it's when I take Rose's blood pressure that I lose my poker face. 180/110!

"Mmmmmm," Rose moans. "There it is again; the feeling that I'm going to be sick." I place my hand on her belly.

"That's a contraction Rose. Next time you feel queasy put your hands there."

The girl does what I say and I notice her fingers look like little Vienna sausages.

Mrs. Lincoln looks worried. She's an attractive woman, with light brown skin and very large brown eyes. "It's normal to feel stomach-sick in labor, isn't it?"

"Yes, many women do. Can I get your blood pressure one more time, Rose?"

"Is it high?" Mrs. Lincoln asks, observing my concern.

"I'll tell you in a moment." I put my finger to my lips, indicating they should be quiet. "Yes, her pressure is very high."

"What is it?" asks the father.

"180/112."

"What's it supposed to be?" Rose's mother wants to know.

"140/90 or lower."

Rose moans again, this time placing her sausage fingers over her belly. "Oh," she says. "I see. That sick feeling is the contraction and now I feel pressure in my rear too." She squirms in the bed and sweat beads on her brow.

Mr. Lincoln steps out on the porch to get a

smoke. I motion Mrs. Lincoln to follow him while their daughter puts on the gown and Daisy takes the rocker. I need to tell the parents what I think is going on, but I don't want to say it in front of Rose and make her blood pressure go higher.

I clear my throat. "I believe your girl is very ill. What she has is called toxemia, which can seriously affect her and the baby. The wisest thing to do would be to take her to Boone Memorial Hospital in Torrington, but I don't know if they take colored women in labor there either. We could call them...The trouble is, if she gets jittery, she could have a seizure." *And she could lose the baby or maybe die,* I think, but don't say it.

"Could bouncing up and down on the country roads bring on a seizure?" the father wants to know.

"Yes, I thought of that." Outside, grey clouds roll over Hope Mountain propelled by a powerful wind. A storm is coming. I can feel it. We are entering the land of prayer now.

Seizure

"A seizure would be bad, right?" Mr. Lincoln wants to know. "She could lose the baby, right? We can't chance it," he says. "Please can't we stay here? Can't you help her?"

"I'm only a country midwife. They have medicine in the hospital," I explain.

"Ma'am, can I go to the bathroom," Rose calls out interrupting our deliberations.

"One minute!" I go back inside to attend to the patient.

"I don't think you should stand up, Rose, but I can give you a bed pan." The girl growls like a cornered bear.

"Nah. Nah. Nah. Never. Nah." She shouts and stares at me fixedly. "No. No. No. Ne. Nah."

What's happening? Rose seems confused. Her eyes roll back until the whites are exposed. Her chin juts out. She goes rigid and then she begins to shake. The whole metal bed clangs like a dinner bell. Foam comes out of her mouth.

Outside it begins to rain on the tin roof. "Mrs. Lincoln! Mr. Lincoln!" I call. They slam through the door, bumping into each other.

"Oh, Lord God! Is this what you were talking about? A seizure?" The woman falls on her knees and tries to hold onto to her daughter who is flinging about. Daisy starts to cry and covers her eyes. The man does the same on the other side of the bed, but while Rose is seizing something else happens. Her water bag pops and a small head with dark hair suddenly shows on the perineum.

"Turn her on her side!" I order. I know I should put a stick in Rose's mouth to prevent her from biting her tongue, but so long as she's still breathing, that's the least of my worries.

"Hold her leg up, please." I say in my calmest voice and the little girl, Daisy, rises and tries to comply.

"Baby doll. Baby doll." Mrs. Lincoln croons.

I have everything ready across the room, but there's no time for my sterilized gloves. I check for a cord and am relieved I don't feel one, then cupping the infant's head, I maneuver the shoulders

156

and within seconds a wet screaming infant is in my hands. A few minutes later the placenta shoots out with about a pint of blood.

Rose has stopped trembling, but another seizure can come any minute so I wrap the wailing baby in a towel and hand him to Daisy. Mr. Lincoln's brown face is now as gray as the clay along the Hope River. "I need some air," he whispers.

"I better go with him. He fainted at the doctor's office when he got a shot last time," Mrs. Lincoln says, hurrying out the door.

"Look, Mrs. Midwife," Daisy whispers. "Rose's waking up!"

The young woman is semi-conscious after her seizure, so before anything else happens I grab the vial of Mrs. Potts' hemorrhage medicine and pour a few tablespoons into her mouth. "Drink this, Honey. You need it." Her lids flutter open and then close again, but she swallows it down. The new mother is already lying on her side and when I settle the little one next to her she opens her eyes. "Oh, look! A little bird," she says and falls back in a daze.

"Let me unbutton your gown, Rose. Your baby is hungry. Also if he nurses, it will help keep you from bleeding." The infant roots around and when he attaches, Roses eyes open wide and stay open.

"Holy-moly!" she exclaims. "His suck is so strong. How does he know to do that?"

"Nature's way, I guess. Do you know you had a seizure?"

"A fit?"

"Yes. It happened because your blood pressure

157

was so high. Do you feel better now?"

"My headache is gone. I never had such a headache." She stares at her baby and then in the quiet she begins to sing. *"Hush, little Baby, don't say a word. Mama's gonna buy you a Mockingbird."*

It's an old timey lullaby I used to sing to Danny and the girls when they were little. *"And if that mockingbird don't sing,"* Daisy and I come in. *"Mama's gonna buy you a diamond ring.*

May 25, 1956,
Birth of female infant, 6 pounds 2 ounces, to Rose Lincoln in the Baby Cabin. Rose's parents, Mr. and Mrs. Lincoln showed up unexpectedly after they were turned away from Liberty Memorial because they're colored. The girl was very ill with high blood pressure and had no prenatal care. Labor was fast and just after she seized, she popped out the baby. Blood loss one pint. The infant was fine and Rose's blood pressure went down right after the birth. The girl's father didn't have any money because he'd lost his job in Pittsburgh, but Morgan Mining recently hired him to drive truck, and I'm sure he will give me something. They were very appreciative of my service.

16

Struggle

"Another bus boycott," Dan tells me. It's eight in the morning and we're sitting at the kitchen table drinking coffee before we go out to clip the wings of two dozen laying hens that a farmer in Delmont gave Dan in return for delivering his prize bloodhound's five pups.

Over Dan's shoulder, I glance at the paper. **Florida Coeds Arrested for Inciting Riot.**

"What's the story?" I turn back to the stove, where I'm making breakfast.

"Shall I read it out loud?"

"No, just summarize as I fry some ham to go with these eggs."

Dan takes a sip of coffee and shakes out the paper. "Well a couple of days ago, two female students at the all-black Florida A and M University in Tallahassee paid their ten-cent fares on the city bus. Because there was standing room only back in the colored section, they took seats in the white section that was practically empty. When the driver asked them to move, the girls refused. The driver stopped the bus and had them arrested for inciting a riot."

"That doesn't sound like much of a riot!"

"Well, the plot thickens. The story got in the

paper and the girls were named in the article. That night the KKK burned crosses on their front lawns. Now the whole student body at A and M is refusing to ride the bus and urging all other black passengers to boycott too."

"Bitsy would say 'Halleluiah!'"

"You sound doubtful."

"No...I'm very supportive. It's just that the southern whites seem so bigoted and so willing to use violence. America is becoming a battle zone."

Dan holds out his plate as I serve the eggs. "The Quakers believe change can come through non-violent action," he says as he takes a bite.

"Like what Gandhi did in India?"

"He achieved independence from the all powerful British Empire without a shot fired."

"But can colored people in America achieve such justice without bloodshed?"

"Well, Gandhi was an exceptional leader. We'll just have to see if someone like that appears in the United States. Ready to do the chickens? That will get your mind off the struggle for justice."

"Yeah, right!" I respond laughing. "It will just be another kind of struggle!"

The process of clipping chickens' wings is something I've never really enjoyed, but it's necessary. In the last three nights we've lost four of the new hens, because they've flown over the fence.

The hardest part of the procedure is catching the birds. Years ago, I was afraid I'd hurt them when I grabbed their flapping wings. Now, I'm afraid the chickens will hurt me. Their long yellow talons are pointed and sharp *and* they have beaks!

Since Danny was a boy he always loved to help clip our chicken's wings, but this year he's nowhere around. With only the two of us it will take hours.

"Hold her still now!" Dan says using a pair of heavy shears to trim the long feathers on each wing. There's no feeling in feathers he tells me. It's like cutting your hair or your fingernails. Next we dip the chicken's foot in a coffee can of blue paint to show that's she's been clipped. Finally, we let her go free, but the next time things don't go so well. When we open the chicken-coop door, three hens fly out and it takes twenty minutes to corral them.

"Whew! Pretty tricky bunch," I exclaim when we are down to the last few hens. "Danny would enjoy this. Have you seen him in town?"

"I saw him once and asked him to join me at the Hilltop Café for a sandwich, but he said he had to go see someone about playing music…He's staying in Delmont with some fellow he knows from high school."

"Are you sure it's not a young woman? He could be just hiding it."

"Pretty sure. He said his name was Billie. I guess that could be a girl."

Finally, Dan grabs the last chicken and hands her to me, but she struggles and scratches my arm.

"Hey watch it! Don't let her go!" he yells.

"Sorry…So *is* Danny ok?"

"He will be, Patience."

"You sure?" I ask looking into his gray eyes, but he doesn't answer.

Summer

17

June 1956

Surprise

Since Rose delivered I've visited her twice and her high blood pressure has resolved. The swelling in her face, feet and hands is gone too and she looks like a different person. Last night, her mother gave me an envelope with fifty dollars in it. I couldn't believe it!

I stop writing in my journal for a moment and gaze across the newly plowed garden. This is the first day in two weeks that I haven't planted something and the neat rows of spinach, Swiss chard, radishes and kale are just starting to emerge. I'd be working out there today, but after the thunderstorm last night the ground is too wet, so instead, I go around to the front of the house to check on my baby tomatoes.

The miniature green house, constructed by my husband from a design he found in *Popular Mechanics*, is a simple affair made of 2 x 4s, hay bales and an old window for a door that's hinged at the top so it can be opened. Inside the frame are 25 small tomato plants growing in tin cans. On a sunny day like today, it's important to check that it isn't too warm.

As I lift up the window, I hear a soft squeak that I think, at first, is a rusty hinge, but it happens again. "Squeak. Squeak." And then I look up. I'm standing almost directly under the lilac bush and I know at once what that sound must be. I've been so busy I'd forgotten about the nest with four blue-green eggs.

Up on the porch, I climb an old stepladder that I brought from the barn and discover four tiny birds, red and featherless, looking toward me with big bulging eyes. "Squeak. Squeak," they cry opening their gaping beaks, hoping for food.

Just then, Howard flies up. "Jay! Jay!" he scolds flapping his wings protectively and raising his feathered crest. Seeing it's only me, not a threat, he backs off making a soft cooing sound.

"Squeak! Squeak! Squeak!" say the fledglings and Howard regurgitates a mouthful of food into each yawing beak. Standing on the ladder, I watch as the mother returns. Then back and forth the parents fly, finding food and bringing it home as the demanding youngsters holler for more.

Night Lights

Tonight Dan is off attending a horse in labor and I'm home alone again. For a while I tune in to *Dragnet* on the radio, but it's not much fun listening alone. Finally, I go out on the porch and sit in the dark, listening to the tree frogs in the woods and the bullfrog down by the creek.

That's when I see them, the first lightning bugs, little twinkling flames in the trees and the grass.

First there's just one and then I see two more and then dozens. This makes me so happy I run out on the lawn and do a little dance. "Fire flies. Fire flies. Lightning Bugs! Boo!" Around and around I twirl, like a five-year-old singing and then I drop into the grass.

Above, the stars twinkle in the black night sky and high clouds sail past. It's a wonderful world and I'm sure all this can't be random. From lightning bugs in the trees to galaxies of stars...it's all a miracle to me, just as when a new baby opens her eyes and takes her first breath.

Once in bed and unable to sleep, I start thinking about Grace Potts. It's been weeks since Bitsy and I looked at her journals. The disgusting scene at the slave quarters, where Dr. Coffman staged the rape, stopped us cold...now I begin to wonder what happened next. I pick up the last of her little notebooks...half afraid and begin...

Hintonville, Virginia,
September 1859

After the staged rape of young Lottie by Leonard, the unwilling stud, the doctor and I didn't speak. We road home in silence and once we got in the door, I ran up the stairs.

"Mother," I called, tapping her bedroom door.

"Come in," she said. Things had been stiff with us lately, but today she sounded pleasant. When I saw her, I burst into tears. I just couldn't help it.

"What ever is it, Grace?" She was lying in bed and when she started to get up, I saw that her feet were swollen and blue. I tore off my soiled dress,

threw it on the floor, and jumped under the covers in my petticoat.

"What is it, Grace? Belle said you went on a call with Father. What happened? Did a mother die in childbirth or a baby? Come now. You can tell me."

I threw my head back on the pillows and lay rigid, staring at the canopy, teeth clamped, still seeing the naked slaves and the man-boy rutting on top of Lottie. Then the tears came again and I sobbed into my mother's soft chest.

"What is it? Child what?"

Finally, I stopped and thought about what I should tell her. The truth, I decided, so, I described the scene. How father tricked me into going to the slave quarters as his chaperone for the females while he inspected the slaves for lice. How he and Mr. Blunt herded all the bondsman into the yard in front of the cabins and made them strip naked.

How he insisted I actually examine the women slaves myself, including their butt crack and genitals. How he made me touch a boy's erect organ while he and Blunt laughed and then how he forced the young man to lie on the girl Lottie.

I didn't tell her how the doctor kept me from running away while he rubbed his stiff man parts on my back. I didn't tell her that my beautiful blue cloak was ruined because that would have made me cry again. I didn't tell her that I felt part of the crime against the slaves; that just being a Coffman made me complicit.

After drying my eyes on the hem of the sheet, I

fell asleep and was only vaguely aware of Mother ringing for the maid. "Grace is ill," she explained. "I hate to ask, but could you and Thelma bring the copper tub upstairs and let her bathe in my bedroom. I know it will be extra work, hauling the water up, but I would appreciate it." She was always like that to our servants, gracious and polite.

A while later, I heard the maid and cook bustle in and begin setting up the bath and I surmised that they'd already heard of the terrible event at the slave quarters. When I was situated in the water and they were gone, Mother hobbled over, pulled up a chair and poured warm water over my head. She poured and poured as if baptizing me, washing away my sins. Then she washed my shoulders and my back with perfumed soap and a soft cloth.

"Wash my back more, please," I asked her, but I didn't say why. "Scrub it hard." She was surprised, but did what I asked. I had played a role in the humiliation of the field hands and, body and soul, I felt contaminated.

Eventually, I had to get out of the water. "Come, Grace. I'll dry you and you can wear one of my nightdresses. At fourteen, you're almost my size now. Then we have to decide what to do."

This caught me off guard. I'd thought my escape to freedom would be secret and solitary, running through the dark Virginia pine woods, slave dogs baying after me. To think that Mother might help, gave me comfort.

"All this time, I thought you and your father were fond companions," she explained. "I was

jealous, I'll admit. It hurt that all you wanted to do was ride around in the buggy with a man who neither loved nor respected me. Has he ever treated you like this before? I should have suspected. He is just like his older brother, Andrew, a lecherous libertine."

I took a deep breath and sat on the bed facing her. "He's never done anything this despicable, but there have been uncomfortable moments, and since our family doesn't go out socially, I didn't know what was normal. He's kissed me. Hugged me. Tried to get me to drink spirits and one time...this is mortifying...he was drunk and he seized my breast.

"For weeks, I managed to be sure we were never alone, but he felt my distance and was angry. What happened at the slave quarters was meant to punish me. I can't live here any more, Mother. Oh, let's go to Philadelphia! There are Quakers there who will take care of us."

"I will think on it. Most of my family has already passed, but I have one cousin in Upper Darby. I'll write to her tonight. The problem is, I don't have any money. Your father, like most men, controls everything."

"He's not my father anymore. I cannot call him that."

"Well you may have to for awhile. We don't want to arouse his suspicion. For the next few days, while we make a plan, I'll tell everyone you are having female troubles and you can stay in my room. And Grace...you saw my legs. That's why I stay in bed so much. I don't know if I can take the stagecoach with you."

"What is it, Mother? What's wrong with them?"

"It's dropsy and gout and it's hurts to walk."

There's a tap at the door. "Miriam?" Dr. Coffman shouts. "Is Gracie in there? We have a woman in labor."

"Grace is not feeling well...You'll have to go by yourself."

"If Grace is sick, I should examine her."

I would like to rise up and spit in his face, but I fake a cough and call back, "Yes. I'm under the weather. I just need to rest."

In the next several days, Dr. Coffman became more demanding. Morning and evening he would bang on Mother's door, but she made excuses. Meanwhile we racked our brains for a plan. We needed time, but the longer we waited the more suspicious the master would become.

"I think I should take the fastest horse we have and head north for Pennsylvania," I offered.

Mother disagreed. "You should take the stagecoach. You could get on at the station in Harrisonburg where no one would recognize you."

For days we went back and forth, but couldn't make a decision. Finally, I had to come out of the room and try to act normal and mother agreed that stealing one of the horses was likely the best plan. The doctor would put runaway slave advertisements in all the papers, but if I kept to the back roads I could make it to Upper Darby in less than a week.

"You promise you'll come to Pennsylvania as

soon as you have money enough for the train? I couldn't bear the sadness if I thought I'd never see you again."

"I promise, but do you know that's why most slaves don't run?" she asked. "It's not because they're afraid of getting caught, but because they're afraid they'll never see those they love again." This was something I'd never thought of.

Hintonville, Virginia,
October 1859

Mother and I were planning my escape when on Friday morning something unexpected happened. It was a blustery fall day, not cold, but windy and wet. Leaves already were flying when Mr. Blunt came to the house, looking for Doctor Coffman. Not finding him, he went to the barn. There, uninvited, he entered the stall that Jammy called home and found the groom reading a week old Philadelphia Inquirer.

When the doctor returned from a bloodletting, Blunt met him on the porch and they went into the parlor to decide what to do. Dr. Coffman knew that mother had taught the fundamentals of reading to Jammy twenty years ago, but in front of the overseer he acted shocked.

Voices were raised. From the upstairs landing I could see and hear everything.

"Well, what are you going to do about it, Blunt? You're in charge of disciplining the slaves," Dr. Coffman bellowed. "If we don't punish Jammy, the

law will and I don't want to lose a good slave to prison."

"Do you really wish him to have 39 lashes? That's the prescribed punishment."

"Yes. And find out, while you're at it, who got him the newspaper."

I couldn't help it...I was so enraged! I ran down the stairs and confronted them both. "I got him the paper!" I lied to protect mother. "Whip me instead. You know I'm a slave, just like he is and I can read too. I can read as good as you can, Doctor Coffman and probably better than you, Mr. Blunt."

The doctor doubled his fist, as if to backhand me, but just then Jammy burst in the door. The four of us glared at each other. Then the bondsman broke the silence.

"I'll take the punishment, but if you ever want me to help you with any of your patients or animals again, Doctor Coffman, you'd better not say another thing about my reading. If you do, I'll go back to being a dumb workhorse like you want me to be."

Blunt threw up his hands in frustration. "Do you wish him whipped here or at the public slave yard in Harrisonburg?" he asked.

Dr. Coffman turned as if to leave, but stopped. "Why should I pay someone else to whip him? That's what I have you for, Blunt. Besides, I want Grace to reap what she has sown. I want her to see this...Set the whipping for five o'clock this evening here by the house. And make sure all the slaves are present, the old and the young too, that way nine and thirty lashes will serve as a group lesson. Hell, invite the neighbors and their slaves too."

And so, dear reader, I stood and watched, along with scores of whites and blacks, as Blunt, with the help of some of the neighbor men, ripped off Jammy's rough gray shirt, tied him to a tree, then took a log and spread his legs and tied them too.

Mother didn't come down, but Dr. Coffman was there, smoking his cigar and counting each lash in a loud voice. "One. Two. Three. Four...." And the white neighbors cheered.

Jammy didn't cry out or beg for forgiveness, but toward the end, as his naked back bled, a grunt would come out of him. Ugh. Ugh. Ugh. Blunt whipped thirty-nine times with cow skins tied to a stick and cut great gashes in the bondsman's brown back, while I bit my lip until I tasted blood.

The next day dawned clear and cold with a light frost on the ground and when I went to the stable to see how Jammy fared, I found he had already built a fire, fed the horses and brought in more hay.

"What are you doing up?" I asked.

"Whether a slave is whipped for something major, like reading, or something minor like stealing a pear," he told me. "He must always work the next day.... I made some willow bark tea for the pain. Could I ask you to pour some more salt water on my back? It stings like the devil, but it'll help the cuts heal." While I worked on his 39 open wounds, Jammy talked.

"I worry about you Miss Grace. I heard what

happened at the slave quarters when you went with your father to delouse the people."

"I didn't think you knew."

"Most of the county knows by now. Word around here travels fast."

"It was terrible. I didn't want to go, but Dr. Coffman insisted. The whole affair was humiliating to both the slaves and me. He's not my father anymore, Jammy. And I'm going to run away...You could come with me," I whispered. "We could go to Pennsylvania and be free."

"I can't run. I have responsibilities."

"To Dr. Coffman?"

"To my wife and children."

"Jammy! How come I didn't know? Do they live at the slave camp?"

"No, my wife and little boy are owned by a family in Staunton. That's where I go every Sunday, and I save every coin the master gives me so that someday I can buy myself, my wife, and my son and be free."

I am stunned by this new information. "I wish you could come north with me now, but if I get away and find a job, I'll save all my money and send it to you somehow."

"Your father will do whatever he can to capture you, so be careful. You know what he's capable of."

"Mother's going to get me some boy's clothes from the laundress, Mrs. Washington, so if anyone sees a white boy on horseback, it will seem less suspicious. My story is that I'm on my way to a private school in Philadelphia."

Jammy considered this. "Take Louis. He's the

fastest horse we have, but don't make it look like you're in too big a hurry. And I can make you a map. It's been a few years, but I once drove the doctor to a medical meeting in Winchester. You'll keep going north from there and then cross the bridge over the Potomac at Harper's Ferry.

"I'll arrange to be somewhere else the day you run," Jammy went on. "So it will seem I knew nothing about it…Tell me when you plan to go and I'll arrange to have a sick call in the slave quarters. The people there will vouch for me… I'll miss you, Miss Grace. You're one of the reasons I get up in the morning."

Early the following Saturday, we tried again. Everyone was gone, so Mother got out her scissors and I watched in the mirror as my dark curls fell.

When she was done, I put on my new set of clothes, a white shirt, black jacket, gray pantaloons and a broad brimmed black hat, perfect for a planter's son, then I looked at myself. "What do you think?" I asked her.

"You look like a handsome young lad," she said in a low voice, wiping her eyes.

"You'll take the train north when your legs are better, won't you? I don't care if we're poor. I'll find some employ. Maybe I could be a school teacher in a one-room school house like you used to be."

"I'll come," she promised putting her left hand over her heart and her right one over mine. "I'll save every penny I can borrow or steal for the railway fare….and I'll come," she said again.

18

Whites Only

Bitsy and I arrived in Torrington around noon for the NAACP protest at Rollin's Soda Fountain. I wore my last year's Easter suit, light blue tweed, with a white blouse and white pumps. Bitsy wore her yellow summer dress with short sleeves, white gloves and patent leather flats, much more sensible for a warm day. I swear she dresses nicer than a model in the Sears and Roebuck catalogue.

Just as the demonstration started, Billy Blaze, from *The Liberty Times,* showed up. As usual, he sported a brown fedora with a card in the band that said PRESS.

"Mrs. Hester!" he yelled, running over. "I might have known you'd be here! Can I get a statement?"

"No, Billy. Not now."

"Later then?" He was as hard to get rid of as a leech used for bloodletting.

"Ok. Maybe later. Let us get organized."

There were policemen, TV cameras and reporters with microphones milling around, greeting each other in low voices. A large white placard on the glass door of the establishment said in bold letters, *No Negroes. Whites Only!* Wally Richards, the young leader of the local NAACP chapter, pushed through the crowd to welcome us.

"Nice signs," he said, guiding us through the line of about two-dozen protesters, most of whom I recognized from the meeting; then he gathered the group in a circle. "Remember, this is a *non-violent demonstration*," he said. "No matter what people call us, please don't argue. We use passive resistance and we're as strong as an oak and bendable as a willow, but we shall not be moved!"

I glanced over at Bitsy, who despite all her concerns about Willie, stood with her sign, looking calm and proud, and I decided to let my friend's face be my light. I was marching for Bitsy. I was marching for Gracie Potts, Old Jammy and Emmett Till and for all the people who'd been told their place was in the back of the bus.

For a few hours, the demonstration went on without incident. Back and forth in the heat we walked. Only a few people insisted on going into the cafe and we let them pass even as they mumbled, "Commies," "Jungle Bunnies," or "Go back where you came from!"

The good news was that we also got support from passing cars. The drivers honked and yelled out the windows. "God bless you."

At one point, Billy Blaze pulled Bitsy and me aside again. "So ladies," he said, reaching for his pocket notebook. "I have to cover a wedding back in Liberty and I don't have much time. Can you give me a short interview?"

"Ok, Mr. Blaze. What do you want to know?"

"Well, why are you here today, for starters."

"We're protesting this particular cafe for discriminating against Negroes but also against all such establishments in America." (I was surprised how easily the words came to me.) "We're demonstrating for freedom and justice for everyone, regardless of race or religion.

"Racism isn't just a problem in the South," I went on. "It's here in West Virginia too. We have to start making changes in our own backyard." I pointed to the sign in the window, "**Whites Only**" and he took a few photos.

"And what about you? Mrs. Cross," the reporter asked.

"That just about says it," Bitsy answered with a big smile. Then we were off marching again, our heads held high. Sometimes I waved at the people in the cars and I tried a smile at a uniformed policeman, but he looked away.

"How long will we do this?" I whispered to Bitsy who walked just a few feet ahead of me. A large thermometer outside the door, advertising Mail Pouch Chewing Tobacco, said 86 degrees, unusually hot for early June.

"Probably until closing time." She pointed to a placard that said Open 9am-7pm. We'd been parading back and forth for five hours. My knee ached with each step and I didn't see how I could make it much longer.

Occasionally a car would still honk, but the novelty had worn off, and the reporters had gone back to Liberty, Delmont and Uniontown to cover weddings, barn raisings and baseball games. Even the police had disappeared and that's when the trouble began.

A jalopy, with a miniature confederate flag tied on the antenna, pulled up to the curb and four young men jumped out and began yelling insults. Then they threw raw eggs. One hit the Reverend right in the face.

"Just keep marching," Wally called, walking up and down the line. "Don't react to the racists. They want to start trouble!"

Fortunately, the young men were poor shots and most of the eggs landed on the restaurant's windows where the yellow yolks ran down the glass.

"What the hell!" For the first time the owner, Mr. Rollins, burst through the door. "Junior Johnson!" he bellowed at the fellow with slick backed blond hair. "I don't like these protesters any more than you do, but I'll have you hauled in for vandalism if you try any more of that. Look at my windows. Who's going to clean up this mess?"

Junior pointed to Bitsy. "Let the Jungle Bunny in the white gloves do it. Next time we see her, we'll do more than throw eggs." I whipped around ready to defend my friend. If I'd got to him I would have bashed the snickering bastard with my sign…

But that's when I fainted.

Concussion

"What's wrong?" Dan yelled, loping across the yard when he saw Dr. Greene from the NAACP protest, helping me out of his late model Packard. "Was there violence?" Bitsy had already parked her

178

motorcycle near the barn and was just walking over.

"No, Dan there wasn't any violence," she responded. "Patience just fainted and hit her head on the sidewalk. Dr. Greene felt it was safer to bring her home in an auto than to return in a motorcycle side car." For some reason this struck me funny and I began to giggle.

"Winston Greene," the man held out his hand to Dan. "I'm an MD from Torrington and was at the protest. There were about thirty people there and your wife experienced heat exhaustion...not serious in itself, but the fall worried me. I think she has a slight concussion. I see you're a medical man too." He nodded toward Dan's white coat and the vet bag he carried.

"Not a physician, a veterinarian," my husband clarified. "Let me get Patience inside and then I'll make you some iced tea."

"I should probably go. Nice place you have though," he said gazing around at the old stone house and the livestock in the green fields.

"Please. Come in, we'll get Patience to lie down on the sofa. I want to hear more about what happened."

A few minutes later, I was situated with a pillow under my head and a sick rag over my eyes. *A sick rag.* That's what Mrs. Kelly used to call it. Mrs. Kelly, my mentor, my friend, my midwife teacher... I got tears in my eyes just thinking about it. Dr. Greene was right. Something was wrong with me. I went from laughing to crying in the time it takes to cut a slice of bread.

In the kitchen I could hear the good doctor and Bitsy tell Dan about the demonstration.

"It was the heat that got her," Bitsy explained, "But she did get a little riled up when the rebel boys arrived."

"They're a bad lot," Dr. Greene said. "Always in trouble and they're bigots, as you observed. One of them knocked the front teeth out of a colored boy who plays trumpet in the Torrington Negro High School band. The cops let the bully go because his Daddy owns the Torrington Hotel. That sort of thing happens quite a lot... (I faded out of the conversation then returned, sometimes listening, sometimes flying over the Hope River on the back of an eagle.)

"Does Patience have any medical conditions?" Dr. Greene asked.

"Not really," Dan said. "Patience and Bitsy are midwives."

"Really! I had no idea. My mother was a midwife in South Carolina!"

19

Duck and Cover

In the days following my concussion, Daniel insisted that I do no work and just rest. At first I slept most of the day, but finally, when my head cleared and didn't hurt anymore, he said I could sit on the porch.

I had forgotten all about the Blue Jay nest and the first thing I saw was Howard who greeted me with a soft coo. Above me in the lilac bush, I could see Lulu and the heads of the nestlings that now had fuzzy feathers and looked as cute as little Easter chicks.

As I watched them yammering for food, I had a lot to think about. Dan had told me Bitsy and Lou had bought the house on Third Street and had quickly moved in. It was a shock and I swung between worrying how it would affect us to being happy for Bitsy and her family. Finally, I went back inside and asked Dan, for my first outing, to drop me off at their new residence when he went through Liberty on his rounds.

"Here, Hon, sit down," my friend ordered when she opened the door of her cute Sears and Roebuck bungalow. "No, *lie down*. I'll get you a pillow."

"Oh, Bitsy, don't start! I don't know much

about concussions, but I'm sure Dan's being over protective."

"Dr. Greene says it can be serious and he's the best Negro doctor in the state. Did you know that Dan and I took turns sitting by your bedside the whole first night?"

"No..."

"We were worried. You were so out of it."

"Well, I'm fit as a fiddle now. Can we watch TV?" Bitsy reaches for the local television schedule in the Liberty newspaper. "Wait a minute, what's that on the back?" I demand.

My friend turns the paper over and stares at a photo of the two of us at the protest in Torrington. "Whoops! You weren't supposed to see that."

"What do you mean?" I reach for the paper and she reluctantly hands it to me.

"Dr. Greene said we shouldn't allow you to get excited. Lou and I were pretty sure this would do it."

I begin to scan the article, published a few days after the NAACP demonstration "**Local Women March for Civil Rights in Torrington**" exclaim the headlines. In addition to the photo of Bitsy and me with our protest signs, there's a close-up of the "No Negroes-Whites Only" placard in the window.

"OK, read the article out loud." I toss her the paper. She clears her throat.

"On Saturday, two local women, in sympathy with the Birmingham Bus Boycott, joined a protest in Torrington organized by the local chapter of the National Association for the Advancement of

Colored People.

"Patience Hester and Bitsy Cross walked the picket line to voice their convictions. "We're protesting not just against this particular place, but against all such establishments who discriminate against Negroes," Mrs. Hester, wife of local veterinarian, Daniel Hester, declared. "We're demonstrating for freedom and justice for all. America should stand for something."

"Not exactly my words, but so far, so good," I comment and give Bitsy a smile as she reads on.

"While the passionate Mrs. Hester continued her oration, people passing hurled insults as well as eggs. Traffic was tied up. Men who needed a cup of coffee before work were blocked, and one woman who only wanted an ice cream cone for her crying four year old was unable to get inside."

"Wait! That's hog wash!" I push myself up on my elbows. "We didn't stop anyone from going into the place. What's with Blaze anyway? Is there much more?"

"You want me to summarize?"

"Yeah."

"Well, he goes on to say that compared to the Deep South, Negroes in northern West Virginia have it good. Here's the last paragraph. 'For many Americans the call for equality in places like Alabama, Mississippi and Georgia is long overdue. The Liberty Times supports the bus boycott in Montgomery. We acknowledge the legitimate concerns of civil rights activists there, but stirring up conflict in West Virginia, just before our local schools will be integrated in the fall, benefits no one and may cause harm. Citizens, no matter how well intentioned, need to raise the American flag, stand behind the values of our nation and leave protesting to the militants in the Deep South."

For a few minutes I'm speechless. "Like we aren't patriotic if we protest segregation? What horse shit!"

"You see why we didn't want you to read it? Take a few deep breaths. I'm going to get you some milk and cookies." While she's gone, I try a few breaths while I survey my surroundings. The framed photos and pictures on the walls are familiar, but I'm lying on a new green sofa and there's a new modern floor lamp and a new rug.

The Crosses are definitely moving up in the world, but they never brag about their good fortune. Bitsy and Lou are generous and give back to the community. Lou makes it a point to hire colored workers and veterans at the mill and they've almost adopted a Negro widow, with seven kids, who live on the other side of the tracks.

"Let's see what's on the tube," Bitsy says when she's back with the cookies. I lay back on my pillow when *Lucy* comes on. "It's a rerun," she tells me, pulling over a TV table. "But it's a good one. Let me fiddle with the knobs on the back. The antenna is a little out of whack."

Soon we are laughing as Lucy and Ethel steal a cement slab of John Wayne's footprints and the police are called in to investigate. At the end of the show in a commercial, a handsome physician in a white coat recommends Lucky Strike cigarettes.

"Thanks, Bitsy…for the cookies and calming

me down. I'm not ashamed we went to that demonstration and it doesn't make us anti-American."

"Well, unfortunately, a lot of people think like Billy Blaze. John Cameron Swayze on the news said many people equate the demonstrations in the South with a communist plot to cause division and destabilize our nation. Only twenty percent support Reverend King."

"Well that's hogwash! What's next on TV?" I ask, getting my emotions under control.

"This is cute," Bitsy says adjusting the volume. "It's the civil defense film they've been showing in schools. Did you know the kids now have bomb drills? When a siren goes off, they have to get under their desks and put their hands over their heads until the all-clear."

"Dum dum - Deedle dum dum - Dum dum - Deedle dum dum," goes a catchy little jingle as a cartoon turtle walks across the screen. Soon a monkey dangling a stick of dynamite on a string attacks him. The bomb goes off and destroys the monkey, but Bert is perfectly safe because he "ducked and covered".

The film then switches to a narrator who explains, with authority, what everyone must do when we see the flash of an atomic bomb. By ducking under something and covering our necks with clasped hands, we'll be saved from a nuclear attack by the Russians. The last scene of the cartoon returns to Bert the Turtle who asks what everybody should do in the event of an atomic blast and Bitsy and I yell together. "Duck and cover!"

"Do you buy it?" I ask when it's over.

"I guess it's good advice. Better than nothing, but I doubt it would actually save many lives. The latest nuclear bomb test in the Pacific was 500 times stronger than what the USA dropped on Nagasaki. If the Russians and the US start dropping those things on each other, we won't have much hope."

"I heard on the radio that the United Nations, Albert Einstein, and a bunch of scientists have called for the elimination of atomic weapons," I offer. "And Dan says Civil Defense just gives us something to do while we're waiting for the next world war."

"That's a pretty dismal outlook...Let's go outside. We can sit on the porch swing, but I don't want you to get overheated...Willie's surgery is tomorrow, by the way, the amputation."

"What? Why didn't you tell me? Oh, Bitsy, I'm so sorry."

"I didn't want to upset you, what with your concussion and all. It's OK. He says he's ready. We are all ready and resigned."

"I'm going to come!"

"You don't have to."

"The hell I don't!"

Gift

The scent of green growing things filled the air and bluebells bloomed along the road, as we left the VA Hospital six days later. Lou drove his new two-toned green Hudson like a hearse, while I sat at his side. Behind us, Will rested across the backseat with Bitsy cradling his head. His infected foot was no longer a problem. The foot was gone.

"How you doing, son?" Lou called out over the low sound of the sedan's purring motor.

"About half," Willie answered, still drowsy from the pain pills the nurse had given him. I was surprised to see the size of the bandage. His leg now stopped at his knee.

"Music ok?" Lou asked, reaching for the radio knob and fiddling with the dial until a catchy tune came on. I turned around to check on Willie, expecting him to be almost asleep, but his eyes were wide open, staring fiercely at his stump.

By late afternoon he was settled in bed in the new house in town and Daniel came to get me.

"How's he doing?" Dan asked first thing, when I got into the Olds.

"All right, I guess. He's pretty drugged up. Doesn't complain much. Bitsy's waiting on him hand and foot."

"Poor kid."

"Danny came by to see him. He brought Will a fifth of whiskey and the latest copy of *True Detective,* but we didn't talk."

"That's quite a present for a guy who just lost his foot. How's Danny look?"

"Fine, I guess...I didn't spend more than two minutes with him."

The next morning, after Dan left to attend the whelping of Mr. Pettigrew's award-winning sheep dog, I went out on the front porch, to smell the good air.   As I turned to go back inside, something caught my eye. Howard, the Blue Jay, was hopping around on the porch. "Jay. Jay. Jay," he called.

"Morning, Howard. How are you?"

He jumped up on an unfamiliar crudely made chest and looked at me. "Jay! Jay!" The chest was weathered and old with leather hinges, the kind a seafaring man like my father might have had.

"What's this?" I asked. Howard hopped toward me; then hopped back, so I leaned down and picked up the box, but before I opened it, I felt sure of what I'd find and I was right; another stack of journals written in familiar script! As happy as I was, I stared up and down the road with suspicion.

"Who's bringing these diaries and why?"   I asked my blue-feathered friend.

Of course he had no answer, so I carried the small chest inside and set it on the coffee table. There were dishes in the sink, eggs to wash and a garden to weed, but I took the first diary out of the box, looked at the date and read for the rest of the day.

Hintonville, Virginia,
October 14, 1859

It was early in the morning on October 14, 1859 that I ran away. The date is forever burned into my mind. Father had gone to a neighboring plantation to gamble with friends, so after Mother cut my hair and dressed me as a boy, I mounted the horse Jammy had chosen and rode away. As I traveled North, the sun rose golden over the Allegheny Mountains and the turnpike became busy with carts and carriages heading to the market in Harrisonburg.

In less than a week, I thought to myself, I'd be in Pennsylvania and be free. Jammy had told me there was a black man in Philadelphia, named Robert Stills, who helped runaways. He was part of what was called the Underground Railroad, a chain of safe houses that led all the way to Canada. "Just ask every African you see in the city," he advised. "Someone will know him. He's famous."

Around noon, I ran into my first slave patrollers. Two men, dressed in black with silver badges, hailed me by holding up their shotguns as a signal to stop and my heart pounded so hard I was sure they could hear it. "Be calm. Be confident," I said to myself.

"Going on a long trip?" the shorter of the two greeted me, a broad faced man with two missing teeth.

"Just a few days, good Sir. I'm on my way to Philadelphia to school. Came home for my horse.

You men out looking for runaways?"

The second patroller handed me a printed advertisement. "You read?" he asked. "Oh, I guess you would since you're going to school. Planter's son?"

"Yes, the Blackwell's from Arbor Hill" I lied.

I looked at the ad and read it out loud. There was a woodcut image of a slave running across a field at the top.

REWARD. $50 FOR RETURN of NEGROE SLAVE ANDY, about 25 years of age, mulatto: a stout fellow, about 6 feet high. Has a film over one eye and whip marks on his back. Ran away October 1, carrying with him the master's blue jacket, an old gray duffel and a kitchen knife. May be dangerous. Speaks both English and French. Whoever captures and conveys to me the above slave, shall have a reward of 50 dollars.
Samuel Mayle, Staunton, Virginia

"No, I can't say that I've seen him. Saw twenty field slaves back a few miles, harvesting wheat, but there was an overseer with them. Good luck," I said. "If I catch sight of him, I'll report to the nearest patrollers." I straightened myself in my saddle, ready to ride.

"Thanks and safe travels!" the fellow with the missing teeth said and we both tipped our hats.

My original goal was to get past Harrisonburg. The next day, I might make it to the bridge over the

Potomac at Harper's Ferry. Then in two more days I'd be in Philadelphia and free. Well, almost free, as free as I could be in the United States, now that the slave catchers could come into the North and make a citizen's arrest.

I camped that night in a piney woods a few yards off a side road, had a cold supper and wrapped myself in a blanket, but despite exhaustion I couldn't relax. Leaves rustled above me, crickets chirped a slow song and an owl called in the distance. I'd never slept outside before and as I watched the half-moon cross the star filled sky, I shifted between fear and joy; one moment worrying about snakes, bears, or slave catchers and the next aware of my body resting lightly on the earth, a part of everything that lived.

Finally, I fell over the edge of sleep and when I woke clouds had come in and covered the moon. There was rustling in the bushes and I froze; someone was moving along the edge of the road. I heard short hard breaths as if the man had been running and I remembered the advertisement for the escaped slave with one cloudy eye, a dangerous fellow, perhaps, but a runaway like me. "Keep going, Andy," I whispered. "Godspeed."

Middletown, Virginia,
October 15, 1859

All the next day I moved north. Patrollers seemed to be at every major crossroad, but I greeted them with a smile and they let me go. Because I looked like a white boy, not one asked for identification.

By late afternoon my legs and derriere were so sore, I could go no further, so I followed the signs to the Wayside Inn, a long two-story brick building with white trim and black shutters. A barn in the back had a sign that said Stable and an empty stagecoach waited out front.

When I boldly went in, I saw a wide fireplace with a friendly blaze, a polished pine floor, multiple wooden tables and a long bar in the corner. A plaque over the bar said, Established 1797. The place was near empty, but two men with badges sat eating their evening meal. I nodded politely at the innkeeper who walked out of a back room, wiping his hands on a white apron. "Greetings stranger," he said with a smile.

"How much does it cost for a bed and a one horse stall?" I asked, lowering my voice to sound like a young man.

"Room for one night is a dollar, but there'd be another fifty cents for your horse. We include hay for the animal and an evening meal for you. Liquor and breakfast are extra. If you want to share a room with another traveler, I can bring down the price."

"No that's fine. And I'll be leaving early in the morning. Can you tell me where to find the road to Harper's Ferry?"

"Oh, you missed that turn, Son," said one of the patrollers across the room, a bearded man with a bulbous red nose.

"It was ten miles back. The sign at the intersection only says Charles Town, but that's also the road to Harper's Ferry."

I must have looked discouraged, because he added, "Don't worry, it will only add a few hours to your trip. Where you headed?"

"Philadelphia...for school."

I handed the innkeeper the coins. "Can I have supper in my room? And should I bed my own horse or do you have a stable hand?"

"We'll take care of it." He handed me a key. "Do you have luggage? I can bring it up."

"Just my saddle bags. I'll get them." I started for the door, but the patrollers called me back.

"Hey, Sonny!" Big Nose called. "What's your name?"

"Blackwell," I answered, using the name Mother and I had chosen. "Patrick Blackwell."

"Well Patrick, you look like a sharp young fellow; can I ask you to look at these posters?" He invited me to sit. "This will only take a minute." Then he pushed a couple of escaped slave posters across the table. "See anyone in your travels that could be these darkies?"

The first flyer I'd seen before. It was for Andy, the runaway that spoke several languages and had one cloudy eye. The second was new and it took my breath away.

REWARD $200 for return of light skinned slave, a fourteen-year-old wench called Grace who escaped from my place just two days ago. Believed to be heading north riding a brown Morgan with a golden mane and tail. Slave is a skilled midwife and can and write. **Reward, also, for the horse, $100.** **Contact Dr. Richard Coffman, Hintonville, VA**

This was a low point for me... I'm sure you will understand. Though I'd been on guard before, fearing I'd be recognized and returned to Dr. Coffman, I believed I could get to Upper Darby and safety before he had time to advertise my escape. I was wrong.

"Sounds like someone really wants that girl back," I said. "If see her, I'll report her to a Marshal or maybe I'll capture her myself! That's a pretty reward," I laughed. The patrollers laughed too.

Once in my room on the second floor of the handsome establishment, I fell back on the bed. I'd disguised myself as a boy, but I'd never thought of disguising my horse. It was the golden mane and tail that distinguished him.

A knock on the door brought me out of my reverie. "Mr. Blackwell? Your supper, sir." I unlocked the door and nodded to a small round kitchen girl who carried my evening meal on a tray.

"Thank you," I said and held out a penny. She smiled and put the coin in her apron pocket. "Thank, you Master. Thank you."

It was a strange world, I thought. Two days ago, I lived as Gracie Potts, pampered daughter of a white physician and planter, but in reality his property, a non-person he could whip or sell or breed whenever he felt like it. Now people called me Young Sir and Master.

Middletown, Virginia
October 16, 1859

In the morning, I took a quick cold sponge bath, and was out of the inn before anyone was up. The groom had my horse ready. "He's been fed and watered, Sir," he told me. "I kept him in the back stall by himself as you requested. Do you have a long ride today?"

"Yes, I'm headed to Harper's Ferry." Just then another man came into the stable and I took that opportunity to lead Louis outside and around the corner, where I could stand on a stump and mount without difficulty.

For two hours, I rode south again, reversing my course, finally spotting the sign for Charles Town. Occasionally, I'd pass farmers in carts, but most people were still at breakfast. At one point I hailed an old man on a donkey.

"Mister," I called out. "Can you tell me if I'm headed toward Harper's Ferry?"

"Oh no, young man! You better stay away from there," he alerted me. "The U.S. armory was attacked last night by a hundred anti-slavery men. John Brown's Raiders they call themselves. The mayor has already been killed and Robert E. Lee and the Calvary are on their way. Thousands of slaves have already escaped and attacked their masters." he exclaimed.

"But if I did want to go there, am I on the right road?"

"Yes, but don't go! It's too dangerous. You might get killed." I nodded and thanked the old

gentleman, but stubbornly continued on towards Harper's Ferry, where I'd find the bridge over the Potomac and freedom.

If I heard gunshot, I decided, I would turn back at once. I didn't have to wait long.

The sun was half way to its zenith when white men in civilian clothes came riding hard, rifles and shotguns slung across their saddles. In the far distance, there was shooting. This is it, I thought. This must be the insurrection I was told about.

To avoid whatever was taking place in Harper's Ferry, I took a side road going west across a narrow valley with the intention of somehow turning north again and getting away from the trouble, but then another group of armed men came riding. One pulled his lathered horse up to me. "It's the black demons!" he yelled, breathing hard. "There are hundreds of them with guns, an uprising! Every white man is needed," Then he rode off. Apparently, every white boy was needed too, even a youth, like me, with no gun.

I could still hear the shots in the distance, sometimes in the direction of Harper's Ferry, sometimes nearer at hand. Ascending the hills on the far side of the valley, I took to a laurel thicket, hobbled my horse and lay down in the grass.

It started to drizzle and I rolled up in my blanket, wondering how the fight was going at the armory. I knew whose side I was on and in my heart I cheered the brave Africans.

20

Stars and Stripes Forever

Daniel and I drove into town for the Fourth of July parade just after lunch. The festivities were scheduled for three, but we left early, hoping for a good place on the courthouse steps.

"Nice dress," Daniel comments as we push through the crowd. I'm wearing a little number I got on sale from the Montgomery Ward catalog, blue with white stripes and my hair is tied back with a red ribbon. Dan looks rather dashing himself in a green polo shirt with a white stripe around the collar and gray slacks.

"Want a soda?" He points to the red metal cooler with the now famous Cola symbol on the side in front of Bittman's Grocery. Still five cents a bottle, I think, the same as during the Great Depression.

"Sure. Remember when just getting a coke was a big treat," I muse.

"And maybe all the sweeter for it," he answers.

While Dan goes over to buy us two bottles, I gaze along Main, noting the signs of post-war prosperity everywhere. Little girls in their swirly skirts, boys with no patches in their overalls, mothers in high heels, fathers leaning against shiny new cars. Though some coalmines are closing since the end of the war, you can't tell it yet.

Far down the street and around the corner we hear the rat-a-tat-tat of a drum and the crowd stirs. The American Legion color guard comes first, with two white men and two black men carrying the American Flag and rifles. The Liberty High School Band follows, playing the Stars and Stripes Forever.

Next come the band from Oneida High School, complete with four majorettes in short shirts and white boots and finally, my favorite, the snappy All Negro Drum Corp from Fredrick Douglas High in Delmont.

All the bands have new uniforms, a sign of the earlier booming times, but the Fredrick Douglas kids don't wear gold epaulets and tall hats. They're dressed in green military broadcloth with high utilitarian black boots, like men in the army. It's their drums and precision marching that set them apart and I can't help but cheer.

Trailing a good way behind them all are the World War 1 and World War 2 Veterans, walking slowly, twenty in all, but there's only one from the Korean War, Willie, sitting tall in his army uniform, pushed in a wheelchair by his father, Lou, who is dressed in his Spanish Civil War outfit. Will's stump is covered by his pant leg and pinned at the knee. I know there must be other soldiers from the Korean War in town today, but only Willie marches with pride.

Everyone stands as the veterans move past and I get tears in my eyes and swipe them away. The tears are not just for Willie; they are for all brave men and women who've fought for their county and for men like my husband Dan, pacifists, who went to jail or served their nation in other ways, because of their beliefs.   Though I think of myself as a citizen of the world, there's something about simple patriotism that moves me. I inevitably get a lump in my throat and I don't even know why.

Next, there are dozens of kids riding bikes, decorated in red white and blue and finally the floats. I'm surprised to see the new hospital has one, yellow and black, the civil defense colors, with Bert the Turtle sitting in a bomb shelter waving and throwing candy.

Bert has lived 1000 years, it says on the back of the big truck. Because he knew how to "duck and cover." How about you?

We are living in peacetime, but even on this summer day *The Cold War* is a dark cloud rolling toward us.

"Here they come!" my husband breaks out in a smile. It's Dan's favorite part. Mares and stallions, ponies and even burros, prance along Main Street, their coats gleaming, hooves washed; ribbons braided through their tails.

"See that pinto," he directs my attention to a beautiful white and brown horse. "See how she limps a little. She tore her back left leg on barbed wire fence last year, a hell of a repair. It took two hours and I had to use chloroform… Did I tell you there's been a horse thief in the area?"

"That sounds like something in a John Wayne

western."

"No, it's true. We need to start locking our barn at night."

Across the street, I catch sight of Sheriff Aran Bishop and his brother, Earl, along with Aran's wife, Cora, and they've noticed us too. "Honey..."

"The Bishop brothers" Dan mutters, as he grabs my hand. "Let's go."

It's not that Dan's afraid of the Bishops; he just doesn't want to get in another fight. If someone hits him, he will hit back. I asked him about it, since he's a pacifist, but he says defending yourself or your family from a bully isn't the same as killing a stranger in organized warfare.

"It was great you and Willie marched in the parade," I told Lou, later in the evening, as we stood on the stone bridge over the Hope waiting for the fireworks to begin. "I was so proud."

"Thanks. It was good for him, I think. None of the other boys who fought in Korea were around today. It wasn't a popular war." Boom!

"They're starting!" Bitsy squeezed my arm. The sound came from the fair grounds. Boom, again, then a white trail of light shot into the sky, Boom, Boom, BOOM.

Three more rockets flared and the colors were reflected in the Hope River down below us. "Ohhhh, say can you see by the dawn's early light – what so proudly we hail ...." Lou began in a loud baritone and Dan joined him. "And the rockets red glare, the bombs bursting in air – gave proof to the night – that our flag was still there..."

West of Middletown, Virginia
October 1859, unsure of the date

All night it rained and then the sleet came and I grew cold. I was camped a few hundred yards off a side road, but it was too wet and dangerous to build a fire. I felt bad for my horse. At least I had a blanket. Louis had nothing, no stable, no barn.

Louis, I thought. That's a dull name. I tried to think of something courageous and brave. How about Noble?

"Would you like to be called Noble?" I asked him. The horse nodded his head.

As I lay, on the ground shivering and listening to the intermittent gunfire and the sound of riders speeding toward battle, I reviewed my assets. I still had some coins. I had a good steed, but food was running low. Perhaps if I went to a farmer I might find an abolitionist who could point me to the Underground Railroad; then again, perhaps not.

I knew one thing, I must continue north to get to Pennsylvania and to do that I had to follow the North Star, a bright orb just past the big dipper. Ever since I'd found out I was chattel, I'd been watching that star, but how could I see it when the sky was overcast, like tonight. I couldn't just wait for the clouds to part. There was one other possibility... Jammy once told me that moss grows on the north side of trees.

By the next morning the sky had cleared and the sporadic gunshots had stopped, so I started out again, always watching for the moss on the side of the trees. The thick brush on the slope thinned as I made it to the ridgeline and there I found a rough trail running in the right direction. "Thank you!" I said to no one, but I felt that God heard me. For hours I traveled the ridge, passing mountain views of such beauty I would stop in my tracks and say "Oh!" out loud.

Toward evening, I discovered a small overhang under a slab of sandstone, not much bigger than a funeral casket, but it would make a nice shelter. That night I ate the rest of my bread and cheese and slept like a dead man, then just before dawn I heard voices.

"Look, a horse!" I heard a low whisper.

"He's hobbled and tied," said another man. They sounded like Yankees.

"Stay down!"

I peeked out of my den and saw four bearded white men and a fifth, light brown, all carrying multiple pistols and guns. They were wild and fierce looking and I feared for my life.

"Do you think it's someone looking for us?"

"Nah, more likely a hired patroller on some poor slave's trail."

"Should we take the horse? If he's a slave catcher he deserves to be robbed," said the brown man.

"Don't be reckless, Josiah. If the slave catcher reports the stolen horse, the law may put two and two together and move the search for us in this direction. We don't need that."

The men stood twenty feet from my hideout

arguing in low voices.

Finally, someone made the decision. "We'll untie the stallion and just let him go. That way, if the rider's a bounty hunter, it will at least slow him down...."

By that time, I'd about had it! I popped out of my hole and said in the manliest voice I could muster, "Excuse me, gentlemen! The horse you're discussing is mine and I'd appreciate it if you left it alone."

"Holy bejeezus! You scared us lad. What's a boy like you doing up on this ridge?" asked the fellow who seemed like the leader. The five dirty and tired looking chaps found rocks or fallen logs to sit on and waited for my answer.

"Are you Yankees?" I asked.

"You reckoned that by our accent. And you're from the south." This was the leader again.

"A planter's son, I betcha. Probably a slave owner." accused the African.

This offended me. "I don't own slaves. I am a slave, an escaped slave. I've been on the run for three days." That shut them up. Who would lie about that?

Finally, the leader spoke again, "Well what in Sam Hill are you doing up here?" He had sandy hair, a sandy brown beard and piercing blue eyes.

"I was on the road, disguised as a white boy, trying to get to Philadelphia, when I heard the gunshots and was told about the insurrection at Harper's Ferry. Fearing I'd get involved or caught, I turned west to stay out of trouble. Now I'm trying to head north again by the stars and the

moss on the trees. Do you know how to get to Pennsylvania? You aren't going to turn me in for the reward are you?"

"How much would we get?" one man asked.

"I can read, write and do sums. I also know some of the healing arts because my owner who was a physician taught me. He's offering $200."

"There's a reward on our heads too."

"How much would someone get if he turned you in?" I asked with a straight face, though I was also joking.

"Ten thousand a piece," said the short balding fellow, laughing at the joke. "Twenty thousand for Owen, because he's John Brown's son."

My mouth dropped open "Were you men part of the raid on Harpers Ferry?"

"Well, you told us your secret. I guess we can tell you ours," said Owen. "We're the last of Brown's Raiders; none of us was actually in the fight. We were ordered to stay back, as a rear guard, to protect the weapons we'd purchased with abolitionist funds. Our leader, General John Brown, my father, believed that after capturing the armory, slaves would rise up and carry out a rebellion across the entire South..."

"But something went wrong," the balding man added, "Someone ratted us out. All we know was that most of the raiding party, 17 whites and 5 free blacks, were killed or captured. We're all that's left."

"I'm going to make a fire," said the balding man.

"Do you think that's very wise, Cook?" Owen

Brown asked.

"I'll build it behind this big boulder...Do you have any food, Sonny?" the man asked.

I shook my head no. "I ate the last of my bread and cheese yesterday."

"We can share," said Owen and he pulled two hens out of a sack. "We lifted these out of a farmer's chicken coop last night. Had a heck of a time catching them, but we've been starved."

The men pulled the bird's feathers and roasted them on sticks and the meat tasted as good as anything Thelma cooked at home in the kitchen.

As we ate, I told the raiders I'd been traveling by day and sleeping at night, but they informed me I had it all wrong. Escaped slaves, they said, slept in the day and moved north after dark. "You can come along with us, if you get rid of the horse," Owen said. Here, I twisted my mouth, looked over at Noble and remembered there was a reward on his head too.

"The horse is a liability," Cook agreed. "A man can slip into the bushes and lie on his stomach if he hears or sees trouble, but how can you hide a horse? Also a handsome animal like that will draw people's attention."

I shared the story I'd concocted; how I was on my way to Philadelphia to attend school, but got lost cutting through the wilderness. "Does that sound believable?"

The fellows all shrugged. "Maybe you should just be bold and get back on the turnpike. What's your name son?"

"Patrick Blackwell. You can call me Pat."

"Well, Pat, I hope that's an alias," Owen said. "If it's not, you better come up with one fast. For today, you can lay low with us, but tonight you'll have to make a decision.

"It's dangerous for you either way. Get rid of the horse and travel with a band of men wanted for treason or keep the horse and risk getting captured by slave catchers. Think on it son; the advantage is, we have weapons and can use them to protect you."

As the daylight lifted, the men put out the fire, wrapped up in blankets and prepared to sleep.

"I've rested all night," I told Owen Brown. "I can stand watch."

"Thanks," he said and dropped into a deep slumber, but the black man called Josiah sat up with me.

"Are you a fugitive slave too?" I asked, feeling we must have that in common.

"No, I was born free in Pennsylvania. I've also lived in Ohio and lately in Canada. I'm on my way back to Canada, now. If you ditch the horse and come with me, I'll take you home to The Elgin-Buxton Settlement, a community of refugee slaves and free black families in Ontario."

"I only want to get to Pennsylvania. Canada is too cold and too far away."

"You're right. It's almost four hundred miles, but if you manage to get there, you are <u>truly free</u>. You won't have to hide your identity or look over your shoulder ever again." That was the end of our conversation. He wrapped up in his quilt, pulled it over his eyes and went to sleep with a grunt.

All day, I kept watch. Once I heard hounds baying in the valley and I worried that slave catchers with dogs were closing in, but they faded away. The sun crossed the sky and as it began to sink behind the distant mountains, one by one, the men rose, stretched, and went into the woods to relieve themselves. I'd already done that an hour earlier, because I couldn't afford for them to see me squatting behind a tree like a girl.

"Let's skip building a fire and find the trail down before it gets all the way dark. Maybe we can steal some more chickens," said Cook.

I rolled up my blanket, saddled my horse and stood waiting.

"That's a big horse for you," Owen Brown commented. "Did you steal him from your master."

"Yes. He's a beauty isn't he? That's why I can't give him up. I think I'll be bold and get back on the road again. Probably the runaway slave ads haven't gotten this far."

"Suit yourself," said Owen. "We're heading cross-country to Chambersburg where Cook's wife is staying, then up to Ohio and finally Canada. If you don't want to come with us, remember the slave catchers are everywhere."

We took a trail down that was so steep the men had to lean on their guns for support. Then, Owen made me a crude drawing showing the turnpike and marked where the tollbooths were.

"You have some money?" he asked, getting out a small leather pouch that jiggled with gold.

"I have enough. If I'm captured I'll never tell that we met."

"Good luck," they all said and then, in a neat line, they began to jog North through the woods and I was alone again.

21

July 1956

Loss of Innocence

It hurts when you give birth. It hurts even more when you're a mother of a child who's in pain.

Today, Mira called me crying and told me she broke up with her boyfriend. I wanted to rescue her. If she was little and hanging from a limb in a tree, I could gather her into my arms, but that wasn't possible. "Do you want to talk about it? I can drive into Delmont and we could have lunch."

"No, I'm a mess and I can't talk if there are strangers around. Let's go to White Rock State Park where there's only a few people and we can sit in the picnic area and enjoy the view."

"I'll pick you up at noon with a lunch basket."

Two hours later, we find a table below the wooden pavilion, looking over the mist and the mountains rolling on, ridge after ridge like waves of stone. This is the sort of view Grace faced time after time, as she crossed the Allegheny Mountains, only she'd have no idea where the mountains would end. I spread a red-checkered tablecloth over the rough wood and take out my sandwiches, wrapped in waxed paper.

"So…" I say when we both get settled on the same side of the bench so we can see the view. "So, what happened?"

"Oh, Mama. I'm so mad! Mad at myself mostly. I thought I loved Ronnie, but he's such an ass. I'd heard him say negative things about colored people before, but I thought he was joking."

"Like what?"

"You know. He'd call someone a Jungle Bunny, or a Coon, or a Burrhead."

"Burrhead?"

"*You know*, because of the hair." I shake my head in disgust.

"I feel so stupid, Mom. How could I not see it? I guess I was just so flattered that he wanted me. He's so handsome and likeable. He played football and basketball in high school and is kind of a big shot in Delmont "

"So what happened?"

"Last night, his family had a get-together with their relations from Beckley and Ronnie wanted me to come. I'd met his Mom and Dad before, but not the rest of the clan. Everyone was watching TV after dinner, and the news came on about the Bus Boycott in Birmingham. All of a sudden they all started yelling and screaming at the protestors.

"I wanted to say something, but I swear, Mom, their faces were red and the veins in their necks were bulging. I'd never seen such hatred and

Ronnie was yelling insults along with the rest of them. If I'd had a car, I would have left right then." She wipes a tear with the back of her hand.

"I felt terrible… angry at all of them, but sick about myself too. I didn't speak out, didn't say one thing! Just sat there with my hands in my lap like a good girl. I'm sure they assumed I agreed with them.

"Later in the car, on the way home, I tried to tell Ronnie how I felt, but he defended his family. 'America is a white country,' he said. 'Made by white men *for* white men. What are you, one of those Coon lovers?'

"After that I shut up and just looked out the window at the lights in the houses. When we got to my apartment, he wanted to come in, but I said no. He tried to kiss me and I slapped him. Then he slapped me back."

"Oh, honey!"

"I know, Mom. He's a weasel."

"Worse…a skunk!"

Here she began to cry for real and I knew it wasn't just the slap in the face or the harsh words that hurt. She was crying for her lost innocence. She had trusted a thug with her body and soul. That innocence could never come back to her. She'd misjudged her lover, mistook his animal appeal for good character.

As we sat together on the bench, I held Mira against me as if she were ten and I thought of Mrs. Coffman rocking her daughter the day Gracie discovered she was a slave. Below us, the beautiful Hope River snaked through the valley, jagged rocks just under the surface.

Cumberland Mountains, Maryland
Sometime in October, 1859

The night I left Brown's Raiders I slept near a brook that sang over the pebbles and stones. In the clear mountain air, the stars dazzled me. There were more than I could ever imagine. The big dipper stood amongst them and the North Star beckoned.

"Follow the drinking gourd," I sang the song Thelma used to sing in kitchen. "Follow the drinking gourd. For the old man is awaiting, for to carry you to freedom – if you follow the drinking gourd." A few years ago, I thought the 'old man' was God and that freedom for the slaves would only come in heaven. Now looking up at the sky, I knew the song meant freedom in this life and by Owen Brown's estimation I was less than fifty miles from Pennsylvania.

In the morning, I stopped to drink at the stream. Kneeling down, when I saw my reflection, it was my hair that alarmed me. I was losing my disguise as a young white boy. A week or so ago, Mother had cut it close and applied some pomade, but now it stood out from my head, wild and nappy, a dark halo and it's texture revealed my true African heritage.

I was proud of that hair and in a strange way, proud to be a slave because it meant I wasn't a slaveholder... Still, as I looked at myself, I realized I must always keep my hat on when around white people and never tip my hat in greeting as most men did. Since, I'd had enough sleep, I decided to first seek food.

For an hour or two, Noble and I wandered in and out of the trees, trying to get out of the forest and back on cleared land where I might find a farmer's garden to raid. Finally, the trees began to space out and I came to a narrow cultivated field. I tied my horse and crept forward.

In the distance, smoke rose from a log cabin and outside there were people cutting wood, two men and a boy. As I walked closer leading Noble, I saw that the individuals were of dark complexion and I almost shouted for joy. "Hello!" I called as I approached. The two men stopped what they were doing and the little boy hid behind them.

"Howdy, Young Master," the older of the two greeted me. "What can we do for you? Are you lost?"

"Yes, a little. I wandered off the turnpike yesterday to get my horse a drink of water and ..." Here I stopped and bit my lower lip to hold in a sob. The friendly older man reminded me of Jammy, same way of talking, same dark brown color, same graying hair.

Apparently he realized I was suffering and also half starved and he stopped his questions. "We're just poor Negroes, young Master, but if you'd do us the honor, we could share our noon meal." I nodded yes, still unable to speak. They called me "Master" as if I was a plantation owner's son.

"Molly!" the older man called to a woman in the cabin, "Set another place at the table."

"How about we picket your horse in the field, yonder, where he can graze?" suggested the younger fellow who had a scar on his cheek from branding.

"My name's Irvin Johnson," he said as he helped me take off the saddle and saddlebags. "That is my pa, Thomas Johnson and Molly, inside, is my wife. The little boy is my son, Junior." When we were finished, he led me into their home, and without thinking, I took off my hat.

"Ma!" the little boy exclaimed. "That white man has hair like us!"

"Also he's no man," Molly said and everyone stared. (Peculiar, that it was a woman who first realized my true gender.)

"Can I sit down?" I asked. "I'll tell you my story...I'm going by the name of Patrick Blackwell, but my real name is Grace..."

Molly untied her apron. "Let's eat first." And so we did; cornbread and brown beans with ham and fresh apple pie. The cook kept filling my plate. "When did you eat last, honey?" she asked

I took a deep breath and pushed my chair back. "Two days ago."

Later, we sat on the porch in the cool autumn sunshine and I admitted I was a runaway slave. I shared that I'd been raised as a white child and only found out three years ago that I was listed in my adopted father's ledger as chattel.

I didn't go into how I feared my father might rape me, had in fact raped me by proxy when he made me watch the young Negro man copulate with

Lottie in the slave yard. I didn't mention the huge price on my head. I didn't tell about meeting Brown's Raiders.

They told me their story too.

"Pa is free," said Irvin. "The rest of us are listed in the census, like you, as his chattel."

"I don't understand. How could a black man own another black person?"

"Let me explain," the father spoke as he lighted his pipe. It was a nice cherry wood pipe. Nicer than Dr. Coffman's and the tobacco smelled sweet.

"Fifty years ago I was born a slave on a plantation near Hamilton, Virginia. I married one of the other slaves, Lydia, who was a seamstress. We had two children who died as babies; a sad time for us. When I was twenty I trained as a carpenter and was then hired out to a shop in Leesburg.

"Lydia was rented out too. We took our wages to the master at the end of each week and he gave us one quarter of whatever we had earned, a generous arrangement. Some slaves don't get any of their pay. Eventually, I became a furniture maker and the wages were even better.

I saved every penny and after four years, I purchased myself. Then I could save every dollar and buy my wife, but before she was freed, Lydia had another baby." He indicates his son Irvin with a smile. "This one made it, but since he was born a slave, it took me another twenty years to buy him and his woman, Molly. Now we all work together in the furniture business and farm these twenty acres.

"My beloved wife, Lydia, God rest her soul, passed just last year, but she didn't suffer. She was

working in the workshop and just fell down and breathed her last breath. Her heart attacked her, I think."

"So why are Thomas, Molly and Junior still listed as slaves? Can't you emancipate them?" I asked.

"I've tried. Years ago, I even went to a solicitor, but he said there's no way you can just sign a paper and make someone free. Each manumission has to be approved by the Virginia State Legislature."

"An act of Congress?"

"Yes. Ever since Nat Turner's rebellion in '31, when the armed runaway bondsmen killed some sixty slave-owners, the whites are afraid of us. They don't want more free blacks roaming around, setting an example. That's why we migrated to these Maryland Mountains."

"I heard about Nat Turner, but that was a long time ago."

"Well, did you hear about Brown's Raiders at Harper's Ferry?" asked Irvin. "Five hundred blacks and abolitionists attacked the Federal armory and stole all the guns. I wish I could have been there."

"You should be glad you weren't! Half of them were killed." Molly grumbled. (The family was quite misinformed, but I didn't correct them.)

"So where are you trying to get to?" Irvin wanted to know.

"I want to get across the state line into Pennsylvania then back East to Upper Darby, near Philadelphia, where I have contacts and can stay."

"I'd keep going north to Canada if I were on the

run," advised Thomas. "It's hotter than a skillet full of bacon around Philadelphia. The more slaves run to the city, the more slave catchers wait on every corner."

"I don't know anyone in Canada. Besides, I've heard it's so cold."

"Slavery has been illegal in Canada and England since the early 1800s," Thomas continued. "You'd be safe there, but suit yourself...we can at least help you get a little closer."

"Tomorrow, we have to deliver a wooden wedding chest to a farmer in Bellegrove, just west of here," Irvin added. "And we know a free black man in Cumberland, Maryland who can direct you to the Underground Railroad."

"We could take her in the chest...but what about your magnificent horse?" Thomas wondered. "With the golden mane and tail, he stands out like a sore thumb. Are there reward posters out on you yet? Do they mention your horse?"

Told them how I saw the poster about me. "The slave catchers don't know I'm traveling as a boy, but the ad described my horse in detail, including the golden tail and mane."

"I can fix that," offered Molly. "Ever heard of stove black?"

"It's what our maid, Belle, always used to make the fireplace grates look so pretty."

"Well, I can make his mane and tail black. I'll do the job today, you can sleep here for the night and we'll take you as far as Bellegrove tomorrow."

"Will we travel by daylight?" I wondered.

"Sure, but don't worry," says Junior. "Ma

always brings the toll-keepers a pie."

As the day went on, the kind family devoted all there efforts to furthering my escape. Molly went to work on Noble, staining his tail and mane with stove black and he began to look like a regular horse.

"Will the color last through a rainstorm or if we have to cross a creek?" I asked.

"I think so. I have a terrible time getting it off of my hands."

Then the men took me into their workshop in the back of the barn. The wedding chest they needed to deliver was made of polished maple with hearts carved on top and in the center a bouquet of flowers with the new couple's initials beside it.

"It's beautiful!"

"Let's see if you'll fit," Irvin said as he opened the lid.

"How long will I have to be in here?" I asked doubtfully.

"Should be only a few hours. Mr. William's farm is right off the turnpike, but he owns a few slaves and wouldn't be sympathetic, so we'll pull off the road and let you out before we get to his house." He helped me into the five-foot long box and put down the lid. I couldn't lay flat, but if I pulled up my knees it was all right.

"It's awful dark in here. Do you think there's enough air?" I yelled.

"You could stay there all night. Air can leak in around the hinges...What do you think?"

"I can do it," I responded as I popped out.

I had another good meal with the Johnsons that evening and afterward the wife got out her fiddle and played for us. If they'd lived in Pennsylvania, I would have stayed there forever and perhaps offered to be their apprentice and learn the furniture trade. Irvin and Junior watered my horse and brought him into the barn with their livestock. Molly made me a pallet in front of the fire. She even washed my filthy boy's clothes and cut my hair again, while I sat around in one of her dresses.

Before bed, Thomas gave me a piece of paper with a man's name on it. "This free black man is a farrier and metal smith," he said. "Tell him we sent you. If anyone is around make an excuse. Say your horse needs new shoes."

The next day, around noon, I was released from the wedding chest near a stream, just off the turnpike and I said a sad goodbye to my new friends. Mounting Noble, I continued west on the turnpike. Once two fellows, with weapons over their shoulders, passed me riding fast; "patrollers," I thought, but no one stopped me.

On the outskirts of Cumberland, I followed a cart loaded with pumpkins into a bustling market square. **Cumberland, Gateway to the West**, *a sign proclaimed. Here, I hailed a boy carrying lumber.*

"Young man, do you know the city?" I asked.

"Pretty well. I've lived here all my life."

"Can you tell me where I can find a reputable inn? Something clean, but not too expensive?"

"The Hotel Potomac would be what you're wanting. It's near the railway platform, but stay away from Shantytown." He nodded to a row of shacks, saloons, and pool halls along a canal that was under construction.

"There are runaway slaves and murderers hiding-out there. Locals never go into Shantytown, unless they're looking to hire a whore. Even the constable avoids it. Too dangerous."

I gave the boy a penny for his help and he hurried off. The sun was sinking and dark would come soon.

22

Cumberland, Maryland
November 1, 1859

In Cumberland, Maryland, I looked for the inn that the boy had recommended. "**Potomac Hotel**" a sign in black and gold letters proclaimed and as I went in, I saw the two men who'd rushed by me on the turnpike

"Well, I guess we have no choice, if we want to catch him we'll have to go into Shantytown," the older of the two growled.

"There will be trouble," the other one said as they left the hotel, mounted their horses, and galloped away.

A balding man inside the lobby, wearing a black vest and green string bow tie, greeted me from behind an oak counter. "Hello, young man. Do you need a room?"

"How much do they cost?"

"Dollar-fifty a night, one meal included."

"Do you have a stable?"

"Sorry, we don't, but there's one just a block away down Center Street. That would be another fifty cents. "Blacksmith Shop" it says on the front. You can't miss it. The barn is in back and though the shop is closed by now, there's a stable boy there all night." Exhausted, I paid for the room and while the host was registering me, I glanced at the date. November 1, my birthday. I was fifteen.

After I let the manager carry my saddlebags and bedroll upstairs, I followed his directions to a tall white wooden building with red painted lettering on the front that said "Blacksmith." At the door to the stable, I consulted the note and map that Thomas had given me. This was a bit of good fortune. The blacksmith was the man the Johnson's had recommended.

"What time does do you open tomorrow?" I asked the stable boy after I paid. "I need the farrier to look at my horse's shoes."

"About seven. He lives near the Narrows and has his own stock to tend first."

Cumberland, Maryland
November 2, 1859

In the morning, I awoke much refreshed, and, taking my luggage, went directly to the stable to check on Noble. Outside the blacksmith's shop, three men were already waiting, two whites with horses and a light skinned brown fellow with a broken wagon wheel. It made me anxious, but I was going to have to wait.

Soon the blacksmith arrived and opened the double door to his building. He was younger than I expected, late twenties if I had to guess, tall and muscular, with a big jaw and dark skin, but it was his eyes that I noted, lively and quick, an intelligent man.

Wearing blue overalls like a farmer and a clean gray shirt with the sleeves rolled up, the man looked us over; he didn't apologize for being late, but laughed. "Looks like a busy day," he said. "All right, who's first and what do you need?"

One of the white men stepped forward and started a story about his lame horse, but the blacksmith raised his hand and turned to the Negro. "What about you Ned, need the spoke in that wagon wheel fixed? Won't take a minute."

He stepped back inside, looked around for a tool, and pounded the metal. The white man, expecting he'd be first, looked at me, assuming I was of his race, and cursed under his breath, "God damn it! The black man always favors the Africans. Ain't fair!"

I nodded as if I agreed, but didn't say anything.

One by one, the farrier took his customers into the dim structure and worked his magic. Some of the horses objected to their legs and feet being examined, but the blacksmith always calmed them. Finally my turn came and I swallowed hard.

"Son!" he called and I entered the big open workshop. Two windows let in the light and there were tools everywhere, hanging on the wooden walls and dropped into barrels. A huge anvil dominated the space and a coal fire in a hearth, kept the room warm.

"I'm a friend of the Johnsons," I whispered as I handed him the note the kind free black farmer had written. Mr. Johnson said you could help me."

The smithy looked surprised. "You some kind of mole, thinking I know something about the Underground?" he snarled, assuming I was a white boy.

"No, you don't understand," I whispered. "I'm a runaway from a plantation back in Virginia. The

slave catchers are after me. There's a price on my head and I need to get to Pennsylvania."

"Well you fooled me!" he whispered with his head low; then he sat on a low stool and examined one of Noble's back legs. "Show me where," he demanded in a voice loud enough for the men outside to hear and I squatted down next to him.

"The Marshals and patrollers are everywhere in town" he whispered. "But they're looking for a girl about your age, riding a valuable brown stallion with a golden mane and tail."

"That's me. So far, I've fooled everyone but the farmer's wife. She saw through me right away and she's the one that used stove black on the horse's mane and tail. Can you help me?"

"Yes. You hiding in Shantytown?"

"No, I was warned not to go there. I have some money, so I stayed at the Potomac."

"Well, you have to get out of the hotel. That's where the Marshals all stay. Leave your luggage here in the stable. Go down the canal to Shantytown and ask for Miss S. Everyone knows her and she'll hide you in her brothel. I'll make inquiries at the church. The sexton's a friend of mine. If the underground isn't running, I'll take you across the border myself, but you need to get further north than Pennsylvania. There are slave catchers everywhere. Big money to be made."

He stood and wiped his hands on his coveralls. "What's your name, son?" he said, again loud enough for anyone to hear.

"Patrick Blackwell," I said. "People call me Pat."

"Well, Pat. This is going to take awhile. I need to forge a bigger horseshoe. I'll send word when it's ready."

Then he said in a whisper, "I'll come for you at the brothel, maybe tonight. They call me Mr. P."

Shantytown,
Cumberland, Maryland

I didn't know how to get to Shantytown and didn't want to call attention to myself by asking a lot of questions, so I walked down the back streets, taking any road that headed downhill toward the canal.

Finally, I heard men working and then I saw them. Some were sawing down old growth trees with two-person saws. Others were chopping off limbs and dragging the trunks away with teams of oxen. Occasionally there was an explosion with black powder as the ground was loosened and then the laborers, both African and white, began to shovel the dirt into the waiting wagons.

In the midst of it all, a red headed water boy ran back and forth with his bucket and dipper.

"Son!" I called walking toward him.

"Howdy, mister."

"Can you take me to the whorehouse ..."

"You mean the brothel? I fear you are too young, sir. Other water boys have tried it and the madam kicked them out."

"You misunderstand. I just need to give her a message."

"Well, I'm sorry, sir. I can't waste my time helping you. The master will whip me."

"How can he whip you, a white boy?"

"I'm an indentured servant, sir. My whole family came over from Ireland and we're bound to Mr. Daniels for seven years. After that, we'll be free and can move west. Almost all the white men

226

working on the canal are bound to someone and rented out to the C and O Canal Company. We aren't treated much different than the slaves, except someday we'll be free and the darkies tell me they aren't never gonna be free."

"Boy!" the man on the horse yelled. "Quit your gabbing and get back to work."

"I got to hurry. Just go along the water's edge where they're digging the canal until you come to a row of taverns," the boy whispered. "Count four from the corner and that's the place." He was running away as he spoke.

"Is there a sign?" I yelled after him, but he didn't answer.

Finding the whorehouse wasn't as hard as I imagined, mostly I was just embarrassed to be seen looking. On the dirt road facing the canal, I noticed a group of men at a window, laughing and pointing at what I assumed must be drawings of the courtesans.

Mother would never say the word whorehouse. When describing Dr. Coffman's card-playing friends as rakes who partook of wine, women and song, she called a brothel a "bed house." Now, here I was, about to go in one.

23

Whites Only

When Bitsy called to tell me there was going to be another NAACP demonstration, this one at Dixon's Pharmacy in Liberty, I was excited.

"It's about time someone challenged Mr. Dixon. His Whites Only sign at the pharmacy and soda fountain is an insult to Liberty. The Mountain Top Café has always served everyone," I said. "The main cook is a colored and he'd quit in a minute if Negroes weren't welcome."

"And Ida May is happy to do your hair, no matter what color you are," Bitsy put in.

"Even the Eagle Theater is integrated," I added with a chuckle, "Though that was because of you and Lou...How's Willie by the way?"

"Better, I guess. We went up to Pittsburgh for his first appointment with the people who make artificial legs. He seemed depressed as we drove there, but was actually a little more up-beat on the way back."

"Have you seen Danny at all? He never comes home."

"Yes. We're seeing him a lot since he and Willie got an apartment together."

"Wait...what do you mean? I thought that's

why you got your house in town, so Willie could live there in comfort."

"No, it's ok. Lou thought I was hovering too much and Willie said he needed some space. We're just happy he's getting out. Since he came back from Korea he's been a hermit. Danny drove Willie home for dinner Sunday night in the old car Lou gave them. I asked him to stay for dinner, but he said he had a gig."

"Gig?" I asked, unfamiliar with the word.

"Music event or job...I don't know exactly. Willie says Danny hangs out at Jim's tavern, drinks free beer, and plays songs for the patrons. Hey, I have to get going. I have a meeting with the AME Episcopal Women's Group. I'm trying to get them involved in the demonstration on Saturday. See you then."

"Wait, Bitsy. I have to tell you something."

"What? I'm running late and I'm kind of in a hurry."

"It's the journals. I found another box of journals on the porch the other day. If you want to read them, we could get together sometime. Gracie Potts has run away from Hintonville and there isn't any more upsetting stuff about her father."

"That's good," she responds. "It was getting to me. Maybe we can read after the demo." Then the line goes dead.

Demo? I thought. So, we're going to *demos* now?

Shantytown, Cumberland, Maryland
November 2, 1859

When the group of men in front of the whorehouse departed, I sauntered up to the window and discovered what they were looking at. Displayed there were framed daguerreotypes of six pretty girls, three whites, one mulatto, one dark African and one of the Asian race that looked very exotic. All of them wore beautiful dresses in the latest fashion and had their hair curled up on their heads. Some also wore golden necklaces or flowers behind their ears. Despite the outside of this lowly establishment, the women looked like queens. I sucked in my air, opened the door and hailed the first person I came to.

She was the dark African called Baby Doll. (I knew this by her photo.) "I'm Patrick Blackwell," I said. "Here to see Miss Sue Ellen."

"You're a little young aren't you, sonny? You have to be at least fifteen."

"I am fifteen," I said and it was actually true.

"OK, young sir. Assuming you are *fifteen, let's go find her."*

*At a closed door that said **OFFICE**, Baby Doll knocked. "Are you busy? You have a gentleman caller."*

"If it's one of those Marshals tell him nobody gets something for free around here, including the Law. Hell, I'll tell himself." She threw the door open, her eyes narrowed to slits. "Who's he?"

"Little squirts told me his name is Patrick Blackwell."

"Of the New York Blackwells?"

"Yes," I lied, trying to remember the given names of the Blackwell sisters who'd become the first women in the country to go to medical school. "Actually, I'm distant kin of the New York Blackwells. But I came with a message from the blacksmith..."

"So...give it."

Despite her fine looks, the madam had a rough way of talking. She was wearing a long silk black dress with black lace covering her ample breasts suggesting if you stared long enough you might be able see them, and she wore her hair up, with little curls in front.

I looked at the door, indicating with my eyes that I needed privacy. Baby Doll closed it and the madam sat down at her desk where she'd been working on some sort of ledger. "So speak," she said.

"He asks you to hide me until the next shipment goes out on the Railroad."

"Hide you? Why? A rich white boy from a planter's family? What did you do, steal a horse or kill a politician?" She thought this was funny and burst out laughing.

I took off my hat to show her my hair. "I'm a runaway."

Like the blacksmith, Miss S. immediately understood. "You're an escaped slave!"

"Actually, I'm my master's adopted daughter, but also his slave." Since I wasn't sure the madam would understand, I told her the whole story, including how my father began to take a cruel and unusual interest in me.

"So you see, I am both Negro and white, privileged and yet a piece of property, a thing. Several weeks ago, with the help of my Quaker mother, I dressed as a boy, stole one of my father's horses and some of his money and I'm now trying to get across the Pennsylvania border."

The madam didn't say anything for a moment. Finally she spoke. "A couple of Marshals were here looking for a girl like you this morning. There's a large reward on your head. If I keep you here, I'd be breaking the Runaway Slave Law and could risk a big fine, maybe even jail time."

"It might just be a day or at the most two. The blacksmith is going to a big church this evening to see if someone can carry me across the border. If you have somewhere safe to hide me, I won't make a peep."

The madam gave a great sigh and then smiled. "Honey," she said. "You've got to go farther than Pennsylvania. It's not safe this close to the border, but I have a place you can hide for the night."

For hours I waited behind a curtain in the brothel's bathing room. Miss S., as she was known, swore me to secrecy and said I was never to say her name outside the brothel. In the Underground Railroad, she instructed me; only initials were used to refer to conductors or agents.

I was given a chair and all the whores, as she called them, knew I was female, so they didn't mind me being in their private area. Sometimes they even talked to me as they made their ablutions and at one point Baby Doll brought me some food.

Finally, late that night, Miss S. led me down the backstairs into an alley where the blacksmith waited in a wagon with my horse tied on the back. He opened a secret compartment that was layered with straw and without a word Miss S. gave me a kiss and helped me get in. She took a quilt and covered me, put the lid down, and we trotted away.

I assumed we were going to one of the several churches that graced the hilly town, but it seemed to be taking too long. Finally, I could tell we were off the cobbled streets and on a dirt road. Then, after another good while, we stopped. The blacksmith got out and lifted the lid to my box.

"Did you fare OK," he asked. "Not too cold?"

"I'm fine, but where are we?" I popped my head out and looked at the blackness. There were stars in the sky, but no moon yet. In the shadows I could see a small white house and a barn.

"This is my place. There are Marshals and slave catchers all over Cumberland. You'll be safer here until the shipment leaves for Washington."

"Wait! I don't want to go to Washington! That's back East."

"I meant Washington City, Pennsylvania. It's the next station on the underground and it's about thirty miles northwest of here. Come on, let's put the horses in the barn."

As we watered and fed them, Mr. P. told me about the Underground Railroad. "Everything is in code," he said. "Most of us, blacks and whites, only know the local abolitionists. I don't know anyone further away than Uniontown.

"Guides are known as conductors. Hiding places

are stations. Agents are people like me who help runaways connect with the underground. Stationmasters are those who hide slaves in their homes. Stations are the safe houses. It's a dangerous business and the penalty for any part of it is six months in jail and a $1000 fine, which could mean that an ordinary person could lose his farm or his business if he had one. He could even lose his life for helping a runaway."

"Why do you risk it?" I asked when we went into his house.

He made a noise in his throat that I couldn't interpret. "I was a slave once, Patrick...."

The Narrows, Haystack Mountain, Maryland
November 3, 1859

We slept for a few hours, me on a pallet and Mr. P., my underground conductor, in his bed. In the morning he started on about Canada as he cooked our breakfast. "I really think you should think more about Canada," he said. "Just a few weeks ago, Joseph Richardson, a free black man living near Chambersburg, was kidnapped by slave catchers when he was out hunting coon and he's never been seen again."

"If a black person doesn't have free papers with him, they can snatch you and under federal law a Negro can't defend himself in court. He's not a citizen. He or she is a non-person. And listen to this..." he paused to crack a fresh egg in a skillet. "The federal judges are paid $10 more if they determine the Negro is a runaway slave and not a

free black person. A Negro can't even testify in his own behalf or bring witnesses. I'll tell you the truth, if I didn't have the blacksmith shop and all my tools, I'd go to Canada in a minute. It says in The Liberator that 1000 slaves a year are fleeing to Ontario."

"You can read?"

"Of course."

"Who taught you?"

The man frowned. "What does it matter?"

"It's just that I only know one other Negro who can read."

He made that noise in his throat again, half chuckle, half groan. "There's a lot more of us that read than white people realize."

"How about you?" the blacksmith asked. "Can you read?"

"Yes. I was raised as a white girl in a home with a library..." Here the truth about my gender slipped out like a weasel.

The blacksmith stopped scraping eggs on to my plate and put the skillet back on the stove. He reached over and picked up one of my hands, looking at both sides. "Girl hands!" he said. "So you're the fourteen-year-old fugitive the Marshals are after, but I thought you were supposed to be riding an elegant brown Morgan with a golden mane and tail."

"I'm fifteen, if it matters, and the elegant horse you mention is in your barn. Molly Johnson used stove-black to color his mane and tail." Here the blacksmith doubled up laughing.

"And me a horse man! You'd think I'd have

noticed that."

"You won't tell anyone I'm female, will you?"

"I'll have to tell the conductor on the Underground Railroad."

Mr. P. prepared to leave for his blacksmith shop. "Don't go outside and don't answer the door if anyone comes," he ordered in parting. "If you do, you jeopardize both of us."

I was surprised that the man used a word like "jeopardize", but that showed my very ignorance. According to the farrier, many blacks were more educated than I'd previously thought. It made sense; why give the white master any hint that you're intelligent and informed.

As a parting gesture, Mr. P. pulled some newspapers out from under his bed and threw them on the table. "Here's something you can read to pass the time. I'll be back around seven. I have to check at the church to be sure arrangements have been made and that there's no trouble afoot. Can you make supper?"

"I'm sorry. I've never prepared a meal. We had Thelma who cooked for us."

"Well, what can you do, besides carry a parasol?"

I lifted my chin. "I can read and do sums. I know about history and medicine and the healing arts, and I can deliver babies."

The man shook his head. "Well, at least that's something." Then he laughed again and went out the door. For an hour, I was in a real snit. Mr. P. really got to me, made me feel small and useless. It wasn't my fault I'd been raised as a planter's daughter and not allowed to do anything but look pretty.

A torn pair of overalls hanging on a nail caught my eye. In my saddlebag, I had a small sewing kit that Mother had given me. When I opened the little wooden box, I found her gold thimble, the one with the rose imprinted on top and I might as well tell you, for the first time since I ran away, I cried a long time. I cried long and hard.

24

July 14, 1956
This Land is Your Land

The Liberty demonstration in front of Dixon's Pharmacy was scheduled for Saturday and the day dawned overcast with red clouds on the horizon.

Dan dropped me at Bitsy's on his way to a vet call at a home in Clifton. He was still fussing about my concussion and worried something similar or worse would happen at the protest, so he made me bring a thermos of iced tea and a parasol in case it got too hot. Though I was sure he was overdoing it, in some ways it made me happy. Since I was thirteen, I've had to look after myself and I secretly love being cared for.

Bitsy, as usual, was dressed to the nines and looked like she was right out of a women's magazine. This time it was a pink cotton dress with a string of pearls, white gloves and white pumps; perfect with her coffee and cream complexion. I wore my old blue flowered number with a white straw hat to keep off the sun.

"Is Mira going to meet us at the demo?" Bitsy asked as we walked down Main Street.

"Demo? You sound kind of hip."

"Got to get with the times!" Bitsy laughed.

"I don't know if she will. She has to find a

ride. I think I told you she broke up with her boyfriend. He used to drive her around in his Ford convertible. His father owns Gibson's Ford in Delmont."

"None of the Negroes in Delmont buy their Fords at Gibson's, because the owner won't hire blacks, not even mechanics," she commented. "Good thing Mira got rid of him."

When we arrive in front of the pharmacy and soda shop, no protestors are there yet, so we stroll on by. "Let's wait until some of the people from the NAACP get here," I said. "Look, Mr. Dixon has moved his Whites Only sign to the front door. He must know we're coming. I didn't like that guy from the first day we met him."

"Here they come," Bitsy announces as four late model vehicles stop in front of the AME Episcopal Church and fifteen sharply dressed people with picket signs get out and are joined by another dozen locals.

Bitsy and I cross the street and join the line at Dixon's, where I set my thermos of iced tea and parasol on the sidewalk, up against the store wall.

There are 30 of us at first, then B.K. Bittman and his strawberry haired wife Lillie, join up. Because she's blind, Lillie and BK walk arm and arm, but the rest of us spread out about five feet apart holding our signs high for all to see. Mr. Dixon stands defiantly just inside the glass door, his dark eyes peering over the Whites Only sign, the large mole clearly visible.

Then Danny shows up and cuts in behind me.

It's the first time I've seen him for weeks and he grins and gives me a V sign for victory, the kind soldiers used to give in the war. Over his shoulder, on a colorful woven strap, he carries a guitar plastered with stickers of cartoon characters, and he begins to strum a few chords, then breaks out in song. *"This land is your land - This land is my land - From California to the New York Island,"* and soon everyone's singing.

Mr. Dixon, with a look of disgust, moves away from the glass and back to the counter. No customers have tried to enter his store, but soon an angry crowd gathers across the street in front of the movie house.

"Hey, Jungle Bunnies! Go back where you came from!" a man snarls. It's Earl Bishop, the Sheriff's younger brother and part-time deputy. A few other hecklers join in with calls of "Jungle Bunnies! Jungle Bunnies! Jungle Bunnies!"

It's a strange duet, going back and forth between protestors and counter protestors.

"This land is your land - This land is our land."

"Jungle Bunnies! Jungle Bunnies!"

"From California to the New York Islands."

"Look, there's Bill Blaze," Bitsy calls to me, just as the reporter's old Hudson screeches up to the curb. He doesn't bother to park in a slot; just hops out, wearing his famous brown fedora with the "Press" card in the band and starts snapping photos. First he focuses on the local people in the picket line. Then he gets some long shots of the whole demonstration and a finally a few shots of the angry red faces across the street.

"Mrs. Hester! Mrs. Hester! Patience!" he shouts beckoning me over, but I just keep marching, so he steps into the processions and walks along side me. "Can you give me a statement?"

I shake my head no, but Danny comes up behind. "Go on, Mom. You can do it."

I *know* I can do it. I just don't want to. Bill Blaze has been clever with his articles and editorials and I can never guess how he'll twist my words. He's criticized our family in the past, but he's also publicly apologized and he was very supportive of Dan when he went to prison for his pacifist views. Finally with Danny's prodding, I relent.

"Ok, Billy, what do you need to know?" I say, strolling along, my sign still over my shoulder; **Justice for All, No More Segregation** it says with a picture of an American flag that I'd cut out of a *Life Magazine*.

Blaze pulls out his notebook and pencil. "Can you tell me why the NAACP has chosen to come to Liberty after the riot in Torrington?"

"Mr. Blaze, you need to talk to the organizers, I can't speak for the NAACP. I'm here because I don't want racism to take over our town. Liberty isn't perfect, but it's a darn sight more peaceful and integrated than many places and I want to keep it that way. Where does this new pharmacist think people are going to get their pills if he serves only whites?"

"Mr. Dixon says he'll pass the Negroes' medicines out the back door. No one will be denied."

"Well, bull shit to that!" There's a devil riding my shoulder now and I don't even care what comes out of my mouth. "Mr. Stenger, the previous pharmacist, was a part of this community for thirty years and he served everyone through the front door, regardless of color. To be honest, I feel the whole town should boycott Dixon. And for your information there was *no* riot in Torrington. All that happened was a few trouble makers showed up to throw eggs and I fainted from the heat."

Just then, an old Ford truck with another Confederate Flag flying from the antenna speeds down the street. The back is full of young white men blaring Dixie through Five and Dime tinhorns and the people on the other side of the road start singing along with them.

"*Oh I wish I was in the land of cotton - Old times there are not forgotten. - Look away - Look away - Look away Dixie land.*"

"Oh, for heaven sakes!" I jump back in my place just as Wally comes down the line.

"Be calm!" the organizer warns us. "Be calm, everyone. Don't give the punks the satisfaction of showing we care. "You. What's your name? Can you get us singing again?"

"I'm Danny Hester."

"Well, do you know *We Shall not be Moved?*"

Danny stops and turns to face the hecklers across the street and strums a few chords as we all gather around him. "*We shall - We shall -We shall not be moved. - We shall. We shall - We shall not be moved.*"

The first egg hits Danny right in the face, but

242

he only laughs and doesn't stop singing. None of us do and soon we're all covered in yellow slime, even beautiful blind Lillie. *"Just like a tree that's standing by the river - We shall not be moved!"*

First Star

"So, I heard it was quite a scene at the demonstration," Dan said as we walked to the barn to do our chores. "Tell me what happened."

"Well, it wasn't as big a scene as the day you got arrested for resisting the draft." I raised my eyebrows, playfully chiding him.

It's been over ten years and the pain of his one-year incarceration has finally faded. We can joke about it now; how behind bars in Moundsville State Prison, he befriended a pet rat named Ronald and was protected by murderer named Bones; how in his absence, I took care of the kids and the farm, delivered babies and battled ice storms, blizzards and wild dogs.

"About thirty people were at the protest, mostly from Torrington, but there were some church people from Liberty and Hazel Patch too, even a couple of coal miners wearing their hard hats. About an hour after we got started, a hostile crowd formed across the street, more opposition than I expected."

Dan set the clean buckets on the floor of the barn, nudged a three-legged stool toward me with his foot and sat down next to our Holstein.

"One of the Bishop men was there, yelling at us. I was so proud of Danny. Did anyone tell you? He came to the demonstration with his guitar and led the singing."

"Well, that's something. Glad to see he got off the bar stool and staggered across the street."

"Dan! You shouldn't talk like that. He might have smelled a little of beer, but I'm sure no one noticed. Anyway, he wasn't drunk and I was glad he was there."

"Well, as far a I know all he's been doing is hanging out at Jim's Tavern. Carlin Hummingbird frequents the bar and he says Danny's always there; he plays the guitar in exchange for beers and bangs out tunes on the piano. Jim probably gives him a few bucks under the table."

"He's a good musician..." I said weakly, leaning my head against our Jersey as I squeezed her teats. Dan, with his big hands, can milk much faster, but he purposely slows to my pace. In the warm half dark, the rhythm of the milk dinging into the pails is like making music together.

"Is there something we should be doing?" I wondered out loud. "Have you talked to Danny?"

"I tried. He's avoiding me now."

"What did you say to him?"

"Last time I saw him, I asked if he wanted to come back and work with me. I told him I could go as high as $2.00 an hour."

"That's good pay! Minimum wage is one dollar."

Dan nodded his head. "I told him he'd be worth it if he could drag his butt out of bed, but he said, 'Nah, I'm fine. I'm concentrating on my music now and Mr. Cross is paying me board and room for living with Willie and helping him get around."

I stopped milking for a moment to let that sink in. "Bitsy didn't tell me they were *paying* Danny."

"Just for the board and room. Lou set up the arrangement. They're worried about Willie and all he's been through. It's probably worth it for them to know someone's looking after him. The thing is, Will might actually be doing better than Danny. I saw him at the Post Office the other day, picking up a correspondence course in bookkeeping."

"Willie?"

"Yeah. The V.A. is paying for it; some kind of veteran's benefit. He was having a hell of a time carrying the box because of his crutches, so I helped him bring it around the corner to their apartment."

On the way back to the house, I stopped and put my bucket down in the middle of the barnyard. Four of our horses grazed on the hillside, the chickens clucked peacefully as they scraped up their feed and the first star was just showing over the mountain.

"Dan, I feel like a tree that's about to fall over, like my roots won't hold. We just have to let Danny go, don't we? We just have to let go of everything and hope there's no windstorm."

Dan smiled his crooked smile and brushed a piece of my hair back over my ear. "Not everything. We don't let go of each other." Then he held me in his arms as the earth slowly turned underneath us.

The Narrows, Haystack Mountain, Maryland
November 1859, I'm losing track of the date.

    Hiding away in the blacksmith's cottage, I
perused the worn newspapers. There were five of
them and they appeared to have been read many
times. One was called The Liberator and not all
their articles were political. There were some
stories about books and travel and women's rights.
This was a surprise, I had not heard of "women's
rights", but there were apparently both male and
female citizens working to promote the equality of
the sexes. They even wanted to give women the vote.
What would Dr. Coffman and his friends think of
that?

    Next, I turned to an 1850 copy of the North Star,
published by Frederick Douglas, a Negro
intellectual and orator, now living in Rochester,
New York. Dr. Coffman hated the man. "Douglas
is nothing but uppity black trash," I heard him once
say. "He was a field hand that learned to read.
That's why a bondsman should never be given an
education. It only makes them want more from the
world."

    I was contemplating these weighty matters, when
I heard the sound of a horse on the road, coming at
a slow trot. Quickly, I placed the newspapers under
the mattress.

    It was not yet six o'clock, so it couldn't be the
blacksmith, but I was wrong. In the growing dusk, I

*heard him go to the barn and care for the horses
and when he entered the house, he was in a good
mood. "Well, it's all arranged. I'm to bring you to
the church before dawn and a free black man will
take you to Uniontown...There is one thing, though,
and you won't like it. You can't take Noble."*

*"What do you mean I can't take Noble? I have
to take Noble!"*

*"Well the conductor says no. It's going to rain
tomorrow and if the stove black on his mane and
tail comes off it will endanger everyone. There are
two other shipments going out with you, another
woman and a man."*

*I snort in disgust, a very unladylike noise.
"Well what will happen to Noble?"*

"I'll buy him from you."

*"No, you can borrow him," I argue. "Maybe
you'll give him back to me someday. Will you keep
blackening his tail?"*

*"Yes. I guess I'll have to. Maybe I can get a
more permanent dye. Some of the prostitutes color
their hair."*

"If we dyed it tonight, could I take him?"

*"No. The conductor says he doesn't want any
questions if he's stopped and he's in charge of this
mission. Maybe if I ever make it to Canada, I'll
bring Noble to you."*

*"You're not going to find me in Canada,
because I don't think I'm going there. You could
bring him to Pennsylvania though."*

*"I really think you ought to go to Ontario.
There's a community of escaped slaves not far from
Lake Erie."*

"Wait. Are you my boss all of a sudden?"

"I'm just telling you; you can't stay in Pennsylvania. It's too dangerous. You have to go further north. You didn't make supper did you?"

"I told you I don't know how to cook, but I did mend your overalls."

"You did? See, I knew you had talents. I should have left a few shirts out too. Sewing is one thing I can't do, except on leather. My hands are too big and rough." He held them out. *They were brown on the top but white on the dry callused palms, just like Jammy's.*

"Anyway, it's fine you didn't cook. Look what I brought home!" He took the lid off the basket he was carrying and pulled out a hatbox and a jug of cider. *"Miss S. asked about you and she had her cook make a meal for us of biscuits and gravy...."*

After eating, we pulled chairs up to the fireplace and I told Mr. P. some of my story, then I asked him how he came to be a free man.

"Let's see. Where to begin?" He threw another log in the fireplace. *"I was born into slavery in North Carolina on a big plantation. This was in 1838 or thereabouts. I'm not sure of the date, because no one wrote it down."*

"You're only twenty-one then? I thought you were older."

"Almost twenty-two. My mother died after my birth and I never knew my father. He might have been the overseer. Some said I favored him.

"When I was nine, they started me picking cotton, but I was a thinker, couldn't keep up, and was frequently whipped. I ran away two or three

times before I was twelve, but I had no plan, just a reckless nature. What helped me most was learning to read. A free black basket weaver who lived down the road taught me. He'd heard from my fellow slaves that I was eventually going to get whipped to death if I didn't settle down, so he took me under his wing. I was a quick study and learned to read books in only a year. They say knowledge is power and for the first time, I felt I had something of my own, something the master couldn't take from me."

As Mr. P. talked, he stared into the flames and I had a chance to study him. He was tall and sturdy with the large biceps and the wide chest of a blacksmith. He had previously shown me his big roughened hands, but it was his face that was most interesting.

He had a strong jaw and very white teeth, a trait I'd noticed in most young Africans. His skin was mahogany and his eyes light brown, almost golden.

"At fourteen," the young blacksmith continued, adjusting the logs on the hearth, "I started thinking about another escape, but it never happened. Instead, I ended up saving the master's son from drowning. The boy, about my age, was a wild one and would ride his horse at breakneck speed all over the plantation.

"We were working in the cotton fields and against the overseer's regulations I was taking a nap down by the river. With so many slaves he couldn't keep track of us.

"Young Master Barron came barreling down the riverbank and the horse stumbled and flipped him in the water. The current was swift and

immediately pulled him down. Without thinking, I jumped in to grab him. I didn't know how to swim either, you understand, but I was tall for my age, so I bounced my way across the bottom of the riverbed to get to him.

"Most of the time I was under the water, but I'd push up with my feet, get some air, and move forward. At one point I felt his arm and I pulled on the neck of his shirt to get his head up so he could breathe. Finally, we made it back to shore and lay on the bank, gagging water and panting.

"That event changed life for both of us. I didn't want Barron to tell the master how I'd saved him, but he insisted. I was pretty sure I'd be whipped for taking the nap, but then something extraordinary happened. The master, Barron's father, gave me my freedom, so you see it was just dumb luck on my part that I'm no longer a slave.

"Barron, because I'd saved him, started looking at Africans differently. When he was seventeen he went to Oberlin College in Ohio, the first university in the United States to have both white and brown skinned students. When his father died, Barron set all their slaves free."

I was silent, imagining the blessing that came from a wild white boy almost drowning. I also liked the way he said white and brown skinned students, as if that was the only thing that separated them, just a thin piece of tissue covering their bodies.

"One more thing before bed," P. said. "You need another haircut. Your disguise as a white boy won't work if you take off your hat."

"Are you a barber too?" I joked.

"Not much, but I have a pair of sharp scissors."

"It's probably a good idea." Once again, I sat in a chair and watched the curls fall.

"So, will you go to Canada?" the blacksmith asked.

I took a deep breath. "Everybody seems to think it's the best idea, the Johnsons, Miss S. and you. Are my traveling companions going there?"

"I'm certain they are. They have family in Ontario who escaped from somewhere in the South last year."

"Good, at least I'll know someone there. And you might come someday? You'll bring Noble?"

In the morning, I hurriedly packed a valise that the blacksmith had traded me for my saddlebags and I gave him a letter to mail to Mother Coffman, in care of her friend the laundress in Staunton, explaining I was going to Ontario and we should meet there; then while he hitched his horse to the cart with the false bottom, I went to the barn to see Noble. It was a heart-breaking time for me, I will tell you. I even let him lick my face with his long wet tongue as I said goodbye.

25

Flight

This morning, after Dan left, I took my coffee out on the front porch to enjoy the sound of the creek and was surprised to see four little Blue Jays out of the nest, hopping around in the lilac bush.

At first Howard was protective, as we all are of our young. He raised his crest and squawked at me in the high-pitched, "Jay! Jay!"

I sat down on the bench and used my midwife voice. "It's all right, Howard. It's OK. There's nothing to fear." Soon he calmed down and perched on the rail looking up at his youngsters with something like pride. The four little birds were now covered with feathers, mostly gray, showing only a little blue, but they had crests and markings just like their parents. For the moment they were not screaming for food and I swear a couple of them were up to something.

They sat very close on a branch and conferred in short peeps, nodding and affectionately pecking each other. The bigger of the two flapped his wings. The other one fluttered back at him and I noticed she had a white patch like Howard's.

Big Boy flapped some more and teetered on the branch; then suddenly he was airborne, fighting hard to stay aloft. For a minute, I was sure he was going to crash, but then he gained altitude and landed in the top of a pine across the yard. Minutes later his sibling followed.

"Jay! Jay!" Howard cheered.

"It won't be long now," I warned my blue-feathered friend. "Your baby birds will be leaving the nest."

After feeding the chickens and hanging laundry on the line, I decided to go into town to see Bitsy. For the past week we've been back at the journals. With the disgusting Dr. Coffman out of the picture we eagerly follow Grace Potts' story.

"Want to read outside?" Bitsy asks. "It's cooler in the shade. Smells good too." We carry the journal out and sit on her new folding lawn chairs.

"Did you hear about Cora Bishop?" my friend asks. "She left Aran."

"How do you know?"

"I was at the House of Beauty having my hair done and Ida May told me."

"What happened? Did she say?"

Bitsy shrugs. "All she knows is that Cora left for Hyden, Kentucky on the Greyhound bus and told the driver she didn't need a return ticket."

"Do you think Aran was punching her around? Remember the bruise on Kitty's face?"

"Probably, but there could be more to it."

"Like what?"

"Well, maybe Aran did something to Kitty and her baby and Cora is leaving before he kills her too." She takes a sip of tea and peers at me with big brown eyes over the top of her mug.

"Come on…You've been watching too many episodes of that Hitchcock show." I laugh. "Let's read."

Cumberland, Maryland
Sometime in November, 1859

The brown skinned sexton of the Emmanuel Episcopal Church in Cumberland carried a lantern in one hand and my satchel in the other as we moved quickly through the dark tunnel under the building.

"These ancient passageways run below the sanctuary and the rectory," he tells me. "We're under the rectory now. The Church was built on the old foundations of the Historic Fort Cumberland where George Washington began his military career. That was during the French and Indian war. You know about that?"

"I've heard of it."

"Well, these tunnels were a way of getting supplies in to the men if there was a siege. Now we use them to hide runaways until we have a conductor from the Underground Railroad heading north. The border is not far away, but it's rough country and it's crawling with slave catchers."

The sexton walked so fast it was hard to keep up. "Watch it," he said, indicating a couple of barrels stashed to the side. "That's black powder left over from when this was a fort. It's too damp to explode, but I don't want someone to fall over it."

At last we came to a T-shaped intersection, where the sexton had set up four platform beds, a table with benches, and a few wooden chairs. A candle was burning in a pewter holder and a young man and woman jumped up when they saw us. The man was over six feet tall, very black and very *muscular. The woman was tiny, almost as light skinned as me, with red curly hair, freckles and a very big belly.*

"Peter and Elsie Lawrence this is Patrick Blackwell, your traveling companion. If possible, we want to get you to Canada before winter sets in and Lake Erie freezes over. We start tonight when the wagon from the brewery comes to the gate."

The sexton pulled me aside. "Can I tell them you're a female? It might be necessary for sleeping arrangements or to use the latrine."

"I hadn't thought of that. I'll tell them." We went back to the table. "Elsie and Peter, please call me Patrick, but I have to tell you that isn't my real name. It's Grace." I waited while they absorbed the information.

"Well, you fooled me!" laughed Peter. Elsie just smiled. Later, I learned that Elsie had been beaten so badly by her mistress in Norfolk that she couldn't get out of bed for a week. That's when they knew they had to escape.

"If it's safe, I'll come back this afternoon and take you up to the church for a prayer service," the sexton announced. "Many abolitionists in the area know of our work here at Emmanuel, but I must remind you never to speak of it. Our lives depend on you."

"I have a question," I boldly interrupted him.
"Yes..."

"Mr. P. said you're an escaped slave yourself. Can you tell me why you stopped in Cumberland, instead of heading right across the border to Pennsylvania or fleeing to Canada?"

"When I first met the Reverend and found out he was a conductor on the Underground Railroad, I told him I was a Christian and I wanted to help other runaways. So he got me forged Free Papers and hired me as a sexton for the church. Hardly anyone knows I was once chattel like you."

"Chattel no more!" Peter hooted. "We're on our way to the promised land!"

"Shhhhh!" Elsie said, suppressing a giggle. "Your big voice echoes in the cave."

After the sexton left us, I got out my blanket and lay down on one of the wooden beds. I'd had a good sleep the night before, but I wasn't sure when I'd get to sleep again. Also, I needed to consider what I was doing. As a group, a large black man, a pregnant redhead and a white boy dressed like a planter's son, was going to be more conspicuous than if I just traveled alone. Then I wondered if I really wanted to go to Canada or was I just letting other people decide for me.

I was more scared now in the hands of the Underground than I had been before. A part of me wished I had just taken the stagecoach as mother wanted. If I had, I'd be in Upper Darby by now...or perhaps not. The coach to Philadelphia passed right through Harper's Ferry and all the trouble that was happening there.

I shivered, but whether from fear or from cold, I didn't know. "Do you need another blanket?" Elsie asked softly and without waiting for a response she threw one over me and tucked me in. She was no bigger than a ten year old with a belly already the size of a small watermelon. About 8 months, I estimated.

With the warmth of the extra quilt, I must have fallen asleep, because the next thing I knew, Elsie was shaking me. "Samuel is back. Do you want to go pray?"

I shook my head to wake up. "Yes, we need all the prayers we can get. I'm scared, Elsie. Are you? Canada seems so far away."

The woman didn't say anything at first. Then she shrugged. "God will take care of the pure of heart."

On that we differed. Plenty of good people have died of starvation, been killed in wars, and beaten to death by their masters. What did God provide for them? Their hearts were just as pure as mine.

Still, I followed the sexton down the dark tunnel, up a short flight of stone stairs and eventually into a large sanctuary where the vaulted ceiling and the beautiful stained glass windows brought a song to my throat. The pastor greeted us each by name and shook our hands. He was a bearded man, with pale gray eyes that looked into my soul.

"We are so proud of you, our brothers and sisters," he intoned in the way of a preacher. "You've sacrificed much for your holy right to be free...." He went on for several minutes, while I looked at the stained glass windows with pictures of Jesus and angels and little lambs; then we sang a hymn.

"Holy, holy, holy – Lord God almighty – Early in the morning our song shall rise to thee..."

That night as we three lay in our underground chamber, our shoes on and belongings at the ready, I heard the church bells ring and a few minutes later the sound of footsteps. It was the sexton with a lantern. "Hurry," he whispered. "The bell is the signal. They're waiting."

In the alleyway, next to the creek, he blew out the lantern. A brewery wagon with high sides stood waiting. Inside the wagon were dozens of wooden barrels of beer and between the rows was a narrow space where we could hide. The three of us had only room to sit with our knees pulled up to our chest and our arms around them.

I felt bad for Elsie, with her bulging belly, and I tried to squeeze tighter to give her more room. Our conductor said his name was Mr. C. and we would be in Uniontown, Pennsylvania before dawn.

As we pulled away, I looked for our guide to thank him, but he was gone.

Scars on the Inside

"How's Willie doing?" I start off when Bitsy and I are settled at my kitchen table cutting up green beans. I don't want to pry, but maybe she needs to share her worries.

While we work, we're waiting for Dr. Greene, from Torrington, to visit us with a patient he thinks might want to deliver in the Baby Cabin. He says she's interested in natural childbirth and has been reading a book called *Childbirth Without Fear*.

"How's Willie?" I ask again, figuring if I was in her shoes it would help to talk.

"Better, physically. He has an appointment to get his artificial leg next week. Lou is taking the day off and we're all going to Pittsburgh. I hope it fits well. I don't know if he can take any more disappointment. This will be the third time we've been up there. The last time the fake leg hurt him when he tried to walk. "

"Dan says Lou's giving Danny room and board for living with Willie. You didn't tell me…"

"I didn't?"

"Come on, Bitsy…"

"Ok. Danny only agreed to the arrangement, if we kept it secret. He didn't think you'd like it."

I shake my head frowning. "He's right. The boy's just drifting; doesn't seem to want to do anything but hang around the tavern and play music with his friends. Free board and room may make life too easy. The setup might be helping Willie though. Dan says Will's started an accounting correspondence course."

Here Bitsy stops. She lays down her paring knife, and shakes her head. "That's the first good thing I've heard. I'll tell you the truth, Patience. I've been so worried about him. Not just about his leg…but so many men come back broken after being in combat. Some can't overcome it and pull the trigger. Willie has scars on the inside *and* scars on the outside. That's why we wanted Danny around, to keep an eye on him."

"He wouldn't harm himself, would he? Nurse Becky's first husband was a veteran with shell shock after World War One and he killed himself. You don't have any guns in the house do you?"

"Lou locked them all up…"

I blow out my breath and pull over another bucket of beans. "I know it's scary, but Willie's making it. He's studying a profession. And soon he'll get his artificial leg. Danny's never endured the trauma of war and yet all he's doing is keeping a bar stool warm."

"He came to the NAACP protest in Liberty; that was something," my friend tries to cheer me. "Come on let's read while we wait for the beans to boil."

Uniontown,
South Western Pennsylvania

The long ride to the next station on the Underground Railroad took most of the day. We left in the dark and it was all back country trails, uphill and down. At one point, Peter pulled out a few apples and we munched them in silence. At last, the sound of the horse's hooves changed; we were off the dirt roads and traveling on cobblestones. I could also hear men's voices and other horses too; in the distance there was the sound of a train.

Eventually, we stopped. Our conductor helped us out and I'll have to admit that after all the hours in that cramped space, I had to hold on to him until my legs straightened out. We were in a workshop of some sort. Early morning light came in the window and an African woman with a pale blue apron and a white man dressed in a long grey coat greeted us.

"Come in. Come in!" he said. "You're the one called Patrick, yes? I'd heard you were a light mulatto boy. That's true enough about the skin, but not the gender, I believe." He laughed as if this amused him.

We slipped into a small windowless room, hidden behind a floor to ceiling cupboard, where the dark woman referred to only as The Cook, had set up a pot of hot tea and fresh bread and butter. There were two beds in the room with plenty of quilts, a small wooden table and a porcelain chamber pot. The room had no windows and we were informed that we would be there until a conductor could be found to take us to Washington City, our next stop.

"Ma'am," Elsie asked, "Do you think you could find something for us to do, perhaps a checker board?"

The cook lit two candles and pulled a small chest out from under a bed where we found not only a checkerboard, but also some copies of The Liberator, along with paper and pencils that had been sharpened with a knife. "We want you to be as comfortable as possible," she said with a big smile.

"Might you have some mending or something I could do for you?" I asked.

"Or if you need anything repaired," Peter offered.

"Could you fix a butter churn?" the cook asked.

"I can fix about anything."

Elsie wanted to play checkers, so we settled down at the table and she beat me twice. This wasn't surprising, since I hadn't played much before. Mother thought such games frivolous, almost wicked, like playing cards.

When we were done, Elsie wanted to lie down so Peter and I played another round and this time I beat him! Now I understood the addiction of games! This was new to me.

In an hour or two, our hostess came to check on us again, bringing the broken butter churn and a basket with some clothes she said I could mend. "These are all children's garments," I remarked as I went through the pile. "Are there little ones in the household?"

"Not anymore. The doctor's children are all grown and gone away to school, up north."

"Our stationmaster is a physician?" I asked.

"I shouldn't have said that. You may have noticed we never use names. Even saying he's a doctor might endanger him. Some people at the church know, but only the abolitionists. Those who want to help the freedom seekers donate these clothes. I thought maybe you could fix up some things for the baby." She nodded at Elsie and pulled a pair of scissors, some thread and a packet of needles out of her apron. "Anything else you can use, like warm socks, take them too."

Peter already had his hands on the butter churn. "It's the gears," he observed. "I'll fiddle with them for awhile."

For the next few hours I laid out the clothes and tried to figure how they could be used. When Elsie woke, I showed her what I was doing and she joined me searching through the donated garments. Peter had finished fixing the wooden butter churn and was looking through the abolitionist newspapers. "Can you read, Peter?" I asked him.

"Just a little. Some of the boys on the docks in Norfolk taught me. This was before my master found out and gave me 39 lashes. I've always wanted to learn."

"I can teach you," I said. "It looks like we'll be doing a fair amount of waiting. Maybe, our hostess will let us take one of the newspapers."

"I don't know," Elsie said. "It might be dangerous, if a slave catcher realizes we can read."

"If a slave catcher gets his hands on us," Peter muttered. "The newspapers will be the least of our worries."

That night as I lay in the hidden room, I began to understand what Mr. P and the others meant when they said the border-states weren't safe for runaways. Though we were in Pennsylvania, a free state, I didn't feel free. Slave catchers were out there, apparently, everywhere. For the first time I began to think that getting to Canada was the right choice.

A few hours later, we heard footsteps, followed by the sound of the false cupboard scraping against the floor as it moved.

"Good news!" the doctor said, carrying in a pot of chicken soup. The cook followed with bread and fruit. "A neighbor is going to the stock auction in Washington City and can take you that far. He assures me he's got a clever way to hide you."

Later, the cupboard swung back again and a black man in farmer's clothes stood with our stationmaster in the opening. "Come quickly," the doctor urged. "Don't forget anything. We'll have no way to get it to you."

We stepped out into the dark and saw a high-sided wagon holding three calves lying on hay. "Where are we going to sit?" I asked with eyebrows up to my hairline.

"Don't worry about that. Look here." The farmer pushed back some hay and opened a small trap door. "Just squirm through and lay on your sides. My Missus put down some old quilts. There's a jug of water in the corner, but don't drink anymore than you have to, because I can't stop if you need relief."

"Let's say a prayer, before we go," Elsie suggested, so we held hands and bowed. "Heavenly Father," she whispered. "Keep us safe from danger. Protect us and help us reach the Promised Land. Amen."

Then we all crawled in and the heavy trap door went down again.

Without Fear

"Wow, can you imagine," says Bitsy marking our place in the cloth bound journal with her finger; "Hiding and then moving and hiding again, all the while trusting the abolitionists and free blacks to protect you. There must have been constant fear. I wonder how many runaways were caught and brought back to their masters…"

The sound of a vehicle cuts short our discussion.

"It must be Dr. Greene," Bitsy says, looking out

the kitchen window. We take off our aprons and smooth down our hair, but when we go outside there's no Dr. Greene. A tall very dark pregnant woman stands in the drive with Wally Richards from the NAACP.

"Hello, Patience. Hello, Bitsy. Dr. Greene wasn't able to come. He's tied up with an emergency surgery in Torrington. This is my wife Victoria."

"So good to meet you," the woman responds with a British accent. In her hand she clutches a small book.

For a minute, I'm confused. Victoria has a British accent, but her beautiful black face is as dark as coal. Fortunately, Bitsy's manners are better than mine.

"Won't you come in for some tea?" Bitsy asks, as she leads the couple in through the front porch door. Our visitors are both dressed as if going to Sunday services, Wally in a dark suit with red bow tie and his wife in a navy maternity outfit with a white collar.

"It smells delightful in here," Victoria comments, breathing deeply. The more she talks the more puzzled I am. She sounds like Queen Elizabeth, but with a musical lilt. Finally I just come out and ask her.

"So are you two from around here?"

Wally bursts out laughing and Victoria stifles a giggle. "We get that question a lot," he says. "I'm from Ohio. Victoria is from London. Her family immigrated from Jamaica."

"My father came to Great Britain right after the

First World War when they needed laborers," the woman explains. "He fought with the Brits as did many Jamaicans."

"So, how can we help you," Bitsy starts out. "Can I see your book? Dr. Greene said you were looking for some place you could have a natural delivery."

Victoria smiles. "I was a nurse with the new National Health Service in London and worked with the midwives there. They do both hospital and home births. I was shocked when I came to the United States and discovered there are so few midwives here, and no one has even heard of natural childbirth.

"Dr. Greene sent me to the obstetrician that most of the university professors' wives go to, a Dr. Fox. I've endured him for 6 months and went to all my prenatal visits, but his idea of a normal delivery is for the woman to lie on a surgical cart, get strapped down with her legs held open in stirrups, and go to sleep. Then he plays the hero, does an episiotomy and pulls the baby out with forceps. I don't want any part of that. We were so excited when we learned you are midwives." She finishes with another wide smile.

"I think we may be able to help. Are you due soon?" I ask, eyeing her abdomen.

"Any time now," Wally breaks in.

"Well, it's important you understand that Bitsy and I haven't been to school to become midwives. We aren't registered nurses. We've learned through apprenticeship and reading obstetrics textbooks on our own, but we've delivered over four hundred babies successfully," I explain.

"There's another thing. The new local hospital is segregated and there isn't a maternity ward for colored women, so if we have an emergency we are pretty much on our own. Torrington is too far away." I let that sink in and when the couple doesn't appear overly concerned, I go on. "Would you like to see the little house we call the Baby Cabin?"

"That was nice," Bitsy said as we waved goodbye to the pleasant couple. "We'll have to flip a coin to see who gets to read *Childbirth Without Fear* first. I can't believe it was published in 1933 and we never heard of it."

"It was sweet how much Victoria admired the cabin. She even took photos for her friends. Did you see that camera? Instant photos! What did she call it?"

"Polaroid," Bitsy remembered the name. "It sure beats my little Kodak Brownie."

Western Pennsylvania
Mid to late November, 1859
For days, maybe weeks, we moved north at a snail's pace, taking back roads and using circuitous routes to confuse pursuers. I lost count of how many basements and attics we hid in. Some were quite comfortable, some were cold, but always our conductors and stationmasters were kind.

One night, we traveled in a wagon under a false bottom, driven by a Mr. A. and his young grandson, Junior.

"Looks like trouble ahead, son. See those men approaching..." Mr. A. says, loud enough for us to hear. Quick as a lick, the cart jerks to a halt. Junior slips off the wagon seat, and under cover of darkness, opens a secret panel and whispers for us to collect our things and follow him. In the blackness, we hide behind boulders not twenty feet away and observe three men on horseback approach our conductor.

"Howdy," Mr. A. greets them pleasantly.

"You're out late." A nasal voice responds. "Where you headed?"

"Home," the farmer answers. "Just getting back from market. I have a farm outside Harmony, eighty acres on Little Creek."

"Seen any darkies traveling the road? We're looking for five slaves that run off a plantation in Maryland."

"Sorry, I can't help. I haven't seen anyone," Mr. A. answers.

"Keep an eye out for them, would you? And report anything suspicious to the Marshal in Harmony."

"Be glad to help if I see anyone."

The riders gallop off and we wait for our conductor to signal us to get back in the cart, but he drives on. "What's happening?" I whisper to Junior.

"Papa can't seem suspicious. He has to continue heading for Little Creek. If the Marshals see him turning around to get us, we'll all be caught. He could be punished with a big fine and

put in jail. Don't worry. He'll be back. We've had to do this before." Elsie is shivering and I put my blanket around her like a cloak.

"Come on," Junior says, taking my hand. "I know a place where we can hide and get out of the weather."

For what might have been a mile we trudged through the dank forest while big flakes of snow began to drift down, melting on our faces.

"Here it is," Junior said, stopping at what looked like a decaying woodcutter's shack.

Once inside, Peter lit a match and you could tell others had stayed in the shelter, fugitive slaves or maybe outlaws. There was a crude table with a stub of a candle in a metal holder and two benches. There was also a fireplace, but Junior said we couldn't make a fire, because slave hunters would smell the smoke.

All night we lay on the earth floor, in the dark, side by side wrapped in our blankets. I could feel Elsie shivering and I shivered too. After a long while, there was light at the one dirty window and we knew dawn was coming.

For two days we waited for Mr. A. to return and at one point we runaways discussed proceeding north on our own, but Junior discouraged us. "It's too risky," he said. "You know there are patrollers out there looking for that other group of runaways. Why take the chance? As soon as Gramps thinks it's safe he'll be back. Not only that, it's still snowing. You'd be so easy to track."

He had a good point about the tracks...so we waited.

And waited.

And waited.

All we had to eat was a loaf of bread given to us by the conductor's wife at our last station then it was gone. Finally on the third day we heard whistling in the woods. Mr. A. was at the door and within a few hours we were secreted in a comfortable attic in his home.

Mrs. A., the chubby cheeked lady of the house, who wore a gray dress and a little white bonnet, laid out three straw pallets covered with quilts. There were fresh baked rolls and cheese and apple pie. She even gave us clean clothes and washed our old garments. Afterward, I asked Elsie to again cut my hair.

"How long have we been traveling together?" I wondered while she combed and snipped with Mrs. A.'s scissors.

"I don't know anymore. Four weeks. Five?" she answered.

I ran my hands over my cropped head. "So, are you discouraged? It seems to be taking forever and every day there's the danger we'll be caught."

"No," she said. "I'm not discouraged. The Lord will provide. We must accept the hardships and the gifts He gives us."

"Come on. Cheer up." Peter whispered as he lay on his pallet listening. "Let's sing!" He tapped out the rhythm on the floor with his hand.

"Paul and Silas bound in jail - Had no money to

go their bail - Keep your hand on that plow - Hold on!"

Elsie knew the words, but I just hummed along.

"The very moment I thought I was lost - the dungeons shook and the chains fell off - Keep your eyes on that prize - hold on!"

It was a song full of power and afterward I vowed not to lose hope again.

26

Fearless

In less than a week, before I'd even finished reading Victoria's book, I got a phone call from Wally Richards.

"It's time." he began without preamble. "Vickie's water broke about an hour ago. Should we hurry over or wait until she starts contractions?"

I didn't have to think twice. "It's almost two hours from Torrington to the Baby Cabin; I'd get started right away. Likely, the baby won't come until late, but you don't want to be speeding down a curvy mountain road while your wife's in labor."

I gave Bitsy a heads up and while I waited, I opened *Childbirth Without Fear* again and skimmed a few more chapters. What I learned was that Grantly Dick Reed was a physician in England who thought more like a midwife than a Doctor of Medicine.

"Good midwifery is the birth of a baby in a manner nearest to the natural law and design," he wrote. "And good midwifery, next to a wise and healthy pregnancy, sets the pattern of the newborn infant and its relationship to its mother."

How could I not have heard of this book? What's so amazing to me is to see in print what I have come to believe…that there is something transformative about human birth, one life coming out of another. Like the author, I've witnessed all kinds of deliveries and have noticed that things go best when the mother is calm, has faith in her body and is supported by loving companions.

Still, there are things that Dr. Reed has, apparently, not seen; women squatting to deliver, or kneeling or even standing. And he doesn't mention women dancing or singing or praying through contractions. By the time I'm half way through chapter five, there's the sound of a vehicle in the drive. Victoria gets out of the car, breathing deeply.

Twelve hours later, Bitsy nods toward the door and we slip out of the Baby Cabin.

"What's up?" I ask as I stand next to her looking out across the fields toward Spruce Mountain. The sky is still gray but you can tell dawn is coming.

"I'm just tired and I don't know what else we can do. She's walked and squatted and rested on her side and still no urge to push."

"The baby's heart beat is still regular and strong. We could take her into the house and get her in a tub of warm water," I think out loud. "That's worked a few times. Dan will be going out on his calls soon. The lights are already on in the kitchen. And then there's the tincture of time. We can wait."

Bitsy shakes her head no. "There might still be two or three hours of pushing. We don't want this to drag on until she's too exhausted."

Just then the door opens. "She's starting to lose it," Wally states. Inside, we see beautiful, strong, Victoria leaning on the bed, whimpering, "I can't do this. I can't do this!"

"Ok," I make a decision. "It's time to go to the house for a bath."

"Really?" Wally asks. "Is that safe with her water bag broken?"

"We'll disinfect the tub. Come on, Victoria. It's time to take a walk. Can you get her bathrobe and slippers, Wally?"

"I can't *walk!*" Victoria wails. "I think I'm going to die."

"Yes, you can. You can walk," Bitsy looks her in the eye. "You can do this!" And the two of us march her out the door and across the yard, just as the sun peeks over the mountain and the clouds burst into flame, red bands across the sky.

Even Victoria, lifts her head. "Oh!" she says. "It's like a prayer. The sky is praying for us." As the next contraction hits, Wally steps over and puts his arms around her.

"Ughhhhh!" Victoria groans leaning over. It's the familiar noise we've been waiting for and I know what it means. We're about twenty yards from the house and when the contraction is over I try to turn her around and head back to the Baby Cabin, but she's locked around Wally, with eyes the size of daisies. "It's coming!" she says.

"Move along, now," Wally says firmly. "Back to the cabin and into bed."

"No! No! I can't move. Ugggghhhhhhhh!" she grunts again and squats lower, so I squat too and put my bare hand on her bottom.

"She's right, Bitsy! Get a blanket and the birth kit. You can run faster than me… Try not to push now, Victoria. Just blow. Blow with her, Wally! Blow like you're putting out a candle."

Quick as a lick, Bitsy's back and throws the blue and white quilt from the birthing bed down on the ground. She's also brought two towels, sterile gloves and the red rubber aspirator, just in case we need it.

"Ahhhhhgh!" Victoria grunts again. I can feel the head crowning, but I dare not take my hands away to put on my gloves.

"Blow! Blow! Get her to blow, Wally. You don't need to push anymore, Victoria. I don't want you to tear. Just ease the baby out." Bitsy kneels down on the blanket, her hands out with the towel across them, waiting for the newborn.

And then it comes. Head first. Shoulders rotate. And suddenly, with a triumphant scream loud enough to wake people on the other side of Hope River, Victoria delivers her baby into Bitsy's waiting hands.

"*Cock a doodle doo!*" cries a rooster.

The kitchen door slams and Daniel runs out. "Everything OK?" he yells across the yard.

"*Yes!*" says the sun, and the sky and the mountain.

July 23, 1956.

Seven pound, 3 ounce, Male infant born to Wally and Victoria Richards of Torrington. They are my first patients to use The Childbirth Without Fear method of natural childbirth. Apparently, this is a women's movement in England, but Bitsy and I have never heard of it. Victoria had quite a long labor, over twenty hours, but it was only just before second stage that she lost her confidence. Bitsy spoke firmly to her, however, and told her she could do it and she did. A few minutes later as we were making our way to the house to run a tub of hot water, she said she had to push. There was no time to return to the Baby Cabin. She had her baby outside, just as the sun rose over the mountain. No tears. Placenta delivered without difficulty and a very small amount of blood. Victoria put the baby to the breast right away. The father was in tears and I will admit it, I cried a little myself.

27

August 1, 1956
War

Just as I'm beginning a letter to the Editor of the *Liberty Times,* the phone interrupts me.

"Hello…" I answer, my mind still on what I want to say about the importance of equal opportunity in America.

"Mrs. Hester?" a male voice rumbles.

"Yes, this is Patience Hester."

"This is Dr. Herbert Andrews, Chief of Staff at the new hospital in Liberty. Judge Linkous, a member of the hospital board, gave me your name. He thought you might be interested in helping organize the bomb shelter at the hospital and assist with the drills. The aim of the exercises will be to determine how well our community is prepared for nuclear war."

This takes me aback. "I've heard of these Civil Defense Committees, but is it really possible to survive a nuclear attack or are you giving people in Union County false hope?"

"Not false. Real hope! If we prepare, the Federal government estimates we can save half of the population, probably more in West Virginia because we're 200 miles away from a primary target."

"Well, you realize I'm not a nurse or a medical

professional..."

"But you're a specialist in women and infant's health. We'd really appreciate it if you would at least come to the first meeting." In the end, I reluctantly agree, but the piss and vinegar has gone out of me and I decide to write my opinion letter later.

Outside, when I come back from the hen house with a basket of eggs, I spy the Blue Jays flying back and forth in the pines. "Jay! Jay!" they cry in recognition.

"So, Howard," I address my friend as I sit on the bench to watch them. "What do you think? Is it possible to survive an atomic war? I've seen the newsreels at the movie house. Hiroshima was turned into a pile of ashes in only a few seconds. An estimated 130,000 people died in minutes and in the next few years thousands more died of cancer.

"Still, I could go to the meeting," I continue talking out loud. "The physician has a point. We in West Virginia live so far away from large metropolitan areas we'd never be directly bombed. It's the radiation that would get us."

Just then a Red-tailed Hawk circles over the farmyard. The chickens see its shadow and run for the henhouse. "Keeeeeeee-ar!" "Keeeeeeeee-ar!" Howard cries, imitating the familiar scream of the hawk and warning all other birds and small animals to take shelter. Instantly, there's not a Robin or Wren in sight.

"Keee-ar!" the half grown Blue Jays cry and fly toward the hawk, fighter pilots guarding their homeland. They swirl around the hawk as he swoops downward, but Howard and Lulu have joined the battle and they force him up. Howard goes so far as to actually make contact, diving at the enemy's head, and the hawk swerves again. As the battle continues they move down the valley and away from our farm.

"Keeeeeeee-ar!" "Keeeeeeeee-ar!"

All birds and animals protect their territory. It's as natural as birth and death. Human warfare is more lethal. *Is it possible to survive an atomic war?* I wonder again.

Daniel would say, "Only by waging peace."

Western Pennsylvania.
Early December 1859

After ten days of discouraging confinement in Mr. A.'s attic, the three of us got a stroke of good luck. A Quaker merchant, Mr. B., carrying a load of barrel staves, would be passing nearby, going north. The staves were to be transported on the canal that ran from New Castle to Lake Erie, and he thought he could make room for us under the lumber.

"Many of the workers on the canals are free blacks," Mr. A. told us. "And they can look after you. Sometimes the barges can travel as fast as ten miles an hour. You'll leave after dark tomorrow. We have to hurry you along because the lake will soon freeze."

That night we were allowed downstairs for a send-off supper, chicken, roasted potatoes, corn bread and home canned peaches. Junior was there, along with both his parents and several other abolitionists. One of the ladies, a plump-cheeked Mennonite woman, brought us warm hats and scarves knitted by the ladies of their church; a nice thought since we are heading into the northland.

Just as we bowed our heads over what looked like the best meal since I'd left the Coffmans, we heard horses come up the lane and Mrs. A. shooed us back into the attic. Downstairs, we heard voices.

"You're welcome to search the whole house, Marshal," the head of the family said loudly. "I know some of the other faiths have secreted runaways, but that's something we Mennonites don't do. We follow God's law, but we also follow the laws of the land."

"I appreciate that," the Marshal said, "But there are rumors to the contrary, so we're obliged to search the whole house...." There was stomping, the sound of furniture moved about, and finally the scuff of boots a few feet on the other side of the thin wall of the attic. I squeezed my eyes shut, hoping I'd become invisible.

"Nothing," said Marshal Layton. "I've checked every room...Let's move on."

I slept that night, but poorly. Before dawn the panel slid open again and Mr. A. knelt in the opening. "We have to go," he whispered. "Word is that another group of patrollers is passing through the county. Come quickly and don't make a sound."

We hastily gathered our belongings and the first thing I heard when we slipped out the door was the far away baying of hounds, not a good sign. Without light, we moved across the yard and around the barn, following our conductor. A fog had come in and we ran, crouching low, through the open fields until we came to a forest.

Here the land began to slope and I could hear water. It must be Little Creek, I thought, the brook Mr. A. had mentioned. Our guide reached out his rough hand, then silently signaled Elsie and Peter to form a human chain and he stepped into the rushing cold water.

What was he up to? In the distance I heard the hounds again and I understood. Jammy had told me of runaways wading through the swamp to hide their scent from the slave dogs. Now we were doing it...step by step, slipping over the rocks on the bottom. In one place I lost my footing and went down on my knees. All this way, all the hardships we'd endured, all the fear and then to be caught only a few days from freedom! It was unthinkable.

Ahead in the darkness, the water got louder and then I felt spray. Suddenly, Mr. A. pulled me to the side and we slipped into a hidden space under a waterfall. It was a room of about ten by ten carved into the sandstone. Peter and Elsie came in right behind us.

"You'll be safe from the hounds and patrollers here," he whispered, dropping my satchel on the sandy floor. "I'm sorry you can't have a fire," He indicated a pit that showed previous ashes. "It could be seen or smelled. Do you have a set of dry clothes?"

"Mrs. A. gave us each an extra set," I answered

in a whisper.

Before he left, our conductor explained that there was a mass exodus of escaped slaves heading to Canada through Pennsylvania just now. Hundreds a day were crossing the border. Free blacks were leaving the U.S. too, because slave-catchers were kidnapping them, claiming they were runaways and returning them to the South for sale at auctions.

"Just remember, no talking. Because of the water, the dogs probably won't be able to follow your scent, but they have keen ears. Don't even whisper."

Our Conductor pulled a crushed half loaf of bread out of his coat pocket. "This is all I could grab as we ran through the kitchen. I'm sorry. Now I have to get back."

"Will you come for us tonight when the man with the wagon shows up?" Peter asked.

The conductor took off his hat and stood listening to the baying of the dogs in the distance. "If it's safe."

After Mr. A. left us in our watery hideout, Elsie and I collapsed on the sandy floor and silently began to get out dry clothes. All I needed was pants, socks and long underwear; my top was still dry. Peter indicated with his hands that Elsie and I should change first while he turned his back. Then I hid my eyes while he changed and we laid our wet clothing on the rocks. All our communication was with signals.

After that, there was nothing to do, but roll up in our quilts and try to go back to sleep. Elsie made a bed for us, with her in the middle, so we could keep warm and I lay on my side looking into the dark.

"Wake up Peter!" Elsie whispered.
"Something's happening."
"What?" He rolled over to face her pulling the quilt off my shoulder.
"My belly."
"You mean you're hungry?"
"No, not that. Something else....Go back to sleep."
Peter rolled back over and began to snore softly, but I got up to get a drink of water with the tin cup Jammy had packed for me and left it on a flat rock near the pool where others could find it.
Elsie started to groan again and I got out my pocket watch. There seemed to be a rhythm to her pains.
"Is it getting light yet?" she whispered sitting up. It had been hours since we'd heard the dogs, so I whispered too.
"You've been sleeping. I don't know what time it is. Is anything wrong?"
She looked down at her bulging abdomen. "The baby's just kicking, but I really need to go to the bathroom. Do you think it's safe to go out in the woods?"
"Just go in the back of the cave. After you relieve yourself we'll cover it with sand. I won't look." I turned my face and closed my eyes, but they opened wide when I heard the pop.
"Oh!" Elsie squeaked and it wasn't a whisper. "What's happening? Oh, no! It's the pain again.

What should I do? Grace, help me!"

28

August 6, 1956
Troubled Times

This afternoon, I went into Liberty for the civil defense meeting at the new hospital. The sub-basement fallout shelter was marked on the door with the now familiar symbol, three yellow triangles in a black circle.

When I entered the windowless room, I had to blink a few times before I could see. All along the walls of the cavernous space, boxes of food were stored next to stacks of narrow mattresses. There were carts with blankets and even some cribs.

As I sat in one of the metal folding chairs set up in the middle of the room, I noticed that all the participants except me were men. B.K. Bittman was there, sitting up front with Billy Blaze, the newspaperman. Reverend Goody of the Saved by Jesus Baptist Church sat behind them and the new pharmacist, Mr. Dixon, was on the aisle. At the last minute, Nurse Frost of Labor and Delivery hurried in and I was surprised when she took the chair next to mine.

Approaching the podium, a squared-off man, in a long white coat with white hair and a brushy white mustache, cleared his throat. "Greetings, citizens and staff. I'm Dr. Andrews of Liberty Memorial

Hospital and I want to welcome you to the first meeting of our Civil Defense Committee."

"Today, we're going to begin with a new film called *Surviving an Atomic Attack*. I think you'll find it informative. After the movie we'll break into committees to discuss our next steps....Ernie?" He nodded to a young fellow in a bow tie who stood next to a movie projector. The lights went off and the film began, on a portable screen, with the same ominous background music I'd heard in the newsreels during World War ll.

A woman stands in a back yard hanging diapers on a clothesline. She looks up, innocently, as a warplane crosses the sky. There's a flash of light, the sky turns black and a mushroom cloud fills the screen.

"Let us face reality," the narrator says in a voice that sounds like Edward R. Murrow. "These are perilous times."

Then the camera cuts to a film of Hiroshima; blasted buildings, a whole city obliterated and on fire. "The atomic bomb destroys in three ways," the Murrow imitator says. "Blast, heat and radioactivity." Across the screen, Japanese men, women and children are in flames running through rubble.

The narrator goes on to inform us how to construct a home bomb shelter, what we should do at the last minute and what to do if there's no warning at all; duck and cover, like Bert The Turtle. All the people in the government's movie are white, as if people who are brown or black would have no interest in survival.

Finally, the narrator closes the production with words of hope and the music changes to the *Stars and Stripes Forever.* "If the people of Hiroshima had only known what we know about civil defense today," he intones, "Many of them would have survived. So act now! Your life, and the lives of those you love, may depend upon it."

The lights flicker on and it's then I notice Sheriff Aran Bishop standing in back and he motions me over. Bishop, a big man with dark hair greased back and a little black mustache leans against the wall in his khaki uniform.

"I'd like to talk to you about an official inquiry, Mrs. Hester. Can you come to the office before you go home?" he asks.

The fuzz on the back of my neck stands up. *What can he want to talk to me about?* "Sure, but what's up?"

"I have some questions for you about the missing girl, Kitty."

"Your niece, you mean?" I say just to be ornery. "Ok, but I've only met her once and I have a few errands to do first."

Afterwards, I stop at Bittman's to sell my eggs and spend about an hour gossiping with Lillie. Then I pick up some chicken feed at the Farmer's Co-op and finally, dragging my feet, I make it to the courthouse by five.

It's been a long time since I've been here, not since old Sheriff Hardman died and I still remember standing behind his desk staring at the wanted posters, half expecting to see my own face.

I knock timidly on the door's frosted window. **Liberty Police** is etched into the glass, something new since I was last here.

"Enter!" a low voice barks. It's Aran Bishop and he sits at the same beat-up old oak desk where Hardman sat, reading a worn issue of *Spicy Detective* with an illustration of a half-naked woman on the cover being stabbed to death by a depraved looking man. Bishop's Stetson hangs on a hook, along with his gun and a holster. "Took you long enough to get here!" he growls.

"I had my errands," I defend myself, looking around. Other than his desk and a rolling chair, there are just two file cabinets and a wooden bench against the wall. An iron door with no window hides the jail cells. "What is it that you need to talk about?"

He closes his pulp magazine and nods toward the bench, so I sit. "We continue to seek information about the missing girl and are interviewing everyone who might shed some light on her disappearance. The hospital records say you did the delivery. I want you to tell me what you talked about?"

Here, I frown. "The girl *Kitty* is your niece, isn't she? And you brought her to the hospital and dropped her off in advanced labor, so you must know there was no time for conversation. Kitty was screaming when we got there, completely out of control because she was so afraid. Bitsy Cross got her calmed down and the baby came a few minutes later. After we cleaned her up and showed her how to breastfeed, I talked to her for a minute about eating nutritiously and getting plenty of fluids. I also told her she would bleed for a few weeks, maybe longer, but if the bleeding was heavy she should come back to the hospital."

"She didn't say anything about a boyfriend or the baby's father?"

"No."

"You didn't ask?"

"I didn't think it was relevant."

"What about friends? Did she mention any friends?"

"No. It was a purely clinical encounter."

"And later, did she come to your office or call you?"

"I don't really have an office and no, she never called me. I never had any personal contact with her again. Maybe she went back to her parents."

"No. Her old man washed his hands of her when she got pregnant. That's how she ended up with us. After the delivery, she was a mess. Didn't eat. Wouldn't shower, just laid around in her bed with that squalling infant and she'd start crying if you even spoke to her. That's why we thought she might have come to you, because of the baby."

"I told you. I only saw her one time. That was at the hospital." The Sheriff picks up a pencil and taps it on the desk, squinting at me as if I'm a witness who's hiding something. "Is that all?" I finally ask, wanting to get out of the room as soon as I can.

He jerks his head toward the door and barks a short grunt, dismissing me. Just a short grunt.

Hound Dog

The last two weeks have passed in shadow, and the ghost of Kitty Bishop still haunts me. Ever since Sheriff Bishop questioned me in the police station, I've worried again that not making a home visit was a cowardly mistake. Was the girl so despondent she killed herself? Was she bleeding too much and walked into the woods and hemorrhaged? Or did she just get on a bus and leave for parts unknown?

Bitsy doesn't carry the guilt like I do and is more philosophical. "Midwives aren't saints," she says. "We're just women trying to help other women. We have lives. We have families. We have our own troubles. We do what we can."

I close my journal and stare at the sunflowers that grow along the rail fence by the creek. How can they still be so beautiful, when I feel so bleak? Just then I hear a truck motoring down Salt Lick. It's the kind used to transport livestock and it pulls across our wooden bridge.

Speak of the devil! Lou Cross pops out from the vehicle's driver's seat and Bitsy gets down on the other side. Between the wooden slats a brown horse watches me with calm eyes.

"Howdy Ho!" Lou shouts. "I just talked to Dan at the Mountain Top Diner and he said I'd be welcome to board Willie's new horse in your barn. Can you show us where to put him? Bitsy can stay for a visit, but I have to get back to the woolen mill." He pulls a ramp from the back of the truck and leads the horse down.

"One second," I call, wondering what the idea is. The gelding is a beautiful animal, chestnut brown with a white tail, maybe something like Grace Potts' horse, Noble, and I show them the first stall in the barn.

Later in the kitchen, over tea, I ask, Bitsy. "So what's the story? Can Willie really ride a horse in his condition? Does he even want to?"

Bitsy tips her head to the side. "We're hoping it will get him out more. Even though he's living with Danny, he just lies on the sofa in front of the tube…What's with Mira, anyway? I saw her sitting outside under the weeping willow tree and waved, but she didn't wave back. That's not like her."

"She's pretty down. She's been home for three days."

"Because of her beau? The racist she broke up with? Good riddance, I'd say."

"Yeah. I guess that's it. She took a leave from Woolworths with an excuse that she's sick. I've tried to talk to her, to ask how she is and all she says is 'fine.' "

"Do you think it would help if I talked to her? Or maybe if we went out together?"

A few minutes later, Bitsy and I stroll across the wide lawn. She carries a tray with three cups of tea and I have a plate of peanut butter cookies. "Whatcha doing?" she calls to Mira.

"Nothing." Mira answers, staring down.

"You look kind of hound-dog," Bitsy teases.

Mira shrugs.

"You ain't nothin' but a hound dog - Crying all the time." Bitsy begins an Elvis impression, complete with the gyrating pelvis. *"You ain't nothing but a hound dog - Crying all the time..."* Finally, Mira gives us a half smile.

"I'm going to keep singing until you start talking," Bitsy warns.

"You aren't as good as Elvis, or as cute either," Mira murmurs.

"She speaks! So what's going on?" Bitsy chuckles.

My youngest daughter lets out a long sigh. "I might as well tell you..." Then she drops the bomb. "I'm pregnant."

Secrets

My timing wasn't the greatest, but I was so distraught I had to speak. Mira had gone on a horseback ride up the mountain and when Dan came home and tossed a copy of the newspaper on the table, I blurted it out.

"Mira's pregnant!"

My words hadn't registered. "Dan? Did you hear me? Mira's pregnant."

"What the hell?"

"She just told me and Bitsy this afternoon. That's why she's been so withdrawn."

"When did this happen?"

"About four months ago."

"She's been sleeping around all this time?"

"Not sleeping *around.* Just sleeping with her

boyfriend. *Ex-boyfriend,* Ron Gibson. Sit down. I'll make you a cup of chamomile tea."

For the next half hour, I explain how Mira came to me and asked about getting a douche bag for extra birth control protection.

"That's when she told me that *they were doing it*, but she made me swear to keep it hush-hush. It was so hard, Dan. I hated not being able to tell you. We never keep secrets."

My husband works his tense jaw. "Well, bloody hell!" he explodes. "What's she going to do?"

"Daniel, don't swear so much."

"Why? Are you afraid the little tramp will hear me?"

"She's not a tramp. And don't say anything about it yet, will you?"

"Why not! It's about time one of us started acting like a parent."

"Dan! I was trying to help her!"

He balls up the newspaper and stomps out the door.

Dinner that night was meat loaf, boiled potatoes, and Swiss chard from the garden. No one said a word, not even *pass the salt and pepper.* Finally, Dan pushed his chair back and let out his air. "So what are you going to do?" he asked Mira. "Do you want me to take my shot gun and insist Ron Gibson make an honest woman out of you?"

Mira looked at me, her eyes narrowed to slits. "Mom! You told."

"Yes, and I should have said something months

ago, but your Dad asked you a question. If you're four months gone, you'll be showing soon. Do you want us to ask around about a private adoption and a maternity home so you can get out of town? I could ask Ida May at the House of Beauty."

"Slow down, Patience," Dan growls. "Give Mira a chance to answer us. You're making assumptions. Maybe, she wants to marry the S.O.B. Or maybe it's not too late to find someone to...you know..." He stops mid-sentence.

"No!" Mira yells, jumping up from the table and knocking her chair over so that it clatters across the yellow linoleum. "No! I won't! Never! It's my *baby*," and she runs out the door.

29

Hidden Cavern, Western Pennsylvania
Sometime in December, 1859

The mother-to-be moaned again and began to swing her head back and forth. I had feared all along that my traveling companion would go into labor before we reached Canada and now it was happening.

"Peter," I whispered. "Peter, it's time."

"What?" He sat up, rubbing his eyes and looked at his wife. "Really? Oh, Lord help us! Here in a cave? What shall I do?"

I sent the worried man to get help, hoping we would be allowed to return to the Mr. A.'s attic, but until he came back we were on our own.

"We have to risk lighting a candle, Elsie. I need to look through my things and find a little birthing kit that I brought with me. Have you ever seen a baby born? Do you know what to expect?"

"Only what some of the other slaves told me. You have a pain and you walk, have a pain and walk, push for a long time and then it comes out your briar patch."

"Briar patch?"

"That's what they called it." She pointed to her nether regions.

"So, you have the basic idea. The pains get closer and stronger and then eventually you'll feel

*like you have to use the privy, but it's not that. It's
a baby's head." Elsie thought this was funny and it
was nice to hear her laugh.*

*Taking a chance, I fixed a candle in the back of
the cave and searched through my satchel to find
my birth kit, a simple affair that Dr. Coffman had
given me before things went bad. For a few hours,
Elsie was calm, but then she got restless. "Where's
Peter," she said. "I want Peter....This is terrible!
Oh! Oh! Oh!"*

*"It's ok, Elsie. You're doing wonderfully. I've
never seen a woman endure her travail more
bravely.*

"I can't do this, Grace. I can't do this!"

*"Shhhhh! Elsie. There may still be patrollers out
in the woods."*

*"I have to get up. I have to walk. I have to get
out of here."*

*"But, Elsie, there's nowhere to go and you'll get
soaked if you try to walk through the waterfall.
Here, get on your hands and knees and rock back
and forth. I'll rub your back."*

*"Oh. Oh. Oh!" Though she tried to hold it in,
her voice rose higher and higher and then suddenly
the pitch of her cries dropped an octave. She was
beginning the birth song.*

*I knew with a first baby Elsie might have to push
for several hours, but just in case, I began
preparing. If Mary could give birth to Jesus in a
manger, I guessed Elsie could have her baby in a
cave. I laid a few items on the top of my satchel and
washed my hands with soap in the waterfall.*

"Do you want a sip of water?" I asked Elsie.

No answer.

"Elsie?" I turned. The girl's eyes were closed and she was on her back, holding her woman parts open and the head was right there.

Within minutes, I held a small brown baby in my hands, wailing and shaking his fists. Quickly, I handed him to his Mama, completely forgetting to hold him upside down or to give him a spank as Dr. Coffman did. Then I covered them both with another blanket.

While I waited for the afterbirth, I recalled that the third stage of childbirth was the most dangerous for mothers. The doctor had informed me that the death rate for slave mothers was 1 in 5 from flooding, but I needn't have worried. Within a quarter of an hour, a blue-purple organ plopped out on the pad. I held the blades of my scissors in the candle flame to sterilize them, and then cut and tied the cord.

When I looked up at Elsie and the infant, I swear this is true; a white light surrounded them.

Waterfall
Northern Pennsylvania

"Holy Cow!" a deep voice said. "The little one has already arrived." It was Peter and our stationmaster, peeking into the cavern.

"We must make haste," Mr. A. whispered. "It's fortunate the delivery is accomplished. There isn't much time. Can she walk if someone supports her? We have to travel about a quarter mile upstream to

the bridge where your next conductor is waiting."

Peter quickly greeted his new son and then helped me pack up. It was rough going, I will tell you, and I felt it was wrong to ask Elsie to move, but what choice did we have? Several times I slipped and got wet, but Elsie and I held on to each other, while Peter carried the baby and Mr. A. transported our belongings.

When we got to the wagon, Elsie, Peter and the baby who they called Moses, were quickly secreted in their hiding place on quilts between the barrel staves, but because I was dressed as a white boy, our new conductor, Mr. B., a Quaker like Mother, said it would be ok for me to ride on the buck seat with him.

"You make a handsome lad," the driver spoke for the first time. "But I was told you are a young lady, a midwife in fact. Kind of young for that responsibility, aren't you?"

"When I was enslaved, I was trained by my master, a physician, to help with his patients," I explained. It was true; I just left out the part that my master was my father, and a scoundrel.

The journey to New Castle took most of the night, and as we traveled along the back roads we met not a soul. Our conductor explained that his barrel staves would be shipped east on a canal boat to the apple orchards of upper New York State. He understood that the captain of the barge was an abolitionist.

"We won't go to the dock yet. First I'm taking you to the home of a local millenary merchant in New Castle."

I soon learned the new stationmaster was a widow, Mrs. G., a seamstress, who employed seven other women in her home to assist with the making of bonnets. Just as the sun rose over the rolling hills, we pulled up to the rear of a handsome brick house and were quickly escorted inside and up the stairs to a bedroom in back.

This time there was no secret panel and with so many women in the house I felt exposed, but Mrs. G., the buxom silver-haired agent, explained that all her workers were fervent abolitionists. One by one, each seamstress took the time to come upstairs to welcome us and to see the baby. Several brought scraps of flowered cloth and said we could use them for diapers.

At Mrs. G.'s home, Elsie sponged off and I had a real bath. The gentle ladies also brought us clean clothes and took all our dirty garments and washed and even ironed them.

While I was bathing, there came a sharp rap on the downstairs front door. "Can I speak to the mistress of the house," asked a voice like gravel running under carriage wheels.

"Yes?" the good lady answered. "Can I help you, Constable?"

"I just wanted to inquire if there was anything I could do for you ladies today. When I saw the lumberman's wagon in the drive it occurred to me that you might need more provisions with a few extra mouths to feed."

"Well, that's nice of you. We are low on cheese if you wouldn't mind bringing some from the

market."

Why is she being so friendly? I thought. She should try to get rid of him! Or was this all some kind of code?

"I'll bring some this afternoon and since I'm on duty tonight, I thought I'd station myself at the end of your drive, in case you have unwanted company."

Now I grasped the situation! The constable was an anti-slavery man. Mr. B. had told me that New Castle was a hot bed of abolitionists. The lawman was even going to guard the house from Marshals and bounty hunters. That night, I slept well.

30

Faith

"If you knew how hard it was to have grown children, would you have had babies?" I ask my husband as we sit on the banks of the Hope River. Below us the water circles in pools, further out are rocks and white water.

"Yeah, probably." Dan takes my hand. "You know when you're younger you don't think much about it. Anyway, I can't imagine life without Mira and Danny, Sunny and Sue."

"Susie and Sunny are doing ok...as much as we know anyway. I'm unsure what to do about Mira." Here I swallow hard over a lump of tears as hard as black gold.

"I blame myself, Dan. I should have talked to the girls more about intimate relationships. I should have tried harder to find her a doctor who'd give her a diaphragm; but I'll tell you the truth, I didn't because I was so shocked she was even having intercourse."

"You mean *S. E .X.*" He grins as he spells the word out. "I still thought of Mira as my little girl. At some point she's going to have to decide what to do."

"I think she just wants to stay home and have her baby out of wedlock and never tell anyone."

"Well, that's not going to work," Dan says. "Word will get out. For one thing, Lou's bringing Willie out to ride his horse soon." He tosses a stone in the river.

"Are you going to be here? I may have to go to town for a Civil Defense meeting. I kind of wish I'd never signed up. The atom bomb seems a long way from West Virginia. Our own family problems are blowing up in my face."

"I'll be gone; the Dresher's Dalmatian is due any day. They'll insist I be there for the whole thing and they're good clients. Remember when you helped me deliver their Corgi so long ago. It was one of our first dates." Here he laughs.

"I thought our first date was when we delivered that foal together and it fell in my lap and got me all bloody. Come on! Last one in is a rotten egg." We dive and the water's so cold I let out a scream.

When I catch up with Dan, I wind my legs around his body, holding tight to his neck. "So, Danny and Mira, they're going to be all right?" I ask for the tenth time as if by his reassurance he could make it so.

"Yeah."

"How do you know?" I look into his grey eyes.

"Think about it. Life is full of hard times. We are up one day. The next day we're down, but we're still alive... all of us." He throws water up with two hands and we watch as it picks up the light and falls like diamonds. "Still alive in this beautiful world."

New Castle, Pennsylvania
November 28-30, 1859
(I finally saw a newspaper today with the date.)

"Grace! Wake up! Time to go." Three days after we arrived at the hat maker's home, Peter stood at our bedroom door. "Mr. B. is outside and he wants to get us on the barge by 5 A.M."

Once again we three, (four now, counting Baby Moses) were loaded in the wagon and transported like freight through the slumbering town. The streets were empty and since I was allowed to sit up front, I could admire the prosperous homes and shops. Our short journey ended at a wharf on the side of the canal where men with carts, carrying all kinds of goods, were already in line.

While Mr. B. went into the lockkeeper's office to pay the fare for the barrel staves, I had a chance to observe the boat we'd travel on. It was a strange affair, shallow, about sixty feet long, but only 12 feet wide with a small house for the crew on top.

When our conductor came back, he was with a black man he introduced only as "Mr. J". Peter, Elsie, and the baby were pulled from their hideout and the new conductor explained that he was the driver of the mules that would pull the boat along the canal.

"There are two teams of mules," the man explained. "And a small stable. That's where you'll hide. The teams of mules must be rotated every 6 hours day and night, so I'll check on you then. The other free black men on the crew, a cook and a helmsman will also protect you. The captain is

white, but he hates slavery and will do anything he can to oppose it."

"So far," the boatman remarked, "There are no other passengers and I don't expect any. People who can afford it take the packet barges that have dining rooms and berths for sleeping."

We said our grateful goodbyes to Mr. B, and then the boatman took us quickly onboard and into the stable. The first two stalls held the mules and the one in the back, a tack room, had clean straw on the floor and five boxes for chairs. It was dark and smelly, but the heat from the mules would keep us all warm.

The first thing I did was spread my quilt over the straw, then Peter got out some bread, cheese and cider that the hat ladies had given us and we had breakfast. Finally, we heard a horn. Someone yelled to the mules, "Giddup!" and with a sharp jerk we were off.

The journey was not as peaceful as I had anticipated. There was an incessant clanging as we passed through each lock, twenty-five of them, if I counted correctly. As we moved north toward the town of Erie, we could tell by the noise that we were passing other line boats going south. Each time there was wrangling and sometimes foul language as we negotiated the narrow canal.

Once in the late afternoon there was even a collision and the swearwords between the two boat captains were enough to blister a grown man's ears. Another time our whole barge ran aground on a mud flat and Mr. J. had to borrow an extra set of mules from another boat to pull us out.

At night, we were allowed up for air and the boatmen would sing, their deep voices floating out into the starry black. "Wade in the water- Wade in the water children – Wade in the water- God's a gonna trouble the water." Peter sang with them.

"It's Meadville," Mr. J. told us when he brought us bread, apples and fresh water for breakfast the next morning.

"Later today you'll be in Erie City where you'll be taken to a safe house on the Underground Railroad. You may have to wait a few days to get passage to Canada, but you're almost there."

"How will they move us through the town?" Peter asked, concerned about the safety of his wife and baby.

"I don't know," the boatman said. "Usually, there's some conveyance waiting at the dock. Don't make a noise until I come for you. If you hear the horn blow five times, cover yourselves with hay."

"I don't like the sound of that," I said, after he left. "How will we protect the baby? If he cries we'll be in serious danger. If the horn blows, Elsie, you will have to put him to breast."

Within an hour we heard the clunk of the boat as it pulled up to the dock, but all was not well. As the men began to unload the barrel staves and produce, a stern voice rang out.

"Permission to board, Captain! United States Marshal."

Hope

Despite Dan's words of encouragement, I continue to lose sleep over Mira. She stays in her room, quiet as a mouse and I have no idea what's she's thinking. When she comes out she doesn't speak to me, except to say yes or no, but I'm almost as bad. I've retreated to *my room* too, just to avoid her.

I once thought of midwives as warriors...but here I am hiding in the trenches. What's wrong with me? I'm heartsick about her pregnancy, that's what, worried about her future and what everyone in town will think. Am I so delicate that I can't take public disapproval? Or is it my own shame that crushes me? *What kind of mother lets this happen? Nice girls don't get knocked up.*

When I stop fretting about Mira, I shift to Danny, but with him I'm not so much anxious as mad. Where the hell is he anyway? Since the demonstration, we haven't seen him. I thought people had sons to help on the farm, to protect their sisters, and to assist their mother and father in old age. Apparently, Danny doesn't see it that way.

My husband and I are conscientious people, devoted to our family and good citizens, but we never sat down with the kids and spelled it out...*"Here's the way to live. Here's how to be a good person, a responsible adult."* We thought they'd learn by example.

As I coil my worries tighter around my troubled heart, a vehicle crosses the wooden bridge. *What now? If it's someone in labor, I'm not in the mood.*

This thought makes me smile. Whether I'm tired, anxious or angry, the sight of a pregnant woman waddling toward the Baby Cabin is enough to *change* my whole frame of mind, but when I go to my bedroom window there's no pregnant woman.

Lou and Willie rattle across the bridge in Lou's green two-toned Hudson. They pull up to the barn and get out. Willie waits by the car while his father saddles his horse and leads him out.

"Mom," Mira yells from the other room. "Mr. Cross and Willie are out by the barn and Willie's walking on his new leg."

"I know."

"Aren't you going to go down and say Hi?"

"No, I'm busy. You go," I grumble. There's no answer. Then I hear footsteps padding down the stairs. She must be curious. Come to think of it, I'm curious too. *How will the young man get up on the horse? Does his artificial leg bend? Can he get his foot in the stirrup?*

Mira greets the men, acting halfway normal. She watches Willie shuffle his way across the grass using two canes. I can't see his face, but I imagine he's embarrassed and doesn't like a young woman observing his weakness.

"Way to go, Willie!" I hear her say. It's the first time in days that I've witnessed her old spark, and I crack the window to hear the rest.

"Step lively now, soldier," Lou orders with humor. At the White Rock Civilian Conservation

Camp, Lou Cross was a favorite instructor of horsemanship until it closed a few years ago.

"Don't let the old man rile you, Willie. Take your time," Mira counters. She's wearing one of Dan's plaid wool jackets so her expanding abdomen isn't noticeable.

"I just like to kid him," Lou laughs. "Willie can mount from that tree stump, but he'll need a way to get up there. Do you have some kind of wooden box in the barn, Mira?"

"Wait a minute. There's something I used when I was a kid and first started riding." She runs to the barn and returns dragging a set of wooden steps that Dan built for her when she was little.

"This is dumb," I hear Willie say, as he struggles up the steps and on to the stump then finally, with Mira's support, flips his good leg over the saddle.

What happens next almost moves me to tears. A look of wonder appears on Willie's face that I haven't seen since he was a boy. I watch as Mira, smiling, holds on to the bridle and walks him around the barnyard and I can't help it; I throw open the window and yell down, "Whoop-i-ki-yi-o!"

Willie looks up and for a minute I'm afraid I've embarrassed him, but he sings right back to me, *"Whoop-i-ki-yi-ay... Back in the saddle again!"*

31

December 1, 1859
City of Erie, Pennsylvania

Through some cunning actions from Mr. J., the lineman, and the captain, the U.S. Marshal was convinced he didn't need to investigate the stable, but we were afterward informed that we were so close to Canada there were slave catchers everywhere. Nevertheless, there was nothing to do but trust in the cleverness of our benefactors. About an hour after we docked, J. pushed his head through the stable door.

"Pssst! Pssst!" he said to get our attention. "Someone just pulled up with a produce cart and we're loading potatoes into it. He wants you to get in these sacks and we'll carry you to the wagon."

"But what about the baby?" I asked. "We can't put him in a sack, not even with his mother."

"Hell's bells! You're right. I didn't think about that."

"You can pass for white, Grace," Peter thought out-loud. "Why don't you put on one of Elsie's dresses and carry the baby out."

I didn't like the idea. It was broad daylight. We'd been told the streets of Erie were bustling with tradesmen, not to mention patrollers, but I couldn't think of a better idea. While Peter turned his back I squirmed out of my pantaloons, pulled a calico gown over my head and put on a bonnet. The baby was of dark complexion, but if I swaddled him in a blanket and held him up to my chest no one would notice.

Peter and Elsie were the first to be carried out in sacks and by the time the Captain came for me, my mouth was so dry I could hardly greet him.

"Your name is Mrs. Clark, of Dayton, Ohio, on your way to visit Mrs. Crowley, your aunt," he informed me. "The conductor in the wagon is Mr. Crowley. He will take you to his mother's house a little ways out of town. They are well known abolitionists and do not hide it. Good luck and God be with you."

I pulled Elsie's shawl around me to protect the baby from the cold and the Captain led me to a cart loaded with the sacks of potatoes. Somewhere in the pile were my traveling companions.

Soon we were on our way. My escort was a clean shaven white man, dressed in farmer's clothes with a fisherman's cap pulled low over his ears and I wished I had some sort of warm hat, myself, instead of just the calico bonnet.

"It will take us about thirty minutes to get to my mother's place along Four Mile Creek," he said in a low voice. In time, we came to a large stone home on top of a bluff. On one side was a carriage house; on the other a barn. We drove into the barn.

"This is my Mother's farm," the conductor said. "She lives alone with one servant since my father died. I live just up the road on an adjoining farm."

He helped me down and assisted Elsie and Peter out of their burlap bags, then took us inside. The

*lady of the house herself met us at the kitchen door
and ushered us into a parlor as nice as the
Coffman's parlor in Hintonville: striped green satin
furniture, Tiffany lamps, and blue velvet drapes
which were kept closed. "Sit down. Sit down!" she
said, treating us like we were royalty.*

*"The city is crawling with slave catchers," the
son informed her. "I need to work on getting them
passage to Canada on a fishing boat as soon as
possible." Then he turned to us. "This is the last
leg of your journey, but you won't be safe until you
cross the Canadian line out on the water and we are
always watched."*

December 4, 1859
Four-Mile Creek, Erie Pennsylvania
  *After a good dinner of ham and potatoes,
applesauce and creamed carrots, cooked by the
household servant, a free black woman from Ohio,
we were escorted down to the cellar. A panel in the
wainscoting of the dining room opened. It led to a
ladder that went to the basement where straw
mattresses and quilts were arranged. It wasn't the
best place we'd ever stayed, but it was far better
than the cave on the creek or the woodcutter's
shack in the forest.*

  *That night, baby Moses was fussy. Every few
hours, Elsie put him to the breast and he would stop
crying, but her nipples were soon sore. In the
morning the poor woman was exhausted, but the
cook brought her some cabbage leaves and told her
to put them under her chemise. When I asked how*

that would help, she didn't really know. It was just something she'd learned from another runaway who was also breastfeeding.

As before, people from the church had delivered extra garments to this railway station. I couldn't decide if I should take a dress or two. There were some that fit me, but I had grown used to my disguise as a boy. Finally, at Elsie's urging, I picked three gowns, a green one with a lace collar, a black one with tiny white stripes and a blue calico. I would have to find work in Canada and maybe the dresses would help me.

For breakfast the next morning, we were invited up to the dining room where a meal of poached eggs awaited us. When we heard a horse coming, Mrs. C. ran to the window and peeked out between the heavy drapes, but it was only her son.

"Criminy!" our conductor said when he came in all bundled up in a rubber mackinaw. "That was quite a snow last night."(Staying in the basement, we'd not even known there was a storm. Winter was closing in fast.)

"Yes," Mrs. C. said. "How long do you think 'til the waves settle down and the fishermen go out on the lake again?"

"Day or two. I'm going down to the docks today to see what I can find out." He turned to Peter. "If we can find a boat crossing Lake Erie, I'll have them wait at the mouth of Four Mile Creek. There's a tunnel from the basement to the stable and from there you can get down to the creek. I need to show you how to get into the tunnel if there's ever a

search of the house by Marshals."

The conductor advised us to keep our satchels packed so that if we needed to leave in a hurry we'd be ready. The signal he said would be three raps with a broom on the floor above us, three raps, a pause - then three raps again."

"Have any runaways ever had to escape through the tunnel in a hurry?" I couldn't help asking.

"Once or twice," he responded.

Shelter

"Life in a fallout shelter where everyone has adequate sanitary water and nutritious food supplied by the Federal Government can be surprisingly pleasant," the narrator of a new Civil Defense film began.

A middle aged white man is shown drinking water out of a plastic barrel with a hose. He walks around the room greeting adults and children, who are eating, smoking, or playing cards.

"There's enough sleeping room in this shelter for fifty people and basic medications too." He shows us a first aid station. Another man sweeps the walls with a Geiger counter, looking for radiation, I guess. Though what he would do if he found some, I have no idea.

I glance around the hospital basement, picturing it filled with 50 adults and children, babies crying, K-rations cooking on a gas stove and the heavy smell of sweat and fear. The soundtrack of the short film crescendos and the narrator closes with a reminder that the United States of America, our great county, can survive if we're prepared. Then the lights come on.

I'm surprised when Dr. Andrews cheerfully asks us to stand and sing *America the Beautiful*, a song that's supposed to make us feel proud of our country, but all I can think of are the photos in the paper last night of a crowd of whites cursing the bus boycotters in Birmingham.

As the meeting ends, I go up to the hospital administrator and ask the question I've wondered for weeks. "Doctor Andrews... It's obvious that there are thousands of people living around Liberty and there's not room for everyone here or even in the basements of churches in town. In the event of a nuclear attack, who decides who'll get in the shelter?"

The man clears his throat and looks around to see if anyone's listening. "Hospital workers and emergency personnel and their families will come first," he says in a low voice. "Then town officials and law enforcement and finally those on the Civil Defense committee. You don't need to say anything about this. We'd prefer that you not, but we'll soon be issuing Civil Defense Shelter admission cards. You and your family will be included, of course." With that he turns to the projectionist pretending he has a concern about the film, but I know he's just avoiding more questions.

As I prepare to leave, still stunned by his answer, Miss Frost stops me. "Mrs. Hester," she whispers. "Would you like to join me for a cup of coffee in the cafeteria?" This takes me aback. *What now?*

"I have a few minutes," I answer, "But I'll have to leave by four to feed the chickens." As soon as I say it, I'm embarrassed. Nurse Frost, I'm sure, has no interest in chickens.

The hospital canteen is on the second floor and she leads me to the main elevator. I have never liked elevators and I usually take the stairs. Such electric contraptions seem dangerous to me, but Miss Frost must be used to it, because without even blinking she presses the button that points UP and away we go.

"Good morning, Miss Frost," one of the cooks says as we enter the mostly empty cafeteria. "What can I do for you?"

"We're just getting coffee," the nurse responds. "Although those donuts look good." The cook pours coffee into two heavy white porcelain mugs and then with a grin she gives us two donuts.

All this time, I'm wondering what Miss Frost has to say for herself. Does she have some new ideas for the Fallout Shelter? Is there a turf war going on between her and Dr. Andrews that she wants to explain? Could there be some hospital gossip I need to know about? Finally, we find a table in the corner.

"Cream or sugar?" she asks, pointing to my cup and pushing the plate of donuts toward me.

"Just cream."

"How many chickens do you have?" she asks.

"About fifty. I sell their eggs at Bittman's Grocery."

"Wow. We only have four hens, but that's

316

plenty for a small family. It's just me and my husband."

"I didn't know you were married. I've always thought you were *Miss* Frost."

"Almost everyone calls me Miss. I'm used to it. At first, I corrected people, but now I just let it go…There's something I want to talk to you about." *Here it comes*, I think.

"Our family is growing," she whispers. She puts her hand on her abdomen and when I glance over the table, I notice a sizeable bulge under her white nurse's apron.

"I didn't know. Is it a secret?" My eyes scan the room and take in a table where other nurses on break, in white uniforms with white caps, sit smoking and laughing.

"No. It's common knowledge, but here's the hitch. I don't want to have my baby in the hospital."

"But you *work* here. You're the head nurse of the maternity ward."

Mrs. Frost bites her lower lip and waits a moment before speaking. "Patience, I'll tell you the truth. I cringe at every delivery I go to. I cringe when I have to admit a patient, stick her in bed and shave her pubic area."

"You do that? I didn't know."

"Yes, and I then have to give the woman a hot soapy enema, start an IV and administer a dose of Twilight Sleep."

"I've heard of Twilight Sleep. A patient once told me she was sedated with it during her labor, but not enough to dull the pain. She said she screamed and cried, but no one helped her. I thought maybe she was hallucinating."

"It's true. The women go completely bonkers with pain and fear. They scream and thrash around. They try to get out of bed. They're like wild animals. You can't comfort them, because they can't hear you and can't understand. We have to strap them to the bed which has high sides like a cage, but no one from their family even knows, because they aren't allowed in the Labor Ward."

"Don't the patients protest?"

"Twilight Sleep is an amnesiac. It prevents recent memories. The mother just wakes up in a daze and in a few hours she's given her baby, *that is… if the baby's ok*. Some infants are so sedated from the medicine that we have to work on them to get them to breathe and watch them closely for twenty-four hours."

"So why are you telling me all this?"

"Because I want you to help me have my baby, but I don't want anyone to know. Dr. Andrews is my doctor, and if he found out, I'd be fired."

"But if you hate your job anyway…."

"Not all of it. My plan is to get transferred out of labor and delivery as soon as I can. When I come back after having the baby, *if I don't get canned*, I'm going to ask to work in the Emergency Department….Here, if you have time, I want to show you something." She reaches into her pocket and pulls out a small paperback, as if it's a state secret. "Have you ever seen this?" she whispers, glancing around to be sure no one's looking.

I take the small volume and am surprised, for the

second time in recent months, to see a familiar title, *Childbirth Without Fear.*

"Yes. It's recently come to my attention."

"Will you help me?" she asks, almost begging, tears in her eyes.

I silently nod yes and press my hand over hers. How can I say no? I'm a midwife.

Four-Mile Creek, Pennsylvania
December 10, 1859

The days we were confined in Mrs. C's basement were some of the worst of our journey. We were so close to Canada, and yet still stuck in the dark. I was so tired of the dark!

All during our journey North, we had scurried from damp basements, gloomy secret rooms and caves into hidden compartments in wagons, under hay or between barrels of beer.

Finally, early one morning, while everyone slept, I wrapped a cloak around me and crawled through the tunnel into the stable Mr. C. had mentioned.

From the open barn doors, I gazed on a meadow of uncut hay, golden in the rising sun. I couldn't help my self. I had to feel that light on my face.

Wading into the tall grass, I raised my hands in salute. "Freedom!" I whispered and a flock of large Mourning Doves shot out of the loft. "Freedom!" I whispered once more. Then I scurried like a mole back through the tunnel and into my bed.

We were in the basement for another three days when finally our young conductor brought us good news. "I've arranged passage with a fisherman who's returning to Canada across the lake tomorrow. It's a journey of some 30 miles across the water, but you should be in the Promised Land by evening."

Mrs. C. and her kind cook asked us up to the dining room that night for a goodbye feast. All our clothes had been washed and even ironed again. The good mistress had also gathered a whole layette for the baby, which brought tears to Elsie's eyes.

The only thing that dampened the party was the headlines of an old copy of The Erie Weekly Observer, lying on the side table in the parlor, **Captain John Brown, Abolitionist, Hung for Treason**.

"Abolitionist John Brown rode from the jail to the gallows on top of his own coffin," the first paragraph of the story read. "The defender of black men was executed by hanging just before noon on Dec. 2, 1859, in Charles Town, Virginia."

Tears shot to my eyes and I couldn't hide them, thinking of Owen Brown, John's son, and the other Raiders who helped me when I was lost in the mountains.

"It's a sad day for our cause, is it not?" Mr. C. said, misinterpreting my reaction. "John Brown was a brave man and will go down in history as a martyr. Some say he was crazy to attempt such a bold raid, but no one questions his courage."

The very next day, early in the morning, our conductor awakened us. He was carrying a lantern and without a word he motioned that we should follow. Twice I bumped my head as we scuttled through the tunnel back into the barn.

"From here, we must slide down the steep side of the bluff to the water," Mr. Crowley whispered. "Peter, you take care of Elsie and the baby. I'll take care of Grace."

"Call me Patrick!" (I was dressed again as a young man and it offended me that he thought I'd need help.)

"Ok, ready?" he opened a secret door at the side of the barn and I saw what he meant. It had snowed again in the night and we stood at the edge of a ravine that pitched straight down to a rushing creek.

"From now on, no speaking, not even a grunt if you stub your toe. We'll be traveling behind several farmhouses. It's about a half mile to the lake." The man took my satchel under his arm and grasped my hand; then we slithered down the steep snowy slope.

At the bottom, we carefully picked our way along the ice-covered rocks that edged the water. Once I stepped in a puddle. The sharp cold made me gasp and the abolitionist farmer gripped my hand sharply, indicating I should be quiet.

Finally, the creek opened onto Lake Erie, a great inland sea as smooth as silk with ice lacing the edges. Somewhere, over the horizon, was Canada, but I could not see the land, not even a tree.

Autumn

32

September 1, 1956

Warrior

"So what do you think I should do?" I ask Bitsy on her day off from the woolen mill.

"What's the issue?"

"The nurse, Miss Frost, wants to have her baby at the Baby Cabin."

"Just be sure she knows the risks and the benefits of home birth, like you do with everyone."

"Well, I don't want to get in trouble with the medical people at the hospital."

"Come on Patience! That doesn't sound like you. I thought you were a rebel, a warrior!" Here Bitsy smiles and puts her arm around me as we stroll across the barnyard together.

"I *was* a warrior once...I used to be. Life has worn me down." I give her a half smile.

"Do you believe in what we do?"

"Yes."

"Maybe you should go to the hospital and witness one of these Twilight Sleep deliveries Miss Frost told you about. Maybe then you'd be more committed to home birth and helping people even if it was a small risk to yourself."

"Could I do that?"

"They have student nurses in hospitals, don't they? You told me that Susie and Sunny were going to do OB rotations in the maternity ward in Martinsburg. Maybe Miss Frost could get you in as a student."

"Mmmm, maybe. I'll think about it…but I have something else I want to talk to you about."

"Mira? How's she doing?"

"Better. She's been riding her horse with Willie whenever she can. I think it's cheered her up. He was even kidding her about getting fat the other day and she didn't storm out of the room, so I guess she either told him her secret, or he figured out that she's pregnant."

"Yeah, he knows."

"Well, she wants to have her baby here."

"No surprise."

"I was wondering if you would be her midwife."

"What do you mean?" Bitsy pulls away and stands staring.

"It's just that I'm Mira's Mom and I bring all those mother-daughter conflicts with me. I think she needs a midwife she respects."

"You don't think she respects you?"

"Not really. She knows how upset Dan and I are about the pregnancy. To me, my daughter getting knocked-up represents my failure to teach her to take care of herself and to Dan it's his failure to protect one of his girls from danger. She needs a midwife with clear eyes and an unburdened heart."

"Ok, I'll talk to her." We watch from the porch as Mira and Willie trot down Salt Lick Creek, past the rail fence, past the golden sunflowers.

"Race you!" says Willie as they come into the yard.

"Is that safe for Willie?" I whisper to Bitsy. "He could fall off."

"When you've been in combat, almost died, lived for six months with a painful bone infection and end up with one of your legs amputated, riding a horse is relatively safe...Let's read. I can't believe this is the last journal."

U.S. Shore, Lake Erie, Pennsylvania
December 13, 1859

When the fishing skiff finally sailed into the mouth of Four Mile Creek, it was smaller than I expected. The wooden vessel had only two sails and was about thirty feet long. The Canadian Captain was a free black man who'd lived across the lake for the last ten years and he'd brought a half grown white boy as his guide because, according to Mr. C., the old seaman was going blind. Since he was Canadian and wasn't worried about the United States laws against helping runaway slaves, we were allowed to use his full name, Hamilton Waters.

The boy threw an anchor into the shallows and helped us in. I was glad I was wearing pantaloons but I felt sorry for Elsie, whose woolen dress got wet and thus weighted.

"Thank you, Mr. Waters," our conductor said. "Good sailing."

"If the Lord's willing, we'll be on the shores of Canada by evening." Waters replied as he began to row and I saw that his eyes were coated with white.

Elsie, the baby and I sat in the bow and at first it

was pleasant and rather exciting to be moving so smoothly over the water. I'd never been in such a boat before; certainly not one that smelled of fish. Peter asked about the watercraft.

"It a twenty-five-foot skiff," the Captain told him. "Fishermen like me use it to empty the seine nets."

"What do you catch," Peter inquired and I remembered that he had once been a seafaring man himself.

"Trout, Cisco and Whitefish," Waters explained. "In general Lake Erie is shallower than the other Great Lakes. We pull the nets into the shore and unload the fish. See there," he pointed to men on the beach tending their catch.

"Can I row awhile?" Peter asked and then he began to sing, no longer in a whisper, but in his good strong voice. "When Israel was in Egypt's land - Let my people go - Oppressed so hard they could not stand - Let my people go - Go down, Moses - Way down in Egypt's land - Tell old Pharaoh - Let my people go."

All at once, Peter stopped singing. "Is that a boat following us?" he asked the nearly blind fisherman. I had fallen asleep to the gentle rocking, but was immediately awake. Mr. Waters pulled a firearm from beneath a canvas tarp.

"I cannot see so well... Boy, be my eyes!" he ordered the lad who accompanied us and handed him a brass spyglass.

"Two strangers in a rowboat, sir. They're wearing black hats, like the bounty hunters. Not village fishermen, I'd wager."

"What are they doing out here so far from

*shore?" Peter asked, his eyes tight. Elsie moved
closer to me as if I could protect her.*

*"We're still in U.S. territory and you're
runaway slaves. If they can catch us, you're gold in
their pockets."*

"Oh for heavens sake!" Bitsy exclaimed. "Was
that really the last page? The journals can't stop
there! Did you look through the wooden boxes?
Are you sure we didn't miss one."

"I'm sure. You want to check yourself?"

"No. It's just that I can't believe her story just
ends. Maybe they made it to Canada and Grace
didn't have time to write anymore."

"Or maybe they got caught..." I said with big
eyes.

After Bitsy left, I sat for a minute, staring out
the window at the cold wind tearing the last of the
leaves off the willow trees. It took months for
Grace, Peter, Elsie, and little Moses to get to
Canada; 400 miles on horseback, in carts and
wagons and boats, relying only on the courage of
strangers. And they weren't the only ones. There
were tens of thousands of escaped slaves, perhaps
one hundred thousand, running from dogs and
patrollers, sneaking through thick woods, wading in
the dark swamps...seeking freedom, a human right.

Calamity

It's Labor Day and Dan and I decide to skip the parade in town. It's so hot, even Dodger's hiding under the porch.

"I have an idea," Dan says. 'Let's go for a swim in the Hope while the parade is on, then after all the commotion is over have dinner at the Mountain Top Café."

"Kind of a date?"

"Yeah. You and I went from being neighbors, to being friends, to being pregnant in a few months and then in the next twenty years raising a brood of four. I think we deserve a few dates."

By five o'clock we're cleaned up and are on our way into town, looking forward to dinner in the well-loved café, but as we take the turn at the intersection of Salt Lick we come upon a disaster. A coal truck is lying on its side, with the coal spilled all over the road. Next to it is a logging truck that appears to have jack knifed across the dotted line.

"It must have just happened!" Dan says, pulling over and jumping out of the car. We both run for the coal truck first, because we can see the driver of the logging truck is already out, sitting on the running board, apparently uninjured.

Dan crawls up the side of the dump truck and looks in the shattered window. The engine is still running, and smoke billows from under the hood. "Get back, Patience!" he commands. "This thing could explode."

"Then *you* better get back too!"

"The driver is alive. I have to get him out."

"But is it safe to move him? Is he conscious?"

"Get my medical bag," Dan orders. "It's in the Olds." By the time I grab the keys out of the ignition, open the trunk and find the bag, Dan is pulling the driver out by his arms. If the man's neck is broken, this could kill him, but if the truck explodes while the man's still inside, he will be dead for sure.

I drop the bag in the road and run to help Dan and that's when I realize it's someone I know; Rose's father, Mr. Washington. He gives me a weak wave of recognition. Just then, a car stops on the other side of the mountain of coal and a farmer climbs over to give Dan a hand.

Since they have Mr. Washington out and safe, I turn to the driver of the lumber truck. "Sir, are you able to walk? I need to move you down the road, in case there's an explosion."

"I don't know what happened! I was coming around the curve and I lost control. Some of the logs must have shifted. Is the other fellow OK? He looks bad. Is he OK?"

"He's alive. Come on. Can you walk? You can sit in our car until help arrives. What's your name?"

"Junior Tulley.... Oh, holy dammit to hell. I'll probably get fired."

For an hour we wait for an ambulance, while Junior keeps worrying out loud about his job. It's sad, I think. He probably didn't do anything wrong, but he's probably right. He'll get canned.

Traffic is held up going both ways for a half a

mile and soon more local men, hearing about the accident, come running with shovels to clear the road. Eventually, Aran Bishop arrives in the black and white cop car, siren blaring, bossing everyone around. "All right men, stand back. I need to investigate the crash. Where are the drivers?" Someone points down the road where they're loading Mr. Washington in the ambulance. "I said stop shoveling Hester, and you too Mr. Hummingbird." Dan looks at Bishop out of the corner of his eyes and throws down his tool.

It isn't until seven that we make it to town, but the Mountain Top Cafe is still open. "That was a real mess," I reflect as we wait for our orders.

"West Virginia has some of the most dangerous roads in the Nation," Dan muses. "They're curvy, steep, often poorly repaired and trafficked by logging and coal trucks."

"I hope Mr. Washington will be OK. He and his family just moved here from Pittsburgh."

"I'll call the hospital in the morning," he says.

Afterward, we walk arm-and-arm down Main and stop to look in the window of the new Ben Franklin Store. It's closed because of the holiday, but the display of pencils, crayons and notebooks reminds us that school will start soon.

"I wonder what will happen on the first day of classes."

"It will be chaos as usual." Dan laughs.

"I meant what do you think will happen with the State order to integrate? I've seen people picketing.

There's more opposition than I expected."

"Well, there are a lot of prejudiced people, Patience. You can't fight them all."

"You and me together, could," I joke. "For a pacifist, you're pretty good with your fists."

"I haven't been in a scuff for ten years."

"Too old for it now?"

"Too mature," he snaps back with a crooked grin.

33

Twilight Sleep

Without the diversion of Grace's journals it's been a rough few days and the darkness has again folded over me.

Basically, whenever I have time to think, I feel like a failure. I've nurtured hundreds of pregnant women, but have failed with my own children, one unmarried girl pregnant and one son singing for beers at Jim's Tavern. Susie and Sunny are still bobbing along the river of life, as far as I know...but one wrong step and they too may be towed under.

The trouble is, I can't talk to Dan about it. He will just give me a hug and tell me I worry too much. And Bitsy, living in town, involved with her new job at the woolen mill, is rarely available.

When the telephone rings, I fight my way out of my gloom to see that outside the sun is still shining. "Hello," I answer.

"Hi, Patience," It's the nurse, Abby Frost. I wanted to tell you a student nurse just called in sick and I could use a hand today. You told me once that you wanted to see what a routine hospital delivery was like."

"OK, I can come right away, but I don't have a nursing uniform."

"That's fine," Abby answers. "The hospital supplies clean white scrub dresses. Just wear some sturdy looking shoes and some kind of hose. Also Patience, this won't be the kind of birth that you're used to. Do you promise to be professional?"

"What do you mean?"

"Well, no deliveries on the floor!" she says with a chuckle.

Within an hour, I was standing at the entrance to Labor and Delivery unit on the second floor of the hospital staring at the metal sign that said in bold letters, **Authorized Personnel Only**. A young man smoking Lucky Strikes and an older woman knitting booties were sitting next to each other on metal chairs lined up against the wall. I knocked on the heavy door, but no one answered, so I knocked louder. Finally, the head nurse came to the door.

She was working alone today, she said as she guided me into the inner sanctum, and caring for two patients. One was a mother who'd had a cesarean section five days ago and didn't need much attention. The other was a twenty-year-old homemaker, now two weeks past her due date, being induced with an oxytocin drip.

"Helen, this is Mrs. Hester, a visiting nurse," Abby introduced me. I smiled, but didn't say anything.

"Is it gonna hurt terrible?" the girl asked us. Again, I was silent.

"Not so bad," Abby Frost answered. "After the medicine is injected, you won't feel the pains."

Soon things got moving. Abby told me to shave the woman's pubic hair and give her a warm soapy enema, a strange experience for both the patient and me. Next, she started an IV drip of oxytocin in saline water and left me to labor-sit while she tended her other patient.

"I wish my Ma could be with me," Helen said. "I didn't know they had rules against it…And my poor husband Wyatt…Would you go out to the waiting room and tell him how I'm doing every now and then, Nurse?"

"I'll try to…"

Within an hour, the patient's eyes got big and she looked at me with alarm. "Is that it? Is that the labor pain?" She was sitting up in the high-sided adult metal crib and when she moaned Abby returned. After a few more contractions the nurse got out a hypodermic syringe and a bottle of clear liquid.

"Are you ready, Helen? When you wake up, your baby will be here."

"Is that the Twilight Sleep?" the patient asked.

"Yes. It's a mixture of a sedative and a pain reliever." I noticed she didn't mention it also contained the amnesia medicine. The patient made a bad face when Abby gave her the injection but she didn't cry out and I admired that.

"Is that all there is to it?" I whispered.

"No," Nurse Frost said under her breath. "It's just the beginning."

The Black Hood

When Helen was heavily sedated, Abby had me assist her in putting cotton in the patient's ears and a black hood over her eyes. Next we covered her arms with cotton batting.

"What's all this for?" I whispered.

"The hood and the ear plugs are to decrease stimulation. The sleeves are to prevent her from bruising herself when she bangs on the side of the crib. Finally, we'll need mittens to keep her from scratching us."

I felt like I was entering a torture chamber and when she pulled out leather restraints I was *sure* I was. "Is all this necessary?"

"It's for the patient's safety." Abby shrugged and tightened her mouth. Finally she lifted the sides of the crib and tied a canvas cover over the top.

"Surely women don't want to deliver this way, like caged animals."

"Most won't remember it. A few do, and they're traumatized."

Soon, I saw what Twilight Sleep looked like. Helen began to scream with contractions. She clutched at the bars of the cage and begged for someone, anyone, to please make the pains stop.

Over the next five hours, I did my best to comfort her, murmuring the usual midwife phrases. "You're doing fine, Helen... The contraction is almost over," but there was no way to touch her through the bars of the crib. Every few minutes the nurse would get up to increase the oxytocin, until the pains were coming 3 minutes apart.

In a few hours, Helen began to thrash so much Abby was afraid she was going to tip the bed over, so we had to put her in four point restraints, her arms and legs attached to each corner of the crib with belts made of leather. At that point tears ran down my cheeks.

"Do you see why I hate my job?" Abby asked. "You don't have to stay if you don't want to."

Maybe she's right, I thought. *I've had enough of modern obstetrics,* but just then I heard a familiar sound. "Uggggh!"

Abby heard it too. "I need to call Dr. Andrews and tell him she's about to deliver," the nurse said as she ran to her desk in the hall.

"Uggggggggghh!" Helen grunted again and again.

"You better tell him to hurry," I yelled after her.

Twenty minutes later we had the patient in the delivery room, (the same green tiled one where Kitty gave birth). The patient was still thrashing and delirious and once she knocked me on the side of the head, but we managed to get her tied on the table with her arms stretched out like Jesus on the cross and her legs in stirrups, open as wide as a barn door.

It was a terrible sight, but I had no time to think about it because Dr. Andrews arrived just as the top of the infant's head began to show. Abby and I were now dressed in sterile surgical robes with green masks over our lower faces and I was positioned at the head of the cart where I could whisper to Helen and try to keep her from struggling.

"Hello, Helen," the physician said pleasantly, as if the terrified girl could hear him. "Forceps please, Nurse," then he took a pair of scissors in his gloved hand and cut open the woman's vagina.

What was he thinking? The head was right there! Birth was imminent!

When he inserted the giant metal spoons around the head, the baby delivered almost immediately and I was shocked to see him grab the floppy infant by the ankles, hang her upside down and give her a whack, just like Dr. Coffman did back in the 1800s. Abby's eyes caught mine; probably worried I'd start tearing up again, but I was nowhere near crying. I was livid with anger.

For a few minutes, the doctor and nurse worked on the gray-blue baby, but finally she breathed. Then the physician stitched the patient up, took off his sterile gloves, tossed them on the surgical table and walked out the door without a word of thanks to us, or even "Goodbye."

"You should go home, Patience. I think you've had enough. Do you understand, now, why I can't have my baby here?" Abby said.

In a dark mood I walked to my parked vehicle. Tomorrow, Helen would remember none of this, but she'd lived through a rape and I'd witnessed it.

Sundown Town

So much has happened in the last few days. First there was the coal truck accident, then the Twilight Sleep delivery, then on Sunday, when Dan and I went to Bitsy and Lou's house for dinner, Lou announced that he was going to challenge Aran Bishop for Sheriff in the November election.

"But how can you run the woolen mill and also be Sheriff?" Dan wanted to know. "Both positions are full time and being a cop will require evening hours, sometimes weekends."

"Well, we're sick of Aran Bishop and his brother running the town," Bitsy exclaimed. "Bullies like them can infect the whole county. If Sheriff Bishop continues harassing coloreds or anyone who looks different or who is down and out, it gives everyone permission to do the same."

"Power corrupts they say," Lou continues, "And word amongst the Negroes in Liberty is that Bishop plans to turn this community into a Sundown Town."

"I don't know what that is." I come in.

"Sundown Towns are places with a law that all Negroes, Mexicans or Native Americans have to be off the streets and out of the city by six PM," Bitsy explains. "Aran Bishop is trying to institute the plan by using intimidation and fear, basically making his own laws. He's not going to get away with it though."

"So… back to Dan's question," I persist. "How are you going to do all this?"

Lou rises and puts his hand over his heart as if he's already a politician. "I'm going to turn the woolen mill over to Bitsy."

I stare at my friend. "You could run a factory?"

Bitsy laughs. "Willie's going to help with the books and Lou will assist us in the evening if there's anything we don't know. Right now the mill is stable. Since the Korean War ended, we aren't supplying the military with blankets and fabric for uniforms, so we're just making soft wool plaid for men's shirts and women's skirts. I know all the machines from being a supervisor on the factory floor. We have fifty-five employees. Willie is already learning to do payroll and accounts."

"Well, we'll help you with the campaign, however we can," Dan stands and shakes Lou's hand. "Here's our first contribution." And he pulls out a tenner.

"Thanks, friends," Bitsy says. "We'll need you. There's a lot to talk about!" And I've never seen her look happier.

"I might as well tell you," Dan says as we drive home. "Mira and Willie are an item." I sit staring out the car window at the fall wild flowers, golden-rod and purple asters along the roadside.

"Did you hear me?" he asks.

"I heard. I'm just trying to grasp what you're saying. Are you sure? Maybe they're just good friends…"

"They weren't kissing like friends."

"Oh, Dan! Where did you see this?"

"I was coming out of the barn last night and saw

them down by the bridge."

"But Dan, she's pregnant. She can't be *dating* someone. What will people think?"

"Is it important what they think, Patience?" he asks looking sideways.

I'm embarrassed to say it, *but I do care.* Once an orphan in Chicago, then a woman on the run, I'm part of the community now. I gave up my membership in the International Workers of the World. I joined the Red Cross. I'm on the Hospital Civil Defense Committee, for God's sake.

Now my youngest daughter is knocked up by one man, and recklessly playing whoopee with another!

34

Go Back to Africa

Today is the first day of school in Liberty, and Reverend Jerome has asked some of us from the church to be at the elementary school to help escort the first colored children into their classrooms. As luck would have it, Bitsy and Lou had to work and at the last minute Dan got a call from a farmer, so I went alone.

"Race Mixing is the Devil's Work. Integration is Communist. No Darkies in Our Schools" read the protestor's signs. There must be a hundred of them.

Holy Cow! How did the Communists ever get involved in all this? Then I remember the Red Scare of Senator McCarthy. For the last fifteen years people have lived in constant fear of Russian spies, so for some these words make sense. Communism is bad! Integration is bad! So integration *has to be* a Communist plot.

I park in the lot across from the two-story brick building and immediately seek out the colored families, a group of about thirty, on the other side of the street. Amongst the group are Mrs. Lincoln, Rose's mother and Rose's little sister, Daisy, talking with Pastor Jerome.

"How's Mr. Lincoln?" I ask the woman. "Is he OK after his wreck?"

"He couldn't work for a week, but he didn't lose his job at the coal mines, thank the Lord," Mrs. Lincoln answers. "The insurance company blamed the logging crew. He's back on the job now."

"Oh, hello, Mrs. Hester." Reverend Jerome is trying to get everyone organized. "Can you be the sixth-grade escort?"

Daisy, still wearing her metal leg-brace, has a red plaid dress on, nipped at the waist with the full skirt that's in fashion. Her hair is braided and tied together with a gold bow at the bottom. All of the other beautiful brown children are also dressed like it's Sunday.

"Hi," I say, standing where Jerome wants me. "First day at your new school, Daisy? I'm proud of you. I'm going to accompany you inside." She gives me a tightlipped nervous smile.

"It's time," Pastor Jerome calls as he looks at his watch and leads us toward the school doors. Daisy and I are right behind him, both limping a little, holding hands. The group is almost to the edge of the sidewalk when Sheriff Bishop shows up in his squad car, siren blaring. He jumps out, blows a whistle and raises his hand like a traffic cop.

"Hey Bishop," I yell when the pastor walks across the street towards him. "Let the kids cross! The Supreme Court says they have a right to be here and it's your duty to uphold the law." Meanwhile, the mob of white demonstrators moves closer and begins to chant, "Go back to Africa! Go back to Africa!"

What the hell! This is ridiculous! These are not burly union miners on strike or brave suffragettes marching for women's rights. These are just scared kids entering a new school. They were born in the U.S. and have never even seen Africa!

I take Daisy's hand and lead her across the street while the cop and Reverend Jones are arguing. My young partner is shaking all over now, but her face shows no fear. Aran Bishop blows his whistle over and over and looks right at me as if daring me to take another step, so I do. I take three, then three more, pulling little Daisy along.

Outside the playground fence, four white boys glare at us with so much hate, Daisy almost falls over, but I pull her up. Then one of them snatches her braids and rips off her ribbon. That's when I lose it. I grab the kid's collar, ready to throttle him, but Reverend Jerome runs over just in time.

"Keep moving," he says. "Think of flowers, Mrs. Hester. Think of trees. Think of the Hope River rippling over rocks in the sunshine."

"Go back to Africa! Go back to Africa!" the boys howl, a pack of hyenas working together to bring their prey down. The white adult crowd is even worse. "Go home jungle bunnies! Go back to Africa!"

Tears run down Daisy's brown cheeks and I am so mad, I feel like crying too. *Think of flowers. Think of the trees. Think of the Hope River rippling over the rocks in the sunshine*, I tell myself as step by step we march past the faces brittle with hate.

And then something unplanned happens. I begin to sing. "*My country tis of thee, sweet land of liberty. Of thee I sing!"* The white demonstrators are caught off guard and for a moment they're silent. Then the colored children and Reverend Jerome come in singing with me. *"Land where my fathers died - Land of the pilgrims' pride. - From every mountainside let freedom ring!*

Crossroad

"Did you have a good day?" Dan says with a grin, as he steps out of his boots and drops his overalls at the back door.

"Yuck! You stink…" I say as I pinch my nose and throw them in our Maytag on the back porch.

"It was a hard surgery," he tells me. "The cow had swallowed a wire. I had to open her second stomach and all her undigested food sprayed everywhere."

"Yuck!" I say again.

He throws the *Liberty Times* on the table and heads for the bathroom to wash up. "You're in the paper again," he calls over his shoulder. "Billy Blaze must think you're especially photogenic."

There I am on the front page, but I'm not singing *My Country Tis of Thee* or bravely holding Daisy's small hand, I'm grabbing the eighth grade boy's striped shirt. I don't even remember seeing Bill Blaze at the school, but of course he would be there.

"Well, it's lucky, my photo isn't the only one," I call to Dan. "The picture of the racist women rolling their eyes and howling is realistic, and the one of Reverend Jerome leading the colored children into the school is great." I sit down to skim the article. **First Day of Integration in Liberty Schools is a Mixed Success**, the headlines read.

"So what was going on when you assaulted the kid?" Dan asks, clearly amused. "I've told you before that you're a hothead."

"The little brat had just pulled Daisy Lincoln's braids and torn off her pretty hair ribbons. Luckily, Reverend Jerome calmed me down. He probably won't ask me to be a chaperone again, though. Is the article supportive of the segregationists or the colored kids?"

"Here let me read you a little. It's short."

"America stands at a crossroad. The Supreme Court, on May 17, 1954, ordered all public schools to integrate, but they didn't specify how or when. They left that up to the states. West Virginia has only partially complied, but our time in Union County has come.

"Americans all say the same Pledge of Allegiance, all sing the same national anthem, have all fought in wars to defend our freedom. In this community white and black have worked together in the mines for one hundred years. Their children have gone to separate schools, but no longer.

It's time to stand up for what we say we believe in...Liberty and justice for all."

35

Picture Show

For Dan's birthday we decide to go to a movie in town. During the Great Depression, this was unthinkable, but now at 50 cents each, it's an affordable treat. The theater is already packed when we get there, but the usher in his green uniform finds us seats in the balcony. It's a musical, *Oklahoma*.

As the golden lights along the walls dim and the blue velvet curtains open, the sound of trumpets fills the theater. On the big screen, *World News* shows a city street where peaceful black and white citizens move along the sidewalk, pushing baby strollers and carrying shopping bags.

"This is Birmingham, Alabama. But Birmingham is not all it seems," the announcer tells us over the background music. The camera cuts to a colored pastor giving a speech to a crowd. It's the now familiar Reverend Martin Luther King.

"For almost nine months now, we, the Negro citizens of Montgomery, Alabama, have been engaged in a non-violent protest against injustice on our buses," King pronounces. "And during our protest, we have, substituted tired feet for our once tired souls…"

After the Birmingham segment, we're treated to a comical skiing tournament with many amazing stunts, a fashion show in Paris, and at the end a piece on the National Civil Defense Program, "Operation Alert".

Finally the feature film opens with the overture, one of our favorite songs. *"Oh what a beautiful morning - Oh what a beautiful day!*

Three Sheets to the Wind

A few hours later, as we step outside into the now cool evening, we encounter a scene so troubling I want to rush back into the dark theater and hide. The town squad car is stopped in the middle of Main Street, with its red and white lights flashing. In the alley next door, men's rough voices echo off the brick walls.

"Leave me alone. Get your hands off me," a slurred voice yells. "Get off me you S.O.B!"

"It's Danny!" Dan yells. I grab for his arm but it's too late; he's already loping toward the commotion and he breaks through the crowd. "What the hell," I hear him shout.

"Get up, you dog," another man growls. "Stand back folks!" It's Aran Bishop, wearing his uniform and a white cowboy hat like he thinks he's John Wayne.

"Get your hands off him, Bishop!" Dan growls back.

"Leave me alone, Goddamit!" Danny yells and then I hear a hand slapping his face.

Now I'm pushing through the throng of people that's rapidly gathering, some still humming *"Oh what a beautiful morning - Oh what a beautiful day."*

This is another low point for our family. Our son is sprawled on the cobblestones in a pool of his own piss, drunk as a skunk. "Let go of me Pa!" he slurs.

"I'll handle it from here," the Sheriff says.

"No, Aran, I'll take him home and sober him up. If there's a fine for drunk and disorderly, he'll pay it tomorrow."

"There will be more than a fine. He's going in the drunk tank for a couple of days."

Dan pulls his son up by the back of his shirt and flops him roughly against the alley wall where he wobbles for a minute before sliding back down. As he falls, Danny's eyes catch mine and I shoot my son a look of contempt that conveys all I feel; disgust, hate and despair. *I'm through with you* my expression says, and then I wheel away and head back to the movie house while the crowd whispers and gawks.

"OK, Bishop!" Dan says as I leave. "You can have him, but no rough stuff. If you hurt one hair on his filthy head, I'm coming after you."

"You and who else?" Aran barks. "Your little woman?"

Tightrope

This morning, Dan went back to Liberty to get his son out of jail, but he insisted I stay home. "You'll only get in an argument with the Law and it'll make matters worse," he explained. Actually, I was glad Dan didn't want me to come. I was still hopping mad, and not at the Sheriff. My jaw ached I was so angry with Danny. The kid was a wastrel, an alky, a bum!

While I wait for my husband to return, I get out my journal and go out on the back porch. It's hard for me to admit all the shame and embarrassment that has come to me lately. I feel like such a bad mother. How is it *my* children have turned out this way? One is a drunk. One is unmarried and pregnant, and if someone is reading this, thinking "Poor soul, nothing like that will ever happen to *my kids*," let me give you a tip. The road ahead is rocky and winding, with twists and turns you can't imagine. There will be times when you'll lie in bed praying for your children. You will pray to your God and then pray to the moon.

When I close my journal and look out across the fields, I notice Howard out by the garden. *What is he doing?* He flies toward the woods and then returns with an acorn and pushes it into the soil. He's burying the acorns, storing them for winter! So too, it is with our sorrows. We shove them down deep, but under our hearts they still put out roots.

A few hours later Dan motors into the drive and I watch him get out of the truck *without* Danny. "When I got to town," he tells me plunking down next to me on the steps, his brow furrowed, "No one was in the Sheriff's office and the secretary down the hall said they were out on patrol.

"The lockup is in back behind a steel door, so I couldn't even see Danny or talk to him while I waited. An hour later, when Bishop returned, he told me our son had already been released, because they busted up a fight out by White Rock and needed the cells for other inmates."

"Well, for heavens sake! You'd think the kid might have called."

"Well after that, I went over to Jim's Tavern to look for him, but Jim hadn't seen him. Next, I went to their apartment, but no one answered. Finally, I drove out to the woolen mill, where Willie was doing accounts, to see if he knew anything."

"And...?" I wait for the rest of he story.

"Well, that's the end of it. No one knows where Danny is or what's become of him, but the old Plymouth that Lou bought so that Danny and Willie could get around is gone too."

I suck in my upper lip. Outside, Dodger whines to get in. I'm balancing on a tightrope between anger and fear. "What the hell?" I finally burst out, pacing to the sink and then back to the door to let the dog in. "Where could he be?"

"I don't know, Patience, but I can't spend another whole day wandering around looking for him. I have to make a visit to Mr. Hummingbird's farm tomorrow to check on that horse that has laminitis. Maybe Danny just took a ride to blow off steam and he'll be back tomorrow."

"Who'll be back tomorrow?" Mira waddles into the kitchen rubbing her expanding belly. She bends down to pet Dodger. "How you doing, puppy?" she coos and runs her fingers over his smooth brown fur.

I look at my husband, not knowing if we should share the news of our son's disappearance. "It's probably nothing," Dan says. "I went into town to get your brother out of jail and he'd already been released. He took their old jalopy and he's nowhere to be found."

"Does Willie know?" Mira asks quietly. "He needs someone to drive him around, especially now that he's working at the woolen mill."

I shake my head in confusion. Why is Mira, all of a sudden more concerned about Willie than her own missing brother?

36

Moonlight

At two this morning, Mr. Spraggs, a coal miner who keeps a few cattle and horses on the side, called to tell Dan that one of his horses was having belly pain. The animal was restless and sweating, breathing hard and trying to lie down and roll over. I could hear the conversation as my veterinarian husband lay in bed with the receiver at his ear.

"Got to go," he said when he hung up. "It sounds like colic and it could be bad." Dan has told me before that he always treats colic in horses as a potential emergency, because a horse can die surprisingly fast.

"Want me to make you a thermos of coffee while you dress? It's cold out tonight."

"Sure. That would be nice. You're a peach."

"Sometimes, I'm a peach," I laughed. "Sometimes I'm a sour pickle!"

Downstairs, I started a fire and set the metal pot on the stove. Then I poured the hot brew in Danny's old Roy Rodger's thermos bottle. By the time my husband hurried downstairs, I'd screwed on the red lid and wrapped a cheese sandwich in waxed paper.

He gave me a smile when he took my small offering and stared at the picture of the famous movie cowboy on the side of the lunch bucket. "I wonder where our Danny is tonight," he said sadly.

"Somewhere warm and safe, I hope," I answered as he went out the door. "And sober," I added under my breath.

Back in bed, but unable to sleep, I chase my fears across the bedroom ceiling. First, I turn to Danny. My mind is a searchlight seeking him out, but I come up empty. "Where is he?" I think. "Slumped in some bar down in Charleston or worse yet, wrecked in a ditch out in the country?" Then the worse horror of all...he couldn't be so ashamed he'd do himself harm, could he? Months ago, Bitsy worried Willie could shoot himself. Now, I am dancing with the same fear.

When I'd gnawed that terrible thought to the bone, I started on Mira, still wondering what she planned to do about the baby. Our daughter refuses to discuss adoption, but in these times unmarried girls rarely keep their infants. Is it fair to let the baby grow up a bastard when, with a little effort, we could find him a couple who couldn't have a child?

Finally I move on to young Daisy. How was she doing in that hostile school? What kind of courage would it take to face those racist jackals each morning?

In the end, frustrated with my insomnia, I pull on my pink chenille robe and go back downstairs. The fire is low in the heater stove and I poke at the coals. On impulse, I tie my robe closer, step into my rubber boots and slip out the door. Looking up, my mouth falls open. The sky is a parachute of silk, lined with silver clouds. When the moon peeks through, I raise my arms in a prayer; only two words, *Help Us,* but I feel the moon answer.

"Here is the truth," the smiling orb says. "Children grow in their own mysterious ways. And just because they seem broken, doesn't mean they won't heal."

Intruder

As I stand gazing at the moon, I become aware of slow footsteps in the distance.   Crunch... Crunch... Crunch... Crunch...   I pull my robe closer and duck behind one of the huge old willow trees at the back of the yard. The sound seems to come from the road.

Crunch......Crunch......Crunch......Crunch, very slowly.

It could be a deer, but it sounds heavier, maybe a bear. For a moment, I consider running for the kitchen door, but I don't want to be caught out in the clearing. The footsteps stop near our mailbox.

Quietly now, a shadow emerges. A person, on a horse, stops at the bridge, gets off and approaches the house. He slips past the big lilac bush. Mira is inside, fast asleep in her upstairs bedroom with Dodger beside her, both unaware of the approaching danger. Our canine used to be a good watchdog, but in his old age his hearing is going and maybe his eyesight too.

I come to a decision; if the intruder tries to break in, I'll grab a stick and run toward him, screaming profanity in the lowest voice possible. (I once used this trick when the hooded KKK attacked Bitsy and me at the house with the blue door and it scared the bloody *bejesus* out of them.)

The trespasser steals onto our front porch and I take a deep breath, preparing myself to mount an attack, but within seconds he reverses his course and walks quickly away, back toward his horse. A few minutes later, I see him mount and Crunch, Crunch, Crunch, faster now... he hurries away.

For a moment, I stay behind the tree, frozen, in the cold moonlight, wanting to be sure the stranger is gone. What could he have wanted? I heard no sounds of an attempted break in. Finally, I decide it's safe to run home and quick as a chipmunk, I scurry to safety.

In the country, we don't usually lock our doors at night, but once inside, I check every entrance, then still shaking, I crawl into bed.

Tracks

First thing the next morning, when Dan gets home, I tell him what happened. Concerned, he hurries out on the road to look for tracks.

"You were right," he informs me, when he returns. "It was a horse. There are hoof tracks right by the mailbox. shoeprints too."

Just then, Mira wanders into the kitchen, looking for something to eat, and I flash him a look, not wanting him to scare her, but he misses my signal.

"Your Mom was outside last night and saw someone stop in the road on horseback. Whoever it was came up on the front porch and then left in a hurry. When I went out just now, I found this. He drops a burlap sack on the table. "It worries me to leave you gals alone here at night."

"What were you doing outside, Mom?" Mira wants to know. "Talking to the moon?"

"I was just walking around." I tell a white lie.

356

The fact is she knows me too well.

"Really!" she rolls her eyes. "So what's in the bag?"

"That's not the point, Mira," Dan growls. "It's not safe now for you and your mother alone here at night. I'm going to put new locks and chains on all the doors and I don't want you walking around outside after sundown, Patience."

"We seemed to cope OK when you were in the Moundsville State Prison, Dad. We made it through ice storms and blizzards…"

"And a wild dog attack!" I add.

"Well, I still don't feel right leaving you while someone's sneaking around in the dark, coming right up on our porch like that."

"What's in the sack, anyway? Is it heavy?" I ask.

"Hold your horses." He gets out his pocketknife to cut the string and pulls out five more of Mrs. Potts' notebooks. "What the hell! Where are these coming from? The journals are entertaining for you and Bitsy and have historical significance, but I don't like the idea of someone skulking around on our property."

"You're right," I agree. "It's getting creepy!" but as soon as everyone leaves, I open the first journal trying to remember what was happening to Grace. Then I remember… They were out in the middle of Lake Erie and slave-catchers were after them.

Lake Erie, United States Water
December 13, 1859

"Stop in the name of the Law! We're Federal Marshals!" the two men in the rowboat behind us called.

The young lad serving as the lookout on the fisherman's skiff handed Peter the spyglass.

"He's right, Captain," Peter said. "There are two men with black hats and there's no doubt about it; they're gaining on us. What can I do?"

"Should we hide?" I asked our conductor.

"No point, they've already seen you," Mr. Waters said as he opened the sails and turned the skiff to the East so that we could catch the mild breeze. "We can outrun them. They aren't used to the lake."

For a while, the rowboat seemed to close in, but Peter took the oars again, and as the wind picked up and the sails filled, we pulled ahead.

"How far to the Canadian line?" Peter asked.

"Don't rightly know. I just go by feel," the old man answered.

I could not turn away, but kept staring, willing the Marshals to give up.

"Looks like we're going to hit some rough weather," Peter said as the sail grew taut and we bounced over a wave. When I turned back the next time, the men were still there.

I looked over at Elsie. She was clutching her baby with the shawl wrapped around her. Water sprayed over the bow and the breakers crested with white foam on top.

As the wind blew harder, the waves rhythmically sloshed us back and forth, the swells topping six feet. Each time we went over one and slammed down on the other side, it felt like the boat hit a boulder. We bobbed and weaved and when I dared to look back the next time, I noted the slave catcher's boat was too low in the water.

"Looks like they're in trouble," Peter observed, shouting over the roar of the wind.

There was no shoreline now, in front or behind. The black clouds at the horizon soon filled the whole sky and rain pelted my face. I untied the only life preserver on the boat and put it on Elsie.

"Is there anything I can do?" I shouted to Peter, but neither of the men answered, so I folded my hands in prayer. "Thank you God for getting us this close to freedom," I whispered into the wind, "And if it be thy will, help us make it through this storm to Canada." When I glanced over, Elsie was praying too.

Finally, after what seemed like hours, I could feel the wind shift. The sails were still full, but occasionally they began to flap. Then the waves slowed and gradually the sky lightened.

"Are we going the right way?" Peter hollered.

"Believe so," the old captain replied with confidence, but then I remembered he could hardly

see.

The boy pointed ahead and I saw, at last, in the distance what might be a tiny line of trees. "Is that Canada?" I asked and he shook his head yes.

"It's Canada!" I yelled at Elsie and she smiled. "It's Canada. Canada!" I couldn't help shouting over and over. I wanted to stand up and throw my hands in the air and when I looked back our pursuers were gone, whether back to Pennsylvania or down to the deep, we did not know.

Finally, as the sun came out and the rocking slowed, Peter was able to crawl forward to Elsie and took her face in his hands. "Are you OK?" he asked and she nodded.

"Moses is fine too. See, he's still sucking." She smiled through her tears.

Then Peter the big man raised his hands and began to sing again. I had never known a person to show such joy.

"Glory, glory hallelujah! - Glory, glory hallelujah! - Glory, glory hallelujah! - For ever, evermore!"

37

Promised Land

It's been a busy week. I brought in the rest of the winter squash and stored it in boxes in the cellar and canned the last of the tomatoes, but today Bitsy had a day off from the woolen mill and I shared with her how the new journals had come to us. She wasn't so much concerned about the stranger on the porch as intrigued.

"I can't believe it," she said, "After we thought we'd read the last one. Did Grace and her companions make it to Canada, the promised land?"

"Yes. It was heroic. The U.S. Marshals were right on their tails. Why don't you read aloud while I clean up the kitchen?"

December 14, 1859
Port Burnell, Ontario

I had never been on a steam locomotive and I'll admit I was scared. Trains ran faster than the fastest horse. Doctor Coffman had read aloud the stories from the Charlottesville paper. Sometimes they went so fast the freight cars went off the tracks.

As I stood on the platform waiting with my satchel at my feet, I hoped I looked respectable. I'd changed into one of the dresses the church ladies in Erie City had given me and wrapped myself in a woolen shawl. Would people still think I was white? I didn't feel white anymore. There was one other person standing nearby, an older Negro man in a black suit and string tie.

"Is this where I wait for a train to Elgin?" I asked shyly. He put on his spectacles and studied me for a moment. "God be praised. Are you new to this land?" he asked me.

I surmised that this was some kind of code, so I answered in kind. "God be praised, I just got here last night in a fishing boat."

"You came through the storm?"

"Yes. Mr. Waters brought us. My companions, two other escaped slaves and their baby, went on to Toronto, to work with the Toronto Anti-slavery people," I whispered. "And I now travel alone."

"You don't have to whisper any more, little lady. You're in the Promised Land. As it happens I'm going to Chatham, Ontario, which is close to Elgin, so perhaps we can sit together." I didn't know if my anxiety about riding the locomotive was obvious, but I appreciated the offer.

A few minutes later, we heard a faint faraway hum and then the blast of a whistle. I stepped back in fear as the engine roared up, its round front window glaring like an eye and the smoke stack belching a cloud of black smoke. The very platform below us shook and then the whistle wailed again, a long wild scream.

"Right on time," my companion said looking at his pocket watch. "My name is Wallace Sinclair

and I'm well acquainted with the Elgin Settlement and the Buxton Mission. Do you have a contact there? It's a big settlement now, over one thousand residents on 9000 acres."

Meanwhile the train, with a blast of steam, halted in front of us. Bumps and crashes ran along the cars, the engine stopped and people began to get out. Another brown man in a black uniform with shiny brass buttons and a matching cap helped me up the steps into an almost full coach.

"Do you have your ticket?" The man asked as he took my satchel and placed it in an overhead compartment. I nodded numbly and sat down next to Mr. Sinclair on a burgundy-upholstered seat.

Then, without warning, we were off with another shrill whistle and blast of smoke. I was both elated and terrified. I wanted to sing. I wanted to dance and laugh. I also wanted to cry. It was going so fast and along with the clickety-clack of the tracks the car swayed back and forth.

"Tell me about yourself, little lady," Mr. Sinclair said, probably to get me calmed down.

"My name is Grace Coffman, and I was raised as a white girl, by a Virginian family, I explained, "I didn't realize I was in actuality a slave until I was twelve…"

Fool in Love

After Bitsy leaves, I stand to admire my eight Mason jars of tomatoes, gleaming like rubies in a shaft of sunlight.

"Hi Babe!" Dan greets me, coming in from his

rounds. "Done already?"

"Yep. Who do you have there, one of your patients?"

"He's not a patient, he's ours. Name is Max." He stops and leads a black and white dog over to me. The medium size canine has expressive ears, kind intelligent eyes and long fur. "When I passed through Oneida today, I stopped at the county dog pound. Max had been there for over three weeks, twelve days longer than usual, and was due to be put to sleep. He's only two-years-old, but no one had claimed him. When he saw me he jumped up and danced on his back legs, so I brought him home. He's an Australian Shepherd mix and they make good watchdogs. I'm going to run him around the edge of the yard so he learns what he's supposed to guard."

"Is Dodger going to be ok? He's used to being an only dog." I lean over and scratch Max behind his ears.

"Oh, he'll be fine."

Old Dodger doesn't even get out of his box when he sees the new canine, just lifts his head, then drops it again and goes back to sleep.

"He's a beautiful animal. No one claimed him?"

"Nope. John, the county dog catcher, found him abandoned in a shed, half starved." Dan opens the back door. "Come on Max," he yells. "Let's run!"

"Come on, Dodger..." I say with a laugh, "lets go out and watch them run!"

"Any news from town?" I ask later over dinner, meatloaf and winter squash fresh from the garden.

"I saw Lou at the Mountain Top Café and he told me he's going to buy Will a Fordamatic so he can get himself to work. You know, one of those new models with the automatic transmission so he can drive with one foot and not have to shift."

"Are the people still protesting in at the school?"

"I didn't see any. Loonie Tinkshell at the Shell Station told me a TV crew from Delmont was in town yesterday and most of the protestors hurried home, pronto. Probably didn't want their mugs on the boob tube…What did you do today?"

"I cleaned off the garden. Piled the old tomato and pepper vines on the compost and piled up the stakes….one other thing…I called Sheriff Bishop and asked him to file a missing person report on Danny."

Dan frowns. "What did he say?"

"Said it wasn't time yet; that Danny was a grown man and might just have moved away. I don't think that's correct. I'm going to check with the cops in Delmont."

Dan blows out his air. "Bishop is probably just too lazy to do any extra paper work, but in a way, he's right. Danny's a grown man."

"Anyway, it was worth a try. I do worry, you know."

"Well here's something that might cheer you," he says, changing the subject. "There's a dance at the Lion's Club tonight. Lou and Bitsy are going with Willie and Mira. It's a good time for Lou to shake hands with the voters. Do you want to go?"

"To be honest, I'd rather relax by the fire."

"Me too," Dan says with a grin.

"Are we getting to be old fogies?" I ask.

"Nah. We both just like being home more than we like hanging out with drunken crowds."

"Good point," I laugh, turning on the radio.

"Earth angel, earth angel - Will you be mine?" croon the Penguins.

Dan pulls me into his arms as he sings along and for a minute I'm safe. I am at peace and all my worries are gone.

"I'm just a fool" he sings *"A fool in love with you – Earth angel, earth angel..."*

Smoke Rising

This morning, Nurse Abigail Frost was supposed to come to the farm for a prenatal visit and to see the Baby Cabin. I was a little peeved when she cancelled.

"I'm sorry to phone you so late," she excused herself, "But I'm having to cover extra shifts when the other nurses don't show. I think they're exchanging information and calling in sick when we have a patient on Twilight Sleep."

"In a way, I don't blame them," I gently counter, wondering if Susie and Sunny will ever have to attend a writhing out of control woman, wrapped in cotton gauze and strapped down for her own protection.

This was the second appointment Abby had canceled, but I tried to be sympathetic. "As Head Nurse, it must be hard to be the one that always has to cover. Are you doing OK with your pregnancy?"

"Fine, I guess. The baby's moving a lot and I think she's headfirst. No contractions or anything. I skipped my appointment with Dr. Andrews last week. He keeps trying to push the drug Miltown on me, a tranquilizer all the women are taking."

"Do they even know if this Miltown is safe in pregnancy?"

"I'm not sure. I guess so. Andrews advised me that with the stress I'm under it might do me some good, but I turned him down."

Before we hung up, she scheduled another visit.

After a cup of herbal tea, I was ready to face the rest of the day. Outside it was the kind of morning that makes you want to roll around in the autumn leaves. White puffballs of clouds dotted the sky. Some of the trees still held their color, red maples amongst the golden oaks, mixed in with the evergreens up on Hope Mountain.

"Want to go with me to put Lou's handouts in the mailboxes along Salt Lick Road?" I asked Mira when she came into the kitchen. She was standing by the sink in her bathrobe even though it was ten in the morning.

"OK. Can we ride the horses?"

"That's a nice idea. I'll get them geared up while you dress."

A half hour later I'm saddled and ready with Mira's handsome brown five-year-old, Bunny, and my old horse, Dusty, a gray speckled Morgan. Tying them to the porch rail, I stick my head in the kitchen door, "Mira! Ready? And don't forget the flyers on the coffee table in the living room." When she waddles out, I hand her Bunny's reins and give her a boost as she mounts from the steps.

"Where shall we start first?" she asks. "Hazel Patch? I think people there would appreciate Lou's position on civil rights. Maybe we can get support from Reverend Jerome." We guide our horses out into the road, but stay off the asphalt, because it's hard on their feet. The first mailbox is a half-mile away.

"Should we take the flyers up to the house and talk to Mrs. Moffat?" Mira wonders. I glance at her profile and decide that even with her heavy coat on, she still looks very pregnant and this makes me wonder what people in Liberty say when she's campaigning for Lou; a young woman eight months pregnant with no wedding band.

"No, just leave the flyer in her box. I'm pretty sure she walks down for her mail every day. Next stop is Mr. Lester."

"Race you!" Mira says and takes off at a gallop.

"Mira!" I yell, trotting after her. "Be careful!"

When I get to Mr. Lester's drive, there's no Mira. *What the heck?* It's hard to know if she rushed on past or turned down the lane.

I decide to go up to the house and that's when I see her, across the mowed hayfield. She's already talking with the old man, a thin fellow wearing a red plaid hat with ear flaps that hang loose. Her horse is tied to a rail fence and is nibbling grass. As I ride up, Mr. Lester lifts his hat.

"Howdy-do," I call. "I haven't seen you for a coon's age."

"I don't get out much. Don't need to. Don't want to. I'm a little bit of a hermit." He grins and I see that one of his front teeth is missing.

"Me too." I admit. "I'm happy at home. Did Mira give you a flyer about Mr. Cross running for Sheriff?"

He holds it up and replies, "I'm no friend of that S.O.B., Sheriff Bishop. I was just telling your daughter, I called him the other day because someone's been stealing my chickens."

"A chicken thief! That sounds like something from the Great Depression."

"You betcha! Bishop told me it was probably a fox. Then in a week or so, it happened again. That time I found footprints. Smallish. Could have been a kid. Bishop still refused to investigate. Said he had bigger fish to fry. I've lost five now and I'm keeping my shotgun right near the back door."

"Oh, Mr. Lester," Mira says, rubbing her belly. "You wouldn't shoot a child, would you?"

"Probably not, but I'd fire into the air to scare him and if I could catch the little bugger, I'd haul him into the cooler."

"Well, if Lou Cross becomes Sheriff, he won't be like that. He knows our livestock are important. Can we count on you to vote for him?" Mira continues, speaking like a professional canvasser.

The man runs his hand over his grizzled chin and pulls on one flap of his red cap, shaking his head. "I haven't voted since Franklin D. Roosevelt. He was the last good one."

"But this is local. This is important," I come in., "Tell you what. On Election Day, I'm going to come by. If you're willing, we can go vote together at the church in Hazel Patch."

"Well, we'll see," he says, as he picks up an armful of wood. "If I don't get inside my fire will go out." He glances up at his stone chimney.

"Awful nice talking to you," Mira says, stepping on the bottom of the rail fence and mounting her horse.

"That was interesting," I say as we walk our

horses back down his lane. "I'm not surprised Sheriff Bishop didn't want to drive ten miles out in the country to catch a chicken thief, but I wonder how many other people he's irritated."

I look back at Mr. Lester's cottage where only the chimney, now billowing white smoke, shows over the treetops. A few miles away a similar vertical cloud appears over a rise and I wonder for a moment whose house that is.

"OK, Mom. You've been quiet for a couple of miles," Mira says turning her horse and walking companionably beside me. "What's on your mind?"

"Well, your Dad says you're sweet on Willie," I begin. "Do you think that's appropriate with you being pregnant with another man's baby?" I don't try to put any sugar on it, just say it right out.

"Willie says he doesn't care whose baby it is. Bitsy and Lou raised him and loved him as if he was their own. He wants to marry me."

I glance around at the gold and red trees and the smoke rising off in the distance. This wasn't what I expected. "And you said...?"

"Well, I said *"no."* I don't need any man's pity. I can raise a baby on my own."

"Do you love each other?" I ask. "If he asked you to marry him and you *weren't* pregnant, would that be different?"

"Maybe," she says, then like a cellar door banging shut, she cuts off the subject. "Can we not talk about this anymore?"

This is a moment that must come to many

mothers; a time when she looks at her child and sees that the young man or woman isn't who she expected. They are their *own* person, with thoughts and dreams that are foreign. And with that knowledge comes a sharp pain as the ghost of the placenta separates. The person she gave birth to, breastfed and raised has drifted away, like smoke over the trees.

Threats

For three days, I hardly see Dan. He's off doing tuberculin testing in the next county because six months ago Fred Gardner, the vet from Delmont, died when he got kicked in the head by a horse. How easily one's life can end. The man goes out in the morning to do a simple castration, something he's done a hundred times before… and by evening he's gone.

This morning, talking on the phone, I cheerfully told Bitsy about our trip on horseback to hand out leaflets and I was surprised she showed so little enthusiasm. Finally, I came out and asked, "Bitsy, what's wrong?"

The line went as silent as frozen earth in December.

'It's Lou," she said, "He's getting threatening phone calls telling him his days are numbered if he doesn't give up the Sheriff's race."

"Oh, Bitsy. I'm so sorry. Is he going to drop out?"

"Hell no!" she responded with vigor. "But don't tell anyone about the calls, OK? Just Dan. We don't want word of the threats to get to Bill Blaze. He'd write a newspaper story and it would bring out all the rest of the crazies."

"I don't know what to say, Bitsy. Do you think it's some of Aran Bishop's friends?"

"Yeah, probably, or maybe Sheriff Bishop himself."

"Mom! Someone's here." Mira yells when I put down the phone. Out the window, I see a tall thin man in a white fedora standing at the front door. The stranger sees me looking at him and tips his hat. He's a youngish fellow, clean-shaven with a deep cleft in his chin and a very pale face.

"Yes?" I say through the crack in the door, thinking he might be a Fuller Brush salesman. Dan has installed new chains and bolts since we had our night visitor and I promised him, day or night, I wouldn't open the door unless I knew who was out there. The man leans down to my height, "I'm Edmund Frost, Abigail's husband. Are you Mrs. Hester?"

I was planning to spend a few hours reading Mrs. Potts' journals, but I could hardly use that as an excuse. "Yes, but I thought Abby had her OB appointment this coming weekend?" I answer, unbolting the lock.

"Well, her water broke last night. She wants to know if you will still do her home birth."

Home birth? I think. *I thought she was coming to the Baby Cabin.*

"Oh, of course, but you could have just telephoned," I say, trying to sound nice, even though I'm steamed. I don't have my things ready for a home birth. I haven't made a visit to their house. I've hardly done any prenatal visits.

"Well, our place is rather hard to find. Abby asked me to drive you." The guy looks confused and uncomfortable.

"Edmund, I have to ask. Are you onboard about the home birth? This is a family endeavor."

"Yes. Yes. I'm all for it, if Abby is. I've read her book, *Childbirth Without Fear*, cover to cover."

"Well, it will take me a few minutes to get ready. Is Abby having contractions yet?"

"Very mild, she says, about ten minutes apart and the fluid is clear. She didn't seem worried."

"Do you want to sit in the kitchen?"

"Oh, the porch is OK. It's pretty out here."

Thirty minutes later, I've got everything packed and we're on our way, but I soon see what Mr. Frost meant. The trip to their house takes over an hour on back roads and is almost next to White Rock State Park.

Finally, we turn down a dirt lane, pull up a long hill and arrive at a small yellow cottage with white trim and a stone porch that looks out toward the white cliffs in the distance. The view takes my breath away.

Inside the cozy home, Abby is pacing the floor carrying her copy of *Childbirth Without Fear* clutched to her chest like a Bible. Her husband slumps down in a big easy chair.

"Are you comfortable, Abby?" he asks.

"I wouldn't say I'm *comfortable*, but I'm doing OK."

"Any contractions?" I ask. She's standing in a long white nightgown swaying back and forth like a ballerina and she nods yes, with a little smile.

"Maybe you could give me a sign when you get a pain so I can tell."

She holds up a finger and I realize she having a contraction right now. A few minutes later she has another one and that's when I notice there's sweat on her upper lip.

An experienced midwife uses her eyes and ears to determine how labor is progressing; the change in the woman's voice, whether she's sweating, increased bloody show. Even nausea or vomiting could mean progress. From the feel of things, I'm guessing Abby's five centimeters. She lifts her index finger again and I note that her breathing is deep and even, eyes closed, as she sways. At the end she looks at her nurse's watch and I look at my pocket watch, the one Mrs. Kelly gave me.

"Five minutes apart," she says. For a few moments, Eddie holds Abby in his arms, then she lifts her finger again and starts to sway. I decide to get out my birth supplies, then for an hour I sit in a rocker, quietly murmuring words of encouragement.

Next to me on a coffee table is a small book of poetry that I've never seen before. *The Prophet by Kahil Gibran* and I skim through a few poems until I read one that knocks my socks off. *"Your children are not your children. They are the sons and daughters of Life's longing for itself."* If I were not sitting here in this yellow cottage on top of a mountain attending a woman in labor, I would burst out in tears.

"Eddie!" Abby breaks my reverie. "Can you get that list of things I want you to read aloud? These contractions are really hard." She bends over a chair and sways some more while the man rummages around in a drawer.

Apparently, his wife had made a list of positive quotes about childbirth that she wants to remember and Edmund with his deep voice reads like a pastor saying a prayer. Every contraction he recites a new passage. Sometimes he even reads one twice. "Be courageous, Abby. You are a mother lion."

"Labor is hard work. That's why they call it labor."

"You are stronger than you know."

"Be brave. All great things take time."

When the contractions are two minutes apart, Abby's voice begins to rise and become almost frantic. Then the moans become groans and she kneels on the floor as if something's dragging her down. "It's coming," she says. "Aghhhhhh!"

Edmund looks at me wildly. He's been her rock, but he's about to crumble. "When this is over take a deep breath," I instruct Abby. "You too, Eddie."

"Can you check me?" Abby asks. "See if it's time?" Holding on to her husband, Abby crawls up his body like it's a ladder and then moves to the bed and flops down.

"Oh no! Here it comes again," she screams as if she sees a locomotive roaring down the tracks. I pull on my sterilized gloves. The exam needs to be fast, because contractions usually hurt more when the woman's on her back.

"Good," I report. "The head is very low and the cervix is fully dilated...no wait, only 9 centimeters."

"Ughhhhh!" Abby growls again and reaches her hands out to Ed to help her out of bed. Next thing I know, she's down on her knees on the floor, her forehead pressed into the side of the mattress.

"Abby, wait. Don't bear down. You're going to tear your cervix if you blast the baby out. Blow! Blow like this!"

For twenty minutes, Abby valiantly tries not to push but it's a losing battle. Maybe it's OK for her to push now, I say to myself; so I get her back in bed, hoping I'll have good news, but I'm disappointed.

"Abby," I start out. "The rim of cervix is getting thicker in front. It's not a good sign." Edmund looks scared. Abby looks determined.

"It's called a cervical lip," she says like she's lecturing a group of student nurses. "You need to reduce the lip...I've seen it done scores of times...Excuse me," she raises her finger for a contraction. "Read, Eddie!" she commands and when she's done we all take a deep breath.

"You are stronger than you know," Eddie says. "You are stronger than you know."

"Can you do it, Patience? Please! I'm tired and this hurts so damn bad!" It's the first time I've heard her swear or even act distressed.

"I'll try."

"Just use two fingers. The cervix is flexible like rubber. I'll push and you hold the cervix up."

I don't usually intervene in a labor, unless it's a malpresentation, like a hand presenting or a breech and I'm afraid I might do some damage, but I agree to try. With the next contraction we work together and I'm surprised to feel the swollen cervix slip back over the baby's head.

"Aghhhhhh!" Abby yells, pulling on her husband until she's into a squat and Eddie roars along with her.

"Aghhhhhh!" A lion and lioness facing each other.

Once the cervix is out of the way, it takes only five contractions, then blow, blow, blow and the baby's head is out. Abby's list of affirmations flutter to the floor as Edmund reaches for the wailing infant and hands him to Abby.

"It's just like Dr. Reed said," Eddie says, tears streaming down his face. " 'The birth of a baby, when labor is allowed to go naturally, brings the sweetest outcome.' Thank you Patience. We never could have done this without you."

October 16, 1956. At 7 pm, Abigail Frost delivered a six-pound, fourteen-ounce female infant without major difficulty. The one problem was a persistent cervical lip that held the baby back until she convinced me that I could stretch it over its head while she pushed and it worked. Her husband, Edmund, was a great help. Both he and Abby had read the new book from England, Childbirth Without Fear. So many women are afraid to give birth anymore. They rush to the hospital for the Twilight Sleep. Nurse Frost knew first hand what that looked like. The baby, named Maybelle, cried right away and there was such peace in the home, I didn't want to leave.

38

Attack

For a week, I've spent almost every day with Mira, putting up Lou's election flyers, and by Thursday my knee is killing me. So instead of walking, Dan and I decide to help out by driving out in the country to inspect the three polling places in designated churches. It's a fine sunny day and I enjoy talking to the pastors, but as we return through Liberty, a squad car and an ambulance speed past us, sirens blaring.

"They're turning on Third," I observe. "That's where Bitsy and Lou live. Let's check it out."

"I don't want to get in the way if there's a real emergency," Dan says, but he follows the sirens and we're shocked when we see the vehicles pull up in front of our friends' house. Bitsy is standing out on the street with a neighbor comforting her and smoke billows from a broken front window.

"Is anyone hurt?" Dan calls as he runs over.

"No," I hear Bitsy say. "Lou and Willie are at the mill and I was in the backyard. I'm fine."

Seconds later, Billy Blaze is out in front taking pictures of the new white ambulance, the broken window, the fire engine and eventually Bitsy and me . "Can I get a statement, Mrs. Cross?" he asks. "Rumor is that your husband has been getting threats? Is this because of his stand on civil rights? Any connection to you participating in the NAACP protests?"

Bitsy is somewhere between crying and punching the newspaperman in the face, so Dan leads the reporter forcefully away and I put my arm around her shoulders. That's when I feel how much she is trembling. She's not fine at all.

Night Visitor

Tonight will be the third time that Dan has stayed in town to guard Bitsy and Lou's house. From 6 pm to 6 am, he sits in the porch swing with his shotgun on his lap; then he gets up and goes off to work.

"Lou had shutters installed over all the windows when Mr. Hummingbird came to replace the window glass," Bitsy tells me when I bring them a chicken pie. "I feel more secure when we close them, but it also feels like a fortress. One thing is good though. The TV station out of Delmont came by and did a spot about the bombing for the local news.

"The attack actually worked in our favor," she says with a smile. "You should have seen the story on the screen. There was our poor little house, with the broken window and Lou standing on the porch saying he refuses to withdraw from the Sheriff's race, no matter what. The reporter even compared him to Martin Luther King when his house got bombed." Here she barks a short laugh and I'm glad to see she's back in the game.

Later, at home, Mira and I sit in front of the fire, listening to *Break the Bank* on the radio, with Dodger and Max curled up at our feet. It's a cold night and the winds of winter whine at the door. "Time to get the storm windows up," I comment, but Mira is looking at a book Willie bought her in Torrington.

"What are you reading?"

"*Dr. Spock's Common Sense Book of Baby and Child Care.*"

"Learning anything I couldn't teach you?" (This is said as a joke, but Mira takes it seriously.)

"Mom, that's not funny. On the back cover it says that *Common Sense Baby and Child Care* is the second best selling book after the Bible. Doctor Spock is a pediatrician and the most important thing he recommends to new parents is to trust their intuition, to pay attention to the baby and love him. Love is more important than routines, he says."

"There's something I want to talk to you about, Mira...You know your father and I are still concerned about how you are going to raise...."

Just then Max stands up with stiff legs, both ears forward as if he hears something.

"Wonder what Max's problem is?" I ask.

"Probably needs to go outside and do his duty," Mira responds. "I'll put both dogs out before I go to bed. Will you bring them in and lock up? I'm beat."

"Sure, honey."

There goes my chance for an honest mother-daughter talk.

After I bank the stove for the night, I call the dogs in, but a few hours later, Max is growling again. *What the heck?* He's down in the kitchen pacing around. Click, click, click, go his claws on the linoleum. *Maybe there's something outside, a wild animal or maybe a person!*

Just in case, I go downstairs and crack the door to let Max out. He pushes past me, growling low in his throat and I quickly lock the door again. It's probably just a raccoon trying to break into the chicken coop, I reassure myself.

For an hour I wait for him to come back and while I wait I turn to the journals.

December 14, 1859
Ontario, Canada

It took about four hours to get to Elgin, and during that time, I began to relax as Mr. Sinclair told me about the community. A Presbyterian minister, Reverend King, a Scotsman who inherited slaves when he married into a planter's family in the South, started the community. Mr. King didn't believe in slavery and wanted to set his bondsmen free, so he brought them to Ontario. With the help of Lord Elgin, the Governor at the time, they formed the Elgin Community, 9000 acres to be sold at cost to runaway slaves and free blacks. Each family owns their own land and a small home.

"Ten years ago the citizens were powerless, non-persons," Mr. Sinclair exclaimed. "Now they

have the three essentials of happiness; someone to love, something to do and most importantly, hope."

As he talked, our train moved at great speed past raw wilderness. Occasionally, I caught a view of Lake Erie, its water tranquil and blue.

Finally, the conductor called "ELGIN, BUXTON SETTLEMENT!"

Saying goodbye to the kind Mr. Sinclair, I gathered my few belongings and was assisted by the conductor out of our coach. On the platform were two other persons of African descent and I immediately tore off my bonnet so they could observe my short frizzy hair.

"Excuse me," I said. "Do you live here?" They both nodded yes.

"Do indeed," the man said in a soft southern accent. "Can we help you?"

A strong wind whipped my long dress around my legs and I pulled my bonnet back on. "I'm looking for Reverend King and his church. Could you tell me where to go?"

"Just come along with us, sister," the woman greeted me kindly. "We're part of the community and can take you right there. Where you from?"

"Virginia," I announced without fear, "I'm a runaway slave."

"I'm Marion Griffith and this is my wife Mary Ann. We came into Canada from Tennessee as fugitives five years ago and have almost paid off the fifty acres we homestead. I'll even be voting in the next provincial election." He was proud and I thought he deserved to be.

As we began to walk, I pulled my wool shawl tight over my shoulders. Soon we passed a family singing as they cleared brush along a fencerow. "I got-a wings, you got-a wings - All o' God's children got-a wings." It was strange to see brown people working their own land and singing their own songs in their own way for the pure joy of it and no overseer with a whip watching over them.

"That's Ezra Sharp and his brood of ten," Mary Ann said. "Their mother died in childbirth two years ago, but he went to Windsor and got him a new wife."

When we finally arrived at the church, I said goodbye to my new friends. A pale man, in a black frock coat was standing at the door and I'll tell you the truth, after coming all this way to this community intended for former black slaves and black freemen, I was afraid the way I looked might disqualify me.

Pushing down my fear, I threw back my bonnet again and hailed him. "Are you Reverend King?" I called. "I bring greetings from our mutual friend, Mr. Sinclair of Toronto,"

The pastor studied me for a moment, then he spoke. "Welcome. I hear by your speech that you're from the South and I suspect you've had a long journey."

It was then that I almost fell to my knees. "Yes," I said, starting to cry. "It's been a very long and arduous trip. I hope you can help me."

The kind man took my satchel. "I know you're cold and weary," he said, with a touch of a Scottish accent. "But we have to do something before I take you inside."

We went around back, into what looked like a barn and he pointed to a large brass bell inscribed with one word, Freedom. "We ring it at 6 AM and at 9 PM every day to remind the community that we are free. We also ring it when an escaped slave arrives. Would you do the honors?"

I think I was only supposed to ring it one time, but I couldn't help myself. I rang it until my arms ached. I rang it for Peter and Elsie and Moses. I rang it for all escaped slaves and those slaves still in bondage.

Outside in the yard, the intermittent barking continues. By this time my eyes are drooping and I'm ready for bed. Over and over, I call at the door, but Max won't come in. Finally, I lock up again. *If the dumb dog wants to roam around all night, so be it. I'm going to sleep.*

39

Lawman

Lou won! And in just a few months, on January 1, he'll be Sheriff!   At the victory party, he made a speech.

"I'm just so filled with emotion," he said. "It's been a tough couple weeks, not just for me and my family with the threats and the bomb, but for all of Union County as we cope with the integration of our schools.

"I've always spoken of the community as 'we'. It's so important that the *we* include everyone, immigrant miners, teachers, farmers, nurses and shopkeepers… brown, white, and in-between.   And it's vital that law enforcement in Union County be the guardian of the peace. Thank you everyone for all your support. Now let's party!"

As the crowd in the American Legion Hall, cheered, Bitsy put on some music, a new Top Twenty number by Shirley and Lee. *"Come on baby - let the good times roll – Come on baby – let me thrill your soul!"* and she and Lou began to jitterbug. Willie and Mira followed. Mira was

387

clearly pregnant, but it didn't slow her down and though Willie didn't move his artificial leg, he moved his hips like Elvis Presley and gave her a twirl.

"Might as well join them," Dan said, pulling me out of my chair. *"Come on baby let the good times roll – Roll all night long!"*

Destiny

In the days that following the election, I was surprised that Aran Bishop didn't challenge the results and I wondered if he had something up his sleeve.

Our happiness for Lou and Bitsy and the whole community was tempered only by my ever-constant worry about Danny. There was anger too. He could at least send a postcard or call us, the jackass!

Mira is another matter. Last week she moved into town with Willie; shacking up, unmarried and unashamed, in the apartment Will and Danny once shared. Bitsy and Lou seem fine with it, happy even, as if they're just any middle-aged couple expecting a grandbaby, but I've had a hard time feeling their joy.

Grandbaby, I think, as I stir cream in my coffee. Though I'm not going to be Mira's midwife, I *am* going to be someone's grandmother.

"Hey, Gramps!" Dan looks over. "We're going to be *grandparents*. Do you think about that at all? Most people get excited about the first grandbaby."

"Mmmmmm. I guess we've just been so busy with the election and everything, it hasn't been on my mind. Maybe I should make the baby a cradle or something."

"For me, it's not *just being busy*. I've never really accepted the pregnancy. I might as well face it, though; this is going to happen. I can't choose how my kids live, but I can get on the train and help make it a good journey."

"Good plan. So what are you going to do?"

"Well, for starters, I'm going to take a present to Mira…a house warming present for their place in town!"

The apartment in the alley where Will and Danny had once lived is not as bad as I imagined. For one thing, there's a red wooden window box where someone, probably Mira, has planted artificial geraniums from the five and dime store and under the window is an old-fashioned bench where a person can sit in the sun in the morning.

I knock on the heavy oak door that looks like it's been there for a hundred years. Music is coming from a radio inside, so I know someone's home.

"Hi Mira," I say, smiling when she answers.

"Ma!"

"Surprised? Can I come in?"

"Ahhhh, sure…. I was just painting the walls. Sorry, the place is a mess."

The small dwelling appears to have only three rooms; a tiny kitchen, a bedroom off to the left and a living room that's about the size of my pantry. A can of white paint sits on a sheet of newspaper on a table.

What surprises me is that it actually feels homey.

There's an old sofa, which I recognize from Bitsy's house on Wild Rose Lane, covered with Mira's quilt and an easy chair with a lace doily on the high back. A wooden fruit crate covered with red flowered fabric serves as a coffee table and a floor lamp stands in the corner. The walls are all white except for the brick one in front and white curtains hang over the windows.

"This is nice," I comment.

"Oh, Mom," Mira laughs. "You don't have to say that. It's kind of a dump, but we're fixing it up."

"You could come home. You and Willie and the baby could live with us."

Mira wipes her hands and sits down on the sofa, patting the cushion next to her. "That means a lot, Mom, but we want our own place. Bitsy and Lou asked us if we wanted to move in with them, too."

"OK, then," I respond. "I brought you some linens from the closet at home and also some kitchen things?" I hold out a worn cloth satchel.

"Thanks, she says with a big grin."

"I brought you some baby clothes too. Do you have much yet?"

"Just the diapers that Lillie Bittman saved from her babies and a stroller we got at a flea market."

"Also, here's the book the nurse, Abby Frost, used for her delivery, *Childbirth Without Fear*. "I don't know if you'll read it. It's about natural childbirth, which is actually the only kind you've seen."

"I'll read it. It might help Willie, too. He's awful nervous."

I begin to get out the newborn things women have given me over the years. Mira spreads them out on the makeshift coffee table; tiny shirts and nightclothes, booties and hats. Then for the first time, she lets down and cries, big gulping sobs. "Oh, Mom, I'm so sorry. I know you hate me for embarrassing you and not being the good girl you wanted."

"We all make mistakes, Hon," I say holding her in my arms. "And sometime the mistakes can lead us in the right direction. I'm sure it was your destiny to be this baby's mommy, just as it was my destiny to be yours."

Mira takes a big breath and wipes her eyes on her shirtsleeve. "Thanks, Mom. Do you want to feel the baby?"

I place my hand on her belly and it moves!

40

Wolf Pack

An hour later, as I leave Mira and Willie's little apartment, I notice three young men swagger out of Jim's tavern. Slicked back hair and black leather jackets, Greasers, Mira would call them.

"You S.O.B., what you think? If there's pussy involved, sure I want some," boasts the tallest of the three. "I don't care if it's white, brown or black, so long it's wet and tight." The men howl like a bunch of wolves.

The tall one, noticing me, holds up his hand. "Wait, isn't that the bitch that was in the paper? The one that walked the little pickaninny into the school, the woman that tore the white boy's shirt on the first day of classes."

This is not good. To get to my car, I have to walk past them, but men like these are my worst nightmare. I could pop back into Mira's apartment, but I don't want to bring trouble to her door, so I hotfoot the other way down the alley and hurry around the corner toward Main. Unfortunately it's a Sunday evening and all the shops are closed so there's nowhere to hide…Hearing footsteps, I look back and the men are right behind me.

"Hey Bitch! What's your hurry?" the little guy

yells.

I've dealt with wild dogs before, but this time I don't have a rifle, so I grab the empty metal newspaper stand in front of Dixon Drugs and hold it up like lion tamer's chair. Just then, there's a sharp short siren wail and the town patrol car pulls up to the curb. It's Aran Bishop, still Sheriff until January 1st.

Oh, great! I think. *Now he's going to harass me too.* But I'm wrong.

"What's up, punks?" he yells out the window. "I thought I told you I didn't want you in town after sundown."

"It's not sundown yet, Sheriff!" sasses the little man. "Anyway, I thought the Sundown Rule was only for coons?"

"It's for any *undesirables* and that includes you. Now get the hell out of my town or I'll throw you in the cooler for public intoxication!"

"Asshole!" yells the tall one and gives him the finger, but the three slouch off slowly and climb into a rusted green Ford with a huge Confederate Flag painted on the hood.

"Where's your vehicle?" Bishop growls at me.

"Just down the way."

"Well, you better get in it. I'll sit here and watch. Those punks are trouble. Hustle now."

Once in the Olds, I lock all the doors and watch as the green coupe roars out of town and the Sheriff drives off in the other direction.

I've been in difficult situations before, car wrecks, blizzards, ice storms and mining wars, but I've never felt like a deer stalked by wolves. The fact that Sheriff Bishop had to rescue me is humiliating. Then I laugh. *I probably could have handled it. After all, I had the newspaper stand as a weapon.*

Red-White. Red-White

A few minutes later on my way home, a car with bright lights speeds up behind me. *What the hell?* As it passes on a curve, I slam on my brakes and veer off on the berm. It's the green Ford with the confederate flag and the town cop, right on its tail, lights flashing, then the siren comes on.

Good for you, Bishop, I think. *The jerks are drunk and deserve to be stopped.* Then taking a deep breath, I pull back on the road.

Five miles later, I come around a curve and see, with horror, the squad car again. It's flipped over against a bank of trees, red and white lights still flashing.

I pull up behind and jump out. "Aran! Are you OK?" On the other side of the vehicle, the cop's crumpled body has been thrown against an oak.

A quick check reveals his pulse is rapid and weak, too fast to count; not a good sign. He's gasping for air and when I pull open his uniform to look for blood, I discover the left side of his chest is crushed in like a cannon ball hit him. There are no lacerations, nothing to bandage. *What to do now?*

I try to remember where the closest phone is, so I can call the ambulance; two miles back, I estimate. *What to do? What to do?*

Bishop is a big man; two hundred pounds, maybe two-twenty. I imagine dragging him to my vehicle over the rough ground and trying to pull him into the back seat, then speeding back to the hospital, but I fear I would only injure him more.

With this kind of trauma, the ribs have probably punctured his lungs and maybe even his heart. He might be bleeding internally. I sit on the ground with his head in my lap, a situation I could never have imagined. I keep talking to him and feeling his pulse. If anyone comes along I know they'll be able to see us with the emergency lights still flashing. Red-white. Red-white.

"Hold on Sheriff. Hold on," I call to him and his dark eyes flicker open.

"Patience Hester…" he whispers.

"You're going to make it," I say, knowing his survival is unlikely. "Hold on."

"I can't get my air, Patience. Am I badly injured?"

"Not so bad, Aran, but I should get help."

"No, don't leave!" he whispers. The man closes his eyes and coughs up red blood. With each labored breath he gurgles some more. "Don't leave me," he pleads then passes out again.

"I won't. Someone's sure to come." I smooth his dark hair and wipe blood off his chin. "There's something only a few people know about me, Aran. I might as well get it off my chest, since we have some time…Make a confession of sorts.

"When I first came to the Hope River I was on the run. Do you remember The Battle of Blair

Mountain, Aran, back in the twenties, when thirteen thousand striking miners in southern West Virginia fought hand to hand with the union bosses and their goons? Well, I was right in the thick of it and I killed my first husband, Ruben, a union organizer, when I tried to get a Pinkerton man off him. It was an accident, Aran, but that one misplaced blow shattered something inside me."

He makes a weak smile and opens his eyes. "You never called me Aran before," he says.

Then the man, once my enemy, dies.

41

Slow Dance

We bury Aran Bishop without fanfare beside his brother Beef Bishop who died in the wildfire of '35 in the little cemetery on Wild Rose Road. It's a cold afternoon, spitting flecks of snow and the only one from the Bishop family to join us is the last of the three brothers, Earl. Because Aran died in the line of duty, four cops in uniform arrive from Delmont and one plays Taps on his bugle.

When Dan and I get home, we're surprised to see Lou's car in the drive and Bitsy's motorcycle parked next to it.

"What's this?" Dan wonders, but when I see smoke rising from the Baby Cabin, I immediately think of Mira and run around back. Just before I get to the door, I stop and take a few breaths. *I am not the midwife*, I remember, only the birthing woman's mother and a guest.

Inside I hear moans and try to gauge by her voice where Mira is in labor. (It sounds like close to five centimeters, I decide) I tap on the door and stick my head in. "Where you been?" Bitsy asks, her hand on her hip.

"Burying the Sheriff. I mean burying Aran Bishop, the *former* sheriff. I would have come sooner if someone would invent a phone you could carry in your pocket."

Willie and Mira stand in the middle of the cabin, holding each other as if they're dancing at the high school prom and a portable phonograph in a little box like a suitcase is playing *Earth Angel*. "Hi Mom!" Mira says with a twinkle in her eye. "Glad you could make it."

"Glad to be here! Looks like you're doing great." Then I hurriedly pull Bitsy out on the porch. "Everything OK? Baby head down? Heart tones good? Is she leaking fluid?"

"Everything's fine, Patience. Baby vertex. Heart beat 142 a minute. Mom's vital signs are normal and no leaking yet. I haven't checked her, but her contractions are every four minutes and from the way she's acting, I'd guess she's 6 or 7 centimeters."

"Cat's pajamas! I was guessing five. Willie doing OK, too?"

Bitsy smiles. "He read every page of *Childbirth Without Fear* and he's doing great. Now go wash up and change"

"Good idea!"

Inside the house, I give the men a report on Mira's labor progress, then take a shower and within thirty minutes I'm back in the baby cabin with a thermos of hot raspberry tea. The music has stopped, but no one's removed the needle from the recording, so I lift the phonograph arm and the scratching stops.

The contractions are now every three minutes and Mira's voice is rising. Soon, I imagine, she'll say she can't do it anymore and get mad at Willie because he isn't massaging her back the way she wants him to.

I pour some tea into everyone's cup and hold Mira's up to her lips when she's in between contractions. "You're doing great, Honey," I tell her and kiss her cheek.

"How long now? How long will this last?" Mira wails with the next contraction and Bitsy and I look at each other. She's nearing the end.

"Not much longer," Bitsy responds. "Just take the contractions one at a time like you're moving bricks from one spot to another. Don't think about how big the pile is. Just do the work."

Feeling somewhat non-essential, I sit down in a chair and check the records Willie and Mira have brought along with their phonograph. "Would you like more music? This is a good one, *Love me Tender* by Elvis Presley."

"Yes! Yes!" Mira says. "Oh no, here comes another one!"

"You can do it," Willie encourages. "I'll hold you. Just bounce a little if it makes you feel better."

"Love me tender. Love me sweet. Never let me go," the singer croons and I can see that the music helps Mira relax. Willie takes her in his arms again, her head on his shoulder.

Soon. Soon, I think. The urge to push should come soon and I glance at my watch. It's 6 o'clock and already dark. The contractions march on at 2 minutes apart. Periodically, Bitsy checks the baby's heart and it's perfect. Then it's 7:30 Then 8:00.

Finally, Bitsy clears her throat. "Mira...Willie. I want to talk to you. For a while it was clear you were making progress. I could tell by your voice and how frequently the pains came, but nothing's changed for a couple of hours. We can go another hour if you want, or I can check you right now."

"What do want to do, sweetheart," Willie asks.

"I don't know. I can't think."

"We'll wait another 60 minutes, Ma." Willie makes the decision. "You said the baby's doing fine, right?"

Calypso

So we journey on, but there's no change in the labor pattern; it's a flat desert with no horizon in sight. I put on a new record, hoping it will change the cheerless mood. It's Harry Belafonte with *Jump in the Line*, a Calypso number. This should liven things up.

"Shake, shake, shake, Senora - Shake your body line - Shake, shake, shake, Senora! Willie starts wiggling and shaking his artificial leg, which makes Mira laugh. In ten seconds, the mood changes from hard work in the coalmines to fun on the bank of the Hope River.

This is what we've been missing; Joy. We've all been so quiet and respectful. This is something I've learned over the years. Mothers in labor don't always know what's best for them, and it's the midwife's job to be creative and make suggestions.

"Dance, dance, dance Senora - Dance it all the time," we sing together between contractions. All of a sudden, Mira stops wiggling and her eyes get big. "On no," she says. "I have to poop. Mom, Bitsy, Willie! Get me a pot or I'm gonna go right on the floor. I hurry to bring the white enamel potty with the lid and wire handle from the cupboard.

"Just squat down," Bitsy says. "But don't strain too hard." It's a small room, so we step out on the dark porch to give her some privacy.

When she tells us she's done, we return and have her lie down, but there's no need for a vaginal exam. With the next contraction, a silver dollar's size circle of hair shows at the opening.

"Holy Cow!" says Willie. "I can see the head, Hon! It's right there!"

"What do I do now?" Mira asks, looking at Bitsy and then at me.

"What do you want to do?" Bitsy asks.

"Well, have the baby, of course!"

Once she starts pushing, Mira's body takes over and her grunts become roars. "Agrhhhhhh!" she bellows, and we bellow with her. Then all of a sudden the head is out. Gently, Bitsy feels for the cord, flips it over the head and within seconds a wet and crying baby is in her hands.

The little girl reaches out her arms and Bitsy gives her to Willie, who gives her to Mira.

"You did it!" he says, kissing her hair.

"*We* did it!" Mira answers.

After things are cleaned up and the baby is examined, weighed and snuggled in a clean blanket, I go to tell Dan and Lou, but they already know. They'd been sitting silently on the dark porch listening the whole last thirty minutes.

"Is that how all births go?" Lou asks. "I'm exhausted!"

Then we all crowd around the mother and baby. *"Happy birthday to you! Happy birthday to you! Happy birthday, dear...."*

"Wait! What's her name? Does she have a name yet?" Lou asks.

November 17th, 1956. 7# 5 ounce baby girl born to Mira Hester at 8:35 PM in the Baby Cabin, into the hands of midwife Bitsy Cross. Present were the patient's friend Willie and the patient's mother, me. One small tear, but no need for stitching. Estimated blood loss, 1 cup. Of note, the mother had very little urge to push. We waited and waited. Finally, when the head was almost on the perineum, we told her to go ahead and push anyway and then the urge came.

42

Glory

Mira named the baby Gloria, Glory for short, and she and Willie stayed in the Baby Cabin for almost a week. Bitsy didn't need to, but she came over every morning just to visit and one day I got out the rest of Mrs. Potts' new journals.

"I'm sorry I started to read them," I apologized. "I know you said it was all right, but I always feel guilty."

"Of course you couldn't wait," she laughed. "It would be like sitting at a table with warm carrot cake in front of you and a fork in your hand…You've got to take a bite. I'll read them from the beginning someday when I have time. For now, just catch me up on what's happening."

I summarized as quickly as I could. "Well, Grace has finally made it across Lake Erie into Canada. She separates from her companions, Peter, Elsie and their baby…and makes her way to a community of free black farmers…"

December 16, 1859
Elgin Buxton Community, Ontario, Canada
For two days I stayed at the home of Reverend King and his wife, Jeremiah, and at night I lay under the warm quilt in their extra bedroom and wondered who I was. One drop of African blood

and by law, in the United States, you were African, but I was so diluted by white masters my African blood barely showed. By candlelight I held up my arms and stared at them.

Whiteness was useful for blending in with the Europeans, the people who had stolen the land from the natives and then kidnapped Africans to work that land, but to me my color, or lack of it, was an object of shame. It made me a "Coffman" and I hated the Coffmans, all of them, except Mother of course.

During this time, I met a few of the leaders of the community who'd come here years ago and already paid for their homes and their land. In addition to farming, some worked at the local lumber mill; some taught in the school; some labored laying tracks on the railroad for cash and I sensed they didn't know what to do with me, a single young woman, without a father or husband to look after her.

"Tell us what you know how to do so that we can find a suitable place for you," Reverend King asked at a meeting of the elders.

I had thought about this. "I can sew. I can play the piano. I can read. I can do sums. I have an education in history and the healing arts..."

"Can you cook and clean? There are several widowers with children that could use a good cook. And we have a new hotel that can use a chamber maid."

"No, I'm sorry." I wanted to explain that the curse of slavery for the white woman was that she

didn't know how to do anything but sew.

The men scratched their heads while Mrs. King quietly served tea. "There's an empty house on plot 44," she said softly. Most men in Virginia would think it presumptuous for a woman to speak at a male gathering, but none of the Elgin men seemed to mind.

"That's true," said the Reverend. "You could stay there temporarily. Edward Matthews passed away from fever last year, and his wife and children moved to Toronto to stay with kin."

"Could I buy the farm on lot 44, make yearly payments like the previous owner?" I asked boldly.

Several eyebrows went up. "I mow the fields to keep the land cleared," a farmer named Layton spoke for the first time. "In return, I get the hay for my animals. I think the young lady has a right to the homestead. If she isn't able to make the payments we can take the farm back. What do we have to lose?"

And so it was decided, the farm would be mine, and the next day we went to see Lot 44.

Reverend King walked with me down the dirt road and as I looked around, I noted how flat the land was. Almost every homestead had a log cabin of about the same size, each with a long porch across the front and a wooden fence surrounding it. Most had one or two old trees, left for shade when the forest was cleared.

"Do you like the houses?" pastor King asked. "They're all about the same size so we can raise a cabin in a day with twelve men. A barn takes

longer. In the summer we have contests to see who has the most beautiful flowers. The gardens are all gone now, of course, and soon there will be snow."

I shivered at the thought. I'd heard about Canada. There would be polar bears, grizzlies and wolves.

43

Spirit of All

This Thanksgiving, because we had a newborn in the family, we decided not to go to the community celebration at the Hazel Patch Chapel, but to have our own feast at home.

The morning dawned clear and cool, but warmed up when the sun peeked over Hope Mountain. The first thing Dan and I did was call Sunny and Sue in Martinsburg to wish them a happy day. As student nurses, employed and trained by the hospital, they had to work, but promised to be home for Christmas.

It was strange not to have Danny home either. With all the excitement of births and deaths, we had forgotten that now that Lou Cross was Sheriff, he could file a Missing Person Report; not that I expected it to do much.

Thinking about our lost son, I felt tears in my eyes, and I quickly put on my jacket and went outside. The leaves were mostly gone now, except on a couple of oaks, but the daisies and snapdragons had lived through the frost and made a nice splash of color.

"Jay! Jay!"
"Hi, Howard," I answered without enthusiasm.

"You trying to cheer me up?" Just talking to him brought a smile to my face. It was so silly.

"Jay!" he answered and flew to the fence.

"Our boy is gone," I told him. "He hasn't called or even sent a postcard. We don't even know if he's alive or dead."

Howard cocked his head and made the soft call he used when he was feeding his hatchlings. "Tweet, tweet, twitter, tweet." I would never have known that Blue Jays sang like that unless I'd heard it myself, and I felt Howard comforting me over my loss. "It's OK," he said. "My children leave every year. Sometimes they come back."

I thought about that. The little troop of young Blue Jays must have already migrated south and only the parents were left.

"Sometimes they come back," he said it again.

"Thanks, Howard." I smiled and brushed away the last tear.

For our Thanksgiving feast we had mashed potatoes and bean casserole from crops we had grown. Dan shot a wild turkey and roasted it in the oven. Bitsy insisted on making four pumpkin pies, two for us and two for the Hazel Patch folk, and I whipped cream from our Jersey cow's milk. For the first time, Mira and Willie, who were still staying in the Baby Cabin, came into the house for the meal, and then Lou surprised us by reading a short prayer.

"As we give thanks for this feast, let us think of those who have no food. As we give thanks for our friends and family, let us think of those who are lonely. Help us to reach out to those in need and to defend the defenseless. Amen."

There was a pause in the festivities while we all rested our eyes on the floor, and then Bitsy broke the silence with her own prayer.

"Rub a dub. Thanks for the grub! Yay, God!"

Discovery

As usual after a feast, most of us just wanted to take a nice nap, but Bitsy was determined to take her pies to Hazel Patch. "Come with me, Will?" she asked. "It will be nice for you to get out. You can sit in the sidecar of the motorcycle like old times."

"I'll come if we can ride the horses," Will said.

This was something new. I hadn't seen Bitsy on a horse for five years, but eventually the two saddled up and trotted off with the pies in a picnic basket.

As the sun crossed the sky and shadows stretched across the dry yellow grass, Lou began to pace the kitchen floor and worry about his wife and son. Finally, he made a call to Reverend Jerome at the Hazel Patch Chapel where they were having their feast. It turned out the two had left the community about two hours ago.

"Where the hell could they be?" Lou grumbled. "It gets dark early this time of year. I guess I should go look for them. Want to come, Dan?" Just then we heard horses clopping across the wooden bridge and Betsy's voice singing... *"Hush-a-bye. Don't you cry – Go to sleep a little baby. – When you wake - you shall have – all the pretty little horses."*

She was still riding my horse and carried a baby against her chest. Willie rode his gelding and led a pinto pony on a rope. Draped over its back was a limp body, wrapped in a quilt, her long red hair almost touching the ground. I didn't need to see her face. The hair was the giveaway. It was Kitty.

"Not long after we left the preacher's house in Hazel Patch, we saw a wisp of smoke rising over the trees," Bitsy tells us when they get inside. "I wasn't sure who lived there, so for the fun of riding we decided to investigate. At the crossroads of Salt Lick and what used to be Horse Shoe Run we turned into the brush."

"It was rough going," Willie added. "But eventually, we came to an overgrown pasture and at the end of the field, a small house."

"It was Mrs. Potts' old place and someone was living there," Bitsy took up the story again. "Willie hollered 'Hello! Hello!' a couple of times, not wanting the occupant to rush out with a shotgun, but no one answered."

"The place was a wreck," Willie added. "Almost falling down, torn tin roof, broken windows covered with boards. We knocked a few times, but when we heard an infant cry we just busted in."

"I never saw anything like it," Bitsy went on. "The baby, though emaciated, was clinging to her dead mother, eyes as big as saucers." Here she stopped and pulled back the blanket so we could see the little one's face. Dan was warming a bottle of cow's milk and he brought it over.

"No kidding," Willie exclaimed. "Kitty looked like the photos of the dead prisoners at Auschwitz, nothing but skin and bones, her ribs showing. We figured she must have died in the last twenty-four hours, because her body didn't smell yet. Apparently, she'd been rationing the food she'd either harvested or swiped and giving the baby most of it."

"Despite the still smoldering coals in the fireplace, the room was cold and damp," Bitsy explained. "Empty bowls had been set on the floor. It looked like the mother, knowing she was too weak to survive, had prepared the food for the infant and left it, hoping against hope that someone would come."

After I got some clean flannel blankets and some diapers from the Baby Cabin, I went out to the barn where Dan and Lou had placed the young mother's body on a table in the tack room. There wasn't much I could do. She was already wrapped in a clean sheet. I tried to comb her hair, but it kept falling out. Finally, I took the ribbon from my own hair and gave her a low ponytail of what was left of her long red locks. Standing in the barn in the lantern light, after the men had gone back to the house, I took Kitty's cold hand.

"I'm so sorry," I whispered. "So sorry. I didn't know..."

44

Will the Circle be Unbroken?

The discovery of Kitty Bishop's corpse had to be reported to someone, of course. Since Aran Bishop had died and Lou was now the official Sheriff, he took his wife and his son's statement, then called the new hospital to have an ambulance come and take the young mother away.

An hour later, the medical crew arrived, including Nurse Abigail Frost. Lou handled the transfer of the body, but when Abby came in the house and saw the baby, she wanted the infant admitted for IV fluids immediately.

"She's dehydrated and half starved," she insisted, but the little girl still clung to Bitsy. Finally Lou said they'd bring the baby to the emergency department in their own car. He didn't want little Mary to be with her dead mother one minute longer.

While the medics and Lou were loading the corpse, I took Abby in the pantry. "What are you doing here in uniform?" I whispered.

"When a part-time nursing position opened in the ER last week, I had to go for it. Then when I heard the squad was heading to your place tonight, I asked to come. I can't believe it's Kitty," she said. "I really thought she'd just run away."

"Did Dr. Andrews ever find out you had a homebirth?" I couldn't help asking.

"He did. 'You'd think a maternity nurse would know when she was in labor!' he ribbed me. I claimed the contractions were so irregular, I thought I was just constipated and when the baby came, Eddie had to deliver it. Ed's job at the university is only three days a week and so far one of us is always home with Maybelle."

After Bitsy and Lou left with the baby, the rest of us just sat in silence. Finally, I roused myself. "Anyone want coffee? Or raspberry tea, Mira?"

"Yes, I guess I should have some." she said.

"Pumpkin pie?" I asked, but after seeing the body slung over the back of the horse, no one had any appetite.

Later in bed, with Willie and Mira and little Gloria back in the Baby Cabin, I found Dan's hand. "What is the world coming to?" I asked. "How could this happen in a civilized country? Was the girl mentally ill? I've read that can happen when mother depression turns into psychosis. Or did she just not know where to turn?"

"Maybe at first she was just trying to get away from the Bishops. Maybe she thought she could survive on her own, living off the land or maybe she was afraid if she went to the authorities her baby would be taken away. I guess we'll bury her in the cemetery on Wild Rose Road after the autopsy. I can make a pine casket in the morning."

"Can we pray for her?" I asked and he squeezed my hand under the covers.

"Spirit of life...we ask your help in accepting the death of young Kitty Bishop. Tell her that her baby, Mary, is still alive and we will be sure she gets good care," I said. Tell her that nobody blames her, that there is something very wrong in our world when mothers and babies don't have food and shelter and love. We will do our best to change that. Amen."

Then Dan drew me close and I cried.

Shifting Sands

Two days later Mira, Glory and Will packed up and moved back to their tiny apartment. Dan went back to work and I cleaned up the Baby Cabin. It was almost like normal, except Kitty was dead, buried behind the house with the blue door on Wild Rose Lane, and the baby had been admitted to the hospital for hydration and treatment for worms.

After my work was done, I got out my mending and turned on the radio to listen to the *World News*. The news was not good.

While we were having babies, celebrating Thanksgiving, and dealing with the death of a young mother, General Nikita Khrushchev declared the Russians would bury us and Fidel Castro began a revolution in Cuba. These are troubled times and I feel the sand shifting under my feet.

I once was a member of the International Workers of the World. After the Rosenberg trials in '53 where the couple were accused, convicted and executed for being spies and giving the Russians assistance building their first A bomb, I burned all my copies of *The Daily Worker*. I'll admit it, my leanings are still for the common man and against the big bosses, but the days are long gone when any American dare be a Communist sympathizer.

To cheer myself, I go back to Mrs. Potts' journal. There were only a few pages left.

December 17, 1859
Elgin-Buxton Community, Ontario, Canada

At last the Reverend and I came to the cabin that was to be mine if I could manage to keep up the payments. The hay fields were neatly mowed, but dry thistles as tall as my waist, broken branches, and piles of leaves surrounded the dwelling. The door was unlocked and when we went in my hand flew to my nose. Some animal had taken up residence and left a calling card. There were leaves inside too, along with cobwebs in the rafters and wood chips all over the floor.

"Don't worry about the smell," The Reverend said. "I'll help you clean it up. Look, Mrs. Matthews left some of her furniture." There was a handmade table with benches, a tin bucket, a bed and a wooden rocker, also a few tin plates, a chipped cup and a bent spoon. On each wall, a six paned window let in the light.

"Do you want me to start a fire and bring in some water from the well?"

"Yes, that would be nice," I said.

Before he went out for wood, Mr. King handed me a broom that leaned in a corner and, not wanting to show my ignorance of such things, I began to sweep. Before he left for home, the Reverend presented me with three candles, a loaf of bread, some cheese and a handful of carrots.

"This isn't much but it will get you through the night," he said. "Someone will come over soon to cut the weeds around the cabin and I'll take you to

the community general store for provisions." Then the pastor left.

That first night in the little log house, I sat in the rocker and stared around my humble abode. The glass windows stared back at me, making me feel small and alone. It was clear I had to leave Virginia, wasn't it? Dr. Coffman could do whatever he wanted with me; rape me, sell me, whip me until I bled, even shoot me for trying to escape if he was angry enough.

"There's no going back," I said out loud. "So I'll have to go forward. At any rate, I am free." I said it out-loud a few times to convince myself. "I'm free! I am free!"

After that, I fluffed up the musty mattress. Jammy had told me he replaced the straw in his tick twice a year and I planned to do the same thing as soon as I could. I made my bed with the clean quilt and linens Mrs. King had lent me and hung my few clothes on the pegs on the walls. Then I set my matches and knife on a shelf, along with my medical supplies, my sewing kit, a medical book I'd stolen from Doctor Coffman's library and my Bible. Finally, I lit a candle and sat down at the table to eat my simple meal of bread and cheese and make a list of what I would need from the general store, which was almost everything. Fortunately, a few gold coins still jingled in my purse.

Just before bed, I remembered the flowery needlepoint that Mother had given me and I put the small frame on the mantle. "Send out thy Light, Oh Lord," it said. "And thy Truth let it lead me."

That was the end! There were no more of Grace's diaries, so I closed the notebook, put another log in the heater stove and tried to imagine the rest of the story.

Journey

After Dan and I milked this morning, he asked if I wanted to keep him company on a visit to a farm near Oneida. "It's an interesting case," he told me. "A goat ate an arrangement of plastic flowers off his owner's porch and I had to surgically remove them. Today I need to check the incision."

"No, that's OK," I laughed. "I think you can handle it."

The truth is, I wanted to go back to Kitty's hideout and see for myself where she'd been living, but I didn't think Dan would like it. An hour after he was gone, I dressed in warm clothes, went out to the barn and saddled up Dusty.

As I passed the intersection to Hazel Patch, I slowed my horse to a walk. Finding the overgrown entrance to Horse Shoe Run wasn't as easy as I imagined, but after fighting my way through the brush, I finally discovered the clearing and in the distance the crumbling cottage. A few starving chickens were still out in the yard.

I am not a believer in ghosts, but there was something eerie about the place as if Kitty's spirit still lingered. Just in case, I knocked at the door. Amused with myself, I even called out. "Hello! Hello!" Then, hearing no answer, I stepped over the threshold. The room that I entered was partitioned off with blankets to concentrate the heat

420

around the hearth. A small stack of dead limbs for firewood still sat in the corner.

As Bitsy had described, there were an assortment of bowls arranged around a pallet that was covered with torn quilts. Two candle stubs had been pushed into bottles and an old axe leaned in the corner. There were a few books stacked on a shelf, one a leather bound volume named *The Theory and Practice of Midwifery*, published in1856, probably stolen from Dr. Coffman; the other, *The Farmer's Guide to Horses*, 1850.

When I poked around behind the partition, I noticed a chest with a curved top and when I opened it I almost choked on my tears. There were piles of little shirts and pants, things the old midwife had saved from her four children that died of typhus and underneath the clothes, a surprise, two more of her notebooks.

The trip home on horseback with the journals, the two old medical books, plus four live chickens in a gunnysack tied on behind me was not pleasant. For one thing, it had started to rain and the rain turned to sleet. For another, the chickens were squawking. By the time I got back, it was almost dark, and I was shivering with cold. Dan's truck was in the driveway, so I went right inside.

"Can you put these chickens in the hen house and give them some extra cracked corn and warm water?" I asked as I pulled off my wet jacket. "I found them at Mrs. Potts' old house and I'm surprised they're still alive."

"Patience, you went out to that old place by

yourself? Here, sit down; I'll make you some tea."

"Thanks buddy...I just felt like an adventure."

Later sipping Campbell's Tomato Soup and eating leftover cornbread for dinner, I told Dan what I'd seen at Mrs. Potts' house, the squalor, the poverty and Kitty's brave attempt to survive. Finally, I showed him the books and the journals I'd found.

"Son of a gun!" Dan exclaims. "So it was Kitty that was leaving the journals on the porch all along. And did you see the paint on the chicken's feet?"

"I didn't notice."

"Well those were our chickens. Ee marked their feet with blue paint last spring?"

"So the chicken thief wasn't a fox." I smiled sadly.

Winter Again

45

December 1, 1956
Change in the Weather

Snow, snow, snow and more snow, coming down in big flakes like feathers and covering the ground in just a few hours. There's something about the first snow that I love; the same with the first crocus, the first swim in the river, the first firefly, and the first hint of red in the maple trees. They're events that mark the turning of our lives.

I'd planned to go to town today, to see Mira and the baby and to visit Bitsy and tell her about what I'd found in Kitty's hideout, but the roads are too bad and we're not going anywhere. When I try to call her, the phone lines are down.

Bored as a sunflower in a rainstorm, I pace the floors, until Dan growls. "Patience, for God's sake, sit down or go do something useful." He's lying on the sofa in front of the fire reading the old book about horses, so I take a deep breath and decide to look at the new journals. I was saving them for Bitsy, but she's so busy I doubt she will mind...

December 18, 1959
Buxton-Elgin Community, Ontario

My first few days in Canada were surprisingly pleasant. For one thing it was warmer than I expected, almost like Virginia in early winter. I attended church on Sunday and made note of the many families in all shades of black and brown, some as light as me.

Mr. King and I made a trip to the general store and stocked up on provisions. I even bought a pair of scissors, some ribbon and a few yards of flowered cotton to make curtains for my new abode, though I realized afterward that until I had some income I'd have to be careful with my last coins.

For two days, men in the community came to clear the yard. They cut the brush and tall weeds. They sawed up the fallen branches and stored them under the porch for fuel. On the fourth day, the weather changed. While I was bringing in firewood from where the men had stacked it, a stiff wind came up, almost knocking me down. The air temperature dropped and it started to snow, little pellets, coming in sideways. I just made it into the house as the wind slammed the door behind me and within minutes I was cut off from everything.

For twenty-four hours the snow rages, and to conserve wood, I push my bed near the fireplace. I don't even try to cook. Finally, the snow stops as abruptly as it started and I begin to see people out on the road. One very black man, wearing a long coat and western hat, drives a sled pulled by two horses and he stops and comes up on the porch.

"I saw the smoke coming out the chimney," he said. "I'm Chester Lee. Do you have enough food and firewood?" I assured him that I did, but he insisted on stomping through the snow, up to his knees to bring in two more armloads from under the porch.

To pass the time, I made up my cloth curtains and hung them from nails that were already there. Then I had an idea. I used some of the extra gingham and stitched up a bonnet. It wasn't elegant. I didn't have any fancy lace, but I knew I could buy some at the country store.

My idea was to try to sell bonnets to ladies in the community. If I couldn't sell them, maybe I could barter for services. It was a plan, anyway, and I went to bed that night fired with visions of the fancy creations I could make. Life was good right then. I was independent. I was free.

Gratitude

"Hiya!" says Bitsy. "I didn't know you were in town. Come for the free samples?"

Mira and I had been out on a walk with little Glory, when we saw the sign in the window. "Bittman's Welcomes Everyone. Come in and try our new soft ice cream." My friend has Kitty's baby, Mary, on her lap and they both give me big smiles. I plunk down on the seat next to her and reach out my arms for Mary.

"I've never had soft ice cream," I say. "Thought I'd try it, especially since it's free."

Mary is a changed child. When Bitsy and Willie first found her, she was dehydrated and hardly had any fat on her body. I'll be honest, I wasn't sure she would live. Now she looks at me with her brown eyes, no longer sunken in her little face. She's still small, but growing, and her blond hair is turning a little red. "You've done wonders with her, Bitsy. What does she eat?"

"Everything. I give her formula whenever she cries and she reaches for table food now."

"So what's the plan?" I ask, noticing how maternal Bitsy seems. (I know for a fact that she and Lou tried for a baby for years. Now she's forty-five.)

"You've done wonders with her. Is the welfare department getting involved?"

My friend smiles tenderly. "Lou checked with Judge Linkous to see if we could adopt her and the Judge says if none of the Bishops object, it should be easy. The only one left in the family is Earl, and he's selling the farm and moving away, so he signed the papers." Mira's baby is fussing and she whispers something to Lillie Bittman, then takes Glory upstairs to their apartment to breastfeed.

"I don't want to discourage you, but can you handle a baby, Bitsy? I thought you were going to be the manager of the woolen mill while Lou was Sheriff."

"Mira said she could babysit a few days a week and I was thinking of getting a playpen and taking Mary to work on the other days."

"I can't believe this!"

"Aren't you happy for me?" Bitsy asks her eyes filling with tears. "You don't know how hard it's been for me to be a midwife and watch mothers, reach for their newborns and cry out for joy. I was always grateful to have Willie as my adopted son, but Lou and I have been trying to have a baby for the last twenty years. The one time we did get pregnant, I lost it. Now I have Mary and I won't give her up."

I want to be supportive, but secretly I can't help worrying. The baby had such a hard beginning! No one knows what the trauma may have done to her. Still, Bitsy will be an excellent mother and she's my friend.

"Of course I'm happy for you!" I reach out to giver her a one armed hug. "And I can help too."

A few minutes later, Mira comes back and I make note again of her shiny gold wedding band. She'd just told me the big news an hour ago. She and Willie had secretly married before Glory's birth, so he's legally the baby's father.

I gaze at the radiant new mothers and healthy little girls and smile. There are moments when you look at life and say to yourself *our cups runneth over...* but then I remember Danny.

Celebration

As soon as I had a chance, I told Dan all the news. Willie and Mira were secretly married and Bitsy and Lou are adopting Mary. To celebrate, he insisted we pick up a red velvet cake at the Mountain Top Cafe and get everyone together for a celebration. A few hours later, we were all settled in front of their television with cake and ice cream on our TV trays.

"This is swell of you to bring us a party," Lou says. "And there's a great show on tonight, *Gunsmoke*, a Western. I saw it last week." Before the episode starts, a new's special comes on and I think, *Oh no…more angry segregationists!*

"Is the Highlander Folk School, in Tennessee, a vanguard of the Civil Rights Movement?" the newscaster asks over a background of blue grass music. "Or a Communist Training Ground?"

The camera moves across a schoolroom showing black and white men and women in earnest conversation and then shifts to a large pond where adults and children of both colors swim in the sunshine.

"Established during the Great Depression, the Highlander's program is based upon the belief that education can be used to empower ordinary people," the reporter tells us. "At first the school focused on building the labor movement and strengthening the unions, but at the end of the Depression, the school turned to the issue of civil rights. Both Rosa Parks and Reverend Martin Luther King attended workshops here before the Montgomery bus boycott and they both credit the school with inspiring them."

Background music rises and a mixed group of musicians is shown on a makeshift outdoor stage singing a song I've heard before. *"This land is your land – This land is my land – From California…"*

"Now, as Highlander has become more prominent in the struggle for racial justice, outraged white citizens are accusing the institution of being a Communist training school and the question looms, after twenty years, can the school survive?"

"Wait!" I shout. "That's Danny!"

"Where?" Bitsy says jumping up and almost knocking her TV tray over.

"On the stage. Sitting next to the young man with the banjo. That's him and that's his guitar. Remember he had all those silly cartoon stickers on it and the hand-woven strap?"

"It's him, all right," Willie shouts. "Son of a gun!"

"What the hell?" Dan growls, "The bastard!"

"From the Redwood Forest - to the gulf stream waters," the folk singers harmonize. *"This land was made for you and me!"*

"We have to go down there," I announce as soon as Dan and I are in the car and on the way home.

"Calm down, Patience. We don't even know for sure if it's him and even if it is, the son of a bitch could have called us. He could have at least told us where he was and that he was safe."

"I need to see him, Dan. You don't know this but when he was drunk in the alley that night and fell on the pavement in a puddle of his own piss, I looked right in his eyes and gave him a look that said... "Go to hell! I'm through with you."

"Maybe we could just call Highlander and make sure it's really him."

I shake my head stubbornly and stare through the

windshield. "I need to see him. I need to touch him, Dan. He's my son. Our son."

Clouds have come in and it's snowing again, white confetti that blows into the windshield. My husband reaches across the seat and tries to pat me on the knee.

"Two hands for beginners," I say and I brush him away.

A Fool's Errand

For two days we try to call the Highlander Folk School. I even telephone Wally Richards at the NAACP office to see if he has any suggestions. Bitsy heard on TV that there's a winter ice storm in Tennessee and she wonders if the phone lines are down.

On the third day, at dinner, Dan says I should give up. "If our son wants to see us, he knows where we are. You don't even know for sure it's him; the picture was blurry. Running after him is a fool's errand."

"You could come with me if you cared."

"Patience, you're going off half-cocked!"

"What's that supposed to mean?"

"You're being a hot-head. Impulsive."

This really gets me! Half crying, I rise, purposely dump what's left of my cornbread on his head and run up the stairs. I don't even turn to see his expression. Just yell over my shoulder. "How's that for impulsive? I'll go to Tennessee by myself!"

Upstairs, I fall on Mira's bed sobbing, but before I'm down for the count, I pack a change of clothes and Mrs. Potts' last journal. Then I leave my bag in the hall.

"Tick. Tock. Tick. Tock. Tick. Tock." goes the Big Ben alarm clock next to my bed. Dan, sleeping across the hall, may be right. I'm being rash, but my heart's been unmoored since Danny left. *I have to go.* I need to tell him I love him. The last time I gave up on someone, it was Kitty, and she ended up dead.

Flying Solo

I wake to sunshine and the smell of coffee. The alarm clock didn't go off; it's already nine and I have to stop at the bank. Downstairs, Dan's flipping flapjacks and he's put my suitcase and a road map by the kitchen door. "Hungry?" he asks. He's trying to be nice.

"Thanks, Honey," I respond, just as nice. "I'll eat a few cakes and have a cup of coffee while I'm getting some food to take on the road."

"Already got it; apples, cheese, bread, butter and a thermos of tea. Need anything else?"

"Maybe some of my oatmeal cookies. No chance you changed your mind about coming with me is there? We could have a nice trip."

"No, I'm sorry. I thought about it overnight and actually called the vet in Torrington this morning to see if he'd cover, but his wife said he's laid up in Boone Memorial with kidney stones and needs help covering *his* practice. If I left, with the hospital and Jim Gardner, the vet from Delmont, dead, that would mean no veterinarian for three counties."

"Thanks for trying," I say, taking his hand and kissing his warm palm. "I guess I'll be like Amelia Earhart."

"How's that?"

"I'll fly solo."

The bank is already open when I get to town, so I withdraw fifty dollars and then swing by the Texaco station to have Loonie Tinkshell fill up the tank.

Four hours later, I stop at a park called Pinnacle Rock and eat the sandwiches Dan made for me. My plan is to go directly south through the mountains of West Virginia, then pick up Highway 58 across Tennessee. It's not the shortest route, but it's easy and I hope to avoid any bad weather.

To keep awake, I listen to the radio and sing along to the songs I know. *"Sixteen tons and what do you get? - Another day older and deeper in debt..."* When my knee starts to hurt, I take a break and walk around at a roadside rest.

The truth is, I may act brave, but I'm not an experienced motorist. I drive around Union County and into Delmont and Torrington, but I've never taken a cross-country trip before, certainly not alone.

By four, I'm already thinking of dinner, but I push on. "This is a mission, not a vacation," I tell myself, talking out loud, to stay awake. Finally, at 7:30 my knee's burning so bad I *have* to stop.

The first three motels I pull into all have signs

outside that say Whites Only and I'd rather sleep in my car than stay there. Finally, I locate the Parkway Motor Court that caters to Blacks. As I plunk down my eight dollars, I have to ask, "Ma'am could you get in trouble for renting to a white person?"

The elderly manager, with a nametag that says Marge, responds with a cackle. "Nah. There's no actual *law* against Blacks and Whites staying in the same hotel, it's just the custom in these parts.... If I say you're welcome, honey, you are."

Then she holds out a little green manual that says on the cover, *The Negro Motorist Green Book*: *Hotels, Garages, Service Stations, Taverns, Beauty Salons, Barbershops*. "Lots of travelers coming through here buy one of these," she tells me. "White or Black, if you don't want to give your money to a racist, this little book will tell you where to go."

It's only a buck, so I buy one; then the nice lady takes a key off the wall and escorts me to my door. It's been a long day, but so far, not as hard as I'd feared. I turn out the lights and crawl into bed, missing Dan. The fact is, I depend on his warmth. I hate it when we don't support each other. I take a big breath and smile. He did make me pancakes!

46

Only Two Girls Now

By eight the next morning, I was on the road again. After a few wrong turns going around Knoxville, I finally picked up the route and began to relax. An hour later, I pulled off at an Esso station. It wasn't in the Green Book, but my gas gauge was on empty and I had to pee. If there was a Whites Only sign, I decided, I wouldn't make a fuss about it, but a moment later I was relieved when a sharp colored man in a white uniform ran out to serve me.

"Fill'er up?" he greeted me pleasantly. The name embroidered on his shirt said "George Robinson."

When I returned from the restroom, George was washing my windows. "Are all Esso attendants like you?" I asked.

"You mean are they all colored or are they all this helpful?" he laughed.

"I mean, are the stations integrated; do they serve both Black and White? I'm trying not to go to places that discriminate."

"I bet I know where you're headed…" He put the window squeegee back in the wash-bucket and took a blue cloth to wipe away streaks: then he opened the hood to check the oil. I smiled and waited.

"You're on your way to the Highlander School."

"You're right. How did you know?"

"Locals don't ask questions about race, so I figure you're one of those civil rights people. The truth is that Esso's been supportive of colored people owning and working in their stations for years. If you're looking for gas, that's where to go."

"How about directions, are you good at that too?"

George took me inside where he drew a map to my destination and gave me a free cup of coffee. There was a photo of his handsome family on the counter, his wife, a boy and three girls.

"I have three girls and one boy too," I shared.

"We only have two girls now," George said softly, picking up the picture frame and staring at the kids. "We lived in Red Boiling Springs then. A few years after the photo was taken, little Ruby got pneumonia and couldn't breathe. They wouldn't take her at the nearby white hospital. She died in my wife's arms in the car before we could get her to Meharry, the colored Hospital in Nashville.

I take a big breath, absorbing his sorrow. "That isn't right," was all I could say and then I mumbled, "I'm sorry."

George brushed away the grief he carried like a smooth stone in his pocket and smiled. "One more piece of advice, if you don't mind, Ma'am. A lot of people around here are up in arms about the Highlander School. They don't like race mixing. They don't like brown and white children swimming together in the pond, and they don't like civil rights, so I wouldn't say much to anyone about where you're headed.

"A white boy, from New York, on his way to Highlander, got beat up by some local toughs a few weeks ago. It was in the paper and everything. The editor called him a Communist Agitator, but I'd met the fellow when he stopped here for gas. He was just a college kid wanting to help out."

"Thanks, for the advice...and thanks for everything, Mr. Robinson," I said and shyly laid a one-dollar tip on his desk.

"Much obliged," he said with a grin and was gone at a run to serve the next customer.

Road to Freedom

Highlander Folk School it said on the wooden sign, supported by two tall poles, one on each side of the gravel track... but I didn't drive in.

Maybe Dan was right; I was on a fool's errand. What was I going to say, anyway? Would people laugh when I announced I was Danny's *mother* searching for him? Would Danny be angry and send me away?

Finally, I took a deep breath. "Might as well face the music," I thought. "I'm on a mission."

The gravel track led through a small grove of trees and then opened on to a field dotted with a half dozen structures, all constructed of wood and stone, some with porches or open decks. The grass was green, mowed short, and there was a large pond below one of the buildings. It looked like a state park.

Unsure where to go, I pulled over at the edge of the grassy clearing and approached a group of white and brown men playing horseshoes. "Hi. I think my son might be staying here. His name's Daniel Hester. Would anyone know him?" (I knew that sounded dumb, but how could I reveal that the loss of my son had blown a hole through my heart and I was heavily bleeding.)

"*Dan the Man*? Sure we know him," a big fellow who reminded me of the black opera singer Paul Robeson, answered with a smile. "He's up at the Meeting House jamming with the old time country band." He pointed the way and when I got closer, I saw that the buildings all had signs on the front; Mens' Dorm. Womens' Dorm. School House. Meeting House. Library. Dining Hall.

A group of men and women were leaving the library and from an adjoining building I heard singing, *"Just like a tree that's standing by the water..."* It sounded like Danny! *"Just like a tree that's standing by the water - We shall not be moved..."*

Entering a large wood-paneled room, I observed a circle of musicians, some standing, some sitting. There was a blond banjo player who reminded me of the actor James Dean, a young colored woman fiddler with a blue scarf wrapped around her head, Danny on the guitar and a white man I recognized only from newspaper photos, Pete Seeger, the folk singer that the House Committee on Un-American Activities has labeled a subversive because he refused to testify against his friends.

Danny's hair is different, longer in front with sideburns, and he's looking away. Seeger starts the next verse in his reedy tenor and everyone comes in, even me. *"On the road to freedom – we shall not be moved. - Just like a tree that's standing by the water - We shall not be moved."*

It isn't until a bell outside clangs a few times, that the jolly group begins to disband. Danny slaps the banjo player on the back and smiles. "See you later?"

"Time for dinner everyone and don't forget," announces a woman in a purple dress who I think might be the leader. "There's a discussion on racial justice back in this building at seven and then country dancing at nine."

"Hi, I'm Zilphia Horton, one of the two co-coordinators of the Center," she says as she passes me. "Did you get registered for the workshops?"

"Actually, I'm not here for the programs. I just dropped by to see…Daniel Hester." She looks me over and nods.

"Mom!" Danny whips around. "Holy Cow. How did you get here?"

"Drove the Olds." I smile, but I don't give him a hug, afraid I'll embarrass him in front of his friends or worse, get publicly rebuffed.

"Is Dad with you?"

"No. He couldn't come." By this time, the singers have all gone to dinner and we're alone in the room.

"Is Dad OK?" he asks frowning.

"Oh, yes! It's nothing bad. He's just covering

the vet work for three counties and no one could sub for him. We saw you on TV and got the phone number for the Folk School, but never could get through."

"That TV show caused us plenty of trouble. As you might imagine, an interracial civil rights and social justice school isn't exactly popular in the South, and someone cut our phone lines. The telephone company wasn't any too anxious to repair them, because we had a bomb threat that week too, but they finally came yesterday...Do you want some grub?"

I hold up my hand. "Bomb threat?"

"Yeah, it's no big deal. We get them all the time and nothing ever happens. A few weeks ago, Jack, the banjo player you saw just now, got beat up in town, but nothing since then."

"Before we go to the dining hall and while we're alone, I have something to say." Danny takes a deep breath, probably expecting a reprimand, but I continue. "The last time I saw you, you were drunk in the alley by the movie theater and I threw you a look of hate that would freeze hell. I don't know if you saw me, but I've felt bad about it all this time. What the look said was *I'm through with you!* Then I turned and walked away, do you remember? A few days later you were gone. I've regretted it ever since."

Danny takes another big breath. "I saw your face and I knew how furious you were. The worst part is, that at the time, I considered *myself* the victim; no one respected *me*; no one knew who I really was... or cared.

"For about a year, I'd felt like I was always under pressure to be someone I didn't want to be… so I drank booze to hide from you and from Dad and to hide from myself. I was close to going under when I got arrested and I had to get away. I'm so sorry."

That's when I stood up and hugged him. I didn't say "Oh, it's all OK." I just hugged him.

Better Than All right

The food in the dining hall was delicious, we sat with Jack, the banjo player and the fiddler woman, named Tancy, and everyone helped clear the tables and wash up. I was checked in and assigned a lower bunk in the women's dorm with a lumpy mattress, but I didn't care. After the evening program, Danny and I sat outside, bundled up, and he explained that he was one of the few paid employees at the school.

"I take care of the mowed grounds and the flowerbeds and repairs on the buildings, a perfect job for a farmer's son," he explained to me. "Occasionally I work in the vegetable gardens, but in my free time I attend meetings and play with the band.

"It's what I love, Mom. I was never cut out to be a vet. I don't have the same nervous system as Dad. I hated holding a bull while he dehorned it. I could never put an animal down, even if the animal was suffering. I knew Dad thought I had a knack for vet work and wanted me to go back to vet school and become his partner... you both told me that over and over again, so many times..."

"I'm sorry," I said. "I didn't know we were making you feel bad. Your Dad's sorry too. I'll make a collect call from the school's office later and let him know I found you, but before I leave Highlander I want us to call him together. Can we do that? Just to say hello?"

"All right, unless they cut our phone line again," Danny teased.

Over the next few days and into the evenings, I met along with the other participants in small groups where we talked about what we wanted to change in society and how we might organize in our communities to create that change. And we didn't just *talk*; we role-played, sang freedom songs and watched movies.

I spent time with Danny and his friends too, including Jack, the banjo player from New York, the one who'd gotten beat-up by the thugs in town. The Highlander Folk School was so much fun that I wanted to come back and bring the whole family, Lou and Bitsy too and the babies.

Finally, on the night before I left, Danny and I made the call to Dan. I stood outside the office door to give him some privacy and there were tears in his eyes when he came out. Is everything OK?"

He wiped his face and said. "Better than OK. I love you, Mom."

At ten, I crawled into my bunk and looked out the small window at the moon, remembering what the silver orb said to me that dark night back at home.

"Children grow in their own mysterious ways, not yours. And just because someone seems broken, doesn't mean they won't heal."

47

A River of Hope

The first stop I make on my journey home is at the red and white Esso station on Route 58, to fill up with gas and say hello to George Robinson. "Did you make it to your destination, Ma'am?" George asks as he puts the nozzle into my tank. "You were on your way to the Folk School."

"You remembered! I spent the last three days there and I brought you a present."

"Now you didn't have to do that!" Mr. Robinson finishes filling, replaces the nozzle, wipes his hands on a blue towel and takes my small gift, wrapped in wax paper.

"It's a loaf of carrot cake from the school."

I could tell he was touched and this time he not only checked my oil, but refilled the water in my radiator too. The second carrot cake went to Marge, the elderly colored clerk at the Parkway Motor Court.

Again the old lady welcomed me and even gave me a hug, and then she walked me to my room, stumping along with her cane. "Let me check to make sure everything's nice and tidy," she said, stepping across the threshold. "You're a brave little lady, traveling all over the country by yourself. Are you ever afraid?"

"Yes," I admitted, "Sometimes."

"Well, honey," she said. "Just remember, if you ever feel alone, there's a great river of hope that connects us."

Now, tucked in bed, I think of her words. "A river of hope"... In these dark times, I need to remember.... "A River of Hope connects us."

At two a.m. by my pocket watch, I wake when the people in the next room come back from a party. Listening to them laugh, I roll on my side, fluff up my pillow and think about Danny and Jack. Danny didn't say they have a special relationship, but he told me they're planning to travel together next summer, performing at rallies and civil right's demonstrations and even on the radio. Pete Seeger has offered to help them. *And* I saw them holding hands more than once.

I'm familiar with women loving women and men loving men. I roomed with Mrs. Kelly, my midwife mentor, and her lover Nora when we lived in Pittsburgh. It's society's prejudice and the laws that concern me. Even though Alfred Kinsey, the social scientist, documented in his research that 10% of all people are primarily attracted to the same sex, it's still illegal in every state to be open about it, with punishment as much as twenty years in jail. Despite my concerns, I smile to myself, Danny has someone to love, to make music with, to travel with and I've never seen him look happier.

Outside my window, the welcome sign continues to blink. Red - Green. Red - Green. Welcome All. Welcome All.

Red – Green. Christmas is only a week away and I haven't done anything!

To get in the holiday mood and help myself sleep, I quietly sing one of my favorite carols. *"Oh, come all ye faithful - joyful and triumphant. O come all ye citizens of heaven above..."*

Finally, to quiet my busy mind, I pull out Mrs. Potts' journal and begin to read.

December 19, 1859
Elgin-Buxton Community, Ontario, Canada
  The evening after the storm there was a special church service. Everyone in the community had survived the blizzard, and the children had made red and green paper chains and decorated a spruce tree for Christmas.

  "Last year," Reverend King told me before the service, "A boy was lost in the snow and found after the thaw, frozen, about two yards from the family's porch, a great tragedy. We try to take care of each other, but the northland can be harsh. Tonight's service will be a memorial to the child and all the settlers we've lost over the year to illness and injury. It will also be a celebration of survival."

  Earlier, as I'd looked over the congregation, I'd noticed a few pregnant women, and after the service, I asked one of the ladies what her plans were for her delivery. "Is there a midwife here or a physician from town who will come out to the settlement?"

  "No," she answered in a voice as golden as honey. She was a small girl, about twenty-five, with

a pleasant round face and she told me her name was Amana Lee, wife of Chester Lee who'd brought in my firewood a few days ago.

"There's a doctor in town, but he won't take care of Africans, even those like us who never saw Africa. Canada is The Promised Land, but there are still people who are prejudiced and he's one of them.

"We're hard working Christian farmers!" she continued, getting worked up. "Everyday we learn new things. We never ask for handouts, but Dr. Braddock still thinks we're beneath him! When it comes to giving birth, the women in the community are in God's hands."

"I've delivered a few babies and have trained as a nurse," I admitted.

"Miss Grace, a nurse and a midwife! Would there be a charge?" Amana said it so loud, people near us turned in surprise. "Dr. Braddock charges the white people two dollars!"

"I wouldn't ask for anything, but you could bring me wood for the winter and I could use some extra potatoes and carrots. Whatever you can spare."

From that day on, I was called on for cuts and scrapes, for fevers and chills and one time even an amputation of a hand after an accident at the sawmill. I never saw so much blood, but with catgut suture from my birth kit, I was able to close the wound and save the man's life.

Elgin-Buxton Community, Ontario, Canada
December 22, 1859

Amana Lee, the pregnant woman from church, started her pains just after noon and Chester came for me by foot at dusk. It was just above freezing, but the snow was gone. As we walked to his farm, I felt my low-heeled button shoes get wet and then wetter.

"Amana and I came to Canada from the Carolinas four years ago," Chester told me. "We traveled north by water to Philadelphia in a tobacco ship where the captain hid us under a stack of tobacco leaves. In Philadelphia, William Stills, the black abolitionist, was able to get us on a train to Niagara Falls and into Canada. It only took one week." Then I told him the story of our trip by land for almost two months and he agreed my journey was much more arduous.

Finally, we arrived at their cabin to find only Amana and their neighbor, Mrs. Davis, present. The husband Chester went on to his brother's home next door to wait. It was strange how nervous I was. I could deliver Elsie's baby in a dark cave by myself, but with old Mrs. Davis watching, my hands shook as I laid out my supplies.

Holding on to the back of the wooden rocker, the young woman swayed back and forth, while the auntie hummed a tuneless song and tapped a rhythm on the heavy pine table. I'd heard such music in the slave camps before and wondered if it

448

was something from Africa.

There wasn't much for me to do, but whisper words of encouragement. "You're doing fine, Amana....Keep it up...Your baby is waiting to meet you." I made her some strong tea with honey and watched as she swayed and moaned, swayed and moaned, riding the waves that seemed to get stronger.

Amana whimpered and her brown knuckles turned white as she gripped the chair again and again. "I don't think I can do this anymore!" she said shaking her head back and forth.

"Is there a chamber pot?" I asked Mrs. Davis. She found a metal one with a handle behind the door and carried it over.

"Oh, no! Here comes another one! I can't. I won't. I can't. I won't." She chanted.

"Now, child," the older lady stopped her. "The midwife wants you to empty your bladder and you have to do what she says...As soon as this pain is over, we want you to squat."

Amana shook her head no, but she did what the Auntie told her and I learned a good lesson. A midwife can't always be asking her patient to do something. Sometimes, she has to tell her what to do.

Between the two of us, we got the expectant mother to tinkle in the pot, but then she refused to get up. "Ummmmph," she groaned deep in her chest.

Mrs. Davis and I looked at each other. "Are you feeling pressure?" I asked. "Amana. I need you to answer me. Is that the baby? Are you feeling the baby at your opening?"

"I don't know...it's something."

"Then let's get you back in bed."

"She can deliver like this," Mrs. Davis whispered. "The midwife in the slave camp let the women push their babies out however they want to."

"But I can't see what's happening!"

"Ummmmmmmmmmph!" the patient grunted.

"You can feel. Here, let me take the pot away and lay down a clean sheet." Between the Auntie and the patient, I was a willow blowing back and forth in the wind.

Here I stopped reading the journal and smiled, thinking of all the births when I'd felt the same way and remembering the first baby I'd seen delivered when the mother was on the floor. There's been so many since then….

"Amana. The baby will be here very soon," I tried speaking firmly. "Mrs. Davis will sit in the chair behind you for support. If you want to deliver this way, we can do it, but it's very important that you pay attention to me. I'm going to touch you down below now, but I'm only feeling for the baby's head. I won't hurt you."

"Don't you want a warm wet flannel?" Auntie Davis asked.

"A warm rag?

"Yes. To help her stretch."

"Heavens!" I exclaimed. "I never heard of this."

The old woman folded a cloth, dipped it in warm water and held it out. Then she sat down and let the mother lean against her.

"Ow! Ow! Ow!" Amana cried and when I put my hands between her legs the head was right there.

"OK, I'm going to put a cloth around the opening to help you stretch. The baby is almost out, but you must take it easy. Open your eyes, Amana."

With the next push a wailing infant dropped into my apron and when the new mother looked down, she was as surprised as if she discovered a raccoon in the pantry. "It's a baby!" she exclaimed, her eyes wide open. "But why is it so pink? I wanted a brown one!"

Auntie snorted a laugh. "Honey, they get darker with time!"

The hours following the birth were like sitting in a tranquil pool of light. The helpful old woman built up the fire and brought Amana some broth. I examined the baby, head to toe as Dr. Coffman had taught me. He was a good-sized infant and looked at me with such wise eyes.

Finally, Mrs. Davis tidied the room, while I helped Amana put the baby to breast again. I was surprised when at the end of cleaning up, the old woman pulled an axe from under the bed.

"Works like magic every time," she said.

My eyebrows shot up.

"You know," she explained. "The axe cuts the length of labor. Cuts the pain."

49

Lost

By noon the next day, I was back in Bluefield, West Virginia, where I saw a sign for another Esso station that was connected to a tourist trap called The Indian Village. I was making good time and needed a break, so after gassing up and using the rest room, I parked in the lot and went into the store.

An hour later, I came out with two pair of the cutest beaded baby moccasins I'd ever seen, a real leather cowboy hat for Dan, a mug with Geronimo on it for Lou, and four imitation silver Navaho bracelets for my girls and Bitsy. My Christmas shopping was done!

As I got back in the car, I looked up at the sky. The temperature was dropping and heavy gray clouds boiled over the mountains. It was already two and if I want to be home by dark, I'd better get moving!

Spruce and firs. Bare maples and oaks. Naked sweetgum trees with little balls on them. There aren't any houses or even signs, but I feel sure I'm on the right road, so I just keep following a rushing creek that seems familiar. Sometimes cars pass, heading down the mountain and they all have their headlights on, so I do the same.

Then the rain hits, a real downpour, big heavy drops that overwhelm the wipers. This is not good! The road ascends with a cliff on my right. There's nowhere to pull off and nowhere to turn around, so I just keep going, my hands gripping the steering wheel and my head jutting forward to see through the rain.

I turn off the radio to help me concentrate and take a deep breath. Twice, I almost slide off the pavement, but regain control. Finally, after driving like what seems more than an hour, I spy a small sign on a metal post, a state marker, **Welcome to Virginia** it says. Not West Virginia, *Virginia!*

Well this is just swell! Somehow, I'd made a wrong turn after leaving the Trading Post and I'm now across the border, *in the wrong state.* In another five miles, I come to a second sign. "**Rocky Gap State Park**," it says, with an arrow pointing to the left.

Taking a deep breath, I stop in the middle of the intersection, trying to decide what to do. The rain has turned to sleet on my windshield. If I head toward the state park, there might be a cabin to rent, but if there isn't, I'll have to retrace my steps to this crossroads and somehow get off the mountain before dark.

No, it will be better to turn back toward Bluefield now, where there's a telephone to call Dan, who's expecting me, and probably a motel. Carefully, I back to my left in the intersection and then to the right in an attempt to turn around. It took me three tries… and I ended up in a ditch.

Refuge

I used to scold Dan for swearing, telling him "Little pitchers have big ears", now I pound on the steering wheel and swear like a coal miner. "Damn! Damn! Damn it to hell!"

It's already four o'clock. Night's coming on fast and I have no way to call for help, so I pull on my gloves, put on Dan's new cowboy hat and get out of the car. Then I curse some more, when I slip on the ice.

Stepping forward, I fall again; this time on my bad knee. Finally, I just crawl to the trunk where I discover I forgot to bring the snow chains! It's then that I hear the growl of a truck. "Help! Help!" I yell, waving the hat like a cowgirl.

"Howdy, Miss," a thin man with a long white beard greets me through his truck window. He doesn't get out, but glances at my vehicle down in the ditch. "Looks like you're having some trouble."

"I am! I was headed the wrong way and got lost. This is the first place I could turn around and …well you can see, I backed into the ditch. Can you help me?"

"No darlin'," the old man says in a strong southern accent. "Not tonight. I can get you out in the morning though; for now you better come home and stay with my missus and me. My name's Hollis Slocum."

The whites of his blue eyes are reddened and his nose is covered with veins, but he doesn't sound drunk, so I decide to take a chance. The alternative would be to sit in the car all night with the heater on and the gas gauge sliding toward empty.

"How far is your house?" I inquire as I get my purse and suitcase out of the Olds and lock up.

"Only a little bit down the road," he answers, as he points toward Rocky Gap.

The cabin where Mr. and Mrs. Slocum lived was not just "a little bit down the road". It must have been five or six miles. Finally, we turned onto a narrow dirt track that led through an ancient spruce grove to a clearing where a log house stood. Smoke rose from a stone chimney and a golden light shown through the windows.

When we entered, the old man, who appeared to be nearing ninety, set my suitcase on the floor. A tiny woman turned from the wood-cooking stove. Glancing around, I saw that they used only kerosene lamps. Probably the electric lines had never come this far, or possibly the Slocums didn't want it. What shocked me was the wallpaper on the inside of the log walls. It was made of newspaper and covered every surface, every nick and cranny.

"Ma," Mr. Slocum addressed his wife. "I brought home a *damsel in distress*. Got something warm to eat? Found her stuck in the ditch back at the turn. I'll take Rebel down in the morning and pull her out."

"What's your name, honey?" the lady asked. "You can call me Ma." Her thin white hair was twisted up in a bun and she wore a flowered apron.

I took off my coat and looked for somewhere to

hang it. "Patience Hester. I'm from Liberty, West Virginia, on my way home from visiting my son in Tennessee. (There was a confederate flag over the fireplace so I didn't mention the Folk School.)

"I *thought* you sounded like a Yankee, the way you talked," joked Hollis. "But we won't hold it against you."

Soon we were sitting around a wooden table, eating the cornbread and ham hocks that Mrs. Slocum had prepared.

"Do you have a farm here?" I asked. "It was almost dark when we came in, but I did see a barn."

"Not much of a farm anymore," Hollis answers. "We had to sell most of the land to the state park back in the Great Depression. The money helped us hang on during the hard times. Now we just have thirty acres of trees and meadow. We keep a cow and two workhorses; still put up our own food from the garden, just like we always did."

"What about you?" Mrs. Slocum asked sitting down in a wooden rocker. "You a city girl?"

"Hardly. I've spent the last thirty years on a farm. I'm a midwife and my husband is an animal doctor. We live about the same as you, only we have electricity now."

"We manage just fine without it," Mrs. Slocum explained.

That night I slept on a feather mattress, the first I'd been on in twenty years, with a down quilt over me. Mrs. Slocum even gave me a nightcap to wear on my head.

"It gets mighty chill on a night like this," she

said "and there's no heat in this room. There's a chamber pot and some tissue in the corner if you have to go. You know how to turn down the kerosene light before you blow it out?"

I smiled. "I've used them a lot. And Mrs. Slocum, I want to thank you for your hospitality."

"What are neighbors for?" the old woman said. "It's a hard world and we help each other when we can."

For a while I lay in bed thinking about the people I'd met on my trip; white, black and every color in between... Most were kind and I felt we were all more alike than we were different. I'd been sure that all white southerners were racist, but that was *my* prejudice.

I pictured the red flag over the mantle in the other room and wondered what it represented to these people. To me the confederate flag was a hateful symbol of a culture that believed in slavery, that it was OK to *own* people, but maybe that wasn't always the case.

Maybe the Confederate flag meant something else to the Slocums. I still didn't like it, but maybe it was a symbol of regional pride, a celebration of the rebel spirit that didn't have anything to do with racism. If Bitsy had been stranded, would Hollis Slocum have brought her back to his home? Would Mrs. Slocum have fed her and lent Bitsy her nightcap? I thought that she would.

Finally, I got out my flashlight and opened the last of Grace Potts' journals. There were only a few pages left. It was hard to believe that the little books were really all gone. Maybe I hadn't searched the old cottage hard enough. Maybe I should go back. Was there an attic or a cellar? I couldn't remember.

Elgin-Buxton Community, Ontario, Canada
December 23, 1859

Another six inches of snow fell over night, but this time it was soft as feathers and so light it was like walking through water. For helping with the birth of their baby, Amana and Chester gave me a present of high top leather boots made by the cobbler of the Elgin shoe shop. Mrs. Davis, the auntie, gave me an old wool cape and scarf, asking me if I'd teach her to read. It almost brought tears to my eyes. She must have been sixty years old and she wanted to learn so she could read to her grandbabies.

I thought about the stories the masters in Virginia used to tell their slaves about Canada; how runaways would freeze to death or starve if they went there. Yet, here I was. The wolf of winter howled at my door, but I was surviving and I was free.

And here's more good news. Today, I sold my first bonnet to Reverend King to give to his wife Jeremiah for a present. "She's not well," he explained. "And I thought the colorful fabric might cheer her. Most people don't know, but she suffers from melancholia and it's often worse in the winter." When the good lady proudly wore it to Bible study, I got orders for three more.

December 24, 1859

On the day before Christmas, I put on my new boots and wool shawl and headed for the general store to buy more fabric, some gauze for bandages, a tin of boric acid, and a vial of belladonna for my nurse's bag. I also purchased some treats for the children, red and white candies.

Back home in Virginia, the slaves all came to the planter's house on Christmas morning, where the mistress threw them sweets and the master gave the adults whiskey. I was pretty sure there would be no whiskey here, but didn't know what else might be expected.

On the way home, I made note of a dark brown horse, tied to the split rail fence near the Reverend's house. The steed looked tired. A saddle blanket had been tied over him and a bucket of water was placed near his head. Another freedom seeker had just arrived, I imagined. As I passed by, Reverend King came out and called to me, "Miss Blackwell, There's a man here asking after you." Immediately, I thought of a slave catcher and looked for somewhere to hide.

"Not to worry," the minister said in his Scottish accent. "He's of African descent, someone you know from the South."

Unsure what to do, I walked toward his house, a cabin like the others, but with shutters on the windows and a swing on the porch. A tall man with dark skin came out of the door.

"Mr. P!" I exclaimed. "Mr. P. from Uniontown, Pennsylvania! And that must be Noble, tied to the

460

fence." I ran over to my horse and greeted him by pressing my face against his nose and rubbing my hands along his back and then I began to cry. "His tail is still black..." I managed to choke out while almost crying.

"I told you I'd bring him to you some day." Mr. P. said.

After I composed myself, we conversed at the pastor's home for a few hours, but I could see Reverend King was tiring. "I must prepare for the evening service," he excused himself and I asked Mr. P. if he would walk me home.

"I have a barn, but no hay," I explained. "Have you eaten? I can cook a little now. Johnny cakes and beans, if you'd like."

Mr. P. laughed. "Well that's something. I brought some mending if you have the time and I purchased a big sack of oats for Noble before coming to Canada. It was a relief to get here, I can tell you. There were slave catchers everywhere in Detroit and I feared, despite having free papers, I'd be picked up and sold South as a runaway"

Sitting in front of the fire, we talked about the slave trade and the slave catchers. One of the underground conductors that helped me get to Canada, Mrs. C., the hat maker, had been arrested by Federal Marshals in New Castle, but the jury had let her go.

Soon it was time for the Christmas Eve services. I was expecting some excitement, some sort of frolic like the slaves had back in Virginia, but as we walked along the frozen road toward the church, those who passed us were dignified and quiet, even the children.

I was dressed as a woman and Mr. P. complimented me on my wool frock, the one the Erie church ladies had given me. My hair was braided and done up on top as I'd seen the other women of Elgin do and Mr. Potts looked handsome in a long gray coat with a flannel vest. When we went into the church, he took my arm and we found seats toward the back.

At the end of the service, the two of us handed out my candy and then as the newest member of the community, he was asked to ring the Freedom Bell. He rang it twelve times in celebration of the Savior's birth.

Walking home through the Canadian night, we caught sight of a bird I'd only seen in books, a Snowy Owl, floating through the trees. So many stars dotted the night sky that joy bubbled out of me and I started to sing....

"Go tell it on the mountain - over the hills and everywhere. - Go tell it on the mountain, - that Jesus Christ is born." Mr. P. knew the song and sang with me. By the time we got home, we were laughing so hard he had to help me up the front steps.

Later when the blacksmith went to the barn to check on Noble and bring in more wood, I prepared a pallet of extra quilts for him in front of the fire and slipped into my white flannel nightdress that the church ladies had given me. Then I made tea and *when he came back we sat in the firelight and talked some more about the future in the Promised Land.*

It was a cold night and it's not like I meant it to happen. I had no experience in love or the ways of men and women, but Mr. P. did not sleep on the pallet that night. I invited him into my bed.

"You can call me Alfred if you want," he said. "Alfred Potts."

So I did.

50

Rebel

I woke at dawn with Mrs. Pott's last journal on my pillow, feeling it was I who'd found freedom, safety and love.

Through the wall, I heard someone stirring the fire and I sat up in bed, grateful for the frilly nightcap the Missus had lent me. On a dresser, I noticed a young man in uniform and at breakfast I asked the couple about him.

"Is that your son's photo in the other room?"

Hollis looked at his wife, waiting for her to answer and when she didn't, he spoke. "That's our only child, Gene. He was killed in the Great War."

While the Missus did the breakfast dishes and her man went out to the barn to put the harness on his horse, Rebel, I tossed together my things and slipped a two dollar bill under the son's picture, because I knew if I offered the old couple money they wouldn't take it. A few minutes later, Mr. Slocum trotted up on a massive gray workhorse.

Standing on a stump, I climbed on behind him, gripped my suitcase and waved goodbye to Mrs. Slocum. A fierce wind had come up and whipped the old man's long white beard back in my face, but I was glad to have him to cling to.

For what seemed like an hour, we plodded back to the highway, ice-covered branches tinkling over our heads. Finally, I caught a glimpse of my blue Oldsmobile, back wheels still down in the ditch. Once Rebel was chained to the car, he pulled it out without difficulty, then, as casually as if we'd see each other tomorrow, we said goodbye.

Road to Freedom

"Hello?" Dan's voice sounds strained, when I finally call from the first pay phone I find back in Bluefield.

"Hi. It's me."

"Are you all right?"

"Yeah. I had some car trouble, nothing serious. I got turned the wrong way after stopping for gas and ended in a ditch across the Virginia line. A kind family took me in for the night and pulled me out with a work horse this morning."

"Were you hurt? Is the car ok?"

"Everything's fine. The only bad part was I had no way to call you. The people didn't have a phone; no electricity either. It was an adventure. I'll tell you about it later and I promise I'll be home for dinner. Will Sunny and Sue be there?"

"No, that's something I ought to tell you. They called last night to tell us they won't be coming home this Christmas."

"The hospital won't let them off?"

"No, it's not that. They're going to spend the holidays with one of their girlfriends whose parents have a vacation place on the coast. They promised to be here for Easter."

"They don't want to see Mira's new baby? Who are these people they're going to stay with?"

"It's not our business, Patience. Our children are growing up."

"OK…" I respond without enthusiasm, but the truth is I'm devastated. This Christmas will be our first without any kids at home.

Determined to keep my mind on the road, and not make any more wrong turns, I get back in the car and force myself to stop fretting. The twins are adults, Dan's right, and like Howard's troop of little Blue Jays, my chicks will fly away too.

On the way back to Union County, I only stop once and that's for gas in a little town named Sutton. There's snow on the ground, but the roads are still clear. Passing through Liberty, all the Christmas lights are on in the stores. Someone had even put lights on the stone bridge over The Hope and I stop for a minute to look down at the colors reflected in the rippling water.

When I finally pull into our drive, I get out and take a deep breath. Then I take three more and raise my hands to the sky where the moon sails in and out of the clouds.

Home

Turning, I notice the golden light shining from every window, making a halo around the house. My husband has put up colored lights on the porch rail and the shadows of the bare willow trees lean on the snow. Then Dan is there, taking my suitcase and leading me inside. The whole house smells like Christmas. It smells like home.

"Tired?" Dan asks.

"Exhausted."

"I made meatloaf."

"Maybe later. For now, I just want to sit with you. It's been a long trip and I need to tell you about it."

"I talked to Danny again last night," Dan says. "I was worried because you weren't home; then I called him this morning to let him know you're OK. Everyone at Highlander was concerned. And, did you hear the big news?"

"No, what?"

"The Montgomery Bus Boycott finally ended. The protestors actually won. There will be no more segregation on their buses."

"That's great, Dan. Every time people stand up against injustice, it gives the rest of us courage to do the same. I want us to go to Highlander someday. It's a great place. Oh look, you put up a tree!"

In the corner is a fresh cut spruce, fully decorated with strings of lights and glass balls. Dan turns off the table lamp and pulls me down on the sofa next to him. "This isn't so bad, is it?" he asks. "Christmas with no kids at home; just the two of us? We're free!"

I let out my breath in another long sigh, letting the chains of anger, fear, and guilt drop off my heart. What's left is just the warmth of the fireplace, the fragrance of the spruce and Dan's solid body next to mine.

"Did you know that Esso gas stations actually cater to colored people?" (I picked an odd place to start my story.) "They employ Negroes and actually promote them. I met this black man, George Robinson, at an Esso station in Tennessee. His little girl died of respiratory arrest, because the segregated white hospital wouldn't take her. He was the best gas station attendant I've ever known..." And then I started to cry.

"I just want everyone to be happy, Dan. I want our kids to be fulfilled in their work and friendships. I want the world to be fair. I want George Robinson and his family to be respected and safe... and the lady at the motor court where I stayed..."

"These are troubled times, Patience. There are revolutions and counter-revolutions around the world. There's fear of nuclear war, but we can still find happiness here on the Hope."

"I used to think our family should be happy all the time. I wanted us to be perfect."

"Nothing is perfect or permanent," he says, kissing me softly. "Peace comes and goes, shifts like the weather. You want a rum toddy?"

"Sure." Outside, a sudden blast of wind and sleet rattles on the tin roof.

While Dan quietly bustles around in the kitchen, warming cream and getting sugar out of the pantry, I stare at my arms, thinking about Gracie Potts, George Robinson and Bitsy. They are called *colored*, but all three are different colors.

My skin is *colored too*, pink with freckles, but it's not our skin that defines us. It's something inside. Our courage. Our compassion. Our laughter.

"So what else did you do, besides make friends with Mr. Robinson, the Esso attendant, and get lost in the boonies?" Dan asks when he comes back from the kitchen.

"At Highlander we made music, had meetings, square danced and Dan...I should tell you about Danny. He has a friend named Jack, another musician and I think they're in a relationship...."

"I know, Patience. He told me over the phone. It will be OK. We each have our own life to live. Mine is right here with you. Let's sing one of the songs you learned at the center."

"Here's one, I liked. There were so many. *Oh freedom. Oh freedom, Oh freedom over me. And before I'll be a slave. I'll be buried in my grave and go home to my Lord and be free.*"

"I know that one from when I was in the Moundsville State Prison. We sang it at night in the cell block," Dan interrupts and then begins to sing the next verse. *"There'll be singing. There'll be singing. There'll be singing over me. And before I'll be a slave, I'll be buried in my grave and go home to my Lord and be free."*

"Here's another one. It's new," I tell him. *"We shall overcome. We shall overcome. We shall overcome someday. Oh deep in my heart. I do believe..."* Here my voice catches.

"Why does singing get to me?" I ask, resting my head on Dan's shoulder.

"Because music is the voice of the heart," he answers. "We sing when we're happy. We sing when we're sad. We sing when we're scared and to summon our courage."

"Music is the song of the heart," I repeat. "The song of the heart."

Discussion Questions

1. The opening scene in the book presents a chaotic and scary view of unprepared childbirth. Do you think young women are better prepared now?

2. As students we learned about the tragedy of slavery in history class. Does reading about it in a novel make it more real?

3. If you were born a slave, do you think you'd have the courage to try to escape?

4. Bitsy and Patience are best friends but of different races. Is this common? Why do we tend to be close to people who look like us?

5. Is it harder to be a parent to a two-year-old or a parent or a twenty-year-old?

6. Have you ever known a soldier who came home from war broken in body and spirit like Willie? How can we help veterans today?

7. In the 1950s and 1960s the threat of nuclear war was very real. Are we headed back in that direction?

For Further Reading

The Life and Times of Frederick Douglas by
Frederick Douglas

Harriet Tubman: The Moses of Her People by
Sarah Bradford

*The Underground Railroad: Authentic First Hand
Accounts* by William Still

Incidents in the Life of a Slave Girl
by Harriet Jacobs

Black Slave Owners, by Larry Koger

The House of Bondage by Octavia V. R. Albert

*Equiano: The Interesting Narrative of The Life of
Gustavus Vassa, The African*, "by himself"

Born in Bondage by Marie Jenkins Schwartz

Orlean Puckett; The Life of a Mountain Midwife
by Karen Cecil Smith

*Slavery by Another Name: The Re-Enslavement of
Black Americans; the Civil War to World War 2*
Douglas A Blackmon

Remember: The Journey to School Integration
Toni Morrison

On-Line Resources

www.naacp.org

www.history.com/civil rights

www.midwife.org

www.mana.org

www.blacklivesmatter.com

www.wvculture.org/history/Owen-Brown's-Escape

www.highlandercenter.org/history

www.atomictheater.com/history/cold war

www.millercenter.org/mcarthyism-red-scare

Places to visit to understand more:

www.usatoday.com/50-places-to-visit-during-black-history-month

Thank you for reading this book. If you enjoyed it and found benefit in it, please let me know and write a review on Amazon.com or your favorite on-line site

We are far more connected than we know and we are far more alike than we are different.

Maybe the branches of our family trees touch.

Patricia Harman

patsy@patriciaharman.com

www.patriciaharman.com

Made in United States
Cleveland, OH
05 May 2025